SLAVE OF AKRONA

by Gregory Urbach

Dedicated to the memory of my brother,
Kevin Urbach

Who died too young,
and too little mourned.

Table of Contents

Cover by Adam Lovell
Floating Spaceman by Grayson Bowling
Technical support by Kwei-lin Lum

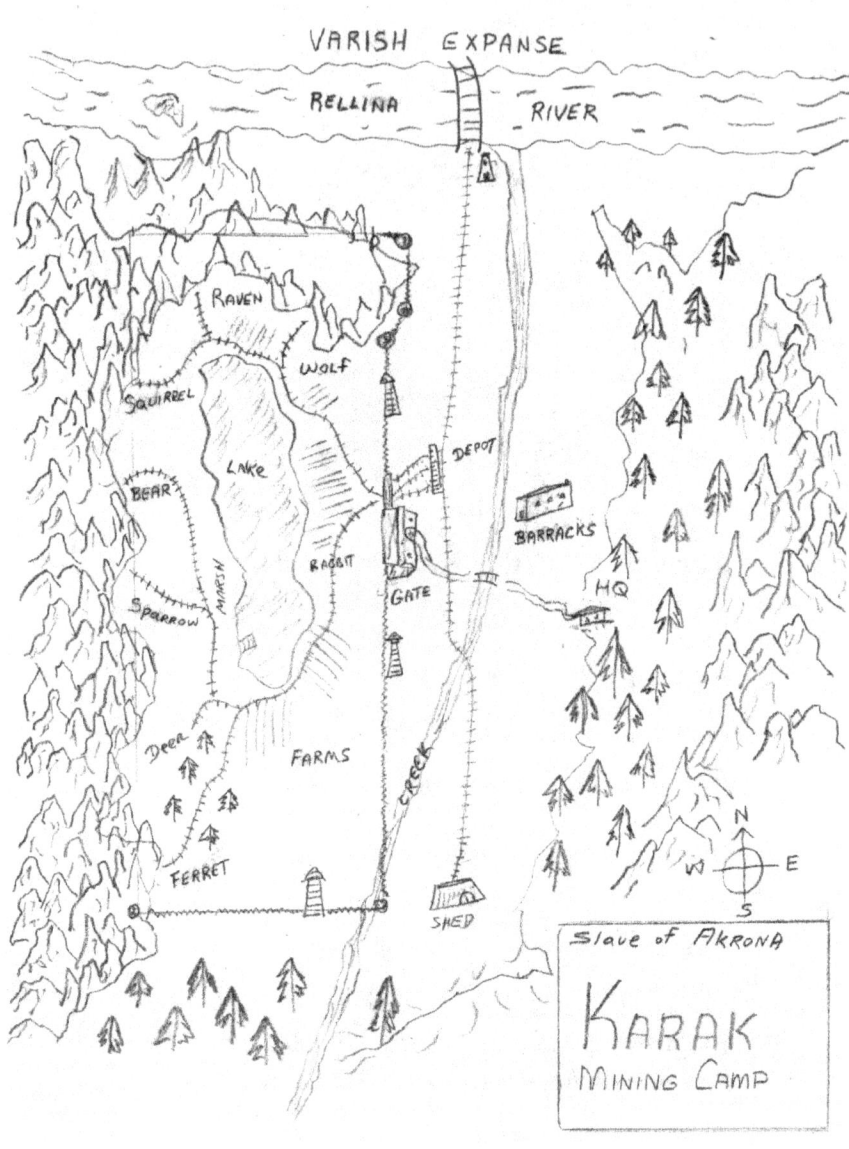

Chapter One
FROM THE DEBRIS FIELD

The castaway floated through an endless void. His battered spacesuit no longer provided visuals. The sensors were off-line, the com link silent. The recycled liquids had grown stale. What little physical sensation he felt was sporadic, mixed with long periods of deep slumber.

How long have I been in this state of nonexistence? he wondered. *Days? Weeks?* It was difficult to think.

Why am I not dead?

His thoughts wandered back to the last few minutes of the battle. The alien battlecruiser was bombarding Earth from high orbit. Burning forests. Pulverizing cities. Earth's small defense fleet had slowed but not stopped the invaders, and now only a desperate ploy might save the planet from conquest.

When was that? How long ago?

He remembered standing alone on the bridge of his half-built spaceship when an energy blast tore the vessel apart. But that had been expected. Necessary to the plan. He floated free of the shattered hulk to hide among the wreckage.

The battlecruiser loomed closer, six hundred meters long, fifty meters in diameter. A fearsome juggernaut that Earth's fledgling technology had been unable to stop. The hull gave off a blue glow. A neutralizing energy screen that had frustrated every weapon the fleet had deployed.

The planet was below him, much of it shrouded in black smoke. In the other direction, barely visible as tiny streaks of light, Earth's remaining warships were ambushing the invasion's supply transport. In a battle that had started in the moons of Jupiter, the invaders had underestimated their prey, and now they were paying a price.

Forced to break off the bombardment, the alien battlecruiser was rushing to the assistance of their beleaguered companions when a

1

small enemy warship got in their way. An enemy they quickly brushed aside, or so they thought.

Drifting through the battlecruiser's energy screen, the young soldier's brain had suffered a short interruption before the biological nature of his wiring brought him back to consciousness. And the nuclear warhead tethered to his belt survived the transition as well.

Once inside the enemy's neutralizing energy screen, the battlecruiser was just another warship. A mass of technological devices and life forms enclosed within a thick hull. He hand-cranked the nuclear warhead's battery back to life until the ignition sequence showed ready.

Should I trust the timer? he remembered thinking.

He had promised to use the timing device rather than set the bomb off manually. He was barely twenty-nine years old, a daring leader with high hopes and a bright future.

But what if the timer doesn't work? Is one life such a great price to save a world?

He set the timer, hoping it would work despite his doubts, but his hope was quickly frustrated as glare from the sun obscured the timer's readout.

Was the timer counting down?

He shaded the readout with his hand trying to see if the priming sequence had activated. It was no good. The glare was so bright that even his meteor suit's sophisticated sensors couldn't detect the readings.

The timer is probably working, he thought. *It tested fine in the lab. If I jump free now, it still might be possible to escape the blast. Maybe. No. I shouldn't take the chance. This trick will never work a second time.*

Tears welled in his eyes as he looked toward the world he was trying to save. He regretted how his death would affect his wife, who didn't take loss easily. His friends would mourn him. He had spent his whole life knowing he might eventually die in battle, but this was more difficult than expected. It's one thing to hold the line against a fearsome enemy, but to push a switch in cold blood? To suddenly vaporize into countless sparkling atoms?

It couldn't be helped. This was his plan. His responsibility.

An airlock opened on the side of the alien warship as an enemy head poked out, the long narrow face visible through the transparent space helmet. The large black eyes were staring in surprise.

Now that his presence on the hull had been discovered, there was no choice. The Arikhan soldiers would soon be swarming out. Grey had never truly believed in a religion. Those who had raised him thought such superstitions foolish, but he had his doubts. To not believe felt so dogmatic. In his experience, life was full of questions that science would never answer.

He said a prayer. A prayer for his family and friends. For his world and the future he might have had if fate been more kind. And he put in a word for himself, asking that his faults, of which there were many, might one day be forgiven. It was Thursday, September 2nd, 2088. The warhead was ready for activation. He pushed the lever.

How long ago was that? He didn't even know if his sacrifice had been worthwhile. Did the bomb go off? Was the warship destroyed?

The floating seemed to go on forever, interspersed by long periods of dreamless sleep. Then, at last, there was a new sensation. The deathlike cocoon was no longer drifting. There was noise on the outside, muffled but clear enough not to be his imagination. He heard a thumping sound.

What's going on? What happens next?

Nothing happened.

Sleep came again, lightly this time, with nightmares exciting his breathing. If his body wasn't so dehydrated, he would have been sweating.

He woke up. Something was banging on him. Or on the suit. There was a grinding. Cutting. Drilling. The visor broke loose and, in a blinding flash of white light, his eyes were free of the darkness. He couldn't see at first, it was too bright, but gradually he made out two humanoid forms hovering over him. He was in a white paneled workroom. Power tools were attached to the walls. Enclosed shelves prevented containers from spilling to the floor. He was in a spaceship. An engineering department. A voice was speaking, but it wasn't an Earth language. It was Arikhan.

"The thing is alive," a croaking voice complained, the final word cut by the angry lash of the alien's long gray tongue.

Grey squinted against the light. The technicians leaning over him were bipeds, slightly more than two meters in height, with leathery brown skin reminiscent of large lizards, but they were not reptiles. More birdlike, with stubby bill-like noses, high cheekbones, and darting black pupils peering out from pale yellow irises. They had muscular arms, flexible legs, thin necks, and narrow heads. Their hands were shaped like claws, each of the four digits ending in hard, pointed nails. Webbed membranes covered the sides of their heads instead of hair, and only holes showed where their ears should be. The thin mouths hid evidence of ivory fangs well-adapted for tearing meat.

Grey had met Arikhan before. What he knew of their eating preferences could be unpleasant.

"Can we claim it for our pens?" the other alien asked, the dialect marked by a distinctive provincial accent.

"The Linyet Leader must decide," the first replied in disappointment.

"None expect a living specimen," the hungry one said. "Perhaps only we should know? Who found it if not us? Have we not earned first taste?"

"We have earned first taste, yet the Linyet Leader awaits our report. She will not be pleased if our words lack truth."

"Where am I?" Grey asked in English, his throat so dry the words were barely whispered.

He felt dizzy, more asleep than awake, but even with his senses dulled he still preferred the aliens not know he understood their language.

"Seartan, it speaks!" the male alien shouted, jumping back from the workbench with twitching shoulders.

"By Sherra's mystery," Seartan said, reaching for a weapon mounted on the wall.

The alien need not have bothered. Grey realized now he was still in the Quexelian meteor suit he had worn during the battle, the suit's hibernating functions having kept him alive while drifting in space. But he was too weak to get up, even if he could free himself of the

4

suit's grip. Talking was difficult. Thinking even harder.

"Faytro, what tongue does it mutter?" Seartan asked.

"The words are unfamiliar. Not Akronos, nor any of the cursed marauder languages," Faytro said. "The thing must be barbarian."

"Does that mean we may taste it?" Seartan asked.

Faytro snapped his moist tongue sharply against the roof of his mouth, indicating a negative response, and used a steel wedge to pry the suit open. Eventually the chest plates spread far enough apart for the unusual occupant to be removed.

"The thing has no meat," Seartan sighed with disappointment.

Faytro pulled the prisoner from the suit, laying him on a nearby workbench where Grey saw the outfit for the first time. He was shocked at its condition. The bulky outfit was charred. Bent. Expended. It was no surprise the aliens hadn't expected to find a living creature inside. As a mangled piece of space debris, it hardly looked worth salvaging.

The meteor suit hadn't permitted underclothing. Except for his gold wedding band, he wore nothing as he lay on the workbench. It didn't matter to the aliens. They would no sooner clothe him than they would a cow or pig, humans being primarily an exotic food source. And he had to agree with the alien's assessment; his body was wasted to skin and bones.

"Where am I?" Grey asked in Arikhan, fighting a temptation to add a clip to the edge of his words as the alien scout Mordari had always done.

The male alien studied him coldly. The Arikhan did not appreciate surprises. None would describe them as a curious race, nor an inventive one, having taken their technology from conquered worlds. But Grey knew they could be crafty, and this alien was clearly wondering what a strange food creature was doing floating inside a piece of space junk.

A third alien arrived wearing a long white tunic and carrying a black leather satchel. Unlike the slate gray tunics of the technicians, which were frayed at the edges, this tunic was crisply pressed. The slender female peered into Grey's eyes, stuck a gloved foreclaw down his throat, and poked him hard in the abdomen. Grey replied with a grunt and tried to push the annoying claw away.

"Give it water," the intrusive alien ordered.

"Yes, yarbel ky," Faytro said.

It's a doctor, Grey realized. He looked out a porthole, trying to fix their location. Was Earth nearby? The moon? Had the alien invasion proved successful after all?

"Quickly!" the physician demanded. "Food creature, my name is Pamaro, yarbel ky of the Link. Do you understand my words?"

Grey had to think, which wasn't easy. He wanted to sleep again. Link was not a group word for the Arikhan. Could it be the name of their ship? Impossible. Other than the battlecruiser, the only surviving enemy spacecraft was a colonial transport called *Bhast*. Both of the escorting warships had been destroyed. There was no fifth ship.

"Link," Grey whispered.

"Yes, the Link," Pamaro said. "Where did you come from? Are you from Akrona? Were you trying to escape? What happened to your vessel?"

Faytro returned with a container and a tube, then sat Grey up and helped him sip the fluid. It tasted like brackish water. He spit some out.

"Not so much at once," Pamaro cautioned, taking over the duty. She helped him drink slowly, studying for clues to his origin.

"It has no water for many days. How long was it out there?" Pamaro asked.

"The thing passed through the gate three seasons ago in a debris swarm. We found it while clearing the 12th degree approach," Seartan said.

"We thought it salvage," Faytro added.

Gate? A stargate? Grey wondered.

The Quexelian entities had told him of stargates. Intense rings of resonant energy established around a sun, permitting interstellar travel along subspace dimensional paths. But Grey knew Earth had no stargate, and even if the technology was available, assembling the complicated energy fields was said to take years.

"It's an interesting creature," Pamaro said, forcing a greenish liquid down Grey's throat. The fluid was thick and tasteless but for a lingering beefy tinge. Grey felt a burning inside.

"Sad the metallic covering is ruined. It may come from Gorthan, or perhaps Ballor," Faytro said.

"This creature is not Gorth or Ballorian," Pamaro said, using a scanner to study Grey's biology. "Human, obviously, but it carries genes not in our database. It may be from Rog."

"If the marauder world sends spies, much will be the retaliation. Too long has been the truce with those treacherous food creatures," Faytro complained.

"That is for the Council of Warriors to decide," Pamaro cautioned.

Grey was only able to follow bits and pieces of the exchange, his Arikhan not sophisticated enough to comprehend many of the subtleties, but the word spy wasn't hard to decipher. He would have liked to know more, but soon he was asleep again.

* * * * * *

He woke up, gradually realizing he was no longer on a spaceship. It was a planet, the gravity similar to a large moon. The room was dark but not blacked out. Small, like a cell.

"The prisoner moves," a guard said outside a metal screen.

The tall Arikhan was dressed in a common blue tunic that hung nearly to the knees, khaki trousers, and high black leather boots. A sidearm was holstered on its hip. The glint in its large black eyes displayed a contemptuous curiosity.

Grey sat up to take a deep breath. He felt a little stronger. There was a trace of green liquid on his lips. No doubt a nutritional concoction from the yarbel ky. But he was still incredibly sleepy. He had hardly opened his eyes before he wanted to doze off again.

Someone had put a scented pad beneath him to absorb waste matter. He had always thought the Arikhan an orderly species, but this exceeded his expectations. The cell had a tiny window high up on the wall and a thermos of water lay nearby. A brown blanket with an itchy texture lay across his legs. He had no clothes.

Soon a broad-shouldered military official arrived, sliding the steel grid open and squatting to study the captive. The alien had intense black eyes and wore an olive green tunic decorated with three silver swamp leaves. The insignia of command. The alien's skin was a leathery brown but highlighted with blue around the neck, cheeks and chin, indicating a higher caste than the average Arikhan foot soldier.

"I am Cordaris, Varbatro Leader of the Akrona Contingent," the veteran commander said. "For whom do you spy?"

Grey pretended not to understand the question, though he grasped most of it. The alien leader waited a moment before striking him across the face with the back of his clenched claw. Grey blinked and tried to shake off the blow. He was struck again.

"Speak or other means will be discovered," Cordaris said.

"I not spy," Grey said in broken Arikhan. "Don't know. Confused."

The alien hit him harder. Blood swelled in his mouth. Grey perceived little choice but to accept the beating. What could he say? He didn't know where he was or how he got there, and his last conscious act was setting off a nuclear warhead to destroy an Arikhan battlecruiser. Hardly an act likely to endear himself.

"What is this? An ornament?" Cordaris asked, noticing the slender gold band around Grey's finger. The ring slipped off easily. "There are etchings within the band. If the scratches are words, we will decipher them."

"Slaves have no written language," the tall guard said.

"They did before the conquest. Confess, spy. This trinket has betrayed you," Cordaris said, waving it in Grey's face.

"I sorry, being of great superiority. I lost. Not spy," Grey answered, putting his forehead to the floor.

Cordaris raised the clenched claw again but held back. The submissive creature before him did not appear courageous enough to lie. Nothing but skin and bones, it could barely kneel without losing balance. Cordaris lowered his fist.

"Tomorrow, be ready to speak," Cordaris ordered.

Grey was brought more food. Not much, but enough. It had a strange aftertaste. Drugs? He ate it anyway.

The next day Cordaris returned and beat Grey again, this time at greater length. Grey still played dumb, and the effects of his drugged food made it easier.

Typical lizards, he thought, using the derogatory nickname they had gained on Earth. *They want information, but drug my food, believing it will make me compliant. They don't understand people who are willing to die rather than submit.*

After the third day, Cordaris sent a surrogate to do the beatings, an ambitious junior officer named Amartro. The assistant was stocky and strong, but not very bright. His face was wider than average for an Arikhan, the black eyes set deeper. The skin was a deep brown with no trace of aristocratic blue. Only one bronze swamp leaf showed on his dreary olive green uniform.

"You will speak," Amartro demanded, pinning Grey against the wall and punching with a closed claw.

Lacking any sense of subtlety, Amartro seemed to believe that force alone would achieve his goal. Sometimes the prisoner was beaten several days in a row, sometimes with days of solitude interspersed between the interrogations.

Accustomed to more clever adversaries, Grey came to view the Contingent minions with ill-disguised disdain. As the sparse feedings continued, giving him just enough strength to endure the questioning, he fixed it in his mind to forget everything. To forget his name, past life, and anything else Amartro might find interesting. He learned to use the drugs, draining his mind of useful information.

Several weeks later, even the Arikhan came to feel their efforts were futile.

"You show much fortitude, food creature," Amartro said one day, crouching comfortably outside the cell.

Grey looked into the black eyes, sensing a change. Having failed, Amartro had decided to change tactics. Knowing that Arikhan, as a rule, would rarely resort to guile, Grey was surprised.

"Take this," Amartro said, sliding a roll of baked grain across the floor.

Grey studied the roll for the briefest moment before eating without comment. It was good.

"You must tell me your secrets," the ambitious guard said, lashing his tongue lightly.

"Tell me what to say, and I will say it," Grey meekly agreed. Though without sincerity, a lapse he hoped the alien would fail to notice.

"The secrets must be yours. I already know my own secrets," Amartro said with a sly dipping of his eye-rings.

Finishing the bread, Grey sat cross-legged in the center of the cell, tipping his head down.

"I will say what you tell me to say," he repeated.

"Then you will die," Amartro threatened.

"It has happened before," Grey replied.

* * * * * *

"Shall it be sent to the pens? It might be worth slaughtering if the butcher can add enough meat," Sub-Leader Talatron asked, a waddling disgrace to the bronze swamp leaf on his tunic.

Cordaris, Talatron, and Amartro stood outside the cell, apparently contemplating a decision. Having grown up on a lunar mining colony subjected to lighter gravity deterioration, he had spent much of his early life underweight. That changed when he finally visited Earth, though he didn't reach 5'10 until his early twenties, and didn't weigh 175 pounds until years after that. Women generally found him good looking with his unruly brown hair and thoughtful gray eyes. He weighed considerably less now.

"It may yet be a tool of the marauders, or a test by Central Planning of our diligence," Amartro warned.

Cordaris lowered eye-rings, gazing at the prisoner in contemplation.

"Feed it for a few days, then send it to the mines at Karak," the Varbatro Leader ordered.

"The creature is too weak. It will not survive a season in the mines," Talatron protested, thinking the stubborn animal might have just enough flesh on his bones for a decent lunch.

"It shall be as Sherra wills," Cordaris said, ignoring his subordinate's suggestion with a sharp click of his tongue.

"As Sherra wills," Talatron agreed with reverence.

Cordaris dipped eye-rings in respect. Amartro silently walked away. Grey knew Sherra to be the most honored deity of the Arikhan, the goddess of their prosperity, but it was the first time he remembered her intervening on his behalf.

The sun was not yet up when he was escorted from the concrete cell several days later. Days in which he had mostly slept. The guards had obeyed the order to feed him, usually a thick gruel, but he didn't mind. He had never been particular about what he ate, and he had decided the whole experience was just a fevered delusion, so it didn't matter.

The floor beneath his bare feet was cold. Of the two armed guards, one was portly and shorter than most Arikhan, the other a head taller than Grey but unusually thin. They were not well-dressed, their common blue tunics showing age and leather boots requiring polish. The smaller guard, Larbatro, did most of the talking, expressing satisfaction at getting away for the day. Colatron, the taller of the two, said little but didn't disagree. Neither spoke to their prisoner or expected much of him.

After tying Grey's hands behind his back with a leather strap, the shorter guard put a rope around his neck and pulled him toward the door, but they received enough cooperation that dragging wasn't necessary. As he stepped outside the crude cinder block building, Grey looked up at the dark sky, searching for the comforting stars of home. He thought he should be able to see several of his favorite constellations, but they weren't there. None of the stars looked familiar.

Even before sunrise, the air was warm. A small yellow moon was visible above the horizon to the west. Judging by the gravity, Grey felt the planet might be smaller than Earth but larger than Mars. Akrona? He tried to remember if Mordari had ever mentioned such a world, but she had rarely discussed the extent of the Arikhan Empire.

They walked down a crude path between two wooden maintenance shacks, reaching the foot of a long asphalt runway. It was an airport. Or spaceport. Probably both, and not very large, having only three hangars. Grey recognized a sho'kara set on the edge of the tarmac, a large cigar-shaped Arikhan cargo transport. The airbase was surrounded by simple rock walls, guarded by an occasional stone tower. The conquerors of Akrona appeared to have little need for high-tech security.

He was led to an area where several boxy ground vehicles were parked, all hydrogen powered, none bigger than a standard Earth ground runner. The six-wheel transports, known as a sho'kara, were large enough for eight passengers and a modest amount of cargo. Painted in a dark maroon with jagged yellow stripes on the doors, the protective coating was beginning to peel. Grey was pushed into a rear compartment and the hatch locked. The vehicle was fast but noisy. Either poorly built or poorly maintained. The Arikhan were not known for their engineering skills. He rolled on his side and went back to sleep.

The red sun was high in the late afternoon sky before the vehicle slowed to a stop. The hatch opened and Grey was pulled out, blinded by the blazing light. The heat felt good on his pale skin, at first, but without protection it quickly became uncomfortable.

"Forward, food creature," Larbatro said, pushing him toward a ramshackle building perched on a low hill surrounded by tall leafy trees. The one-story structure was made of slat-board, the roof covered in gravel and tar. Much of the green paint that had protected it from the elements was missing.

Grey complied with the guard's order as best he could, but his legs were weak, the warm air difficult to breathe. It felt strange having no clothes, public nudity not being part of his culture. He tripped going up the rough stone steps, scraping his knees, and had to be dragged into the comparative coolness of the headquarters.

It wasn't much of a command center. He noticed a large meeting room, a cramped bunk area to the left, a kitchen back to the right, and a few offices located down a rear corridor. The floor was sanded wood. The walls were poorly painted in drab jungle green. The beam ceiling showed traces of sunlight, stained where it leaked in the rain. After seeing the impressive military outpost the Arikhan had briefly maintained on Europa, Grey could hardly believe this shabby cabin was inhabited by the same species.

"What skinny piece of meat is this?" a broad-shouldered alien said, storming into the main room where Grey had fallen on the floor. The alien appeared to be a high official with intelligent red-brown eyes and the voice of authority. The olive green tunic indicated a post of leadership but there were no lapel pins to indicate rank. His skin was a dry blue, unlike most Arikhan, who were brown.

"A prisoner taken by the Contingent Leader. Cordaris sends it to your mines," Larbatro explained.

"Does the Contingent Leader now interfere with production?" the annoyed official asked.

"Yes, Sarden Leader Gamtro," Larbatro said, boldly straightening to full height.

"Hold your place, ranker. Even a lowly camp leader may put such as you on report," Gamtro warned with a sharp glare, his cheeks flushing.

"Do so, but still must you accept this gift," Larbatro insisted.

The guard defiantly clicked his tongue and kicked Grey in the ribs, rolling him over to Gamtro's leather-booted feet. The prisoner lay flat on his stomach, not moving for fear of being stomped.

"It has no meat. Take it to the pens," a tall guard said, emerging from the rear corridor wearing a brown leather tunic and tan trousers. A yellow swamp leaf indicated he had once been a warrior before being reduced to this obscure outpost.

"Nabbatron, if the slave has no meat, what good is it in the pens?" Colatron replied, offering a rare remark.

"What good is it here?" Nabbatron protested.

"Perhaps it will be eaten by your slaves? No doubt they long for a taste of blood in their mort," Larbatro suggested.

Gamtro rapidly clicked his tongue against the roof of his mouth, an Arikhan way of expressing amusement, and waved the guards away. They hurried back down the flagstone steps to their sho'kara and departed before the Sarden Leader could change his mind.

"Get up, food creature," Gamtro ordered.

Grey struggled to his knees and put his forehead to the floor in the posture of submission. Gamtro was pleased.

"Give it water and put it to work," Gamtro ordered his subordinate.

Without another thought on the subject, Gamtro returned to his office where an old wooden desk and a communications globe awaited

13

his attention.

With hands still tied behind his back, Grey was taken to the outside steps and allowed a drink of cool water from a copper faucet. He considered begging to have the bonds removed, but decided not to. He was too weak to provoke trouble for which he was unprepared.

From the staircase atop the hill, Grey saw some of the sprawling mining camp on the other side of a narrow valley. Karak looked to be several thousand acres of dry brush and scrub forest stretched below a long series of steep cliffs. Vibrating pale blue energy waves, probably a force field, surrounded the entire area.

There didn't seem to be any security within the enclosure itself, only small groups of weathered tents and huts. Sparse gardens were fed from a lake toward the northern end of the compound. Beyond the enclosure to the south, as far as he could see, was nothing but rugged mountains and thick forests. No tracks, no roads. Nothing resembling civilization.

A poke in the back told Grey to move. He gingerly walked down the steps to a dirt path, then across a flat area and over the railroad tracks to the main gate three hundred yards away, splashing his feet in a shallow creek. The rope around his neck hurt as the guard pulled him through a door and up a short flight of stairs into a red brick building. Grey was glad to be inside away from the glare of the sun.

The two-story gatehouse towering above the main entrance to the camp appeared to be the Arikhan contact point with the workers. Out the long broad windows, he saw a network of aluminum tracks bearing ore carts. The tracks appeared to link together just inside the gate before exiting to a long cement loading platform. From the platform, a larger gauge of tracks ran north where a long pylon bridge crossed over a bluish river before disappearing into a vast prairie. Grey guessed there must be processing facilities beyond the prairie, but it was only a guess.

As the sentry pushed him down on rough wooden floorboards, Grey realized that solar powered fans were cooling the building. The plaster walls were painted in the same drab green as the commandant's office. A staff of eight Arikhan sentries were seated on stools around an old communications globe located in the corner, their attention so riveted to the broadcast that he was ignored.

Grey soon realized that all of the sentries were generally lean and similarly dressed in brown tunics and patched gray trousers. Most were between six and a half to seven feet tall. Their rawhide boots were worn.

"An official announcement from the Council of Warriors," a grim voice said from the viewer.

Grainy images appeared in the globe, first of an Arikhan military official, then a picture of an Arikhan battlecruiser. Grey recognized the warship. The last time he had seen it, he was standing on its hull.

"Terrible news, brothers and sisters. The rumors are confirmed. For the first time in living memory, our courageous forces have met with defeat. The invasion of Sol has failed. Farre, Timik, and even Bellerophon, are destroyed," the official said.

Grey noticed the announcer had the shiny dark blue skin of an aristocrat, though even commoners sometimes showed bluish traces, especially when flushed with excitement.

"Bellerophon!" several of the guards exclaimed.

"How can this be?" their sub-leader asked, a female better dressed than the others. "Too well was Bellerophon constructed. Too strong were her arms."

"Your questions are worthy," the high official said, not specifically to this group, but to millions of Arikhan who must have been wondering the same thing. "Much did our forces prevail against the Sol inhabitants, despite loss of the armed escorts, and a lush world of blessed resources lay before us. But a curl struck in stealth at Bellerophon even at her moment of greatest triumph. Demonic magic was practiced, and all aboard were lost. But take heart, for the foul curl was slain, never again to darken our prospects. One day the food creatures of Sol will again be subject to Sherra's mercy."

Grey noticed the high official wore broad silver leaves across her red tunic and spoke in a soothing fashion to soften the impact of the distressing report. He had thought the Arikhan a tougher species. Maybe they had been, he decided, in their past. Before the riches of conquered worlds began to spoil them. The image vanished, replaced by a cloudy screen.

"Not for two generations shall we again tread the path to Sol," a sentry whispered to his comrades, a middle-aged Arikhan with plain features.

"It could be more, Bortro," his sub-leader warned. "Sol is a primitive world without a stargate, inhabited by vicious barbarians. Long will it be before we venture there again."

"Romtra, what of Bhast? There is no talk," Frontra asked, an older female with delicate eye-rings and a pensive gaze. She was the tallest of the females, with long arms and a powerful frame. Perhaps a warrior in earlier times.

"Sad indeed the fate of a colonial transport without escort," Sub-Leader Romtra answered, her opinion meeting with respect. "A thousand of our brothers and sisters must now beg the mercy of food creatures."

Romtra's remark brought much anger.

"We should slay them all," Nabbatron said, the largest Arikhan in the room. "Too weak were our forces. Too much was our confidence. Now the food creatures abide in victory."

"The fate of Sol is for warriors to decide, not sentries of the rear echelon," Romtra lectured.

Nabbatron spun on his heels and left the room with a disgruntled thrust of his shoulders. The others were not unhappy to see him go.

"The Council of Warriors will need more warships, better and stronger than Bellerophon," Bortro said. "If work orders are placed, our production will increase. Duty on Akrona may once again bring prosperity."

"Resources are not what they were a hundred years ago," Frontra cautioned. "Akrona no longer builds warships as in the past. Our labor is much depleted. Too many workers are sent to the pens."

"Production may fill a few orders," Romtra said without much confidence. "Perhaps cargo ships, or courier vessels."

"Let us hope. What promotion may we receive on this Sherra forsaken rock?" Bortro complained, heavier and older than the others.

"Do not blaspheme," Romtra scolded. "Sherra forsakes none of her children. And forget not the prophecy. From the mines of Akrona will be forged the Sword of Sherra. We thought Bellerophon, forged from the minerals of this world, had fulfilled the prophecy. Our greatest triumph may yet lie ahead."

"Blessed is the wisdom of Sherra," the group chanted.

Grey tried to gather bits and pieces of the conversation that seemed to apply to him. Particularly the part about the destroyer of the *Bellerophon* being killed.

If I'm dead, what am I doing here? he thought.

He tried to shake off the haze pressing against his brain, but still felt sleepy. Nothing around him seemed real except the blows of his captors. *This must be another nightmare,* he decided. *At some point, I'm going to wake up. I hope it's soon.*

"What's that?" Romtra said, pointing at the prisoner near the door.

"Nabbatron brought us a new worker," Dhartro said, younger than many in the room but slighter than most.

"It looks like half a worker," Romtra remarked, gaining clicks of amusement from her staff.

Grey glanced up as Romtra squatted down to run her claws through the shaggy brown hair hanging over his forehead, pulling his head back. She was older than her staff, slender but sturdy. The webbing around her head was growing thin. Romtra stared into the prisoner's blank expression, the gray eyes empty.

"It will not last a week. There is no meat," Romtra said.

Romtra untied the rope around his neck, probed the soft flesh with momentary interest, then took out a thick bronze collar and positioned herself to fasten it around the prisoner's neck. The moment he saw the ring, Grey panicked and kicked fiercely at Romtra's midsection. Bortro leapt forward, seeking to pin the prisoner down. Grey twisted, kicked Bortro in a sensitive area between his thighs, and struggled to free his hands, fighting on instinct alone. Frontra joined the fray and eventually the three of them managed to hold the prisoner down long enough to secure the collar.

"The thing is stronger than it looks," Frontra observed, the large female sentry breathing heavily.

"A fighter. Maybe it will last longer than a week," Bortro said, the husky male's eye-rings bent in pain as he clutched the injured area.

"Apparently the creature is only docile until provoked. Keep the paws tied until you release it into the compound," Romtra said, also breathing hard.

Pinned to the floor with Frontra sitting on him, Grey wasn't listening to the conversation. None of it made sense to him.

Once again dragged into the blinding light, Grey passed under an arch into the compound. Frontra led him on a short leather leash, moving slowly because the food creature appeared disoriented.

"You are sent to the lowest camp," Frontra said, veering toward the southern end of the enclosure. "The mines are hot. Work begins at sunrise. No work, no eat. Attempt escape and you die. Obey the rules, perhaps you survive. Do you understand?"

Grey did not respond. He did not understand. Nor did he care so long as no one was hitting him.

"Do you understand?" Frontra repeated. But she saw he didn't. His eyes held a glazed look. He stumbled over the rough dirt path like one wandering in a fog, his tender feet pained by small stones.

They walked for a long time, following a line of ore tracks toward the rocky, tree-studded cliffs above the mines. As they traversed the compound, Grey vaguely noticed a series of widely spaced campsites. Nearest the gatehouse, the tents looked better maintained. Several even had raised wood floors. A handful of people, mostly women tending the gardens, were clothed in sparse cotton tunics or animal skins. They seemed to be growing a crop similar to wheat and a variety of odd-looking vegetables. There were no tractors or plows, only hand trowels and a few shovels.

Closer to the mines, which were spread in a long fishhook along the base of the mountain, the camps looked poorer. An ore cart rolled past pushed by two burley male workers. Human workers, hardly different in size or shape than his own people. The workers wore collars as Grey did. They did not look up.

Near the southern end of the lake he saw a dozen women working small plots. Some had adequate clothing, others wore rags. A few children, all very young, sat quietly in the shade of some run down shacks. Most looked undernourished.

This isn't a work camp, Grey realized. *These are slaves. It's a slave camp!* He remembered reading of such things. It was said that some nations on Earth still maintained similar institutions, though nothing this extreme. Grey felt like he should be shocked, but the impact didn't register. He seemed to be watching an old documentary rather than observing a miserable reality.

At last they reached a decrepit camp pitched fifty yards from the foot of a granite cliff. The mine was nothing more than a rough tunnel cut into the mountain. Trees and bushes grew thickly along the top of the ridge, and a waterfall gushed down the side near the entrance. The creek continued running past the camp toward a vibrating wire fence two hundred yards away. Beyond the fence lay a lush green forest, small portions of which had been cleared away. Grey assumed the trees had been harvested to provide timber supports for the mines.

Set in a clearing surrounded by scraggily trees and blue shrubs, the camp consisted of a few old canvas tents. A large communal tent was held up by four corner posts and two tall center poles, the sides held down by ropes and stakes. Smaller pup tents were arrayed nearby. Only one person was in the camp, a young woman with her arm in a sling. Grey guessed her age at about twenty-five, though her figure was unnaturally thin. She had long auburn hair, sad brown eyes, and vaguely Asian features. She wore nothing but a bronze collar and a ragged yellow tunic.

"Greetings, Frontra," the slave woman said, kneeling on the ground in submission.

"Peace, Myra. Does the wing heal?" the alien sentry asked.

"Yes, mistress. Thank you for letting me rest it," Myra said, bowing her head before looking up. Grey detected respect in the slave's eyes but not fear.

"Damaged workers are not valuable," Frontra said. "Where is Garn?"

"Shalli takes him with her to the gardens," Myra said, glancing at the prisoner but saying nothing until asked.

"You should have more children. We have too few in this camp," Frontra said.

"Clagg would like more children, but food is scarce. This has not been a good year, mistress," Myra dared to suggest.

By her posture rather than words, Frontra seemed to agree.

19

"Garden allotments are improved for the lesser camps. More food will be provided if production improves," Frontra advised.

"Thank you, mistress," Myra replied.

"This is a new worker," Frontra announced, untying Grey's hands and gently pushing him toward the big tent.

"Excuse me, mistress, but it looks like half a worker," Myra joked.

Frontra clicked her tongue in amusement.

"It needs food, but make no rash judgment. The half-meat is stronger than it appears," Frontra said. The alien turned around and showed Myra a dark brown mark on her hip. Myra was surprised.

"He struck you?" Myra asked.

"Not so hard as it struck Bortro. It will be days before the old waddler walks upright again," Frontra said, apparently with satisfaction. "And Romtra's belly will grumble for a week."

Myra looked at the stranger again, trying to see something in his demeanor that suggested such a fierce temperament. Nothing of the sort showed. He was close to her age, desperately thin, of average height, and pale as a bleached bone. The masters had not given him a shred of clothing to wear.

"The food creature does not have all its senses," Frontra explained, anticipating Myra's thoughts. "It may have been drugged while in Contingent custody. In time, it will grow stronger."

"You are generous, Frontra. Always has it been so," Myra said.

"Not always," Frontra corrected before returning to the gatehouse.

"Welcome to Ferret Camp," Myra said in a language Grey didn't recognize.

He stood in one place, looking at the worn tents and a small cooking fire. Other than a few pots and water jars, he saw little else in the way of possessions. Unlike the tents near the gate, which looked newer, these tents were patched. The beds were made of straw tied with reeds into mats.

"Do you accept my welcome?" Myra asked in the strange language.

"Where am I?" Grey asked in English.

"I don't know your words," Myra said, making him sit down near the community tent. Switching to Arikhan, Myra said, "Do you understand the language of the masters?"

"I lost," Grey said in Arikhan.

"You have not been a slave long," Myra said in surprise, replying in Arikhan.

"Not slave. I—"

He reached up to feel the collar locked around his neck. On Earth, he was an engineer. A soldier. A leader. Now he was sitting naked in the dust of a slave camp hundreds or maybe thousands of light years from home. Beaten, confused, and bewildered. He wasn't anybody anymore.

Myra brought him a bowl of soup and slowly fed him with a tin spoon, noticing the empty look in his eyes.

"You need sleep," Myra said. "Eat. Take rest. What is your name?"

Grey thought for a long time, continuing to fondle the collar, but he didn't answer her question.

Near sunset, a teenage woman carrying a baby in one arm and a heavy basket of vegetables in the other returned from the gardens. Small-boned with long blonde hair and vivid blue eyes, the woman would have attracted attention in any culture.

Myra jumped up and took the baby with her good arm.

"How was Garn?" Myra asked.

"Fussy. I gave him tubers to stay quiet," Shalli said, thankfully setting the basket down.

"He grows quickly in his third year," Myra said, rubbing the youngster's red hair and making him laugh. "We must watch that he doesn't gain too much meat."

"The masters say children are no longer taken to the pens. They need workers."

"I don't trust the masters," Myra explained. Shalli nodded agreement.

"Who is that?" Shalli said, seeing a stranger sleeping in the community tent.

"A new worker brought by Frontra," Myra said.

"We have little allotment as it is," Shalli objected. "Wolf Camp is claiming much of the harvest. Raven Camp is making claims, too.

21

Our share is barely enough to feed Clagg."

"Their arrogance is without limit. Before the cave-in, none would challenge Ferret Camp in such a way. Now our numbers are so few, we get nothing. Clagg will be angry."

"Even Clagg cannot fight so many," Shalli said.

"At least we had fresh tunics to wear in the fall. Wolf Camp shares none of the new furs," Myra bitterly remarked.

"What can we do?" Shalli said, tears welling in her eyes. "Our mine is played out. Our quotas unmet. The masters will not bend the share for a camp so poor as ours, and now they give us starving strangers to further weaken our hopes! Isn't it bad enough that Marne and his disgusting wolves grow more difficult to avoid?"

Myra put a comforting hand on Shalli's arm. All had noticed the Wolf Camp leader's unwelcome advances.

"Courtesy seems to mean nothing these days, but don't worry. Clagg won't let those savages touch his sister in such a way."

"I'd be sport for their torment pit if not for Clagg," Shalli agreed. "What do you know of the stranger?"

"Little, other than he doesn't speak our language," Myra said.

"He's mute?" Shalli asked.

"No, not mute. He knows a little of the masters' words. I think he's been sick for a long time. He has no meat."

"Fortunate for him to avoid the pens, but it's not good that he's so ignorant. Could he be a spy?"

"He's not a spy."

"He could be a spy. There have been stories."

"He's not a spy," Myra insisted.

"I don't trust him," Shalli said.

"You don't even know him," Myra said, shocked by her attitude.

"If he's a spy, the men will kill him."

"Frontra brought him to us. She would be displeased, and we have few enough friends among the masters," Myra protested.

Shalli paused in thought, looking again at the sleeping stranger.

"The mines are dangerous. Maybe there will be an accident," Shalli suggested.

Myra glanced over at Grey as he slept in the tent, knowing that

22

Shalli would not be alone in her opinion.

As the sun set over the mountain to the west, the workers began returning from the mine in small groups, twelve men and six women. Eight more women and two young children returned from working in the gardens. All were curious about the stranger who continued sleeping soundly despite the noise.

"We must know if he's a spy," Hernet said, the squat miner holding a stick of timber in his hand. The digger had short hairy arms with tattooed circles on the shoulders. A black beard set off his pale green eyes.

"Push his face in the creek," Cot said, the skinny stonecutter willing to volunteer. Big hands, long arms and a thin neck made him look awkward.

"Be patient. We are yet to hear his words. Have difficult days brought us so low?" Clagg asked, the giant hulk of a man unwilling to tolerate rash suggestions. With a bushy red beard, deep blue eyes, and a stature almost the size of Nabbatron, his presence commanded respect. Many hung their heads in shame, for none doubted Clagg was right.

"If he's a spy, he's a meatless one. Maybe we can trade him to Wolf Camp for some berries?" Hernet said, making everyone laugh.

"Should we wake him?" Shalli asked.

"No one will wake him until morning," Myra said, frowning at the suggestion.

"You're not the leader," Cot protested.

"Do you wish to find a loosening herb in your soup?" Myra asked.

Cot did not laugh, though many others did.

The next morning, just as the sun was rising, Grey woke from a restless sleep. There was unusual movement around him in the semidarkness. At first he thought it was his wife coming home from a late duty tour. He wondered what new problems might arise during the day ahead and happily remembered an experiment he wanted to try with the new step-two variable star drive.

He sat up with a start. This wasn't his sleeping chamber. The bed was straw, the roof a flapping piece of canvas. His heart beat faster with a sense of panic. The nightmare couldn't be true!

"The stranger wakes," someone said in a strange language.

"He's lazy to sleep so late. He'll eat more than he's worth," another complained.

Grey felt around for his clothes only to discover he didn't have any. As the light improved, he saw many others in the camp had little to wear. The men only had breechcloths and a few shirts. Several of the older women had thin cloth tunics, but some had even less. Grey reached for the collar around his neck, testing its strength. It couldn't be removed without tools and there wasn't a hacksaw in sight.

Someone laughed. Grey wondered if they were laughing at him. He started to get up but realized his entire body ached. The legs were sore. His arms bruised. His feet hurt and portions of his face felt swollen. He got up anyway and went outside to look at the fading stars. They weren't his stars.

Grey studied the people preparing for their workday, the camp lit by a cooking fire. They looked like normal humans. Some shorter, some taller. Some with dark hair, others light. Skin color ranged from peachy to dusky brown. Nor did there appear to be any anatomical differences. The only person he recognized, Myra, was busy serving broth to the biggest of the men, a tall muscular giant with a dirty red beard and pleasant blue eyes. Then Myra gave some broth to a small child hardly more than a three years old.

Myra glanced at Grey and smiled, then brought him a bowl of the foreign soup. None of the others smiled or made an effort to speak with him.

Grey didn't care. He wasn't supposed to be there. The more he thought about it, the more convinced he became that he wasn't supposed to be anywhere. He had set off the nuclear device. Destroyed the enemy warship. He was supposed to be dead.

"You need food," Myra said in Arikhan, presenting the bowl.

Grey studied the hot broth for a moment before looking toward the scrubby prairie between the camp and the perimeter fence some hundred and eighty meters away. The wire vibrated in an odd manner, humming softly as it gave off a soft blue glow. Grey ignored the food Myra was offering. He turned toward the fence, walking slowly at first, then more rapidly, stretching his cramped legs into longer strides.

"Clagg, stop him," Myra said with concern.

Clagg began to follow as did several of the workers, but Grey was well ahead of them. He paused briefly when he reached the fence and studied the energy pattern. It was a force field, probably supported by an electrical grid, and nearly invisible, which explained why the enclosure appeared so open. He stepped back, took a deep breath, and threw himself against the shimmering wall of energy.

The pain was explosive, tearing through his nerve endings. He fell back, struggling to breathe, unsure how much of the energy field he'd been able to penetrate. Not very much, he knew. He crouched, caught another breath, and charged again, determined to push through into the forest beyond or die in the attempt. The pain was just as bad the second time, and after a few seconds, he tumbled to the ground, his body quivering. He rubbed his hands together, trying to restore normal feeling. His vision was blurred. He crawled to his knees, gasped for a breath of the cool morning air, and staggered to his feet, ready to lunge again. He was grabbed from behind.

"No, stranger, you'll never make it. No one has ever made it," Clagg said, wrapping his huge arms around Grey's shoulders.

Grey briefly struggled against Clagg's grip, but realized he couldn't break loose without hurting his rescuer. He wasn't prepared to do that. Not yet.

"You work with me today," Clagg said, switching to Arikhan.

"Work where?" Grey asked, his memory of the alien language improving.

Clagg was surprised the stranger not only knew the language of their enslavers, but practiced the inflections as well. Even Akronians never did that. It made Clagg suspicious.

"We go to the mines. There's much work ahead to meet our quota," Clagg said to his workers, waving them toward the cliff.

Grey followed Clagg back to the tents where the women watched with quiet curiosity.

"The stranger works with me today," Clagg said.

Myra gave Grey the bowl of broth again, watched him gulp it down without a pause, and went to pick up Garn. The curly-haired

25

child laughed at Grey's wary expression.

"This is my son, Garn, and you met my husband, Clagg. We'll watch out for you," Myra promised.

"Do not trouble yourself," Grey said in Arikhan, clicking his tongue rudely.

Grey followed the tree-lined path toward the mine entrance, trailing behind several others who were already on their way.

"Don't get attached, Myra. He won't survive," Clagg warned.

"Try to teach him our words, Clagg. The sooner he accepts our ways, the better chance he'll have," Myra said.

"Always taking in the strays," Clagg laughed.

Inside the mine entrance, a musty storage room held the workers' tools. Grey found them primitive after the advanced equipment he'd used mining the mineral rich tunnels beneath Vitruvius. All were hand tools. Picks, shovels, wedges and mallets. Bolts for securing the timber supports, and stacked in the wide entry area, a pile of roughly cut beams. Grey noticed a number of old jackhammers in the corner, but they were in such poor condition they couldn't be used. There was no evidence that anyone had ever tried to repair them.

As they gathered their tools, each worker picked up a luminescent lamp, a filtration mask, and a pair of thick leather gloves. Grey noticed dozens of jars in a cabinet that held dry chemical bases. Though dusty, Arikhan lettering could still be seen on the labels.

"What are those?" Grey asked.

"We do not read the masters' writing," Clagg said.

No one else tried to answer Grey's question. He went forward to study the containers, but Clagg pulled him back, gave him a pair of gloves, and pointed down the shaft.

"No tools can leave the mine," Clagg warned. "To be caught in camp with a pick or shovel means punishment. Understand?"

Grey glanced at the tools but said nothing.

"You should have this," Clagg offered.

He handed Grey a ragged breechcloth made of two hide flaps tied together with leather string. It reminded Grey of something out of an old jungle movie, but he made no protest. Nor did he say thank you.

Grey trailed Clagg down a long twisting tunnel that branched off in a dozen places. He had the impression the mine was about ten years old, and though the surface minerals were nearly depleted, he knew enough about ore trails to guess there were still rich loads waiting to be discovered. Oddly, Clagg bypassed the more promising areas and went to the end of the tunnel. Behind them, two others were laying track to bring the ore carts closer to the work area.

"I'll dig, you load," Clagg said.

Grey did as instructed, feeling the heat of the tunnel. Ventilation was poor and soon he was sweating profusely. The filtration masks were so old they barely suppressed the dust.

"Water!" Clagg shouted after an hour or so.

Within a few minutes, Shalli came down the tunnel carrying buckets of water from the creek. She was sweating also, and for the first time, Grey realized she wasn't wearing any clothing except for her reed sandals. He also noticed Shalli was quite attractive, even by lamplight, with round firm breasts, a slender waist, long legs, and a bushy apex. Apparently, these Akronians were no different than the humans of his homeworld. There was likely a scientific theory for that. But he said nothing to betray his thoughts.

Grey would have liked to work harder but his muscles wouldn't cooperate. He had spent too much time confined to the Contingent prison. And the heat grew worse instead of better. By the end of the day, he was convinced he'd become trapped in a perverse version of Dante's Inferno. His fellow workers didn't care for the heat, either, but they were accustomed to the conditions. And though they talked often with each other, and joked with the females who brought them water, none spoke to him but Clagg. And even Clagg said no more than necessary. Grey noticed Shalli actually looked at him with contempt. It wasn't the first time he'd provoked that reaction.

At the end of the day, the workers poured out of the shafts, storing their tools before emerging into the fading afternoon light. The setting sun was beautiful, slowly dropping over the hill in a blaze of red against a clear blue-green sky.

Campfires were lit to cook the evening meal as the workers returned. When several who had been pushing ore carts to the front gate also came back, everyone sat down to be served. All seemed to have regular sitting areas except Grey. Myra handed him a bread roll filled with steamed vegetables that smelled quite good. The bread roll was snatched from his hands.

"None for you until you earn it. We have no food for lazy strangers," Cot said, tall and skinny with knobby knees.

"Cot, give that back," Myra demanded.

"Let him scrounge from the other camps. They can afford charity," Cot said.

Myra looked to Clagg, but Clagg shrugged. The situation was between Cot and the stranger to work out.

Cot held the bread roll above Grey's head, daring him to do something about it.

Grey looked at the unfriendly eyes watching him and decided it wasn't worth the effort. He backed away and returned to the mine entrance. Jagged rocks allowed him to climb up the steep hill along the side of the waterfall where he disappeared into the stunted trees along the crest of the ridge.

"That's the meanest thing I've ever seen you do," Myra scolded Cot. "And the rest of you should be ashamed."

"He's a spy. He only speaks words of the masters," Hernet said.

"I hope he starves. Then we won't have to kill him," Shalli added.

"Of everyone here, I should think you would understand," Myra said, her voice angry. Shalli bowed her head and walked away.

* * * * * *

Grey scrambled to a point on the hill where he could see most of the compound. It was better than two kilometers wide and several times as long. He guessed the total population at seven or eight hundred, most living near the western cliffs or north beyond the lake. Ferret Camp seemed a poor stepchild, being farthest to the south in the most barren area, but none of the campsites could claim riches. Even the Arikhan headquarters had been no more than a rough cabin with solar collectors for power. Akrona could not be a good place to serve, he realized, and knowing the Arikhan warrior spirit as he did, Grey guessed the sentries would much rather be someplace else. He knew the feeling.

The hill was mostly dry earth and sedimentary rock, covered by scattered trees that looked like oaks and thick clumps of prickly bushes. Around him, growing on the shrubs, he noticed a variety of small berries. Some were red, others purple, and a few were blue. They might be poisonous, but he was hungry and didn't particularly care. He ate several of the small red berries and found them bitter, then tried some of the larger purple ones that smelled like raspberries. They weren't good, either, but not as bad as they could be. He was pleasantly surprised to see many of the trees grew nuts.

As the sun finished setting, Grey found a dry sandy hollow at the base of a sandstone cliff that would make a good campsite. He pulled down several slender tree branches and peeled back enough of the pliant bark to tie them together, making a crude shelter. Just as he'd been taught during his days in boot camp. Little had he imagined how his military survival training would one day be applied.

The sun disappeared, revealing a sea of stars and a small moon. Not the same moon Grey remembered from before. This planet had two moons. He sat back against a crooked stump and studied the constellations for clues, wondering how he had become lost in another solar system. And how he might get back to the world he knew. The odds didn't seem good, but he wasn't ready to accept his unkind fate. Maybe he never would.

The next morning, the work crew arrived at the mine curious to learn what had happened to the stranger. They were surprised to find him already selecting the equipment he wanted, which included a pick ax. They didn't ask the stranger what he was doing or where he had been all night. He offered no explanations. Most of the workers hadn't even arrived when Grey started down the central shaft.

"Do not hurt yourself," Clagg warned as Grey's ax bit into the rock some hours later.

"It doesn't matter," he answered.

"The rock is hard here. There is shale farther down," Clagg said.

"I am not looking for fossils. Chop the shale if you want."

"You have no strength to break the rock," Clagg complained.

"It doesn't matter," Grey replied.

After a time, the heat of the mine seemed to grow worse. Clagg removed his blue cotton shirt as he began to sweat. Another young woman brought them water, a petite brunette hardly more than fifteen called Pie. Grey took no notice, drinking what he needed and returning to work. At the end of the day, as the workers made their way back to camp, he turned toward the mountain instead, climbing up the rocks next to the waterfall and disappearing into the brush. He didn't explain where he was going and no one asked.

* * * * * *

"Where is the half-meat?" Frontra inquired, making her rounds just before sunset. Myra seemed embarrassed. Many of Ferret Camp's workers looked away.

"He resides upon the mountain, mistress," Clagg replied in Arikhan, pointing to a clump of foliage above the mine.

"It seeks escape?" Frontra said.

"No, mistress," Clagg said.

"He does not choose to stay in our camp," Beknar said, an older woman with short-tempered words. Her face was prematurely wrinkled, the black hair tingeing gray even though she was barely forty.

"You know the rules. It cannot be fed if it does not work," Frontra said.

"He works, mistress," Myra answered, coming forward with Garn in her arms. "The stranger is weak, but he tries."

"It needs feeding. Why is it not here?" Frontra asked, a click of her tongue indicating her displeasure. Nearly Clagg's height, she stood with claws on her belt near the shock sticks used to control unruly slaves. Her black eyes searched for an acceptable excuse.

"He is a stranger. He does not want to be here," Cot said.

"He is a spy," Shalli said.

"You are insolent, sister of Clagg. With another, you would be punished," Frontra scolded, her thin eye-rings rising in warning.

"I am sorry, mistress," Shalli apologized, edging backward toward Myra.

"Forgive us all, mistress. The year has been hard with so many lost in the falling mountain. Our camp is not strong," Myra said, raising her eyes to meet Frontra's.

Frontra stepped forward and gently stroked her claw through Myra's soft long hair.

"Sherra does not abandon the faithful," Frontra said. "You are but food creatures, yet still a spark of her grace resides in you. Perhaps the stranger carries such a spark."

Frontra looked toward the hill, squinting against the setting sun. A moving silhouette along the ridge confirmed the newcomer was truly there and not dead in some cavern.

"I will not interfere. Work hard. Your quota is behind schedule," Frontra said, taking a final look at the camp before walking north toward Deer Camp a kilometer away.

"Frontra is kind to overlook your foolish words," Myra scolded Shalli.

"Frontra did not deny the accusation," Shalli said.

"If he's not a spy, why did Frontra not tell us?" Cot asked.

"She could have lied," Hernet said.

"The masters are not good deceivers," Pie disagreed, making room for Shalli to sit down near the campfire. "Their eyebrows twitch upon false words. Frontra rarely twitches."

"Then he must be a spy," Shalli concluded.

"You're all fools," Myra said, returning to the cooking.

"Why are we fools, my wife?" Clagg asked.

"Look at our camp, my husband," Myra said, holding up an old pot and a broken ladle. "We have nothing of value. Not even enough tunics for the girls. What is there to spy on?"

Atop the ridge, Grey prepared to spend his second night on the mountain in more luxury than the first. He returned to the burrow he'd started the night before and pulled enough leafy bushes together to make a brush cave, leaving an opening so he could study the stars. A nearby rocky outcrop allowed him to peer down on Ferret and Deer Camps.

Though hungry and tired, he resisted a temptation to pick the bushes immediately around him. There weren't that many, so he planned to cultivate them instead. There were more such plants farther up the ridge, along with some dry roots and soft nuts. He mashed the nuts with a flat rock, stuffed them into the roots, and ate the awful concoction along with sips of water from the creek. *In time,* he thought, *I'll grow to like it.*

He noticed the tree line ran all the way to the top of the hill a thousand yards away. By peeling strips off the branches, he could twist bindings to hold poles together for a more permanent shelter. He could also fashion snares to trap small animals, assuming he would need fur coverings when the weather turned colder. A fire pit could be dug back from the ridge that wouldn't be visible from the valley. He even considered making pots from the clay of the nearby creek, for the sand and silt was thick with a hardy red base.

Using the moon and starlight, Grey explored the mountain, remembering to save strength for the next day's work. The force field fence retreated far back into the interior. An old shack, long since abandoned, sat on a knoll above a derelict ventilation shaft. He probed the rundown shed, believing it to be an outpost once used by prospectors, and realized the markers he'd seen must indicate the area was off limits, suggesting why none of the human inhabitants ventured so far from their camps. Grey didn't really care about such admonitions. He never had. During his exploration, a second moon rose in the eastern sky.

Having eaten enough to satisfy his hunger, he returned to his new home, glanced again at the stars, and picked up a sharp rock, scratching lines on the soft sandstone cliff near the burrow. It was the beginning of a star chart. With luck, he would eventually discover where he was, and maybe even develop a calendar. Then, after rubbing the stubby brown beard that had begun to thicken in the last few months, he rolled over and went to sleep, knowing the project might take months to complete. It wasn't as if he had anyplace else to go.

* * * * * *

"You work hard," Clagg said in Akronos, helping Grey load an ore cart.

Grey hefted a boulder, his body sweating in the heat, the muscles in his back and arms struggling. Clagg went to help, finding the stone heavy. Grey returned to the end of the shaft, swinging the pick with practiced fervor.

"This is good ore. Richer than we have seen in years," Clagg said.

"Mountain generous," Grey answered with a stilted accent.

"You were right to dig here."

"If must dig, dig something good."

"You should come back to camp."

"I not welcome. Spy."

"We were suspicious, but that was a whole season ago. Frontra often asks where you are. We all wonder."

"I on hill. Everyone know," Grey said.

"Come back to camp. Eat real food. It will make you strong," Clagg encouraged.

"I strong," Grey replied, striking hard with the pick ax and cutting out a sizable chunk of rock facing.

Clagg nodded in agreement. The stranger had gained strength in the three months since his arrival, but more, he knew how to combine his strength with a steady coordination.

Shalli came down the tunnel carrying two water buckets hung on a pole over her slender shoulders. Clagg set aside his shovel, splashed his face, and drank deeply from a clay cup. Grey stood back waiting his turn, not bothering to look at the young woman. She was naked, as before. The camp could not afford to have the few tunics they owned ruined in the mines. On another world, Shalli would have been considered very desirable. Young and shapely, with long blonde hair and big blue eyes. When Clagg handed Grey the cup, he drank thirstily and went back to work without offering appreciation.

"Thank you, Shalli," Clagg said for both of them.

"He works hard. I don't think he's a spy," Shalli said.

"He's not a spy," Clagg agreed.

"Make him come back to camp. I'll cook food for him," Shalli said, watching in the dim light as Grey struck the wall again with even greater force. His shaggy hair was tied back behind his head with birch twine. The short beard was rough but trimmed using sharp flints found on the ridge. The strong lines of sweating muscle sparkled in the lamplight.

"I'll try," Clagg said.

At the end of the day, Clagg stopped Grey as he prepared to climb up the hill. The path was well worn now, his favorite handholds easy to find.

"Come for food. You don't have to stay if you don't want to," Clagg offered.

Grey had no desire to mingle with the people of the camp. His home on the ridge reminded him of his childhood on a remote lunar outpost before changing times complicated everything. Now he had nothing, wanted nothing, and spent his time alone dwelling among the stars, imagining himself in a better place. A place where he still had a loving wife, loyal friends, and important responsibilities.

"Come with me," Clagg impatiently said, taking hold of Grey's arm and dragging him toward the camp. It was a mistake.

Clagg hardly understood what was happening as Grey grabbed the big man's wrist, twisted him around, and then tossed him upside down to the ground with a thud. Nearly half again his weight, Clagg couldn't believe he had been thrown with such ease.

"You can't do that again," Clagg said, getting up and taking a step forward.

Grey didn't wait for the advance, but stepped underneath Clagg's outreached arm and flipped him over in a tight somersault. Clagg was fortunate they were on soft ground. Closer to the rock path, he might have been hurt.

"Maybe you *can* do that again," Clagg admitted, rubbing his butt.

Grey stood ready, feet apart, crouched for a number of different responses. Clagg noticed a predatory intensity in his expression that was unnerving. Almost like an Arikhan when provoked. Clagg felt sure he could beat Grey in a real fight, but it wasn't an experience he would look forward to.

"You don't have to come with me if you don't want to, but I would be grateful," Clagg requested. Then he smiled, the blue eyes sparkling.

Clagg started back to camp, Grey following a few paces behind but ready to bolt at any moment. Many were surprised to see him arrive, and not all were happy about it.

"We have a guest," Clagg said.

Myra smiled. Shalli was not disappointed. Beknar frowned.

Grey accepted a seat on a mat near Clagg and Garn, allowing the child to get close as long as he wasn't touched. Myra brought a loaf of grain bread dipped in broth. Grey hardly had a chance to taste the bread before Cot snatched the loaf away. This time Grey got to his feet, his eyes blazing. Cot held the bread high above the stranger's head.

"You're not accepted by this camp. We don't share bread with spies," Cot declared.

"Give that back, Cot!" Myra shouted, jumping to her feet.

"Be still, woman," Clagg said, pulling her down.

Cot was enjoying his teasing of the stranger. Grey backed off. Cot laughed.

"Cot is not afraid. You should not be afraid," Clagg said, grinning encouragement.

Grey hesitated as the camp looked for his reaction. None understood why Clagg was smiling except Grey, and all he wanted to do was leave. But he couldn't. He had worked with the men of the camp for months. Shared their labors. Their opinion meant something to him, even if he didn't choose to acknowledge it. A glance toward Shalli helped him make up his mind, the pity in the young woman's eyes making him angry.

"Leave now. We have no food for spies," Cot said.

Rather than answer the challenge, Grey grabbed Cot by his collar, put a foot in his midsection, and yanked forcefully as he rolled backward to the ground. Cot was suddenly flying upside down through the air, landing on one of the smaller tents. Cot was still trying to figure out what had happened when he found Grey hovering over him with a foot pressed against his throat.

"My bread," Grey said, reaching out his hand.

Cot handed him the bread. The foot was removed from Cot's throat.

"What kind of fighting is that?" Cot asked, checking himself for injuries.

"On my world, called judo. I not good. Study with priest," Grey answered.

Cot rubbed his elbows as Grey returned to his place near Clagg. Everyone in the camp was staring at him, most frightened. Even Myra looked worried when Garn went to sit near Grey, but to her surprise, he shared the bread with him. Garn laughed.

Though there was less talking than usual that evening, Grey could be seen listening intently, working hard to learn their language. He said little. After the food and a cup of watered grog, he was suddenly gone, disappeared into the dark night.

"He works hard," Hernet said.

"I think he's stronger than he looks," Cot said, rubbing his sore back.

"He would be good for our camp if we can bring him down from the cliff," Clagg said, pleased with the new attitudes.

"What's his name?" Shalli asked. No one answered. "Doesn't anyone know his name? He's worked with you for an entire season."

"I asked his name once," Clagg said, his voice subdued. "His face looked very sad. He said, 'I'm only stardust now.'"

Chapter Two
THE MOUNTAIN

"Tomorrow is the rest day. Maybe you should return to Ferret Camp," Clagg suggested, striking hard with his pick ax at the end of the tunnel.

"We need to shore this roof up," Grey said in conversational Akronos, cutting a niche in the wall to hold a support beam in place.

"Myra asks about you. You make Garn laugh," Clagg said.

Grey stopped, but only for a moment. Though Clagg had just turned thirty, he looked older. Many years of difficult leadership were taking a toll. When necessary, Clagg could enforce his will because of his massive strength, but he preferred persuasion instead. Neither had proved effective with Grey.

"The cart grows full. Should I have Banor roll it to the depot?" Grey asked.

"Our production is up. If we make quota, there will be new tunics for the girls, and warmers for the babies," Clagg said. "If you ate better food, our production would improve even more. I might trade for a fur hat. Myra would like that."

"The crossbeam is weak. Stop while I get another support," Grey announced.

"You've grown irritable these last few weeks. What's wrong?"

"A project doesn't go well," Grey said with a sigh. "That is, the project goes well, but I'm unhappy with the results."

"What project? You live in the weeds like a dire rat. Even on rest days, you never walk among the people. Do you mean the old tools that don't work?"

"No, I've made progress on repairing the jackhammers. It's a different problem," Grey hedged, looking away so Clagg wouldn't see the disappointment.

"Is it the strange words you mumble? The numbers of your language?"

"They're called coordinates. Intersecting lines that specify spatial relationships."

"Like fixing a point in the tunnels, as you've shown us on the maps in the dirt?" Clagg asked, surprising Grey with how quickly he grasped the principle.

They may only be ignorant slaves on a backward, ignorant slave planet, he realized, but they learn fast. They understand complicated principles when carefully explained. And each morning, whether he wanted her to or not, Myra got up early to give him warm soup outside the mine entrance. He knew he should be grateful, or at least pretend to be, but all he felt was bitterness. Bitterness and rage.

I was a hero, he remembered, *even though I never wanted to be. Why have I been abandoned?* The heat of the mine made it worse. *This is hell, he thought. I died and went to hell.* He swung his pick ax with such force the sound could be heard all the way back to the main junction. Then he paused.

No, he was forced to concede. *It's not hell.* He knew Clagg to be a good man. His wife gentle and forbearing. Deserving of better. Even the others aren't so bad, he decided, when they aren't being suspicious. And scared. It embarrassed him that he had made so little effort to help the people of Ferret Camp.

Why didn't I die when I should have? he wondered. *I was ready. It was my time.*

Grey looked up from the ore cart to see Clagg studying him in the lamplight. It was as if Clagg had sensed every thought in his mind, a talent inherent to many good leaders. Grey admired Clagg for keeping his people together under such cruel conditions.

"I want to be your friend," Clagg said.

"They are my troubles," Grey answered.

"Don't be afraid to share your fears. We're all afraid. Afraid the food will be scarce. Afraid our women will go unprotected. Afraid of the pens. Afraid our children will be taken away. Are your fears so much worse?"

"No, they're not worse," he admitted. "But they're all I have."

"Myra would have you live at the camp. It would save her a walk in the mornings."

"The beam is weak. I'll get another support," Grey said.

He walked up the gently sloping tunnel, following the ore track to a junction where timber beams were usually stored, but the only beams left were too short. Then he saw Shalli coming down the shaft, carrying water buckets on a pole over her shoulders, sweat dripping from the soft round curves of her body. Her elfin size reminded him of a fiery young Russian woman who had once hated him, but later became a close friend. Like her, the resentment that had once burned in Shalli's eyes was in the past, replaced with an impetuous curiosity.

"Hello, stranger with no name," Shalli said.

She set the buckets down and removed her filtration mask, revealing a pleasant smile as she presented him with a cup of water.

He removed his own mask, sipped some of the cool water, and splashed the rest on his face and neck.

"Thank you, Shalli," he said, handing the cup back.

"You can have more," she encouraged.

"The others need water, too. Your walk is long."

"I don't mind making an extra trip, and you never take half of what anyone else uses," Shalli said, offering another cup.

Grey looked into her deep blue eyes where the lamplight danced like small sunspots. Though he resisted as best he could, there was no doubt he found Clagg's sister attractive. Shalli found his shyness intriguing.

"You are generous," he said, drinking the whole cup.

"You call me generous? You fill our quota but barely eat our food," Shalli said. "You will not accept the gifts of our camp, meager as they are, yet you teach the men to find better ore. All I bring you is water."

"And a smile," he answered.

Shalli blushed so deeply it could be seen even in the dim light of the tunnel. Grey smiled, too. It was the first time Shalli had ever seen him smile. It was warm. Far from his usual grim demeanor.

Suddenly there was a roar from the far end of the mineshaft, followed by a booming echo. A cloud of dust filled the junction. Grey pulled Shalli underneath a sturdy beam, holding her close until the most immediate danger passed. Their eyes met. Shalli was terrified at first, but the look in his eyes reassured her. There was concern, but no fear.

"Get help," Grey said, pulling up his mask. Then he ran back into the cloud-filled tunnel.

The shaft was thick with dust near the junction but had begun to settle toward the end where Grey had last seen Clagg. Part of the wall had caved in, knocking the ore cart over and pinning Clagg against the opposite side. A single beam of light from a fallen lamp cast deep shadows.

"Watch out. The roof," Clagg grunted, trying to push the cart back.

But strong as he was, there was no chance. The weight of the cart and pressure from the rockslide was preventing him from working free, and it looked like his leg was broken.

Clagg pointed at the timber beam supporting the roof. It had cracked nearly in half. If it gave way, the entire tunnel would come down.

"We must hurry," Grey said, throwing rocks off the cart one after another. The beam creaked, fine dust raining down all around them.

"Run, my friend. The mountain is coming for me," Clagg said.

"I'm not afraid of the mountain," Grey denied, trying to move the stones faster. But there were too many. The beam splintered.

"You're not afraid to die," Clagg agreed. "You're afraid to live. But you must live. After the mountain claims me, how will Ferret Camp meet quota? Many will be sent to the pens. You must live. You must live to help my family after I cannot."

"The mountain will not claim you. Not today," Grey swore.

He stripped off the filtration mask to study the cracked timber for the weakest point. Then, with a deep breath, he climbed up on a boulder and set his feet slightly apart, placing both hands underneath the beam to push with all his strength. The beam continued to bend, small rocks falling down on him.

"No one defies the mountain. Flee now, before it's too late," Clagg begged, struggling even harder to get free.

But Grey did not flee. The more the beam bent, the harder he pushed back, fighting the inevitable with growing anger.

You want me, come get me. You've taken my wife. My world. Everything I once loved. You've left me a slave, dwelling in the desolation of an alien planet, destined for the pens of a rapacious race. And now you want Clagg. You, who have sought to make my life a living hell, would make me abandon my only friend. Make his wife a widow. Strand his people among a sea of enemies.

"No! It stops now!" Grey shouted, not to Clagg, but to the mountain.

He shoved at the creaking timber, his arms, back and legs braced like beams of oak. He remembered the training of Master Shao those long years ago in a Chinese monastery. Remembered the Master's teaching that the spirit may prevail where the body alone would certainly fail. He focused his thoughts, bringing mind and body together into a single unified force, and fought against the mountain. Fought with all the fury and anguish he could command.

The beam stabilized.

Clagg stopped trying to dig himself free, staring at Grey in disbelief as he held the roof in place. Rocks continued to fall amid puffs of dust. He was straining so hard it seemed impossible he could last another second. Yet he continued to hold. He had defeated the mountain.

Cot emerged from the dust, then Hernet and Banor, each going to help Grey maintain the beam. Others arrived just as quickly, and soon a support strut was hammered in place, allowing Grey to step back.

"Hurry," Shalli said, pushing aside rocks as the ore cart was forced back just enough for Clagg to be pulled free. As Grey suspected, his leg was badly broken, but four men quickly picked him up.

"The mountain comes," Cot warned, herding the people through the tunnel as fast as he could. When Cot noticed Grey lingering in the junction, he returned to draw him away.

"Come with us, nameless one," Cot said, daring to grab his arm. Cot half expected to be thrown against the wall, but Grey meekly obeyed.

With a thunderous roar, the mine started to collapse, the beams at the end of the shaft breaking under the stress. A cascade of cave-ins soon filled the tunnel with choking clouds of dirt and rubble, but the rescue party managed to reach the entrance with a few moments to spare. They emerged into the midday sun with sighs of relief and prayers of thanks.

"Back to camp. We will judge the damage in the morning," Hernet said, nursing a bad scrape on his arm. None needed convincing. They were battered, bruised, and frightened. That everyone had survived seemed a miracle.

Grey remained behind as the people of Ferret Camp disappeared down the trail to their tents. He was surprised to find Shalli waiting for him.

"You held up the mountain," she said, her eyes filled with awe.

"I only delayed the collapse for a few seconds," he explained.

"You saved Clagg."

"The mountain was not interested in Clagg."

"You could have run," Shalli said.

"Yes, that's what the mountain wanted."

Shalli did not understand. He who wasn't quite a stranger anymore looked disturbed by what had happened. His breath was short even though the air was clear near the mouth of the mine. He had a faraway look in his eyes. Shalli noticed blood dripping from a cut on his forehead.

"Come to camp. I'll wash your wound," Shalli said, reaching for his hand.

But Grey had no interest in the camp. He turned toward the path leading to the top of the ridge instead, crawled up to the first ledge, and kept on going. In a matter of seconds, he was gone. Shalli watched him disappear with tears in her eyes. Then she followed the others back to camp.

When Grey reached his campsite, he dropped down next to the creek. First he caught his breath and drank deeply of the cool water. His hands were shaking. The muscles twitched. The small of his back hurt. But none of that mattered. Something had happened. Something inside him had changed. A nameless slave had run into the tunnel to help Clagg, but someone different had walked out.

He took another drink, his lips dry from a sense of panic. Then he returned to his burrow for a moment of rest. The structure was sturdy now, well insulated with crisscrossing branches and leaves. A rock foundation kept out the occasional rain. The grass mattress was covered with several sewn hides, not enough for a blanket, but a good start. Clay vases held extra water and stored nuts. A newly made straw hat hung from the rafters while his rawhide moccasins sat on a shelf, but he didn't wear them in the mines, not wanting to appear wealthy. He had started to make a shirt but still needed more fibers. The hillside offered a variety of useful plants.

After calming his nerves, he went to look at the calculations etched on the nearby cliff. Calculations he had finished just a few days before. There could be no mistake. He was eleven hundred and eighty light years from home. And Earth had no stargate. Even if he could escape the camp, steal a spaceship, and fight his way through a chain of well-guarded Arikhan outposts, the closest solar system to Earth with a stargate was a dozen light years away. A voyage of at least forty years.

It had been two years since he battled the *Bellerophon*. His wife was long past her mourning period. He was only a memory now. A statue in a park.

Grey picked up a stuffed root and chewed. The dry plant filled with mashed nuts and berries wasn't bad, but he didn't taste it. Not even the wild spices he had added for flavor. Suddenly he started crying. He tried to stop, only to cry even harder, and there he sat for much of the afternoon, not moving. Having no desire to move, or even think. What would be the point?

The mood swings were over. The vague fears put to rest. He finally knew that his world was gone forever. He was dead. Atomized, only to be resurrected as a slave of the enemy by forces he didn't comprehend.

Who am I now? he wondered. *No one,* he decided. *Nothing. Reassembled molecules.* He reflected on those times in his life when there had been hope. And purpose. His struggles involved great challenges and great risks, but always with a high destiny in mind. *What an ego I had, to think that only I could save the world. Others gave as much as I did. Many gave more.*

He remembered Shalli's words in the tunnel. She had called him generous. What an ironic joke that had been. He didn't eat their food because he didn't want their friendship. Worked hard only out of habit. He avoided their camp so there would be no chance of belonging. He wasn't generous. He was selfish. Selfish, arrogant, and spoiled. He had been a great hero on another world, and now he was nothing.

"Hello. Excuse me," someone called out. "Hello? Where are you?"

It was Shalli's voice coming from the edge of the ridge, growing louder as she approached along the narrow trail through the bushes. He tried to wipe his face, embarrassed by the streaks on his cheeks.

Shalli emerged into the clearing, noticing the well-made hut and its several luxuries. The stranger did not dwell in the weeds as everyone thought, nor was he impoverished. Then she saw the wall where thousands of unfamiliar markings were scraped. Row after row of inscriptions, all carefully aligned. She wondered what meanings the marks could have, and why he had spent so many months making them. He had held up the mountain. Could he speak with the gods through these strange symbols?

"What's wrong?" Grey asked, seeing she had not cleaned up from the cave-in several hours before.

Shalli hesitated to enter the holy place, fearful of the powerful magic. Grey jumped up and took her hand, drawing her forward.

"Clagg is hurt. Thal, medicine woman of Raven Camp, is claiming everything, and still she won't promise to keep Clagg from the pens," Shalli said. Then she suddenly burst into tears and dropped to her knees at his feet.

"Please help us. Please, master, please help us," she begged, the sobs catching in her throat. Grey saw her small hands claw at the ground before daring to touch his ankles, her forehead pressed to the dirt. "We have so little. So little. Now we will have nothing. Not even Clagg."

He lifted her up, firmly holding her upper arms until he had her full attention. The eager blue eyes that had smiled at him in the tunnel only hours before were now filled with despair.

"I will come, but you must never kneel to me like that again," he said, trying not to sound angry. "Do you understand?"

"Yes, master," Shalli said, her lips quivering.

He ignored the lapse and took her down the ridge, assisting to make sure she didn't fall from the sharp rocks. Shalli recovered her composure, and as they walked toward the camp, it seemed she never doubted for a moment he would be able to help.

Every member of Ferret Camp was standing near the community tent as they approached. Grey was shocked to see all of the younger women stripped bare except for their collars, the older women wearing rags. Several men had lost all but their breechcloths. A section of canvas was spread before the tent, and on the canvas was the missing clothing, along with a decorated water jar and Myra's favorite cooking pot.

A woman stood over the pile dressed in a flowing white tunic trimmed with ermine, a bear tooth necklace around her neck overlapping her slave collar. Grey guessed her not quite thirty in age. She was not tall, but kept her shoulders straight. Colorful red and yellow feathers were tucked in her long silky black hair. She held her head high with all the regal bearing of a monarch. At her feet lay a black leather satchel. An Arikhan medical kit.

"Have you nothing else?" Thal said, her dark brown eyes radiating contempt. Her voice was calm and cold, tinged with sarcasm. "Is the life of Clagg worth no more than a few trinkets?"

"Please, Thal, will you save Clagg from the pens?" Myra asked on her knees, her cheeks stained with tears.

"The break is bad. The masters will take Clagg if he is crippled," Thal said. "Perhaps my magics will work. They are powerful. Nothing is promised."

Grey could feel Ferret Camp's distress. It was as Shalli had said. They had so little, and now Thal was taking everything. The fall season was approaching, and though the winters were said to be mild, they were not that mild.

"Can you offer nothing else? I must have more," Thal said.

Grey looked past the group into the tent where Clagg was laying on a bed of thatched grass, then circled around and entered through the back. Clagg's left leg was broken so badly the fibula nearly protruded through the skin. Grey knew he must be in terrible pain.

"I should have come sooner," he whispered, kneeling by Clagg's side.

"You held up the mountain. No man can ask for more," Clagg grunted.

"A man can ask more, when he asks it from a friend. I have not been your friend. While you were in trouble, I was on the mountain feeling sorry for myself. Can you forgive me?"

"All in this camp have seen your pain. Forgiveness is unnecessary."

"I'll try to do better," Grey promised.

"Do you have a name now?" Clagg asked.

"Yes," he replied.

Grey stood up and emerged into the light of the setting sun. All eyes turned in his direction, even the haughty Thal's.

"Who is this? The spy you've harbored?" Thal said, looking him over.

"I am Benjamin, a friend of this camp," Grey said. "Are you a healer, come to treat the leader of Ferret Camp, or a vulture come to feast upon the bones?"

"Do not speak to me, spy. You have nothing to trade. And I truly mean nothing," Thal laughed, pointing at his ragged breechcloth.

All expected Grey to shrink back in humiliation, for there was undoubted truth in her words. He smiled instead. A dark, mischievous smile that gave Thal pause. He walked forward and picked up her medical kit, pawing through the contents.

"Do not touch the magics! You will be cursed. Cast into hell!" Thal shouted.

"I've already been there," Grey replied, finding the expected supplies of opiates, probes and scalpels.

"You will return the magics now," Thal demanded, reaching quickly. He held the prize away from her, meeting Thal's angry look with a subtle grin.

"Cot, Hernet, take her arms," he ordered.

Cot and Hernet were shocked, but Grey's voice of command was so strong they soon obeyed, each grabbing one of Thal's arms. The medicine woman's confidence faded, replaced by a frightened belligerence.

"Release me. Release me now before I unleash terrible evil on you," Thal threatened.

Cot and Hernet looked to Grey, whose face was no longer smiling.

"Beware, witch, for nothing in your bag of parlor tricks can frighten me," he answered, staring into her dark eyes with defiance. "Know that I've trolled the depths and soared with eagles. I've seen planets burn and children sing. I have magic beyond your feeble imagination. Behold."

Grey walked to the cooking fire where an iron pot was suspended over a low flame.

"Bring the witch forward," Grey ordered.

Cot and Hernet dragged Thal to the fire.

"Myra. Pie. Strip her," Grey ordered.

More than happy to obey, Myra and Pie pulled the white tunic and underclothing off Thal despite her struggling. Shalli rushed forward to take the bear tooth necklace. Then Grey took a thin leather strap and tied Thal's hands tightly in front of her. Unlike the poverty-stricken Ferret Camp, Thal felt intensely humiliated to be exposed in such a way. She had forced several women in Ferret Camp to stand before her naked, never thinking it would happen to her.

"Lay her on her belly before the hearth," Grey demanded.

As Thal was laid face down in the dirt, Grey raised his right hand to the setting sun.

"Hear me, High Goddess of the Stars, for this is Benjamin, a traveler from a far land," he said. "Here lies a practitioner of the healing arts strayed from your guidance. She has exploited her people. Abused your gifts. Much does she deserve punishment. Absolve her sins, Great Mistress, and accept her humble submission to your will."

He reached into the fire, hearing a gasp of astonishment from all who watched. Even Thal quivered in horror. But Grey was not seeking to get burned. Slipping his hand discreetly to the side, he wiped the side of the pot until his hand was black with oily soot. Then he held the hand up for all to see and pressed firmly on Thal's bare right buttocks, leaving a clear handprint. He repeated the gesture with his left hand, this time imprinting Thal's left buttocks. She squirmed under his touch, unable to resist.

"Release her," Grey said.

Thal jumped to her feet and spun around. The black handprints looked like branding marks. With her hands tied before her, Thal could not reach back to wipe the marks away. For the barest moment, Grey thought her a fine looking woman, despite her evil ways, with clear white skin, graceful legs, and many female attractions.

"Whip this shameless harlot from the camp, then meet in the tent. Clagg needs our help," Grey instructed.

With all fear of evil magic forgotten, the young women chased Thal from their camp, laughing and throwing sticks at her. Thal fled slowly, her bare feet unaccustomed to the stony ground.

"Thal will pass many curious eyes before she reaches Raven Camp," Myra said to Grey as he washed his hands in the creek. "None will help her until she gets home, fearing the black arts that have been practiced. You didn't tell us you're a magician."

Grey knew Myra was both amused by Thal's embarrassment and apprehensive of his newly revealed powers. He found a piece of soap root to scrub his hands.

"You've known me nearly two seasons, Myra. You were kind to me when no one else would be. Fed me even though I was ungrateful. I tell you now, I'm not a magician. I have no special powers. I saw Thal carrying a medical kit and decided to take it from her. Everything else was meant to scare her away."

"You're not a magician?" Cot asked, glad to have his shirt back. He handed Myra her tunic. Shalli held Thal's ermine collar to her face, feeling the soft white fur.

"I'm not a magician," Grey said.

"Did you not call upon the gods?" Hernet asked, pleased to be back in his fur pants.

"Anyone may call upon the gods. It doesn't mean they'll answer," Grey replied.

"You shamed Thal before the entire camp," Myra said.

"Yes, I enjoyed that part," he admitted.

Myra laughed, partly in relief, then truly enjoying the jest. Others

48

were soon laughing, too. Grey wasn't ready to laugh. Not yet. Clagg's injury was serious.

"I'll need boiling water," Grey said. "And I want the tunic Thal was wearing torn into strips and put in the boiling water. We'll also need two flat pieces of timber and several yards of leather string. Lay Clagg on the straw with his head propped up. Clear away anything that's been soiled."

The camp burst into action, obeying the commands without question. Grey kept his hands clean and returned to the tent while Shalli carried the Arikhan medical kit.

"This is going to hurt," he told Clagg.

"It already hurts," Clagg said. "Did I hear your name? You are called Benjamin? What does it mean?"

"It means man-who-comes-late-to-help-his-friend. Sometimes people just call me Ben, when they're not angry at me."

Clagg smiled, pleasure in his gaze despite the pain. "I'm glad you finally have a name, my friend. Maybe someday you will tell us what it really means."

"Maybe," Grey said.

The first boiled strips of cloth arrived carried on a sturdy branch. Myra brought Grey a clay cup, and after tasting each of the drugs with the tip of his tongue, he mixed a dose of morphine to apply with an injector.

"I've seen breaks like this before," Clagg grunted. "They don't heal well. I am food for the pens. Cot will be leader now. You must help him."

"The break is serious," Grey agreed.

"Thal would make no promises. To lie of this would hurt her magic," Clagg continued.

"My magic is stronger than Thal's," Grey said, stretching the leg out and probing the contours of the bones.

"You said you have no magic," Myra reminded.

"This is a different magic. It's called battlefield medicine," Grey said. "I've been a soldier since childhood. Injured many times. Seen others injured, and sometimes killed. Each time I watched the doctors to learn their skills. This injury is bad, but I've seen worse."

"I'll be sent to the pens," Clagg lamented.

"I say you will not," Grey insisted.

"You've only had a name for a few minutes," Clagg said.

"You have called me friend. It is name enough," Grey replied, twisting the leg for position.

"That is true," Clagg winced. "But the break is bad. Thal would make no promises. Promise to help Cot."

"Did I hold up the mountain?" Grey asked.

"I saw you hold up the mountain," Clagg agreed.

"Then don't doubt me now. Your leg will heal. You will walk. You will be strong. You will not go to the pens."

Clagg rested back as Grey administered another painkiller, doing everything possible to relax the muscles around the broken bone. Once the maximum affect had been reached, he placed his hands along the pressure points of the break, probing deeply with his fingers.

"Hold him," Grey instructed.

Cot, Hernet, and several others took hold of Clagg's arms and feet, bracing themselves. The big man was calm, maintaining his composure. Others crowded in to watch Grey work, fascinated by the furrowed brow that betrayed such intense concentration. All knew Clagg's life was at stake, along with the well-being of the camp. The stranger had assumed an enormous responsibility.

Grey made ready to set the bone and glanced out toward the stars to whisper a prayer. A new moon hung in the east just above the horizon, which he took as a good sign. When he noticed every man, woman and child in the camp watching him, he thought it worthwhile to share his prayer, both for Clagg's sake and his family's.

"Sherra, hear me, for this is Ben, your servant, carried far from the land of my birth. Granted life from certain death. Blinded by your mysteries but dwelling in new hope," he offered, digging for a place deep inside that the goddess might hear. The people were moved by his undoubted reverence, and surprised by his mixture of Akronos, Arikhan, and a strange language they had never heard before. They did not understand all he was saying, but they understood enough.

"Long have I wondered why you brought me to this place, and what meaning it may have. I still don't know the answer. Maybe it's

50

not my place to know, but I have no gods of my own to call upon. This is your world. These are your people. For their sake, I beg your guidance in this moment of need."

Grey glanced again at the new moon. Normally it was pale red, but in the light of the setting sun, it appeared yellow, very much like the moon of his youth. *Is this Sherra's answer?* he wondered. He caught his breath before twisting the bones with a quick snap of his wrists, feeling them slide past the relaxed muscles into alignment. Clagg let out a relieved sigh.

Grey breathed again, sweat dripping down his brow. His silent thank you was so profound that all could feel it even though he barely moved his lips.

"Shalli, give me the splints," Grey said.

Shalli was frozen for a moment, staring with no less wonder than she had in the tunnel. Her hands trembled as she passed him the carefully trimmed pieces of wood.

Grey wrapped the leg with strips of torn tunic and placed the splints as he'd been taught in survival training many years before, tightening the leather ties enough for support without cutting off the blood. Clagg was asleep by the time he was done.

"You did well," Cot said once they were outside the tent.

"Better than Thal has ever done," Hernet agreed. "Your battlefield medicine is stronger than her magic."

"If she ever had any magic," Shalli said. "I think she's false. Her only magic comes from the black bag, which isn't magic at all. It's medicine."

Myra emerged from the tent, tears running down her face, and she hugged Grey with all the thankfulness in her heart. Then she started to kneel in homage, as Shalli had done on the ridge. Grey instantly caught her and shook his head. Myra understood.

"Thal has cured many, but maybe it's as Shalli says," Beknar decided, her forehead wrinkled in thought. "Thal has been using medicine rather than magic. What do you think, Ben?"

"I think Thal has been greedy," he answered, low anger in his voice. "Medical knowledge is a gift that should be shared. Is Thal the reason your camp is so poor?"

"One of many reasons," Myra said. "The cave-in last year. The season we could not keep a full group in the gardens. Our hardships meeting quotas. But we should not speak of troubles tonight. The mountain did not take Clagg. Thal did not loot what little we have. And we have a new member in our camp. There is much to celebrate. We *do* have a new member in our camp, don't we, Ben?"

Grey looked embarrassed when he noticed everyone watching him, his eyes dropping shyly to the ground. A very curious reaction, thought most of the camp, for someone who had been issuing orders with such confidence only minutes before. Grey glanced toward the ridge where he had been living. Where his celestial calculations littered the cliff like so much worthless graffiti.

"Only if everyone agrees," he finally said. "It must be known that trouble follows me wherever I go. Many of my ways are different, and I can't say that will ever change. I would rather live on the mountain than cause dissension among your people."

"Does anyone object to Ben becoming a member of Ferret Camp?" Myra asked.

There was a moment of silence. Then Cot stepped forward.

"Welcome, brother," Cot said, wrapping a bony arm around Grey's shoulders.

"Welcome," Beknar said, touching his hand.

"Welcome from all of us," Hernet said, offering fur pants that Grey could wear over his worn breechcloth.

Pie gave Grey a pair of sandals. Myra found him a worn blue shirt. Shalli came forward wearing her yellow tunic, her blue eyes glittering in the light of the cooking fires.

"Welcome, Ben. Welcome so much," Shalli said.

She got up on her toes, giving him a long kiss on the lips that raised many eyebrows, her arms reaching around his neck and fingers tangling in his long brown hair. Red-faced, Grey gently put her back on her heels. He was, after all, a married man. And at seventeen, Shalli was hardly more than a child.

"Clagg needs blankets. There's still danger of shock," Grey said.

"Our blankets are gone. Traded for serums when the children took spring fevers," Beknar said.

"I've seen Deer Camp from the ridge. They have blankets," Grey mentioned.

"Deer Camp has been warned not to speak with us," Pie said, her soft brown eyes and long flaxen hair setting off her delicate features.

"Deer Camp is afraid. We were friends once, but Wolf Camp is jealous," Shalli said.

"It's dangerous to anger Wolf Camp," Myra explained. "Marne and his wolves have sent many to the pens. Raven Camp will be displeased, too, now that you've put black hands on Thal."

"The black hands looked good on Thal," Cot said, much to everyone's laughter.

"We'll gather grass mats to cover Clagg. Then we'll eat. Everyone is tired and hungry," Myra said.

"I'm going to ask Deer Camp for blankets," Grey announced, tucking in his new shirt and looking for the trail north.

"They won't help," Cot warned.

"I won't be gone long," Grey said before disappearing into the darkness.

"Should we call him back?" Hernet asked.

"Ben cannot be called back. He held up the mountain. He speaks to the gods," Shalli said.

"He put black hands on Thal," Banor said, his big smile missing two teeth.

"Someone should go with him," Beknar suggested.

Before Cot could ask for volunteers, Shalli dashed into the night, following Grey's trail.

Grey made his way along the dark path by moonlight, remembering the route he had seen from the ridge. He had not gone far when Shalli caught up.

"I know a better path," she said.

"You'll be safer back at camp."

"Clagg is my brother. It's my place to help him."

Grey had no argument for that, so he followed Shalli across a ravine and along a line of old ore tracks no longer in use. In daylight it would only have taken a few minutes to reach Deer Camp. Even in the dark, Shalli knew the way well enough that it wasn't long before they saw cooking fires in the middle of a dozen modest tents.

"What are you going to say?" Shalli asked.

"I will ask for blankets."

"They will not help."

"It hurts nothing to ask. I prefer you not mention the mountain or any other stories that may be hard to believe."

"But they're true," she said.

"It's my wish they not be mentioned," he insisted.

"Yes, master," Shalli said.

"Stop that," he demanded.

"Yes, master," Shalli repeated, laughing this time and flipping her long blonde hair over her shoulder. He could not ignore how beautiful she appeared in the moonlight.

"Hello Deer Camp," Shalli said, emerging first into the firelight.

The men in the camp reached for wooden stools that could be used as clubs, the women retreating to the tents. All relaxed when they recognized Shalli. They were curious when they saw the stranger following a few paces behind.

"It's the spy," a craggy woman said, her long gray dress aged but in good condition.

"He's a member of Ferret Camp, and our friend," Shalli corrected.

"We've seen this stranger on the mountain. What brings him to the valley?" a tall young man asked.

"Clagg is hurt. His leg is broken. Ben helped us when Thal would not," Shalli explained. Many in the camp laughed.

"We saw Thal on the lake road. Did this stranger put the black hands on her?" a tall, slim man said, walking forward with the confidence of a leader. But still holding a stool. He wore a faded red leather vest, white canvas trousers, and calf-length rawhide boots. Unlike the men of Ferret Camp, and even his own camp, this man was clean-shaven.

"Yes, Nole, he did," Shalli said in a firm voice.

"You may enter Deer Camp," Nole said, putting the stool down.

"Did you untie her?" Shalli asked.

"Of course not. She showed the brands all the way back to Raven Camp," Nole said. Again everyone laughed. Grey could tell they thought it a good joke.

Grey was offered a stool near the main campfire. Shalli sat next to him on the ground. As he looked around, Grey noticed about forty adults and eight children. All were clothed, but not finely. The tents were in the same aged condition as Ferret Camp's, but there were more of them and generally larger. He saw more cooking utensils, too, but no better in quality.

"Ben, this is Nole, leader of Deer Camp," Shalli introduced. "That's Sal, his dig leader. Next to him is Sal's wife, Bab, and this is Nole's wife, Court. The boy is Turk, Sal's son. Members of Deer Camp, this is Ben, accepted member of Ferret Camp."

The leaders Shalli introduced were somewhat older than Clagg and Myra, being in their mid-thirties. Nole and Court were both tall with long brown hair and green eyes. A nice looking couple. Sal and Bab were even older, traces of gray showing in their otherwise black hair. Grey knew few people grow old in slave camps.

As for Turk, he realized Shalli was making a joke by calling him a boy. Probably seventeen years old, Turk stood half a head taller than average with shoulders that were already wide. Grey wondered if Shalli was teasing Turk because she found him attractive.

The eyes watching Grey were suspicious. He didn't believe them unfriendly, but many were worried. It wasn't a happy camp.

"I treated Clagg's leg. It will heal. He will be strong again," Grey said. "But there is risk of fever. He needs blankets to keep warm."

The circle remained silent.

"You ask us for blankets? For Ferret Camp?" Sal asked.

"For Clagg. The blankets will be returned," Grey said.

Silence again. Many shifted uncomfortably.

"We cannot help. Wolf Camp is angry with Clagg," Nole said with regret.

"Any who help him will have arms broken. Maybe sent to the pens," Sal said. "We are having trouble making quota as it is. Losing someone will leave us short."

"Women who tend the gardens will work the mines instead," a worried young woman said, a baby cradled in her arms. "Fewer women in the fields mean our food allotments will be reduced."

"And there will be no winter tunics for the girls," Bab said.

Now Grey was silent. There were thirty men around the fire, strong and able. But they were miners, not fighters. He didn't know whether to condemn them as cowards or pity their impotence.

"Are you sure Wolf Camp will seek retribution over a few blankets?" Grey asked.

"They've threatened any who help their enemies," Nole said. "Not just Clagg, but others. Lart stood up to them and they broke his arms. He is gone to the pens."

"We won't tell anyone where the blankets came from," Grey offered.

"It will be known. There are few secrets among the people," Nole said, looking around the fire. Grey wondered if Nole suspected informers within his own camp.

"Why is Wolf Camp angry with Clagg?" Grey asked.

"Mostly it's Marne who is angry. He put hands— " Bab started to say. Her explanation broke off. Shalli had her head down.

"Marne wanted me, but not as a wife," Shalli said. "His wolves wanted sport. Clagg beat two of them and said he would hurt more if they didn't leave me alone."

"Clagg cannot hurt them now," Bab said, looking concerned for Shalli's safety. Grey noticed that Shalli was worried, too.

"You have hard problems," Grey said. "Still, Clagg is my friend and needs help. Is there anything I can say?"

"We're sorry," Nole answered. "We like Clagg. Most of us. We wish him well."

Nole stood up, the audience over. Grey noticed he hadn't been offered food or drink as custom would dictate. Deer Camp was frightened.

"Where is Tak?" Shalli asked, looking for a missing face in the crowd. The camp was silent. Many looked away. Court looked ready to cry.

"She isn't well," Nole said.

"Is she sick?" Shalli pressed.

"She is not well," Nole repeated.

Again there was silence. Something important wasn't being said.

"Can I see her?" Shalli asked.

"Do you not hear? Tak isn't well," Sal insisted with an angry grunt.

"Not well? Not well? She is destroyed! My little girl is destroyed! Sherra curse them!" Court suddenly screamed, bursting into hysteria.

Bab rushed to Court's side, holding her in her arms as the leader's wife sobbed.

"Marne's wolves carried her away after she left the gardens," Bab explained. "She fought back. They threw her in their torment pit. Five of them took her, including Marne. That was two days ago. Tak has not spoken since. She does not eat or sleep. She just sits and stares."

"She is destroyed. They destroyed my daughter," Court cried.

Bab tried to calm Court down. Nole went to hold his wife but was unable to console her.

"Where is she?" Grey asked.

"This is none of your business, stranger," young Turk said, reaching to throw Grey from the camp.

Grey caught Turk's wrist, bent his arm backward at the elbow, and soon had the strapping youngster kneeling on the ground in pain. When Turk tried to break free, Grey twisted the arm even more, nearly separating the shoulder. The men of the camp jumped to their feet in surprise.

"I can rip your arm in half. Is that what you want?" Grey whispered in a cold voice.

"No," Turk said, barely able to speak.

Grey released him and turned defiantly on the rest of the camp. Fire blazed in his eyes. He looked like a wildcat ready to pounce.

Shalli felt her heart beating faster. Ben was outnumbered, yet there he stood ready to take them on. She could not remember ever seeing anything so frightening. And thrilling. The men of Deer Camp were not anxious to test the stranger's resolve, stepping back as they looked to Nole.

"Where is the girl?" Grey said, breaking the silence.

"Over here, in our tent," Nole said, sensing a power in the stranger he never would have suspected. And the way he had subdued Turk, with hardly an effort, was taken as a warning. The stranger was dangerous. Not one to be defied without consequences. And yet he had not used force to take blankets for Clagg. It was a mystery that required careful study.

Nole was not alone in his thoughts. Many were startled by the sudden violence, but they were also curious. The adoration in young Shalli's eyes spoke volumes. She was not afraid. She worshipped him.

Grey entered the tent followed by Nole and Court. Huddled in the corner was a young woman hardly much older than Shalli, slightly taller but thin with an attractive figure and dark brunette hair. She stared blankly at a rusty miner's lamp illuminating the cramped quarters. Her face was bruised, her lower lip split. She had a red woolen blanket pulled tightly around her shoulders.

"She doesn't move. Doesn't speak. Even feeding her is difficult," Nole said.

Grey looked at the pain of the parents and glanced past them to see a stricken expression on Shalli's face. They must be friends, he realized. Grown up together. Played little girl games together. Dreamed and gossiped about boys. Now her friend was a shell, staring but not seeing. Grey was familiar with the condition. He even knew a little about possible treatments. He also knew many treatments failed, and the scars would run deep for the rest of her life.

He tried not to think too heavily on the past, but the memories were there. The more he thought about it, the more a desire for vengeance on these ones called wolves boiled in his heart. This wasn't the time.

"Leave us," Grey said.

"We cannot leave our daughter with a stranger," Nole protested.

"If you can leave your daughter to the mercy of a raping wolf pack, you can leave her with me. Now shut your mouth and get out," Grey ordered.

Grey's tone wasn't likely to ingratiate himself with the Deer Camp leader, but Court pulled her husband back and drew down the tent flap, desperate to find help for her daughter. The only noise outside the tent was the crackling of the cooking fires, and after a time, the sound of people quietly eating their meals.

Grey sat cross-legged in front of Tak, not moving or touching her for quite some time. He suppressed his anger, focusing on the young woman only, searching deeply through his experience. What would Doctor Meriwether say? Or Master Shao? Yes, what would the old shaman suggest? Give up? Give in? Feel sorry for yourself? No. Never. Fight back!

This is a hard culture, he thought. *There are no weaklings in Karak. This is a life of challenge and survival. It's also a life of love, with powerful bonds of family and camp. These feelings are still inside her, beaten back by the horror of the attack. Can I draw her spirit forth?*

The miner's lamp flickered against the sides of the dark tent as a gentle wind caused the canvas to rustle. He found a piece of jewelry on the fur, a small silver medallion on a chain that reflected the light. He toyed with the shiny object, letting it slowly swing back and forth where Tak would be sure to see it.

"My name is Benjamin," he said, softly and without expectation of a response. "I've come to take you on a journey. It's a long journey. We'll take it together. When the journey is over, we'll come back together. Court and Nole will be waiting for you. Deer Camp will be waiting for you. Your friends will smile to see you return, and those who hurt you will never hurt you again. My name is Benjamin. I held up a mountain. I once saved a world."

Grey began talking in quiet, carefully modulated tones. So quietly no one outside the tent heard more than occasional mumbling. He told the story of an orphaned child raised on an abandoned mining colony. Of intense loneliness. Of fears, real and imagined. Years of hard work, constant danger, and betrayal. There was the story of the beautiful Russian girl he had failed to save. Who died on an operating table while he could only watch. What followed were dark fantasies of violent death sought in pursuit of deep revenge. And a greater duty that made all of his gloomy imaginings impossible.

And then there was a woman he had struggled to love. But how could he love? He who was raised in such isolation, without parents, family or friends? He who could never love anyone. And then he lost her. Lost his friends. Lost everything because an ancient duty was more important than anything else. But it was no longer a duty bred into him. Not an obligation dictated by necessity. He did love. At last. And it was such a love that it was worth dying for. And he did.

The sun was rising as he approached the end of their journey. His journey, which Tak was allowed to join without pressure to participate. Tears were running down her cheeks.

"Where an old path ends, a new path begins," he said, believing he saw a spark in her eyes. He raised his hand, held the outside of his palm to her mouth, and pushed gently against her lips.

"Bite my hand," he said.

Tak didn't respond.

"Bite my hand," he said again.

She shook her head.

"Bite my hand. Bite hard," he gently ordered.

Tak started to pull back, then suddenly bit into the side of his hand, her teeth sinking into the rough, calloused flesh.

"Harder. Don't be afraid. Don't ever be afraid again. Bite!"

Tak bit harder. She bit until she drew blood. Bit until his blood was running down her chin.

"Now hit me," he said. "Now! Do it!"

Tak let go of his hand and struck him with her small fist, whacking his shoulder. The first blow wasn't hard, but she struck again and then began pounding with both fists as she vented her rage and frustration. Her breathing grew labored, the tears falling freely. Then suddenly she stopped, her gaze steady, looking Grey in the face with big brown watery eyes.

"Court, come here," Grey called.

Court burst into the tent. Within seconds, Tak was sobbing in her mother's arms. Nole followed and Tak hugged him, sad but filled with love for those she had almost lost.

Grey silently slipped out of the tent. The sun was hovering over the forested mountains to the east. Curled in a ball on the ground outside the tent, Shalli had awakened to hear the noise inside.

"You're bleeding," Shalli said, seeing the bite marks on his hand.

60

"That happens to me a lot," he said. "I'm tired. Let's go home."

The walk back didn't take long. He enjoyed the cool morning, looking at the moist vegetation that grew along the trail. The trees and bushes were different than those found on Earth, but in most ways, very similar. He noticed several small birds chirping in the foliage.

"Will Tak be all right?" Shalli asked.

"Time will tell," he said.

"Do you think Tak will be all right?" Shalli persisted, growing accustomed to his way of not answering questions directly.

"Yes, I think she'll be all right," he responded hopefully.

"I'm glad it's the rest day," Shalli said. "Meeting our quota is going to be hard with Clagg hurt. Will it take many days for his leg to heal?"

"It will take at least six weeks. Clagg is big and restless. It will probably take eight," Grey speculated.

"Eight weeks! Without quota the masters won't give us fall supplies. If we all work the mines, there are none to take our places in the gardens. Ben, what are we going to do?"

"We'll make quota. The women will take their places in the gardens."

"Not without Clagg."

"Clagg will be missed, but the others are strong. I think one day young Burne will be even stronger than Clagg," Grey said.

They reached Ferret Camp and Grey went straight to the community tent. Clagg was asleep under a makeshift covering of clothing parts and straw mats, his bare feet sticking out the end.

"We were worried. We sent Wart to spy on Deer Camp, but all was quiet, so he returned," Myra said.

"Marne's wolves went after Tak," Shalli reported. "Five of them had her in their torment pit. Tak wouldn't talk or see. Court was afraid Tak would never speak again. Ben helped her not feel so bad, and now Tak will be all right."

"They could not give us blankets," Grey said.

"I told you, they are afraid of Marne. Everyone is," Myra said.

"When Clagg feels better, I will visit the gardens and see Wolf Camp. I would like to meet Marne," Grey mentioned.

Myra and Shalli had a feeling that Grey didn't intend for his meeting with Marne to be pleasant. He showed no emotion on the subject, going to the back of the community tent and finding a place to sleep.

"Beknar and I will take the older women to the gardens. I don't want you or Pie anywhere near those wolves until Clagg is healthy again," Myra told Shalli. "Now help make breakfast. There isn't much cereal left, but I think we can add some meadow root."

Shalli joined Myra sorting out the last of the week's rations, finding just enough stock for the broth and some wild oats for substance. Soon the rest of the camp stirred.

"Shalli is right," Cot said as Myra put soup over the fire. "I don't know how we'll meet quota without Clagg. The masters will be displeased. But if we can't attend the gardens, we'll have to scrounge roots and bark from the woods."

"We only have ten tunics left for the women, and they're nearly worn through," Banor said, the burly cart pusher resentfully tapping the ground with a stick. "It's bad enough some must wear rags in camp. I don't want them walking to the gardens like that."

"It would be embarrassing, but we've suffered worse," Myra said. "I wish we could have gotten a blanket for Clagg. Every tunic we have still doesn't cover him."

"All the tunics in Karak cannot cover Clagg," Hernet said. Everybody laughed.

"Hello Ferret Camp," someone shouted from the woods. The camp jumped to their feet, the men grabbing branches to use as clubs.

"Who calls?" Cot asked, taking the lead position.

Nole emerged from the ravine near the camp, followed by Sal and Bab. Ferret Camp relaxed, many sitting down on their log seats.

"How is Clagg?" Nole asked.

"He is well, thank Sherra," Myra said, her face flushed red.

Sal and Bab noticed that Myra was not the only half-naked woman in camp. A glance inside the tent explained why. Clagg was covered in a quilt of tunics. The women of Ferret Camp felt awkward but there was nothing to be done.

"Come join us," Myra said.

"Here, these are for Clagg. A gift from Court and Nole," Bab said, presenting Myra with several large woven blankets.

"We have nothing to offer in return," Myra said.

Bab saw Myra meant that literally. Nole took the blankets and forced them into Myra's hands.

"We have our daughter back, and we're ashamed of our behavior," Nole said to all. "Put the blankets on Clagg. Get dressed. We'll sit and talk."

The women rushed to the tent and parceled out the tunics, finding just enough to give each person a bit of dignity. Clagg woke up and soon the leaders moved into the tent. To everyone's surprise, Grey continued to sleep, so voices were kept low.

"Sal, look," Bab whispered when she noticed Shalli and Beknar scrounging unsuccessfully for more food. Sal nodded and left the tent, going to the ravine. A minute later, he returned with several large baskets of grain bread, orange squash and greens.

"We did not wish to insult you by bringing food, but we weren't sure if you had enough. Little is known of Ferret Camp's hardships," Nole explained.

"Pride is a luxury these days," Myra said, handing the baskets to Shalli and Pie. The children smiled to see the orange squash, crowding close for a piece.

"There are a few extra tunics in Deer Camp that no one needs. I'll have Leet bring them over," Bab offered.

"If no one wants them, it will be welcome," Myra said. "I don't wish to be rude, but why the sudden generosity? Have you lost fear of Marne?"

"No, we are still afraid," Nole said.

"I'll put a stop to Marne once I can walk again," Clagg said, still sleepy from the drugs.

"Clagg is only one against many. Even if Deer Camp and Ferret Camp joined together, Wolf Camp is still bigger," Nole said. "And they would call upon Raven Camp, outnumbering us by even more."

"We can't make quota without Clagg. If some of us are injured fighting, it will be worse. We must appease Marne," Cot said.

"That will be hard. Do you know what they did to Tak?" Bab asked.

"We heard this morning. We're very sorry," Myra said.

"She's getting better now, thanks to the stranger. Where did he come from? Is he a spy?" Nole asked.

"Ben is not a spy," Clagg said.

"What does Ferret Camp have to spy on?" Myra asked.

Nole and Sal looked around, seeing nothing worth the effort.

"He put black hands on Thal," Nole said, a question in the tone.

"When the mountain wanted Clagg, Ben—" Cot started to explain.

"Ben is very brave, but he doesn't wish stories told about him," Shalli interrupted, remembering Grey's admonition from the night before. Clagg and Myra looked at her in surprise, but nodded agreement. This made the Deer Camp members even more curious. There are few secrets in such a small community. They would find out eventually.

Just as the meal was being served, a new commotion disturbed the camp.

"It's Nabbatron. Frontra and Nabbatron," Pie warned, rushing into the tent.

The people set aside the food and dropped to their knees as the two Arikhan sentries walked into the clearing. Frontra was calm. Nabbatron agitated. They wore brown leather tunics and large floppy hats for protection from the sun. Their holsters contained various weapons for controlling the slaves, most of them non-lethal but capable of inflicting great pain. No one thought their sudden appearance on the rest day a good thing.

"Welcome to Ferret Camp, masters," Myra said, kneeling closest.

Myra heard Clagg trying to get up and thought of going to stop him, but she could not risk offending the alien overseers. She glanced back to see Grey had awakened and put a hand on Clagg's shoulder, instructing him to stay put. Myra sighed with relief.

"There, in the tent," Nabbatron said, pointing at Clagg.

Nabbatron and Frontra walked past the kneeling slaves and stood at the entrance of the tent. Clagg remained on his back. Grey knelt in homage, keeping one hand on Clagg's arm.

"He is crippled, just as the healer claimed. He must go to the pens," Nabbatron said, his voice a deep growl.

"I am sorry to see it so serious," Frontra said, seeming to agree.

"May I speak, beings of great superiority?" Grey asked in Arikhan, his voice humble. The aliens noticed that his diction was reasonably good for a lesser species.

"Speak," Frontra said.

"The big food creature is not crippled, only injured," he said. "In a matter of weeks he will be strong again and ready for the mines."

"It is a lie. The healer said he is crippled," Nabbatron asserted.

"I put black hands on the healer," Grey responded.

"I have heard much of these black hands," Frontra said, her eye-rings rising in inquiry. "It is spoken of in every camp. In what manner were black hands put upon her? What is the meaning?"

"The black hands were put upon her in the name of Sherra. They show all that her magic is false," Grey answered.

"There is no such thing as magic, and Sherra does not help food creatures. Sherra's gifts are for her eggs alone," Nabbatron said, his heavier eye-rings curling inward.

Grey noticed Frontra flinch at the remark, the webbing around the back of her head ruffling, and had the distinct impression that she disagreed with Nabbatron's philosophy. He remembered, towards the end, that the Arikhan scout Mordari, who he had known in a different solar system under far different circumstances, had expressed similar doubts.

"It hurts none to see if the injury heals. If it does not, he will still be food," Frontra said, adding a gentle click of her tongue.

"They cannot make quota. The camp should be dispersed, the weak harvested," Nabbatron persisted.

A quiet gasp rose from the kneeling slaves. Shalli clung tighter to Garn. Banor took Beknar's hand, hoping it wasn't for the last time. Nole wondered which of his neighbors might not see another sunrise.

"Pardon me, being of great superiority, but your opinion is in error," Grey said.

Nabbatron stepped into the tent, grabbed Grey by his metal collar, and struck him across the face with a clenched claw. It was a hard blow, the large alien having a well-developed physique. The other camp members kept their heads down, afraid to intervene.

"What did you say, food creature?" Nabbatron asked.

"I said your opinion is in error," Grey repeated, only to be struck again so hard that blood splattered on Clagg. Clagg grabbed Grey's elbow and pulled him back, trying to shelter him with his arm.

"Please, master, Ben is a stranger to our ways. If I must go to the pens, then I go. Please do not harm the camp," Clagg said, his tired eyes pleading.

"The leader of Ferret Camp should not beg favors from a coward," Grey said in Arikhan, completing the insult with a sharp click of his tongue. Nabbatron flew into a rage, taking a shock wand from his belt.

"Nabbatron, control yourself," Frontra cautioned, putting a claw on his arm.

"The food creature called me a coward," Nabbatron protested.

"It is only a food creature, why should its words matter?" Frontra replied.

Nabbatron slowed his breathing to regain composure. He knew it wasn't good to overreact in front of the slaves.

"In what manner is my opinion in error, food creature?" Nabbatron asked, releasing Grey as he lowered the wand.

Though stunned from the blows, Grey managed to clear his head. He saw the entire camp was frightened. It couldn't be helped. He adjusted position and knelt at Nabbatron's feet, his forehead pressed against the toes of Nabbatron's boots. Nabbatron was mollified, looking at Frontra with satisfaction.

"Being of great superiority, Ferret Camp will make quota," Grey said. "I would offer a proposition."

"You set terms?" Nabbatron asked.

"A proposition," Grey said, pretending more fear than he actually felt. Not that he wasn't apprehensive.

"Speak," Nabbatron ordered, his tongue clicking in amusement.

"Ferret Camp will make quota. In reward, Ferret Camp would be gifted with new tunics for the women, shirts for the men, and medicines for the children. And a fur hat for Clagg's woman."

"You ask much. What happens when you fail?" Nabbatron asked.

"If we fail, Clagg will go to the pens, and I will go with him," Grey said.

The camp burst into involuntary murmuring, many finding it hard to keep their places. Nabbatron was pleased with the offer and enjoyed the fearful reaction of the camp.

"It will be as you say, food creature," Nabbatron said.

Nabbatron pulled Grey's head up so he could look directly into the slave's eyes. The alien's soft brown cheeks had flushed dark, the blacks of his pupils focused with a malevolent intensity. The upper lip curled back, revealing sharp fangs useful for tearing flesh, and the thick rings above his eyes rose in evidence of his intent.

"Remember this, half-meat," Nabbatron added, his voice lowered to a disturbing snarl. "When you fail, I will personally put you to the spit. Your death will be slow."

Nabbatron wheeled about and left the camp, much to everyone's relief. Even Frontra's, whose wide shoulders quickly relaxed.

"You may rise," Frontra said.

"Thank you, mistress," Myra said, hurrying to check on Clagg before treating the bruises on Grey's face. Grey spit blood and was relieved not to have lost any teeth.

"You are too bold," Clagg complained.

"Would you rather go to the pens?" Grey asked.

"I would rather not take a friend with me," Clagg answered.

"It's a sucker bet. We'll make quota and more," Grey said, seemingly unconcerned.

"Sucker bet?" Myra asked.

"A wager with a foregone conclusion," he explained.

"Only death is a foregone conclusion," Myra said.

"Not in my experience," Grey sighed.

"Come," Frontra ordered, having Grey follow her out of camp where others wouldn't overhear.

When she stopped on the trail around the edge of the trees, he dropped to his knees at her feet.

"Stand up, impertinent food creature. Nabbatron may be fooled by such tricks. He is arrogant, as are all males. I understand you better."

"Yes, mistress," he said, standing up.

"Can this camp really make quota?" Frontra asked, eye-rings dipping.

"I believe so, mistress. It will be hard, but it should be possible."

"You told Myra it is a forgone conclusion," Frontra said.

"The people are discouraged. They need hope."

Frontra took his face in her claw, turning it from side to side, inspecting the bruises and bleeding lip.

"You have made an enemy of Nabbatron," Frontra warned.

"I make many enemies. It cannot be helped," he replied.

Frontra clicked her tongue in approval.

"The healer's instruments must be returned. If you make quota, I will have another kit issued to Ferret Camp."

"Thank you, mistress," Grey said in surprise.

"You need not return her stolen coverings. She was given black hands instead," Frontra added.

Until that moment, Grey hadn't realized that Frontra didn't care for Thal's methods any more than he did. Her attitude surprised him.

"I enjoy you, food creature. But you are rash. Be careful," Frontra warned.

"Thank you, mistress," Grey said, bowing his head in appreciation.

Frontra went north, following the trail Nabbatron had taken. When Grey returned to camp, he found everyone staring at him, their expressions filled with curiosity.

"Is breakfast ready?" he asked.

Chapter Three
FOOLISH GAMBLES

Later that morning, Grey gathered Ferret Camp in front of the community tent. Though Bab had returned to Deer Camp, Nole and Sal stayed to hear Grey's plan. He was glad to see old friendships renewed. Myra and Cot sat near Clagg, who was propped up, the broken leg extended. Shalli sat at Grey's feet, a puppy love in her eyes that had him concerned.

"We can't take what we need from the mountain, so we will have the mountain give it to us," Grey said.

"Will the mountain be so generous?" Hernet asked.

"I don't know. It's possible the mountain will be angry," Grey responded.

"Why would the mountain be angry, Ben?" Shalli asked.

"Because I'm going to blow a hole in it," he said. "The jars in the mine are chemical bases. Some are used for cleansing and purifying ores. Others are used to make explosives. I've used such chemicals before."

He walked to the entrance of the tent, pointing to a section of steep cliff above the canyon separating Ferret Camp's mountain from Deer Camp's mines on the other side of a broad ravine.

"This may benefit Deer Camp, too, if you're interested," Grey said. He could tell Nole and Sal were more than interested, sitting forward on their knees to hear. "We'll need to move our tracks to the edge of the gully. There are rich veins just beneath the surface. There, on the north face, where those two deep crevices come together. After we drop the hillside, much of what we need will come down with it. We'll use the jackhammers I've been repairing to break up the larger fragments and shatter out the ore with sledge hammers."

"How do you know where the mountain hides its treasure?" Sal asked.

Grey thought it a fair question.

"I was raised on a mining colony. My mentors taught me how to search for the best results," he explained.

"Much of the face is solid rock. Bringing it down will be hard," Nole said.

"It would be if we were blasting from the outside," Grey explained. "There's an old ventilation shaft on top of the ridge that drops down into the mountain. I can crawl within fifteen meters of the crevice and set the charges off from there."

"Meters?" Clagg asked.

"About fifty feet," Grey said. "The inner strata are fractured. One blast should initiate a cascade of copper, zinc, and silver. And at least a half unit of Akronium."

The miners smiled. Used as a strengthening element in the construction of spaceship hulls, no mineral was more sought after than the elusive Akronium. Such a discovery would involve many rewards.

"Will the masters punish us for removing tools from the mine?" Burne asked, the young teenager's voice nearly cracking.

"We will not remove tools from the mine," Clagg said. "Nole, can you bring us a roll of yellow ribbon?"

"Danger ribbon?" Nole asked.

"Yes. We'll section off the blast area and declare it a mine, like our fathers did at the old camp," Clagg said.

"A quarry. We'll call it a quarry," Nole said.

"We can move a tent to the area and leave the tools there," Sal suggested.

Soon other ideas were being discussed and agreed on with rapid speed. Grey sat down next to Shalli and Pie, listening to the discussion but not participating. The miners fully grasped his idea and were quickly improving on it.

"You must have priority," Nole said. "Clagg and Ben must not go to the pens. But Deer Camp would like to help and perhaps benefit if there's a surplus."

"Are we agreed?" Clagg asked.

The hands of everyone in the camp went up, which surprised Grey. He had no idea he was participating in a democracy. And he wasn't especially happy about it.

"Are you sure this can be done?" Nole asked Grey.

"Preparing the explosives will take time, and accidents are always a possibility," he said. "I plan to take the materials up to the abandoned shack on the ridge and mix them there. If you hear a loud boom, you'll know it didn't work."

Grey smiled, enjoying his joke. No one else thought it was funny.

Experts at laying track, moving the narrow aluminum rails only took a few days. Workers from both Ferret and Deer Camps participated, excited by the possibilities. None of them saw Grey, who gathered supplies and disappeared into the rocks atop the ridge.

"Tak! It's good to see you," Myra greeted.

Now dressed in a knee-length blue tunic and sandals provided by Deer Camp instead of rags, Myra was joyed to see Shalli's friend looking well. Tak wore a brown cotton dress that came up to her neckline, fitting snugly at the waist.

"I want to help. Mother won't let me go to the gardens, so I've come here," Tak said, her long dark brown hair tied back in a ponytail.

"Only the older women are going to the gardens for now," Myra said, getting ready to leave with Beknar. "When Clagg is better, he and Nole are going to speak with Squirrel and Sparrow Camps. There hasn't been a council in more than a year."

"Marne will not permit it," Beknar said, grouchy in her used gray tunic.

"We must try," Myra said.

"Tak!" Shalli called out, running to give her friend a hug.

Pie followed, just as happy to see their childhood playmate. Myra smiled to see them together again, and was pleased that Shalli and Pie did not have to meet their friend wearing rags.

"Stay close to the men today," Myra cautioned.

Myra, Beknar and the other older women left for the gardens carrying their baskets, singing a song to lighten the morning.

"Where's Ben?" Tak asked as they walked toward the new work area, taking a dirt trail through the thick woods.

"He's on the mountain," Shalli answered, pointing to the hill above the old mine.

"What did he say to help you wake up?" Pie asked.

"I'm not sure. I know he told me a story, and it was very sad. There were other worlds and strange people. And strange machines. Then suddenly I was hitting him. I shouldn't have hit him. I want to tell him I'm sorry."

Shalli laughed.

"Ben wanted to help you, and he did. That's all that matters to him. I think that's all that ever matters to him," Shalli said.

"Not getting enough attention?" Tak asked, her dark eyes showing interest.

"I'll get more, somehow," Shalli swore, clenching her fists.

They reached the canyon and found a large tent erected on a knoll overlooking the new site. Thirty-two men and eight young women were arranging tools and ore carts, looking from time to time towards the ridge. Several members of Squirrel Camp were watching from a distance.

"Is it time?" Shalli asked, jumping with excitement.

"Soon. Wart will go up to see if Ben is ready," Cot said, glancing at the lithe twelve-year-old with wild brown hair who eagerly awaited the signal.

"Let me go," Shalli said.

"I can do it," Wart said, frowning with resentment.

"I've been up there before. Wart could get lost," Shalli insisted.

"It's dangerous," Hernet said. "Wart is fast. If—"

Shalli ran to the edge of the cliff and scrambled up the side, grabbing rock ledges and thick brush to pull herself to the top. In hardly a minute, she had disappeared.

"Shalli grows headstrong," Nole observed.

"Shalli's in love," Tak said, clinging to her father's arm.

The old shack wasn't hard to find. Shalli had snuck up there when she was a little girl even though she wasn't supposed to. She remembered there had been markers in the area warning workers away, but the markers were gone now. She wondered if Ben had removed them, then decided he had. This way, if an Arikhan sentry came to inspect, which was rare, he could claim he didn't know the area was off limits.

He's very smart, Shalli thought with an extra skip in her step.

Though much of the shack was in ruins, Shalli noticed one corner had been repaired. An old door was now a workbench and torn floor boards had become shelves. She saw Grey sitting on a tall stool.

"The device is ready, Wart," he said without looking up. "I'm just adjusting the fuse. Tell Cot it should be in place by midday."

"You should tell him," Shalli said, suppressing a mischievous grin.

He looked up in surprise, double-clutching the blue steel canister on the bench. Shalli hadn't realized he could be startled so easily.

"What happened to Wart?" he said, brow furrowed with displeasure.

"Wart is too slow," Shalli laughed, stepping over and around broken floor boards to reach the workbench. Though the cotton outfit gifted to her by Deer Camp was better than the tatters she had before, it was still revealing. A bit too much, with a low neckline and high skirt. Grey needed to avoid looking too hard. Despite difficult times and a great deal of stress, he was not immune to his natural instincts.

The smelly jars of chemicals were carefully laid out around two mixing bowls. The canister Grey held had a blasting cap sealed with tar attached to a coil of fuse wire.

"Tell Cot and Nole to draw everyone back from the canyon," he said. "And don't come here again. It's too dangerous."

"Too dangerous for who?" Shalli said, pressing close.

"Too dangerous for foolish young children."

"I'm not a child. I'm a woman. Many have already mated at my age," she protested.

"You should mate with one of your own people. Someone your own age," Grey responded.

"You're one of us now, and you're not so old," Shalli said, her hand on his shoulder.

"I have fifteen more years than you. Almost twice your lifetime. On my world, you would be wearing the latest bad fashions, dying stripes in your hair, and spending endless hours on the com gossiping with girlfriends. Soon you would be going to college and studying for a career."

"It sounds like a vile place," Shalli said. "Is that how you spent your middle years?"

"No," he said, sorry to have raised the subject. And embarrassed to realize that, on a slave planet, life can be short. In Shalli's world, she *was* in her middle years. The oldest person he knew was Sal, who probably wasn't more than forty.

Shalli looked into his perceptive gray eyes. She couldn't guess what he was thinking, but something had suddenly troubled him. She remembered seeing the expression before, when an idle remark would transform into a sad memory. She worried for him.

"Is there anything wrong with me loving you?" Shalli asked.

"No, it's not wrong. But I think it would be better if you look for someone else."

"I won't be blind. If I can find someone braver than you, and smarter than you, and more caring than you, then I will mate with him instead. Until I make you change your mind!"

Shalli smiled, blue eyes sparking with hope, and she ran from the shack to deliver Grey's message. He watched her go with a sigh, the firm round figure squeezed into the tight tunic inspiring a sense of longing.

With the explosive device prepared, Grey set it down next to the old ventilation shaft and clawed through some thick bushes to reach the edge of the ridge. He was pleased to see the new track nearly complete, and surprised by the size of the crowd working at the bottom of the hill. Deer Camp had apparently abandoned their own mine, putting their faith in his plan. It wasn't a responsibility he relished.

He waved until he knew Cot and Nole had seen him. He also noticed Clagg had been carried on a litter to sit in the newly erected tool tent. Grey pointed at Clagg and shook his finger in disapproval. Clagg grinned and waved back.

The ventilation shaft dropped straight down into the heart of the mountain, its only access a rotting wooden ladder bolted into the rock wall. Grey assembled a bracket over the shaft, rigged a pulley, and put the canister in a basket along with a solar lamp and some hand tools. Then he started down, feeding the pulley with a thin rope coiled around his shoulder.

He had been in the shaft several times and found it surprising the project had been abandoned. The ore strains running north from the shaft were far richer than those found on the lower levels where Ferret Camp had been working, though access was an issue. He had no doubt the explosive would be adequate for his purpose, having experience with nitroglycerin. But accidents happen, especially as he'd been unable to mix a proper desensitization agent. As much as he would have appreciated help getting down the shaft, he felt more confident handling the volatile mixture alone. Life in a slave camp hadn't prepared the people there for such dangerous technologies.

The branch tunnel appeared. He crawled in, pulling the basket behind him, and secured the rope. Grey remembered the shaft being reasonably straight and long. It would need to be, having about two hundred yards to cover before reaching the north face. He wanted to rig a guideline to draw the explosive along, the roof being too low for walking, but he lacked the time and materials. He would need to crawl, clutching the bomb in one arm and dragging the tools with his foot.

The tunnel was dark. Ominous. He guessed the shaft had been carved dozens of years before with laser cutters, but the equipment had long since disappeared. He growled. He sure wished he had a laser cutter now. Even a life support hood would have been nice, the stuffy tunnel filled with a fine-grained dust.

Deep in the mountain, he encountered a side access blocked by a partial slide. Knowing he would need a place to shelter after setting the fuse, he put the canister aside and dug out enough of the offshoot to reach an old metal hatch.

Grey was startled to suddenly find himself in a large chamber. Lamplight revealed a workbench with testing apparatus and hand tools. It was an old Arikhan research station with no evidence that a human had ever been there. The slide he had dug through was a blocked vent. Another hatch exited to the west. Glistening mineral samples lay in well-organized bins along the walls, and something was sparkling in a tray below the workbench. Diamonds. Dozens of small pink, white, and blue diamonds. Highly valuable, from what he could tell, and even more interesting, two skeletons lay locked in mortal combat, the bones covered by rotting engineering suits. The bones were Arikhan.

Master Shao once claimed Grey had an ability to fathom much with few actual facts. His intuition now asserted itself again. He knew rare minerals had great value in the Arikhan economy, yet this promising area had been abandoned years before. Even slaves had not been permitted to enter. Could it be these two Arikhan, possibly prospecting on their own, told their superiors the upper strata was dry only to work it secretly? Did the position of the bodies indicate the thieves had betrayed each other?

Though not an expert on the Arikhan compensation system, he vaguely knew a mine's surplus provided rewards for the guards and transporters, and most particularly, for the supervisors. Could this discovery be used to benefit Ferret Camp? He wasn't sure. The California gold rush of 1849 certainly hadn't helped the indigenous peoples who lived there.

With a mission to accomplish, he performed a quick clean-up of the crime scene, dug a niche to hide the diamonds, and crawled another hundred yards before reaching the north face. He found no diamond deposits along the route, nor did he expect to. The indications were wrong for such a discovery.

At the end of the tunnel, where a narrow air passage had once penetrated to the surface, he carved out a hole for the explosive and attached the detonator. In theory, a slow burning fuse should give him enough time to crawl clear. He packed the canister in with boulders to give the explosion more force before unreeling a hundred meters of twine saturated with potassium nitrate. It was all he had.

As he prepared to light the fuse, he paused to plan his retreat to the abandoned chamber, taking an extra breath of the stale air. He didn't want to die under the mountain because of an error in judgment, and wondered if the project had been such a good idea after all. But it was too late for idle worries. It would be better to suffer the mountain than be broiled alive on Nabbatron's spit.

Grey struck a flint, blew the spark to life, and crawled away with the speed of a frightened cockroach, reaching the chamber seconds before the tunnel shook. He dove to the floor of the research lab under a workbench, covering the back of his head with his hands as a deafening earthquake shook the walls. The workbench toppled over, his lamp went out, and within seconds all around him was thundering darkness.

From the low hill overlooking the ravine between their mines, members of Ferret Camp and Deer Camp stood side by side in silence. The ore tracks had been laid, the tool tent readied. The mated women had returned from the gardens early to see if the bold experiment would work or become another failure in a long year of disappointments.

"Soon. It should be soon," Wart said, so excited he was jumping around.

Hardly a minute later, there was a low rumble. The ground beneath their feet trembled. Frightened birds flew from their sanctuaries on the hilltop. The spectators looked to the north face of Ferret Camp's mountain that suddenly exploded in a ferocious ball of yellow flame followed by a thick black plume of smoke. Trees and boulders were hurled through the air, and a gray cloud blotted out the afternoon sky.

Through the swirling dust, the spectators saw tons of rock pouring down from a gaping hole in the mountainside, first in a hesitant wave, and then in a crashing torrent that tumbled halfway across the ravine. The people murmured with approval. Some were crying. The young people stared wide-eyed, never before having witnessed such awesome power.

"I've not seen such since we were children," Clagg said, an arm wrapped around Myra. Myra hugged him with relief.

"Long has it been since our people used more than shovels and picks," Nole agreed, kneeling next to Clagg outside the tool tent.

"I doubt even the masters know how to use such magic," Court suggested, hanging close to her husband.

"It's not magic," Wart said. "It's science. Chemicals mixed into the proper combinations. Ben even showed me the markings on the jars."

"When a mountain falls to the ground, I call it magic," Clagg said.

"I think the magic is in the man, not the potions," Nole observed. "Ferret Camp is fortunate to have such a member."

"Ben doesn't seem shy about helping Deer Camp," Myra remarked.

"We're not unhappy that he looks on us favorably," Nole was quick to say. "Though after what he did for Tak, we'd be his friend even if he didn't challenge the mountain."

As the dust gradually settled, they saw the results of the blast, a gaping crater in the cliff wall revealing glistening traces of freshly exposed minerals. Spread across the canyon floor was enough shattered ore to meet several quotas. The excited workers moved forward with their sledgehammers and shovels.

"I should help," Clagg said, trying to swing his legs off the bed of hay bales.

"You should sit still like Ben told you to," Myra scolded. "He has risked enough without you being foolish."

"He should not have made that wager with Nabbatron," Clagg said, shaking his head.

"He is your friend," Myra replied. "Now you must be *his* friend by staying out of trouble."

"Yes, my sweet flower," he agreed, pulling her closer.

"Just because everyone else is in the field doesn't make this our mating tent," Myra protested, slapping his hand away.

"Since when do we need a tent?" Clagg asked, grabbing her hips.

Footsteps interrupted them a moment later.

"Clagg won't be going to the pens this season," Nole said, returning to the tent after completing a survey of the debris field. He was holding several ore-laden rocks and smiling.

"Nor will Ben grace Nabbatron's spit, if the master keeps his word," Cot added, sitting on the ground to shake stones from his boots.

"Ben must love you greatly to make such an offer," Nole said, expressing the awe Deer Camp felt over Grey's wager. An awe shared by Ferret Camp.

"What has happened here? What is this?" Frontra said, marching into the tent without notice. It was rare for the tall Arikhan guard to show such agitation.

Everyone quickly dropped to their knees except Clagg, who could only bow his head.

"We are making a new mine, mistress. A quarry," Cot said.

"A quarry? There was a volcano. Great smoke. Half your mountain is gone," Frontra exaggerated, claws twitching in excitement. Her cheeks flushed black.

"There is still much mountain left, mistress," Clagg said, trying not to smile.

Soon Nabbatron, Bortro, and Dhartro arrived, storming through the area and stopping work. The ore carts were examined and the tent searched. Workers were called up from the debris field, kneeling in groups as their masters gazed about in confusion.

"I would have an explanation," Nabbatron demanded, eye-rings protruding with skin drawn tightly around his face.

"This is a quarry, master," Clagg said. "We had such in the old days. At the gravel camp. The ore is easier to gather."

"Where did you get explosives? How did you learn to use them? Such knowledge is forbidden," Nabbatron said.

"They were used in the old days," Clagg dared to repeat.

"This is a trick to avoid the pens. You and the half-meat seek to trick me," Nabbatron cursed, reaching for a shock wand.

"We seek to make quota, master," Clagg said, his voice angry.

Nabbatron's eyes bulged as he stepped forward with the weapon raised to strike. Frontra stepped in front of him.

"This is my zone. My workers," Frontra declared. "They are working an open mine with my permission. Have you no respect for the proper order of command?"

"You knew nothing of this," Nabbatron said.

"That is for Romtra to decide," Frontra responded.

"No, it is for *me* to decide," a tall Arikhan said, entering the tent unexpectedly.

"Lord Gamtro! Forgive us, Sarden Leader," Nabbatron said, bowing his head.

Karak's commandant wore no weapons on his belt or badges of office on his vest. His supreme authority required no extra trappings.

"Welcome to our sector, Sarden Leader," Frontra said with equal respect.

"Is there an explanation for the cloud of smoke hanging over my camp?" Gamtro asked. "And I would like to know why my guards are found arguing before the workers. Have we fallen so low that honor means nothing?"

"We are sorry, Sarden Leader," Frontra said, eye-rings dipped in shame.

"There is the true cause of our difficulty," Nabbatron said, pointing to the line of tracks where Grey was slowly approaching the worksite.

"Is that the half-meat? It has gained weight," Gamtro said in surprise, his naturally blue facial features turning lighter.

"It works hard. Much does it strive to please," Frontra said.

"Remain here. Raise not your voices again, lest *you* wish to hammer the rocks yourself," Gamtro instructed his staff.

"We obey, Sarden Leader," the sentries complied, thumping their chests with clenched fists.

Gamtro returned the salute with a casual wave of his claw and walked down the knoll to the tracks, reaching a partially loaded ore cart in Grey's path. He glanced in the cart and noticed the contents, a fine grade that would go far toward meeting quota. If enough such carts could be filled, it would mean bonuses for his unit. Gamtro was not displeased.

"Food creature, come here," Gamtro ordered.

Grey squinted against the sun, recognized an Arikhan accent but not the owner, and dropped to his knees next to the ore cart. Gamtro saw he was covered in dust, his face and arms streaked with black powder. The creature appeared blinded by soot.

"Wash," Gamtro said, giving the slave a canteen of water from his own belt.

"Thank you, master," he said, gratefully splashing his face. He looked up but still didn't recognize who he was addressing.

"I am Gamtro, Sarden Leader of Karak. Is it you who blew up my camp?" the aristocratic alien asked in precise Arikhan, the pronunciation indicating an advanced degree of education.

"Yes, Sarden Leader," Grey said, bowing low to the ground.

Gamtro noticed the slave spoke Arikhan fairly well, but with an unusual accent. Not one he had heard before.

"Have you no explanation? No apology?"

"Clagg was condemned to the pens if we could not meet quota, master. Clagg is my friend. Ferret Camp will make quota."

"Now you may be sent to the pens instead," Gamtro warned.

"That is only just, master. I mixed the explosives."

"You are experienced in this art?"

"Yes, master," he said.

Gamtro leaned against the ore cart, looked again at the minerals, and studied the prisoner. It not only appeared submissive, it seemed to readily accept his judgment. But the creature was not stupid. It could not be. Setting such a charge required training and intelligence. And from what Gamtro had seen, the results were precisely calculated. The food creature before him was no common worker.

"This zone belongs to Frontra. She decides what must be done," Gamtro said. "If no offense is given, there will be no punishment."

The slave said nothing. He had not been asked a question, so he remained kneeling with his head down. Gamtro liked that.

"I have heard a rumor," Gamtro said. "It was about a wager. If one lost, it would go to the pens. If the other lost, extra supplies would be sent to a camp. Have you heard this story?"

"I have heard there was a proposition, master. Would it not be disrespectful for a slave to wager against a being of great superiority?"

"Perhaps it would. Wash in the creek and resume your duties."

"Thank you, master," Grey said, backing away.

Gamtro watched him go with keen interest. *A very clever animal,* Gamtro thought. And the Sarden Leader was not fooled by its feigned humility.

* * * * * *

For the next five weeks, Ferret Camp and Deer Camp worked side by side. As the ore carts filled and were pushed to the loading platforms near the front gate, they became hopeful of not merely making quota but exceeding it. They were helped by the two jackhammers Grey had repaired, the loud tools breaking boulders with the speed of ten workers. He was also sure to show others how to operate the devices, especially Hernet, Burne, and Turk, the strapping youngsters allowed to assist in the maintenance.

"The rest day approaches," Nole said as the men walked together to Ferret Camp. "Do you think the quota is made?"

"Clagg has been counting the carts. He says the quota was made on the last double moon," Cot said, taking off his sweat-soaked shirt and throwing it around his shoulders as he often did. The tallest of the group, he was also the most prone to sunburn.

"Clagg is not a good counter," Sal said, wearing a broad brim straw hat against the sun. The oldest of the group, he was more vulnerable to the heat, though many who were accustomed to laboring underground were struggling with the adjustment to working outdoors.

"He has more time now. Ben will not let him walk for fear of bending the leg," young Burne remarked, enjoying a late afternoon breeze. The fifteen-year-old youth was enjoying the new environment, quietly wishing never to work underground again.

"Clagg still does not count well. Does Ben think we made quota?" Nole asked, adjusting his felt hat when the sun moved out from behind a cloud.

"Ben does not say much," Hernet mentioned.

"He seems to dwell much in thought. Is there so much to worry about?" Sal asked.

"It's true he doesn't satisfy easily," Cot said. "We have food now, tunics for the women, and we should make quota. Some believe he should rest more often."

"You don't have so much food," Nole cautioned. "Your tunics are old. Many men have rags for shirts. The women have no fur boots."

"Deer Camp is not wealthy, either," Hernet protested, his round face red. "Just because you have shared some of your cast off—"

"I mean no disrespect," Nole quickly apologized, holding up his hands for peace. "Winter will be hard for us, too. I just say that Ben wants more for our camps. What's good enough for us is not good enough for him."

"As Sal has said, he worries about many things," Cot agreed.

"Mostly Shalli," Hernet said, tugging up his pants as he laughed.

Others laughed as well, especially Medim. Short and stout with long black hair and a thin beard, Deer Camp's young stonecutter had not yet found a mate.

"I don't understand that," Medim said. "If a beautiful woman like Shalli took such an interest in me, I'd have her on her back begging for more. Does Ben not appreciate women?"

"He appreciates Shalli. Many times have I caught his eye on her when he thinks no one is watching," Cot gossiped.

"Does Ben have a conflicting interest?" Nole asked.

"If he does, no one knows of it," Cot replied.

Sal shook his head. "Except for Tak, Shalli is the prettiest unmated girl in Karak. Marne would kill to take her. Maybe he will. Ben surprises me."

"Clagg may know more. If Ben opens his thoughts to anyone, it would be Clagg," Hernet said.

They reached Ferret Camp to discover most of the women already there. Nole ran to Court who was sitting with Myra, Bab, and Beknar.

"Were there problems at the gardens?" Nole asked.

"Not today," Court said, rising to give him a kiss. "Wolf Camp is struggling to make quota. They're too busy to cause trouble."

"The new count begins after the rest day. There might be trouble then," Beknar warned.

"Have the camps agreed to a council?" Myra asked.

"Not yet. Some say they are jealous of our quarry," Court answered.

"We don't even know if we've made quota yet," Nole said.

"Everyone thinks we have. Some feel our quarry is cheating," Court replied.

"That's nonsense," Nole objected.

"It's what some say," Beknar confirmed.

"Look! It's Clagg!" someone shouted.

Everyone looked to see Clagg hobbling along on a pair of thick crutches with Grey and Burne standing nearby to ensure his balance. Clagg was all smiles as Myra ran to help.

"Be careful, you oaf," Myra said.

"Stand aside! If Clagg falls, the earth will shake again!" Hernet yelled.

"Come within reach, insolent cousin. I'll shake some earth," Clagg shouted back, freeing one hand to playfully wave his fist.

"Grip the crutch or I'll send you back to the tent," Grey ordered.

"You speak loudly for one half my size," Clagg boasted.

"I'm only a third your size, but if you don't obey Ben, we'll see who speaks most loudly," Myra warned.

"It's only my leg that's broken, woman. Let's borrow a fur and see which of us makes the most noise," Clagg suggested.

"Clagg!" Myra exclaimed, her cheeks flushing.

Grey guided Clagg to a large rock and made him sit, kneeling to check the fresh splints on his leg. Burne helped secure the knots. Shalli and Tak arrived with water and bread rolls for the returning workers.

"Frontra is coming," someone called from the edge of camp.

The combined camps, some eighty people in all, rushed to the central hearth and knelt, heads lowered as Frontra arrived followed by four heavily laden two-wheeled carts. Frontra ordered the cart drivers to unload the bundles and leave. The Rabbit Camp members, generally better dressed, frowned before departing. Many thought they looked envious.

"Greetings, food creatures," Frontra said, holding up a claw in salute.

Having helped Clagg to the community tent before kneeling at the entrance, Grey noticed for the first time a peculiar inflection in Frontra's voice. When the other Arikhan referred to the people as food creatures, they meant it literally. Frontra seemed to be using it as an expression.

"Welcome, mistress," Myra said, kneeling close to her feet.

"Thank you Myra, wife of Clagg, leader of Ferret Camp," Frontra responded, signaling that it was an official visit. "I bring good news. Your camps have exceeded quota by fifteen percent. You will not work the next two days or on the rest day. Here are the fall supplies for Ferret Camp. Others are leaving supplies at Deer Camp. You have done well."

"Thank you, mistress," dozens of voices answered in unison.

"You may rise," Frontra said. "There is mauck and apple grog in the kegs. Red melon for the little ones. There is also freshly killed venison for your cooking fires. Tonight you have earned much celebration."

Ferret Camp surged forward to the waiting bundles, finding new clothing, boots, hats, blankets, and a pile of sleeping furs. Most of Deer Camp's members went to check on their reward, but they would be back soon.

"These are riches beyond expectation, mistress," Myra said with tears in her eyes.

"The half-meat is much responsible," Frontra said, moved by her sincerity as indicated by the soft clicking of her tongue. "Where is he?"

Grey came forward to kneel at her feet. Frontra thought he seemed very pleased by the excitement. He was almost smiling.

"You have given me much amusement," Frontra said.

"I do not understand, mistress," he questioned.

"Bring me a stool and a cup of mauck," Frontra ordered. "Sit and take heed, for it is rare such good stories are told."

The women hurried to serve the mauck as a stool was found for Frontra. Everyone else sat cross-legged on the ground. Grey continued to kneel until Frontra specifically ordered him to sit back.

"It was obvious some days ago that quota had been exceeded," Frontra explained. "And the quality of the ore is the best found in many years. Sarden Leader Gamtro is greatly satisfied. Each day he has required reports on your progress. He sends praise to Clagg and Nole for the quarry, believing their initiative a good thing. And much has he praised me for allowing it."

There was a mumbling among the people at this. Many looked embarrassed, especially Clagg and Nole. It was Clagg who spoke first.

"Mistress, there is something we must say," Clagg started.

Frontra held up her claw.

"There is no need, leader of Ferret Camp. That is part of the amusement," Frontra explained. "Gamtro knows the quarry was not your conception, and he knows I did not approve use of the explosives. Gamtro sees all with a clear eye. After Nabbatron's outburst in your tent, Gamtro went to the half-meat and threatened him with the pens for blowing up the mountain, yet still did Ben claim the deed as his own."

Now eyes were turning toward Grey, most with disapproval.

"You should not have done that, my brother," Clagg said. "Too often do you risk yourself on our behalf. All agreed to attack the mountain. All should share the punishment."

"All would have been punished if Gamtro had so chosen," Frontra warned. "But Gamtro is a just leader. He was once high in the councils of government before jealousy brought him to his present post. Now he strives to regain his former place. To my shame, I knew this before accepting responsibility for your quarry, confident Gamtro would be lenient. Such is his pleasure that many of these gifts come from him."

"You honor us, mistress, to share your thoughts in this manner," Nole said, expressing everybody's opinion.

"A good story should be shared," Frontra said. "As the quota was reached, and then much surpassed, I went to Nabbatron and reminded him of his wager."

Grey looked up with a frown. Frontra slapped her knees and clicked her tongue loudly.

"Excuse me, half-meat. I should say that I reminded Nabbatron of your proposition," Frontra corrected. The camp members laughed.

"Nabbatron said the proposition was a trick. No payment would be made," Frontra said a bit more seriously. "He also threatened Ben with the pens at the next opportunity. These words were overheard by Lord Gamtro, who flew into such a rage as I have not seen. Nabbatron was drawn into the Sarden Leader's office, and even through the closed door, I heard language that dried my egg sacs. The Sarden Leader berated Nabbatron for losing his temper, hampering production, and compromising the honor of our race. Thus has Nabbatron lost a step in rank, and he pays double on the wager that was not a wager."

Frontra reached into her tunic and pulled out a finely sewn raccoon hat with ear flaps. All were dazzled by the quality. Frontra stood up and gave the cap to Myra.

"With the compliments of Nabbatron, as promised," Frontra said.

"It is beautiful, mistress. It is the most beautiful thing I have ever seen," Myra said, afraid to put it on.

"Remember, the wager is paid double," Frontra said.

She reached into a knapsack and pulled out a lush ermine shawl, holding it up for everyone to see before draping it over Myra's shoulders.

"Myra, you look like a queen!" Shalli said, stroking the soft fur.

"In the bales among the new tunics and foot coverings there is a scarf for each female and a hide hat for each male," Frontra said. "You will also find woven blankets for the little ones. These are gifts from me, purchased from the bonus to be received for your effort."

Ferret Camp was stunned into silence. Frontra had always been kind, for an Arikhan, but this was unexpected.

"Thank you, mistress. There is none in this camp we would rather serve," Clagg finally said, speaking for everyone.

"I thank you, food creatures," Frontra replied. And this time Grey knew without doubt she was using the expression as an endearment, not a menu specification. "You have helped raise me in status. Your quarry will bring much profit. And I believe your new member will provide endless amusement. I am grateful."

Frontra finished her drink and stood to leave, smoothing down the edges of her brown tunic.

"Will you not join our feast, mistress?" Shalli asked.

"No, child. I am going to feast with Bortro tonight," Frontra said, a click at the end of her sentence indicating anticipation. "At sunrise we pay homage to Sherra for our good fortune. All have said duty on this depleted world ends careers. I believe we make a beginning."

Frontra went to the edge of camp and paused beside a sturdy footlocker.

"My promise is not forgotten, half-meat," Frontra said, throwing him a black leather medical bag. Then Frontra departed with a bounce in her long strides. Grey had never seen an Arikhan so happy.

It was fortunate that Frontra gave the camps extra rest days, for they celebrated deep into the star-studded night, making a bonfire of damaged timbers and dancing around the ferocious flames. Four of the young women, Shalli, Tak, Pie, and Leet, were especially energetic, gyrating to the rhythms of the drummers tapping out a primitive beat on hollow logs.

Sitting alone at the edge of the circle, almost in the dark, Grey sipped his cup of mauck and feasted on salted bread sticks. It was a fine evening in his opinion. Myra approached and sat on the log next to him.

"Always the outsider," Myra said, teasing rather than accusing.

"I'm accustomed to it," he said.

"But you would have it otherwise."

"I don't know. Maybe."

"Are the people you come from so different?"

"In some ways, very different. In things that matter, not so much."

Myra put her head against Grey's shoulder, her hands wrapped around his arm.

"Look at the pleasure with which the girls dance," Myra said. "Court was afraid her daughter would never smile again. Tonight she sings. I've known Court all my life. When we were children, we lived together in the desert camp. Before the older workers were harvested and the survivors sent here. I'm so glad you brought her daughter back."

Grey said nothing, but he did notice the contentment of Court and Nole, who held hands as they watched their daughter dance. Myra studied him by the light of the fire, trying to read his thoughts. It had brought him satisfaction to help Tak. Joy to help the camps. But he asked for nothing. Accepted no thanks.

"You're a proud creature, aren't you?" Myra questioned.

"Yes," he answered, not happy about it.

"Such pride is rare in a slave camp. And dangerous," Myra warned.

"I have been programmed to function in this manner," Grey said in his best robotic voice.

Myra laughed, though she didn't understand the implications.

"You're funny, when you want to be. And brave. Any woman in this camp would want you in her furs," she said, squeezing his arm.

"Even you?" he asked.

"I wouldn't object, and neither would Clagg, but you don't want me. You want Shalli."

"She's a beautiful young lady," he said, watching her dance.

Suddenly Shalli tore off her wrap and twisted naked near the flames, shaking her long hair loose and flinging her arms above her head.

"Okay, maybe lady is overstating it," he corrected.

"Everyone says you're fearless," Myra remarked. "The way you held up the mountain to save Clagg, and challenged Nabbatron. The way you won't back down if you think you're right. But I've seen your fear many times. It's different than ours. In some ways, I think maybe it's worse than ours."

"Are you making a point?" he asked.

"Yes, my friend. My brother. I'm saying Ferret Camp is your world now. We are your people. We're happy that it should be so. You don't have to sit in the dark."

"Myra, I accepted this world the day I was feeling sorry for myself while Clagg lay in pain. The shame reminds me that I'm needed. If I wasn't, I would have torn Nabbatron's heart from his chest and made him eat it."

Myra started to laugh before realizing Grey wasn't joking. She saw his clenched fists. Felt the tension.

"The masters are bigger than you. Stronger. They are well-armed. Even Clagg has been dropped by their shock sticks. Could you really hurt Nabbatron?" Myra asked.

"If Nabbatron were first rank infantry, it might be difficult. But he's not. He's a retired ranker put out to pasture a thousand light years from the frontlines."

Myra couldn't tell if Grey was bragging or merely exaggerating, and wasn't sure how to respond. She thought it good that he could defend himself, but feared the violence he might be capable of. She would need to think on it.

"Well, since you won't be eating Nabbatron's heart tonight, maybe you can join the celebration?" Myra suggested. "We owe this evening to you. The people will be disappointed if you don't take pleasure in it. They may think you scorn our ways."

"I don't scorn your ways," he defended.

"Then let's dance," Myra said, pulling him to his feet.

Grey followed her to the bonfire, accepting friendly nods from the camp. Myra waved to Court and Nole, then Burne and Leet, getting them to join in before Grey changed his mind. The hollow logs were beat faster, the mauck served more generously, and Shalli jumped in to take Myra's place, taking his hands as they danced with a daring gleam in her excited blue eyes.

* * * * * *

"There will be no council," Cot reported, returning to Ferret Camp at the end of a long day. "Nole has gone to tell Deer Camp. Bear Camp offered support, but Wolf Camp and Raven Camp refuse."

"What about Sparrow Camp?" Beknar asked, grinding grain on a flat rock to make bread.

"Old Ravo is mad we didn't share the quarry," Hernet said, removing his shirt to shake out the day's dust. The squat miner seated himself on a log near Beknar and slapped her butt, getting an annoyed look in return.

"Maybe Ben can help them find a mine?" Shalli asked, busily placing wood beneath the camp's new stone oven.

"They wouldn't listen," Cot said, sitting cross-legged on a fur while the women found food for him.

"And I will be angry if anyone mentions it to Ben," Clagg said. "What he's done for us is dangerous. He shouldn't risk himself every time we have a problem."

"Is Rabbit Camp no help?" Pie asked, kneading dough for the oven.

"They fear Wolf Camp," Cot said. "The young women will continue to avoid the northern fields for now. Perhaps a few men can join the mated women in the gardens."

"That might cause more trouble," Myra warned. "They broke Rorent's arms. Others have been hurt. Beknar and I will ask everyone to work harder."

The men could only nod, having no better solution.

Shalli and Pie finished their chores and walked away from the group disappointed. As they entered a heavy patch of woods, they found a trail to Deer Camp and started north, picking berries along the way.

"I miss my turn in the gardens," Pie said with a sigh.

"I do, too, but if you had seen Tak, you would not miss being near the wolves. It's even harder on Deer Camp. It sounds like their friendship with Sparrow Camp is over," Shalli mentioned.

"Many friendships are over. I never see Loto or Beez anymore. Why is everyone so mad?"

"I think maybe it's getting harder to make quota," Shalli guessed. "People are afraid the masters will break up the camps. Myra said when they broke up the desert camp, the older workers went to the pens. That's when she lost her father."

"That was twenty years ago. The masters say they need more workers now. They even want us to have babies. I would like a baby."

"Do you want a baby with Burne? Or Turk?"

"They're boys. I want a baby with Ben," Pie said, giggling.

"You're just saying that to hurt me!" Shalli protested.

"I tease you, cousin," Pie admitted. "But I wouldn't mind having a baby with Ben. Many would not mind."

"I'm going to have a baby with Ben. It will be a daughter, and she'll be smart just like he is."

"Have you been to Ben's tent?" Pie asked.

"No, he hasn't treated me like a woman yet," Shalli confessed. "But he will. Now that I'm of age, he has no more excuses. And for all his virtues, he still has a weakness."

"What weakness is that?" Pie asked.

"He's a man," Shalli laughed. Pie laughed, too.

"Where is Ben today?"

"At the quarry, I think," Shalli guessed.

"But it's the rest day."

"He won't be working. Clagg has forbidden him to work on rest days. He goes to pick stones. I think he is looking for something, but I don't know what."

"Ben does strange things," Pie said.

"Yes," Shalli agreed. "Look. It's Tak."

The young women ran to an overgrown trail that led away from the quarry. A creek ran through the area, the trees taller than in the southern portion of the compound. Tak was surprised to see them, quickly signaling for silence.

"What is it?" Shalli asked.

"A secret place," Tak whispered.

They followed Tak down a narrow path into the brush, crawling under thick vines into a hollow beneath tangled purple bushes. Shalli looked out through a hole in the leaves, startled. There, in a clearing, was Grey.

Pie started to say something but Tak hushed her up. Grey had stripped to a loincloth and was standing perfectly still. A pile of sharpened stones lay at his feet. Dangling from tree branches ten yards away were bales of weeds bound together with discarded wire. Behind him, the shallow creek had been damned with logs to form a pond.

"I've seen him here before. This is where he fights the ghosts," Tak confided.

"Ghosts?" Pie said almost too loudly.

The women settled back, watching as Grey began a well-practiced routine, striking forward with his hands, thrusting with his feet, going into a sudden spin and kicking invisible objects high in the air, then landing like a cat ready to strike again. Their young hearts beat faster as the speed of the exercise increased, Grey turning, twisting and dancing with a fierce determination.

As sweat made his muscles glisten, Grey picked up a long staff and performed a new series of exercises, probing, blocking and pounding phantom opponents. Sometimes the staff was a club, at other times a spear. The women had never seen a mere piece of wood look so dangerous. After twenty minutes of vigorous effort, Grey rinsed off in the pond and took a deep drink of the cool water.

"Is that it?" Shalli asked.

"Not yet," Tak whispered.

Grey returned to his starting position to pick up a handful of flat rocks. He looked at the bales hanging from the tree branches and rapidly threw the stones, some underhand, some overhand, all the while shifting from side to side and even spinning around. Every flying stone hit a mark, some with enough force to make the bales swing back and forth.

"Those could hurt," Pie whispered.

"The ghosts will cry tonight," Tak said with a smile.

Once the ritual was complete, Grey bowed deeply to the weed bales and dunked himself in the pond before getting dressed. When he left, he passed near enough to the women that they held their breaths.

"He was fighting ghosts," Pie said in awe.

"I think so," Shalli agreed.

"He's fought them here before. I think he's fought them many times," Tak guessed.

"I wish he would fight Marne so we could go back to the gardens," Pie sighed.

"Don't say that! Not ever!" Shalli shouted. "The wolves would go after him. They aren't ghosts. Marne would break his arms. That's why Myra won't let Clagg fight."

"Don't get upset, Shalli. Ben isn't stupid. He won't let Marne break his arms," Tak assured her with a hug.

"We must always watch out for Ben," Shalli said. "Clagg says he's like a child. He acts on impulse. He won't take care of himself. Let's not talk about Marne anymore."

"Would it be all right to sit in Ben's pond?" Pie asked. "It's deeper than the creek, and I see soap root. We can wash our hair."

"Not afraid of the ghosts?" Tak asked.

"A little," Pie confessed. "But I think Ben has chased them away."

Grey was planning to relax at Ferret Camp for the rest of the day, knowing Clagg was unhappy with his prolonged work schedules, but he decided on a visit to the quarry first while the light was still good. On work days, it was harder to concentrate with so many people around. He was surprised to find Frontra and Nabbatron sitting on stools outside the tool tent.

"Greetings beings of great superiority," Grey said, approaching to kneel at their feet.

"Greetings, half-meat," Frontra said, amused by his salutation.

"Your greeting is returned, impertinent food creature," Nabbatron said, unusually civil.

Grey glanced around, but there was no one else in the area. The quarry was well-organized now, with paths cut through the rock strewn canyon and ore tracks laid to best advantage. Thirty transport carts were lined up waiting for work to resume the following morning. Timber once used in the mines had been made into sorting bins, allowing the best minerals to have priority.

"Your camp progresses well. At this pace, you will exceed quota for the fall season," Frontra said.

"It is my hope that we will, mistress," Grey said.

"See that you succeed," Nabbatron cautioned. "Still do I long to have you on my spit, but a production bonus would be better. Serve well and live."

"Thank you, master," Grey said, pressing his forehead to the ground.

Nabbatron clicked his tongue with impatience and left the quarry, walking at a quick pace toward Squirrel Camp.

"Have I displeased master Nabbatron?" Grey asked.

"You annoy him. He no more believes your acts of feigned submission than I do. He is correct to call you impertinent."

"I am sorry to disappoint you, mistress."

"When we are alone, you may call me Frontra. Now get up from your knees, I think you mock me."

Grey shifted position and sat on the ground cross-legged before her, declining the stool he might have accepted.

"I would not mock you, Frontra. Much have I learned to respect your generosity."

"High praise indeed," Frontra said.

"Now who is mocked?" he replied.

"Why are you here, Ben? Has Clagg not forbidden you to work on the rest day?"

"Clagg makes hard rules, but I have not disobeyed him. The quarry is quiet on the rest day. I come to search the ore for trace elements. Before the next season ends, it will be time to bring down another layer of rock."

"Will you provide warning this time?"

"Yes, mistress."

"Frontra," she corrected, lowering eye-rings for emphasis.

"Yes, Frontra," he said.

"Stand. Remove your body covering," Frontra ordered.

Grey did as instructed, kicking off his rawhide moccasins, peeling off the blue cotton shirt, and dropping the beige knee length britches before standing naked with his arms at his sides. Frontra walked around him, occasionally poking a muscle or testing a reflex.

"You are no longer a half-meat," Frontra observed.

"Working the rock has improved my strength," Grey replied, growing embarrassed.

"You appear uncomfortable," she remarked.

"I am not accustomed to being inspected in such a manner."

"The lack of attire? Is your culture so much different than the slaves?"

Grey did not answer. Did Frontra know he came from another world? What would it mean if she did?

Suddenly Frontra lashed out with her claw, aiming directly at his face. He instinctively ducked aside and fell into a fighting stance: feet set apart, his left hand open and held forward, the right cocked back in a fist. The flash in his eyes sought an angle of attack. For a moment, it looked like he was going to hurt her. Maybe badly. Frontra merely stood her ground, tongue clicking with interest.

"Forgive me, Frontra," Grey said, catching control of himself. He dropped to his knees, head bent low.

"You are no slave. No breaker of rocks. Well do I know the gaze of a warrior," Frontra said.

Grey said nothing. No question had been asked. Frontra kneeled and raised his head, her claw supporting his chin. She looked deeply into his steel gray eyes.

"In your days of the sword, were you good?" Frontra asked.

"That person died long ago," Grey answered, trying to look away. "Now I am a slave of Karak. A member of Ferret camp."

"Answer my question," Frontra demanded, squeezing his face.

"The warrior you speak of was among the first rank," Grey said with a trace of defiance.

"I suspect your words are true," Frontra said, returning to her stool. She reached into her knapsack and took out a black bottle with a cork stopper. "Put on your covering and taste bruna with me."

"Thank you," Grey said, getting dressed and accepting a tin cup that Frontra filled to the rim. "May I ask a question of the zone leader?"

"Ask," Frontra said, taking a sip of her fermented grain brew.

Grey took a sip as well, noticing a fine, copper-cooked taste. Similar to the moonshine he had enjoyed in the lush green hills of another world.

"I am much a stranger to the ways of these people. Nor do I understand the Arikhan methods of controlling their slaves. How is it that Wolf Camp is allowed to wreak havoc on the weaker camps?"

"No camp on this world is permanent," Frontra explained. "As resources in one area dwindle, camps are moved. The societies the slaves develop maintain a hierarchy. Because no guard unit remains intact, it is easier for us to let the workers settle their own affairs provided quotas are met."

"Does not the loss of workers impair efficiency? I have heard the wolves hurt some so seriously they go to the pens," Grey said.

"It is true, but this system has served us well for a hundred years," Frontra explained. "The workers remain under control. Guards from successful camps receive promotions. A wealthy camp may allow a guard to purchase a homestead, establish a trade, or even join a Sanctuary. I hope someday to serve Sherra at the Great Temple of Jurat, if I can afford a post in her lodge."

"Sherra's service comes with a high price," Grey warned.

"I hear the sadness in your voice, Ben. They say warriors stand nearest Sherra's heart. How close have you stood?"

"I have stood in the flames, Frontra. I have stood in the flames so long, I no longer feel the fire," he replied, both hands wrapped tightly around the cup as he drank.

"Or fear it," Frontra observed. "Much have you asked about our ways. And the wolves. Are your questions answered?"

Grey finished his drink and stood up, returning the cup to Frontra.

It was late afternoon. He would not hunt for stones today.

"Yes, your insight has great value. Once again I am in your debt," he answered. The thin membranes above Frontra's eyes rose.

"Perhaps someone should be careful," Frontra advised.

"I will not be rash. If the Arikhan choose not to interfere, the task will be easier."

Frontra clicked her tongue with curiosity.

* * * * * *

As the fall season reached the halfway point, it seemed to Grey that the quarry would exceed quota. He even suggested that Squirrel Camp be allowed to share the bounty, though Clagg and Nole were sufficiently angry with them that no agreements were reached. Then Grey made a surprising request.

"I would go to the gardens tomorrow," he announced.

"What do you know about growing food?" Beknar asked, grouchy as always.

"You're needed in the quarry," Myra said.

"I've worked on farms before, and Clagg now leads the quarry crews," Grey replied. "I've yet to be beyond the border of Deer Camp. Haven't I earned a reward?"

"Working the fields is hard work, not a reward," Beknar said with insult.

"It would be a reward for me," Grey mumbled quietly.

"There could be trouble," Myra feared. "We already ... they ..."

"Wolf Camp makes everything difficult. They are selfish. They envy our mine," Beknar complained.

"Marne and his wolves may slap us a little and make rude jokes, but nothing worse," Myra defended. "We are mated women. At least they still respect that."

"It's not right that they harass you," Cot said, intruding on their conversation. "Maybe Clagg and I should come, too. Tell Marne to leave you alone."

"That would cause more trouble. What if six or seven of them gang up on you? Break your arms?" Myra objected.

"If the wolves want trouble, no one can prevent it," Beknar

grumbled.

"I won't cause trouble. I just want to spend a day in the gardens," Grey pleaded.

"Let Ben go," Cot decided.

"Let Ben go where?" Clagg asked, walking up to the quarreling group.

"Ben wants to help in the gardens," Beknar said, expecting Clagg to object.

"There could be trouble," Myra warned.

"Does our camp grow too small for you, little brother?" Clagg asked.

"Is it such an unfair request?" Grey responded.

The women, particularly Myra, felt embarrassed by the resentment in Grey's voice. They did not wish him angry with them.

"Come with us if you must, but be careful. No fighting. Promise?" Myra said.

"I promise. No fighting when I go to the gardens tomorrow," Grey agreed.

"Have you really been on a farm before?" Pie asked.

"Several farms," Grey recalled, looking forward to seeing a new one. "My skills are only fair, but I learn fast."

"You can use the shovel. Men are best with the shovel," Myra said.

"I've heard Clagg is best with his plow," Beknar giggled in a sultry voice.

"Beknar!" Myra protested with crimson cheeks.

Clagg laughed heartily, putting an arm around her shoulders.

"We have been busy in the furs, but times are good. Maybe we will give Garn a brother," Clagg boasted.

"More children already?" Leet said.

"Should it not be so?" Clagg asked.

"It should be so," Cot agreed.

"It will be so," Myra said, snuggling up to Clagg.

Grey sighed and said nothing. He did not think times were so good.

The next morning, Shalli sat down on a grass mat next to Grey as they ate breakfast, a warm porridge with nut root for fiber. The air was cool, the sky cloudy. So close to the equator, Grey didn't expect snow, but it didn't mean the temperatures couldn't get uncomfortable. He thought more blankets might be necessary.

"Are you excited about visiting the gardens?" Shalli asked.

"More nervous than excited. Meeting strangers has never been my best talent," he admitted.

"I'm so jealous. Pie is, too. We haven't been to the fields for the longest time. Not since they went after Tak. I wish we could go with you."

"I'm glad you aren't," Grey said, finishing the porridge so Myra wouldn't scold him.

The camp began to bustle around them, the men and younger women getting ready for the quarry, the mated women gathering baskets for the fields. All knew that Grey was going with them. Many looked concerned. Grey looked concerned, too.

"Don't you want me with you? You let me help at the quarry," Shalli said.

"This will not be my finest hour. By tonight, you may want one of the younger men after all."

"You won't get in trouble, will you? I don't want you hurt."

"You don't need to worry about that," he almost laughed.

"You're talking strangely. Are you expecting something to happen?" she asked. "It cannot be so funny that you would laugh."

"That all depends on your sense of humor."

"Maybe you shouldn't go. Myra and Beknar don't want you to."

"I'm going anyway."

"I don't think you're going to see the gardens. Or the lake. I think you're going to see Marne," Shalli decided.

Her insight surprised him. At times, Grey thought, Shalli can be very bright.

"I'm not going to fight anybody. I promised Myra," he assured her.

"Promise me," Shalli said, moving so close he felt her breath against his cheek. The nearness of her body stirred feelings he sought to avoid.

"Why should I do that?" he asked.

"Because someday I'm going to be your wife."

"You presume much," he responded.

Shalli suddenly leaned forward to kiss him, pushing him back on the mat. Her long hair flowed around his face. Her lips were soft, the smell of her distracting. Grey's resistance grew weak.

"Promise me," Shalli whispered.

"I'll do my best. That's all I ever promise," he agreed, pinned to the ground.

A stomping foot interrupted them.

"Are you tenting my husband's sister?" Myra asked, standing above them.

"Not today," Grey said.

"Then let's get to work. We don't have all morning to lay around," Myra insisted. "Shalli, I'm leaving Garn with you today. We aren't taking any of the children."

Grey went with Myra, Beknar, and four of the mated women through half a kilometer of sparse woods to a junction of ore tracks. A group of women from Deer Camp were waiting for them, surprised by Grey's presence. Myra shrugged, which answered their questions. Going north, the woods gradually grew thicker, separated by an occasional meadow. The trail was not wide but well-travelled.

Though he had seen most of the compound from the hill, it had been from a distance. Grey grew excited as they veered northeast through a brush-filled ravine. Near the south shore of the large oval lake, a line of tall bushy trees sheltered a wheat field from the wind. A row of rough wooden shacks acted as a tool depot and an area had been set aside for corralling the younger children. Plots farther to the east were growing a variety of crops.

"The fields are empty this morning," Beknar said, seeing only a handful of workers. "Rabbit Camp and some of Sparrow Camp."

"The northern camps work the other shore today," Myra hoped.

"Maybe there will be no trouble," Court said with relief.

Walking past the shacks, Grey noticed the largest one commonly used by the Arikhan guards was no better than the others. The lake was bluish green, reeds growing along the sides, and the surface broad enough to ripple in gentle waves. If it ever held fish, he guessed they had long since been depleted. Which was unfortunate. He knew a stocked lake would attract game birds, adding variety to the camp's diet. Though he had often trapped birds during his days on the mountain, most flocks tended to congregate farther north, near the large river at the mouth of the valley.

Grey liked the smell of the lake, so unlike the dry air of the southern camps. A primitive hand pump, somewhat rusted, was positioned to fill the irrigation ditches feeding the gardens. He studied the mechanism, put his hand up to feel the strength of the breeze, and wondered if he could rig a windmill to make irrigation more efficient.

He turned to study the fields. Acres of good growing land, though tired from overuse. Crop rotation and fertilizer would be helpful. The belt of irrigated land bent east around the lake until ending near Wolf Camp on the far side. A strand of scraggily trees, bearing what appeared to be orange fruit, lined a creek that emptied from the lake into the narrow valley. It occurred to Grey that a series of small dams could provide enough water for an orchard.

Grey looked along the western shore and saw where the land grew marshy. And he noticed an old wooden dock extending out into the lake. There had been fish at one time. Maybe there would be again.

"Going for a swim? Maybe you should work first and earn it," Myra said, coming up behind him.

"You've been angry with me since last night," Grey said.

"I'm worried. Yes, and I'm angry."

"Where's my shovel?"

The morning went quickly. Grey decided he would never identify all of the local vegetation, little of it resembling the vegetables he had grown for so many years on his own. They stopped to eat at midday, making a cooking fire to heat their broth. The break also allowed time to plan which areas to harvest. Near the end of the meal, a member of Rabbit Camp came over to inspect their work.

"Greetings, Carger. This is Ben of Ferret Camp," Court introduced.

The lean, middle-aged woman appeared uninterested. Her clothing was better than Court's, trimmed with strips of fur. She met

Court's smile with a surly frown.

"Have your baskets ready for inspection early today," Carger said, quickly returning to the eastern gardens.

Grey waited until the rude crone was gone before asking questions.

"I know Rabbit Camp helps move ore carts to the loading docks, but I didn't realize they supervise food distribution, too," Grey said.

"They have no mine of their own," Myra said. "They have farms, move ore through the gates, and check to make sure no one exceeds their allotments."

"Such people would be powerful on my world," Grey mentioned.

Court and Myra laughed.

"They are worms," Court said.

As the day progressed, no one from the other camps spoke to Grey or even acknowledged his presence. He couldn't tell whether it was fear or resentment. Not that it mattered. Making small talk with strangers was never easy for him.

Toward the end of the afternoon, the women started gathering their baskets. In the distance, Grey saw the final ore carts being moved toward the loading docks. Before long the men would be returning to their camps. He had enjoyed being among edible plants again, feeling the churned earth beneath his feet, but felt disappointment that his objective hadn't been achieved. Then he heard someone shouting.

"Myra, look," Beknar said, pointing to the western edge of the lake.

"Oh, no," Myra whispered.

Grey looked up from the basket he was packing to see five large, well-proportioned men and a medium-sized woman coming in their direction. Dressed in gray woolen shirts, red leather vests, and deerskin pants with rawhide boots, they appeared to be in their early twenties, except for one teenager. None appeared to be carrying weapons, but the vests were long enough to hide objects in their belts. Grey hardly needed to guess who Marne was. A pace ahead of the rest, and the only one wearing a black bandana, he walked with the confidence of an unquestioned leader.

"Ben! Run!" Beknar shouted.

"Yes, maybe they haven't seen you yet," Myra said.

"They saw me from the dock," Grey said. "Is the big one Marne?"

"They're all big. Leave quickly," Myra pleaded.

Others needed no such urging, grabbing whatever food they could and fleeing beyond the edge of the fields into the brush. Some went east toward Rabbit Camp, a few west toward Sparrow Camp. Grey stood still, watching as the wolves approached.

"They will hurt you if you don't run," Beknar said, clutching her basket.

Grey could not blame the women for being afraid. The gang came on like they owned the world.

"There won't be much trouble," Grey said to Myra. "Take your baskets back to camp. I'll meet you there later."

"Myra, get your basket and come!" Beknar yelled, running from the smoldering fire pit where they had heated their lunch. Myra had no choice but to follow, running from the gardens until reaching the south trail. Then she paused in the overgrown ravine with Beknar and Court. When Myra looked back, Grey still hadn't moved.

"What have we here? A stranger?" one of the tall young men said, thinner than Marne with long brown hair and a ruddy complexion. A heavy drinker.

"Not a very big stranger," another remarked, smaller-boned than the others, hair cut above the shoulders, and squinting against the sun. The runt of the pack.

"What is it called?" the woman said, fingering Grey's cotton tunic and pulling out some of the shoulder stitches.

Half a head shorter than Grey, the female was shapely, with long black hair and a pretty face. Except for her smile, which held no warmth. Her black rawhide outfit showed her curves without displaying much skin.

"Hello, my name is Ben. Of the Ferret Camp," Grey said, finding himself surrounded.

"What kind of name is Ben?" the biggest one said, the one Grey guessed was Marne.

The wolf leader was the oldest of the group, about twenty-five, with long reddish blond hair tied back in a ponytail, a closely trimmed red beard, and blazing blue eyes. The others tended to have darker hair and brown eyes. All looked eager to have unpleasant fun.

"It means wanderer. What are your names?" Grey asked, offering a frightened smile.

"*Our* names?" Marne laughed. "We're the wolves, you ignorant stick. I'm Marne. This is Lace." Marne indicated the slender woman who continued to pluck at Grey's clothing with her long black-painted fingernails. "My mates are Logis, Ar, Carp and Winso."

Each smiled as their names were mentioned, but not in a friendly manner. All of the men were taller than Grey, except the skinny youngster, Winso. Miners or cart drivers, like most slaves in the compound, their muscle tone was good. Grey studied the way they walked and stood. How they held their arms. Their reflexes. Which appeared to see well, and which might be nearsighted. He tried to sense a command structure, determining those most likely to act first if confronted.

"What are you doing in our garden?" Ar asked, a stout pig-eyed brute with a scythe-shaped tattoo on his right cheek.

"I thought this was a community field, but if I'm mistaken, I'll gladly leave," Grey said. He looked for their reactions before reaching down to pick up the half-filled basket at his feet.

"Look, Marne, he's stealing our food," Lace said in a smooth drawl.

"Brothers, we have a thief," Marne announced, thumbs tucked in his wide belt. His clothes were better made than the others, the gray shirt tailored for a tighter fit. He would not want to get them dirty.

"I'm sorry. I meant no offense," Grey said, putting the basket down.

From fifty yards away, Myra, Beknar, and Court watched the encounter. Most of the other women were hiding nearby, crouched in the bushes. From the eastern side of the lake, nearly all of Rabbit Camp was observing as well.

"He should have run. Maybe he can knock one down and get away," Court said.

"He should try," Myra hoped, hands clutched so tightly her

knuckles were turning white.

"You made him promise not to fight," Beknar reminded.

"It looks like he's trying to be friends. They'll hurt him for that," Court said.

Grey was beginning to suspect the same thing, but he continued with a nervous smile, pretending nothing was wrong. The wolves seemed to enjoy the game, walking around him in a circle. The woman tore his shirt open down the back, then ripped it off and threw it on the ground.

"We punish thieves. We punish them bad," Ar said, clearly Marne's second-in-command. He had been the first to speak when the wolves approached. Now his fists were curled, ready for a fight. Grey realized he was the group's enforcer.

"I didn't mean to do anything wrong," Grey apologized, turning around slowly.

"Someone needs to be punished," Carp said, finally speaking up. *A bully seeking to prove himself,* Grey thought. *Brave in a crowd.*

"Please don't hurt me," Grey said, looking scared.

"Didn't someone at Ferret Camp put black hands on Thal? Was it you?" Logis asked, big but not well-coordinated. He limped on the right side, perhaps the result of a childhood injury. He was the youngest except for Winso.

"Me? No, I would never do anything like that. It would be disrespectful," Grey said.

"I think it *was* you. What do you think, Lace? Isn't Thal your friend?" Logis asked, possibly the brightest of the group, as evidenced by the crafty gleam in his eyes.

"Thal didn't like running naked through the camps. Not with black hands on her ass," Lace said, the playful smile turning to a frown.

Ar turned Grey around and slapped him across the face. Not hard. It was a test.

"Please don't hurt me. I'd like to leave now," Grey said, putting his hands up.

"Marne, he'd like to leave now," Carp laughed, hitting Grey with the back of his hand.

From the ravine, Myra saw the blow and was sure Grey would strike back. She had seen him knock Cot down. Heard how he'd thrown Clagg. Court had said how Turk was brought to his knees with hardly an effort. But Grey did not fight back. He didn't even try. The more aggressive the wolves were, the meeker he became. Myra felt embarrassed for him. And ashamed.

Ar slapped Grey again. Carp punched him in the gut. Winso dared to step on his foot. Lace pulled Grey's trousers down to his ankles. Then someone struck him on the head from behind and he toppled over, only to be kicked while on the ground. Lace grinned as she tore off his pants, leaving him naked before his persecutors.

"Please, masters! Please don't hurt me!" Grey shouted so loud that onlookers from Rabbit and Sparrow camps could hear him.

"We should do something," Myra said, getting up to leave the ravine.

Beknar pulled her back, holding firmly. "There is nothing we can do," she said.

"I never realized Ben is such a coward. He should have knocked one down and ran," Court said in disappointment.

"Never have I seen him so afraid," Myra agreed. "Prey Sherra they don't break his arms."

As Grey curled in a ball, Carp dragged him to the cooking pit, dropping him near the hot coals. Ar put a knee against Grey's spine as he tied his hands behind his back with a strip of leather. Carp tied his ankles. Lace laughed as she threw Grey's torn clothes in the pit, watching them catch fire. Grey pulled up his legs to avoid being kicked in a sensitive area.

"Please don't, masters. I beg you," he said.

"It whimpers well," Logis grinned. "Too bad Gronar isn't here. He would enjoy putting this one on its knees."

"Someone said the stranger was brave. This can't be the same one," Ar said in disgust.

"It makes me sick. It's not even a man," Marne remarked.

"Maybe it is," Lace said with a nasty smirk, grabbing Grey's crotch and digging with her nails. Grey screeched and tried to wiggle away. The laughter of his tormentors echoed off the lake.

"What should we do with it? Should I stomp its arms?" Winso asked, looking to Marne for direction.

"It's a spineless bug. When the camps hear how it begged for mercy, they will laugh," Marne decided.

"Let's put black hands on it," Lace suggested.

"A wonderful idea!" Carp eagerly agreed.

Each of the wolves rubbed their hands on the blackened firewood before putting handprints on Grey's body, leaving a dozen charcoal impressions. Carp dumped ashes in Grey's hair. Ar painted streaks on his face. Finally, Lace poured a thick porridge on his lower region and added dirt, grinning as she worked it with her hand into a sticky mud.

"Let's visit the east field. Maybe Gurlap is stupid enough to show his face today," Marne suggested.

"Or his sister," Carp said, smacking a fist into his open palm.

"It's not her face I want to see," Ar said, pumping his hips.

The group walked away laughing, young Winso turning back to give Grey one last kick.

Grey lay on the ground, tightly bound and breathing hard, his body decorated with wolfish humor. Once his attackers were sufficiently far away, he rolled over to watch them go. The fear he had shown was replaced by a steely glint in his studious gray eyes. Hardly a moment later, Frontra appeared from behind the wood shacks.

"You look ready for the spit, half-meat, though the aroma is none too pleasing," Frontra said, squatting down but not touching him. "What if they had broken your arms?"

"They had me worried for a moment," he admitted, struggling to catch his breath. "But I doubted they would break my arms if I groveled enough."

"Did you find out what you wanted to know?" Frontra asked.

"These wolves don't speak well for my species, do they?"

"They are large and strong. Especially Marne," Frontra said.

"Yes, they are large and strong," he agreed.

Myra ran up, panting from the sprint across the fields, and checked Grey's eye where there was a bruise. He looked for Beknar and Court, but they were gone. All of the women were gone.

"Are you hurt?" Myra asked, looking for more injuries.

"Mildly," Grey said, twisting his back.

Myra tried to untie the leather but the binding was too tight. Frontra handed her a small knife so she could cut Grey loose.

"They could have killed you. Or sent you to the pens," Myra shouted. "Why didn't you knock one down and run?"

"They didn't leave much, did they?" Grey said, finding only a few shreds of his shirt.

"Here, take this," Myra said, starting to remove her tunic. "Wash off in the lake before more people see you."

"No, that's okay," he said, declining her offer.

Grey stood up, held his ribs were a hard kick had landed, and walked back toward Ferret Camp wearing nothing but the black hands the wolves had given him.

"Poor Shalli. Maybe she'll find a younger man after all," Myra said to Frontra.

"Why would your sister do that?" Frontra asked, eye-rings going up in surprise.

"We didn't know Ben was such a coward, mistress. Soon everyone will know. He'll be the shame of Ferret Camp."

"You believe Ben a coward?" Frontra asked, astonishment in the tone followed by a derisive click of her tongue.

"You saw everything we saw," Myra explained.

"Yes, I saw everything you saw," Frontra said. "But we did not see the same thing."

Chapter Four
SHALLI LOVES A COWARD

Ferret Camp was quiet. Sullen. Grey had expected some reaction, especially after the jeers he'd gotten from Sparrow Camp and the cold shoulders of Deer Camp, but he hadn't thought his own camp so naïve. In a way, it made him angry, but he knew he had only himself to blame. He didn't trust the camp enough to take them into his confidence.

"Look, Seenar, he's leaving," Hernet said as Grey walked from the camp into the early evening darkness.

Seenar spit in the cooking fire, her dark eyes following Grey with contempt. Hernet went to hold his young wife's shoulders, calming her anger.

"Let's hope he doesn't come back. He shamed us all. Don't we have enough problems?" Seenar asked, brushing her long black hair back to keep it out of the soup.

"We are not all shamed. We should be sad for Ben. He's been our friend," Clagg said in a subdued voice, sitting on a log next to Myra.

"I don't understand. Why didn't he run? We warned him many times," Myra insisted.

"Maybe he was too afraid to run. When a coward's feet freeze, nothing can move them," Cot speculated.

"He didn't look so afraid. Not at first," Myra said.

"He looked afraid when he begged them to stop," Beknar said. "It proves what I've always said, you can never tell about people. Especially strangers. Didn't he hide on the mountain all that time?"

"He did hide on the mountain," Pic said, her heart broken. "I thought he was so brave. Poor Shalli. Poor, poor Shalli."

"We'll try to find someone else for her, maybe from Deer Camp," Clagg suggested. "Maybe she should live there for awhile, until she forgets."

"Where is Shalli?" Myra asked.

"She went down to the creek. I think she's crying. I think she will cry for a long time," Pie said.

"I will, too," Myra said, her eyes red.

Grey went up the trail toward the quarry, knowing the way in the darkness, and then veered down the overgrown path to his private clearing in the woods. He had found a spare shirt but did not dare put it on with his body still covered in gunk. There was much to think about.

A small dome tent set up near his manmade pond was made of old canvas and bent branches, forming a sturdy retreat. He started a fire, put several rocks in an iron pot hanging over the flames, and jumped in the pool to wash the ashes out of his hair. The black handprints were gone but the bruises remained.

Once the rocks were heated, he used a thick stick to lift the pot off the fire and carry it to the tent, placing it just inside the flap before crawling in. When he poured water on the hot rocks, the small tent would become a sweat lodge. He found Shalli sitting quietly in the corner, her head only an outline against the dim light showing through the canvas.

"I knew you would come here," she said, moving over so he could sit down.

Grey poured a splash of water on the rocks and settled down to enjoy the flash of hot steam. He considered finding his shirt, and then decided that in the darkened hut, it didn't matter. She couldn't see anything. Not that she hadn't already seen everything many times. It took him a moment to realize she wasn't wearing anything, either.

"Myra and Clagg will worry," he warned.

"Maybe they should think more and worry less," she responded.

"I can't disagree," Grey said with a sigh.

"This morning, you said today would not be your finest hour. I didn't understand. I wasn't even close to understanding. Now I understand too much," Shalli said, snuggling closer.

"What do you understand?" he asked.

"You're going after the wolves. You're going after them alone because you don't want Clagg or anyone else to get hurt. Today you were watching them. Looking for weakness. Getting them to

110

underestimate you. You risked your life, and gave up your pride, and you've been rewarded with scorn."

"What would make you think all this?" Grey said, not quite admitting it was true.

"Knowing you. I have felt your courage. You cannot pretend around me so well as you think, because I love you. And you know I love you."

Grey poured a little more water on the rocks and sat back against a bale of weeds. Shalli crawled next to him.

"Does it hurt?" she asked.

"The ribs will heal," he said, stroking her hair.

"Not the kicking. I've seen you ignore pain in the mines. I mean the insults."

"It's disappointing, but it can't be helped. The wolves are tough and confident. My only chance is to take them by surprise. Sometimes sacrifices need to be made."

"And you've always made them, haven't you?" Shalli said. "I think that's been your whole life. Now that I know more, I see it in your eyes. The way you talk. The way you study problems. I'm happy."

"Happy?" he asked.

"Yes, I'm happy. I grew up today," Shalli said.

Grey sensed that maybe it was true. There was a maturity in her that hadn't been there before. She leaned up for a kiss. He kissed her.

* * * * * *

Grey appeared at the quarry late the following morning, moving slower than usual. Ahead of schedule for the fall season, he didn't feel bad about asking Clagg for some rest time. Clagg was quiet, merely nodding. Of the forty workers in the quarry, none appeared anxious to look Grey in the face. Except one.

"Ben, come over here," Nole said, putting down his pick ax.

Grey turned from the new scaffold erected next to Ferret Camp's mountain. Constructed with scrap timber from the mines, the scaffold rose in four shaky levels to the blast crater in the steep cliff.

"Yes, leader of Deer Camp," Grey said, stepping back from the lowest platform.

"I'm sorry about your fight with the wolves yesterday. I hope you aren't hurt," Nole said.

"It wasn't a fight, and I'm more sore than hurt," Grey answered.

"Many here are unhappy with you," Nole continued.

"That's not my problem," Grey said, turning to climb the scaffold.

"Wait," Nole said, grabbing Grey's shirt.

Grey turned with an angry flare in his eyes, his brow furrowing. Nole had seen that look before. He let go and stepped back with his hands raised.

"Hear me, Ben. Let everyone hear me," Nole said, nearly shouting. "You gave us this quarry. You gave us summer quota, and the benefits that go with it. You saved my daughter. I don't care what anyone else says, you're my friend. If Ferret Camp is too blind to see your heart, come to Deer Camp. We will always have a tent for you."

Nole turned to those who were watching, especially members of his own camp, daring someone to disagree. None did. Cot walked up, followed by Hernet.

"We were not your friends last night. Nole is right, we become blind too easily. Can you forgive me?" Cot said. The tall miner gazed in sincere supplication, the long arms wanting to reach out.

"And me," Hernet said, standing at Cot's side.

Grey was surprised. Had he already challenged the wolves and his motives became clear, such contrition would have been easy to understand. But these men still thought him an embarrassment to their camp. They were accepting him despite his shameful performance, uncaring what anyone else thought. Grey stared at the ground, not knowing what to say.

Clagg pushed through the crowd.

"I, too, am sorry. I think we all are," Clagg said. "Only so much should be expected of any man. Sometimes we expect more than is fair. That's our fault, not yours. Will you return to Ferret Camp?"

Grey nodded with his head down, unable to speak. Clagg grabbed him in a bear hug, grinning from ear to ear. Cot and Hernet embraced him, too, followed by many others. Grey's ribs hurt but he didn't care.

"Thank you, Nole," Grey said as Ferret Camp's members returned to work.

"It was for their sake, too," Nole explained. "Last night they felt shame. And anger, because they felt you brought that shame on them. But the shame belongs to Marne and his wolves, and those of us who haven't stopped them. It's our shame, and we know it. We're simple people, Ben. Sometimes we don't see the truth right away. But I know this. You aren't a simple person, and you didn't run from the wolves when you could have."

Everyone went back to work, breaking up the better ore stones and loading them into the carts, though there was more talking now. The mood in the quarry had lightened. Grey glanced toward the tracks and saw Shalli, a big smile on her face. He felt she had every right to be proud of her people.

* * * * * *

"The scaffold isn't strong," Grey complained on a late afternoon a few days later, pointing at the wobbly platforms they were using to mine the cliff wall.

"Will you use an explosive to enlarge the crater instead?" Clagg asked.

"I'd rather not. Not until we have a wide enough ledge to drill proper holes," Grey answered.

"The ore is good. All can see the golden veins even from here," Hernet said, looking up at the glistening streaks.

"It would be better to take the riches directly from the mountain. If we cave it down into the gully, much might be lost in the field," Cot added.

"I think so, too," Grey agreed. "I'll ask Frontra for more materials so we can build a stronger scaffold."

"You asked her last week. And the week before," Cot said.

"And now I will ask her again," Grey replied.

"Good timber is scarce," Clagg warned.

Grey looked toward the thick forest growing in the mountains south of the compound. It occurred to him that if they could get large saws, they could cut all the timber they needed. Even produce a surplus to pay for the equipment.

"The masters come," Wart warned, the youngster running from the eastern trail.

Grey cursed under his breath. The arrival of the Arikhan sentries always involved a degree of kneeling and cringing that slowed production, and even though the season still had three weeks left, he hoped to reach quota before the next rest day. Clagg smiled, knowing exactly what Grey was thinking.

"Patience, my brother. Only death lies at the end of our trail. Don't be in such a hurry," Clagg said, slapping him on the shoulder.

"We can die later. Today, I have work to do," Grey growled.

"You will pay us heed, food creatures," Nabbatron said, climbing on a boulder in the middle of the quarry. He wore a new emerald green leather vest and black leather boots. Frontra was also wearing a new outfit. Both had put large yellow feathers in the bands of their broad brim felt hats, displaying a new pride in their service.

The workers came to kneel. A head taller than most of the humans, Nabbatron looked like a giant standing on the rock with his long arms and powerful legs. An excellent psychological advantage, not that he needed one.

Grey kneeled impatiently at the perimeter of the group, anxious to get back to work. Frontra came to stand nearby as if assuring him the assembly would not be long. She, too, knew what was on his mind.

"Good news, food creatures," Nabbatron announced. "It appears you will soon reach quota for the fall season. Sarden Leader Gamtro considers this a remarkable achievement. When the quota is met, you will be granted two days of celebration and a keg of mauck. If you exceed quota by fifteen percent, you will be rewarded with extra clothing, new tents, and solar lanterns."

"Excuse me, master, may I speak?" Clagg asked.

"Speak, food creature leader," Nabbatron permitted.

"Much would we like to earn the Sarden Leader's reward. May we take the rest days at the end of season?" Clagg requested.

Nabbatron clicked his tongue with approval. In line for a bonus, he appreciated the difference those extra two days could make.

"The request is granted," Nabbatron agreed. "Return to your efforts. Do not allow the presence of your superiors to distract you further."

"Nabbatron is generous, is he not?" Frontra said to Grey, her voice low. "Ordering workers to ignore our presence, even on a worksite, is rare for him."

"In this matter, mistress, I agree with Nabbatron. We should not slack off so close to our goal," Grey said.

"What does the food creature complain of now?" Nabbatron asked, approaching at the end of their conversation.

"The half-meat agrees with your decision to keep working. He desires Gamtro's rewards," Frontra said.

"Impertinent, but not stupid," Nabbatron remarked, clicking his tongue approvingly. "Why do you keep asking for more timber? You labor outside, not in a mine. You have enough."

"Excuse me, master, but this timber is either too thick or too thin for scaffolding," Grey said. "We have no bolts or metal straps, only pliant bark and a bit of wire. No heavy tools can be used on the top platform, yet there lies the best ore."

He pointed up. Though the stones littering the canyon floor offered much promise, even Nabbatron could see the shining streaks in the rock face.

"Eventually we can carve a ledge in the rock and tunnel in, but for now, we need a sturdier scaffold," Grey insisted.

Workers in the area shook their heads and looked away. No one else would dare speak to an Arikhan in such a manner. Nabbatron didn't like it either.

"You risk much, food creature," Nabbatron said, drawing his shock wand.

Grey knelt at Nabbatron's feet to accept punishment as he had several times before. Frontra stood aside, not interfering. Nor would Grey have wanted her to. Nabbatron lowered the wand, touching Grey's shoulder. The spark only caused him to flinch. Grey realized the wand had been put on the lowest setting. He looked up at Nabbatron.

"If fitting punishment were given each time you speak impertinently, you would be dead, food creature. How can you serve me if you are dead?" Nabbatron said, putting the wand away.

"If I were dead, master, your cook would need to do the serving,"

Grey answered.

Frontra clicked her tongue in delight at Grey's joke, and Nabbatron seemed to enjoy it just as much. This also astonished the workers close enough to hear, for no one but Grey would have offered such a dark jest.

"I will inspect these platforms, but if you speak falsely, the punishment will not be light," Nabbatron warned.

"Thank you, master," Grey acknowledged, getting to his feet.

As the Arikhan sentries walked to the cliff wall, Grey went to the tool tent where Clagg, Cot, Turk, and Nole were waiting. They shook their heads.

"You're a fool to provoke Nabbatron," Clagg scolded.

"Good timber is scarce," Turk added.

"The best timber goes to the northern camps," Nole explained. "You may be pressuring Nabbatron to provide that which isn't his to give."

"He's a greedy son of a bitch. If better timber would boost his reward, he'd cut the damn lumber himself," Cot declared.

"Nabbatron appreciates the bonuses we bring. His punishments grow less as his rewards increase," Grey said.

"As you would know best of all," Clagg said, frowning in disapproval of Grey's provocations.

"Gamtro would not offer such lavish rewards if he wasn't aware of our progress," Nole concluded. "And Nabbatron will not see the Sarden Leader disappointed."

"The other camps are jealous," Turk said, the young man standing next to Nole. Working outside every day for the first time in his life, his skin had tanned and grown clear. Strapping and square-jawed, Grey still thought Turk would make a good match for Shalli. And as other camps spurned Ferret and Deer camps, he knew the lack of social contacts must be frustrating for young men like Turk and Burne.

"Gamtro may have more ambitious plans than tension between the camps. By spring season I think there will be changes," Nole suggested.

Nole's opinion gave Grey pause. He wasn't sure if a more aggressive leadership was in the people's best interest. On the other hand, good leadership could make the entire compound more productive. Having grown up on a remote colony, he had a hundred ideas on how it might be done.

A noise from the cliff attracted everyone's attention. Nabbatron was testing the strength of the scaffold supports. At the other end of the long structure, Frontra was inspecting grooves in the granite wall where the workers had tried to cut steps with chisels. The effort had only dulled the tools, which she found discarded underneath the lowest platform.

"Master, don't!" Grey called out from the hill fifty yards away.

Nabbatron stared at him and shook the scaffold harder, eye-rings raised in defiance.

"Nabbatron, stop!" Grey yelled, walking from the tent and waving his arms.

The scaffold started to twist sideways, one end bumping into the cliff, the other wobbling. Workers backed away, some trying to grab their tools. Then one of the fragile brackets snapped, tilting the entire structure.

"Run! Everybody run!" Burne shouted, grabbing Wart and pulling him to safety.

"Get away! Get away!" Hernet yelled, carrying Pie as he ran.

The other workers quickly scattered, too, for it was not the first time the scaffolding had presented a danger. Only the two Arikhan overseers seemed confused by the sudden panic of the food creatures.

As the weight of the structure rapidly shifted, more of the bindings started to separate, causing the platforms to break loose and slide in the direction of the tilt. When one of the falling planks hit Frontra on the head, she stumbled against the rock wall, stunned by the impact.

Grey didn't waste another second, accelerating down the slope, hurtling an ore cart, and leaping from rock to rock toward the cliff. Nabbatron finally jumped back from the disintegrating scaffold before seeing Frontra leaning against the wall, blood on her forehead. But with the teetering structure coming down, all he could do was get out of the way.

Disoriented by the blow, Frontra seemed dazed, unsure which way to turn. She felt the side of the cliff, pushed against a leaning timber, and deflected a falling beam with her arm that pushed her roughly into the mountain. Nabbatron desperately searched for a way to reach Frontra, but planks kept tumbling in his path.

Then, out of the corner of his eye, Nabbatron saw a sprinting figure charging the cliff. It was the half-meat, running faster than he thought the creature could move. Just as the scaffold gave way entirely, Grey dove under the lowest platform and pressed Frontra into a niche, protecting her with his body. The structure collapsed in a crashing plume of churning dust.

"Hurry, food creatures! Hurry!" Nabbatron called, rushing to the pile of timbers and throwing the broken pieces aside. His double-jointed knees and elbows allowed him to twist fragments loose. He was quickly joined by others, especially Clagg, whose strength almost matched Nabbatron's.

"Careful. Careful. Prop the beams up," Nole urged.

Nabbatron and Clagg saw he was right and paused to brace some of the broken timbers, lest loose beams sink deeper into the pile. Others hauled the debris aside. Near the bottom, a frame was pinning the victims against the cliff.

"Clagg, help me. All others stand back," Nabbatron ordered.

Standing side-by-side, Clagg and Nabbatron lifted the frame and dragged it away. Nabbatron found Frontra sitting against the cliff, her eyes alert. Grey lay unconscious in her lap.

"Do you survive, sister?" Nabbatron asked, stepping through to help her up.

"Yes, brother. Sherra chooses another day to call me to her altar," Frontra replied.

Nabbatron saw Frontra had superficial cuts and was breathing hard, but otherwise appeared uninjured.

Clagg stepped through the wreckage to pick Grey up. The unconscious body was limp in his arms. Blood streamed from his nose and mouth. Cot assisted Clagg out of the debris, carrying Grey to the tool tent where he was put on a grass mat. There was no tension in his muscles. Pie tore off her tunic to make a pillow for his head. Shalli used her dress to mop the blood. Tak put a blanket over his legs.

"Does he breathe?" Cot asked.

"Not much. Bones may be broken. I'm not sure," Clagg said.

"There's no light in his eyes," Pie worried.

"We need Thal," Tak decided.

"Thal cannot help him. And even if she could, she wouldn't come," Cot said.

Frontra and Nabbatron approached, causing most of the workers to draw back. Several more guards arrived, alerted by the dust cloud and shouting.

"Did someone attack the zone leader?" Bortro inquired, seeing blood on Frontra.

"No. The ladders fell," Frontra said, pointing to the pile of timbers.

"I should not have shaken it after the half-meat's warning," Nabbatron admitted.

The guards put their weapons away and established order. Bortro entered the tent, pushed Shalli and Pie away, and opened Grey's shirt to probe his chest for injuries with his stubby claws. All in the tent grew impatient for the stout guard's verdict.

"Favorable news, Nabbatron," Bortro finally said. "The food creature bleeds inside but will live a few more hours. The meat will be fresh on your spit."

With a grunt of primal anger, Nabbatron struck Bortro with the back of his claw, the force so great the shorter Arikhan sentry was knocked to the ground.

"Offer no opinions, ranker," Nabbatron growled. "Where is Wart?"

Frightened half to death, young Wart came forward to kneel at Nabbatron's feet, his body shaking.

"I am here, master," Wart said, the words barely audible.

"Listen well or it will be you who graces my spit," Nabbatron said.

"Yes, master," Wart nodded.

"Run to the main gate. Run as fast as you can," Nabbatron ordered, switching to a clearly spoken Akronos. "Tell Delatron the half-meat is hurt saving Frontra from the falling wall. He is to summon a yarbel ky from the assembly plant at An'cor with great speed. Most important, food youngling, tell Delatron that by my

119

honor, by the faith of our brotherhood, *do not fail me*. Do you understand my words?"

"Yes, master," Wart said, leaping to his feet and running for the gate two kilometers away.

Nabbatron picked Grey up and carried him to Ferret Camp with Shalli and Tak running fearlessly in his wake. Frontra and the other guards followed, not even looking back at the mystified workers.

"I never thought to see anything like that," Nole said, scratching his head.

"See what? One master strike another, or Nabbatron try to help a food creature?" Cot said, just as amazed.

"I didn't know Nabbatron knew Wart's name," Clagg said. "Hell, I didn't know he knew *my* name."

* * * * * *

Grey woke up during the night at the height of the second moon. He was lying on a canvas cot, the first bed he had been in since—since he had lived on another world under a different name. Shalli was sleeping on a ground cloth beside him. The people outside were quiet but the campfire burned higher than usual. He could smell fresh venison.

"What happened?" he whispered to no one in particular.

A portly Arikhan entered the tent carrying a lantern, squatting next to the cot. It was an alien Grey had never seen before. It wore the white tunic of a yarbel ky with bronze swamp leaf decorations on the collar, an indication of long service. Without speaking, the Arikhan looked into his eyes with a medical scanner and ran its claw over his torso, poking tender areas. Grey noticed tiny stitches near his lower ribs but felt no pain. He was drugged. He felt good.

"The damage was halted in time," the pudgy Arikhan said in a precise, professional accent. "Stay still for three weeks. Do no lifting. Take the medication that stops infection. Do not ever call me to this horrid place again."

The yarbel ky picked up his medical kit and waddled from the camp. Shalli got up as Myra and Clagg entered to kneel by the cot. Standing in the doorway were Frontra and Nabbatron. Grey noticed the two Arikhan were brushing claws and realized for the first time that, despite their feuds, they were fond of each other.

"My debt to you is paid, Ben. Next time, you grace my spit," Nabbatron warned.

"My debt is not paid," Frontra said, eye-rings bent in appreciation.

"Expressions of obligation are unnecessary, mistress. Many times have you been a friend," Grey said.

Frontra lowered her head in acknowledgement and left the tent with Nabbatron, going back toward their quarters outside the main gate.

"You did not call him food creature," Frontra said as they walked a dirt trail through the quiet compound.

"It is not a food creature, so I did not call it one," Nabbatron replied.

"You confuse me, my sometime companion," Frontra said.

"The creature offered its life to save you, my preferred companion. It is well known that food creatures risk much to help each other. Even animals in the wild do that. But for one of them to help one of us is not an ordinary thing. It is not something a food creature would do."

"There are many stories of slaves helping their masters. It is known that some slaves have died for their masters. It is not so unusual."

"It may not be unusual for a slave, but Ben is no slave. Ben is arrogant, impertinent, and annoying, and much does he deserve punishment for speaking boldly to his superiors, but there is no trace of slave in him," Nabbatron explained.

"Have you seen what I have so long believed?" Frontra asked.

"I have no answer. To me, most of them are still food creatures. Maybe I will always see them as food creatures. But not all. I must visit the Shrine at Ra' Pall to seek Sherra's wisdom," Nabbatron said, clicking his tongue softly.

"Blessed is the wisdom of Sherra," Frontra agreed.

While Grey went back to sleep tended by Shalli, the men and women of Ferret Camp hunkered down near the fire, sharing a late night broth.

"There is something I must say," Cot whispered. "After the

wolves, I said Ben's feet had frozen because he was afraid. His feet were not frozen today. He ran very fast even though the logs were falling."

"I have never seen anyone run so fast, not even Wart," Hernet said.

"He could have run away from the wolves, if he'd wanted to," Myra remembered.

"Yes, I think he could have," Hernet agreed.

"Ben is not a coward," Cot decided.

"No, he is not," Clagg said.

"He didn't run away from the wolves, but he didn't fight them, either," Beknar said. "He cried and begged, but he's not a coward. What does it mean?"

"I think Ben is planning something," Clagg said.

"Planning what?" Seenar asked, clutching her new baby, a red-faced infant named Mora.

"We'll need to ask him when he gets better," Myra said. "But if Ben wants people to think he's a coward, maybe he has a reason."

"He's very smart. If Ben does something, there's always a reason," Clagg said. "Let's not say anything to the other camps. Let them think what they want."

"I should not have called him a coward. He's been my friend," Cot said.

"And mine," Hernet said just as dolefully.

"He's still your friend, you big oafs," Myra said. "Now go to sleep. Without Ben our work will be harder tomorrow."

* * * * * *

Grey hated being restricted to a tent erected near the quarry. Even supplied with paper and pencils to plan a new scaffold, the days were long. To keep him from disobeying the doctor's orders, various camp members were assigned to watch him, much to his displeasure. Frontra found the ritual so amusing she even volunteered for a shift.

"What do the bird scratches mean?" Frontra asked, inspecting several sheets of closely scrawled yellow paper. They included charts, diagrams, maps, and machinery.

"They are calculations using a numbering system called Arabic,"

Grey said, propped up by a feather pillow. He finished another page and handed it to her.

"Like the scratches on the cliff above the old mine?" Frontra asked. Grey hadn't known his observatory had been discovered.

"The numbers have similar meanings, but these are for a different purpose. I would like to build a ramp up into the mountainside and run in the tracks. We'll need to select a grade that's not too steep and rig pulleys to control the ore carts, but we'll save six months of tunneling. And we won't need as much timber."

"You are ambitious, half-meat. You make quota. Is that not enough?"

"When quota is exceeded, the guards receive rewards. Nabbatron is less cruel. The people have food, clothing, and a chance to see their children grow. If wanting these things makes me ambitious, then I must be guilty."

"And what do you get, ambitious food creature?" Frontra asked with a teasing click of her tongue. He laughed.

"I have long work trousers, good leather boots, two shirts, and a straw hat to protect me from the sun. What more could any slave want?"

"There was a time when you had more. I suspect you were once a creature of great wealth. And power," Frontra guessed.

"Too soon do you forget the teachings of Sherra, my mistress," Grey said. Frontra raised her eye-rings.

"Instruct me, one of great insight," she said.

"I know what it is to have much. And to have nothing," Grey said, setting aside his paperwork. "Much do I turn to the sacred teachings in my old age, and this I have learned; it is not the clothes you wear that gives wealth, but the strength in your heart. Gain is measured by the happiness of those you love. Power may be achieved one day and lost the next. Wisdom knows that power used selfishly destroys. Power used unselfishly builds worlds."

Frontra rocked back on her stool, clutching the scribbled pages in her claw. Pages that represented both wealth and power if properly applied. She dwelled carefully on his words.

"I must apologize to my friend," Frontra said. "You are indeed wise in the ways of Sherra. More so than many. I did not mean to make light of you."

"Let us not make too much of ourselves, my friend Frontra. We are all dust in the end."

Shalli entered the tent carrying a midday meal and knelt next to the cot.

"Thank you for sitting with him, mistress. He won't lie still unless watched at every moment," Shalli said with exasperation.

"Stubbornness is a difficult survival trait to overcome," Frontra confirmed.

Shalli didn't quite understand, but she rarely knew much of what the Arikhan spoke of. She fed Grey broth and half a loaf of wheat bread.

"The wound heals quickly. You'll be walking again by the rest day," Shalli advised, probing the stitches.

"It will be too late. The season ends on the rest day. We were ahead of schedule until the accident. With me trapped in this tent and our scaffold gone, there's little chance of earning Gamtro's reward," Grey complained.

Shalli looked at Frontra with a question. Frontra's eye-rings dipped.

"It is for Nabbatron to say," Frontra insisted.

"What is for Nabbatron to say?" Grey asked.

Little three-year-old Garn suddenly burst into the tent, jumping into Shalli's lap. His auburn hair was tousled, the bronze cheeks flushed. Shalli smiled. Frontra clicked her tongue and opened her arms. Garn went to sit on Frontra's knee without a trace of fear. Grey had seen Garn do this before, but it still amazed him. Noise from outside the tent indicated the workers were returning from the quarry, their voices excited. And then, abruptly, they fell silent.

"Nabbatron comes," Frontra said.

Shalli took Garn back from Frontra and put her forehead to the floor as Nabbatron entered Grey's tent.

"Leave us," Nabbatron ordered.

Shalli needed no urging, fleeing outside with Garn hugged close to her chest. But she didn't go far, stopping just outside the flap.

"Nothing has been said until now. I would not look a fool," Nabbatron said, standing above Grey's cot.

Grey wasn't afraid, but he was curious. The fearsome guard was behaving very strangely. Even Frontra was acting unusually, her eye-rings curled.

"None here would think you a fool," Frontra said.

"Your camps have exceeded quota by fifteen percent. The rewards are granted," Nabbatron announced.

"I do not see how that can be, master," Grey said, reaching for one of the production charts to see if he'd made an error.

"Nabbatron has taken your place in the quarry, Ben," Frontra said. "For several hours each day, he has wielded a jackhammer and loaded carts. The work proved difficult. Only this morning was the surplus confirmed."

Grey's expression of astonishment was obvious to both aliens. They exchanged glances of satisfaction.

"Do not thank me," Nabbatron ordered.

"I will thank you anyway, master," Grey said.

"You are impertinent. Do not think your weakened condition forbids punishment," Nabbatron warned.

"You did not call me food creature," Grey observed.

"The yarbel ky says your organs are tough. Your body has much muscle and no fat. You would not grace my table well," Nabbatron explained.

"I am sorry, master," Grey protested, "but I believe the yarbel ky is wrong. My flesh would prove most succulent if properly spiced."

The Arikhan sentries clicked their tongues rapidly in amusement. Outside the tent, Shalli was horrified by the conversation and made Garn run back to Myra.

"I have found a bottle of Lafarian wine," Nabbatron said. "Not as strong as mauck, but appropriate for one in your feeble condition. Would you try a taste?"

"Thank you, master," Grey said, passing Nabbatron his tin cup. Frontra stood up and left the tent, finding Shalli cowering outside.

"Come, child," Frontra said, taking Shalli away.

"I don't understand, mistress. Has Nabbatron become Ben's

friend?" Shalli asked.

"No, Shalli, they are not friends. Nabbatron knows the day may come that he would send Ben to the pens. There is no confusion between them."

"Then what does it mean?" Shalli asked.

"Your people are food creatures. I am sorry to say it, but it is truth. Ben is not a food creature. Ben is a warrior, as is Nabbatron. There is no friendship, but there is respect. If Nabbatron kills Ben one day, his flesh will be dedicated to Sherra."

* * * * * *

Winter proved rainy enough that Grey was thankful for the extra clothing and tents. Sensitive to inclement weather, the Arikhan sentries were rarely in attendance, which disappointed no one. Work on the mines slowed but did not stop.

Having a tent of his own, Grey was able to work on his engineering drafts at all hours. Which he did.

"I have a plan," Grey said at the evening meal.

The camp was sitting cross-legged on straw mats around wooden tables cut from old mining timbers. The meal included fresh baked bread, greens, and small amounts of bulb root. The children laughed as they nibbled on succulent tubers, while the adults enjoyed creek water spiced with fermented blue wheat.

"You always have a plan," Clagg answered. "I once thought your plans would mean less work, but they always mean more work."

"We can give back the new furs. And the lanterns. Or the mauck ration," Grey suggested.

"What is your plan?" Clagg asked, smiling.

"Our quarry will last through the season," Grey replied. "In the summer, we'll blast a porch in the mountainside and build a slide down to the ore carts."

"You wanted an earthen ramp," Cot said.

"We don't have the resources," Grey said in disappointment. "In the meantime, it's possible to help Sparrow Camp. I've heard they're having trouble. Bear Camp might benefit, too."

"No. They haven't helped us," Cot instantly objected.

"There is much jealousy. They might betray us to Marne," Hernet said. "We're safe in our own zones. We won't be safe there."

"I don't want anyone from Ferret Camp involved. Only one person needs to come with me the first time. Just to make introductions. After that, I'll go myself," Grey said.

"It's too dangerous," Myra disagreed, setting aside her new sewing kit.

"I'm not afraid," Grey said, chewing on a bread roll with a trace of honey in it.

"That's the problem, you're never afraid when you should be," Clagg complained. "Hernet is right. If you try to help Sparrow Camp, they might give you to Marne."

Shalli studied Grey's expression, wondering if that's what he wanted. Ever since he had recovered from the wound, he had been working out in his secret hiding place harder than ever. Fighting ghosts with his hands, beating weed bales with his staff. If Marne was a phantom, Shalli thought, he could kill him easily. But Marne was not a phantom.

"Maybe Sparrow Camp won't be so angry if they make quota. Even if we fail, it would still be worth the effort," Grey said.

"If *we* fail? You are taking the risk, not any of us," Cot said, unhappy with his friend's lack of caution.

"It's my plan. The risk should be mine," Grey said.

"We'll think on it. I would like to speak with Nole and Sal to see what they say," Clagg insisted.

"The spring season will bring changes," Grey concluded.

"Do you read our future in the stars?" Hernet asked, passing a bowl of greens.

"There will be changes," Grey repeated. "I cannot promise if they will be good or bad, but they're coming. If they're bad, I hope you'll forgive me."

He stood up from the fire, ready for bed.

"You're going to Sparrow Camp whether we agree or not, aren't you?" Myra asked.

"Yes," Grey answered.

"Nabbatron is right about your stubbornness. You would make us angry if we didn't love you so much," Myra said, rising to give him a hug. Many around the fire nodded agreement, some tapping their cups with sticks.

"For a minor risk, many people might have better lives. I have placed my heart at Ferret Camp, but I must take that risk," Grey insisted.

"I'll talk with Nole," Clagg said. "Relations with Sparrow Camp were not always bad. Old Ravo may have a temper, but at times, he can be reasonable."

"Warn Nole there might be trouble," Grey said.

Grey's private tent was large enough for four people, the ground covered by thick grass mats. A low platform held a bed of comfortable furs. A round marble table, a gift from Frontra, held his pencils and paper. A solar lantern allowed him to work at night, which he always did. His files lay in a wood crate on the floor. A rope strung between two poles was used to hang extra shirts and a spare pair of pants.

Tired from a long day, Grey stripped off his clothes except for a light cotton vest, snuggled under the furs, and propped himself up with pillows to study the drawings he'd made of Sparrow Camp's mountain. A few minutes later, Shalli appeared at the entrance, inviting herself in.

"You're setting a trap, aren't you?" Shalli asked, sitting next to him.

"When word gets around that I'm negotiating with Sparrow Camp, the wolves will wonder what it's about. They may suspect I'm seeking protection, being a well-known coward. If they come looking for me in a group, I'll run away. Eventually they'll try lying in wait. The trail through the woods has many tempting areas, which will give me a chance to take them down one or two at a time."

"What if three catch you at once?" Shalli asked.

"That would be harder, but if I can find something to use as a weapon, it won't change the outcome. I once took down two Arikhan infantry with a hunting knife. Marne's bullies are much less skilled."

"Two masters? You killed two masters?"

"Shalli, be quiet. Do you want the whole camp to hear?"

128

Shalli settled down, but she was still shaken.

"I've heard stories, but I've never known of anyone who … who did something like that," Shalli whispered.

"My world was at war. We fought to protect our people," he explained.

"Have you killed others? Other than the two with the knife?"

"We shouldn't talk of this. You'll just be upset."

"No, please. I'm sorry, but you surprised me. I've heard about wars. I know bad things happen. I want to know about you. Who you really are."

"No, you don't," he said, determined to change the subject.

"You think I'm just a stupid little girl, don't you? An ignorant slave," Shalli said, growing angry. "You don't think I can face real problems. But life in our camp is hard sometimes, and I've seen terrible things. Just not the same things you have. How can I learn if you won't teach me?"

Grey sensed she might be right. In the course of his life he had participated in many violent events. Known moments of fear and desolation. Would his experience help Shalli or hurt her? Did he have a right to make that decision?

Shalli watched him think, his brow furrowed as he remembered dark days from his secret past. She struggled to follow the train of emotions the memories evoked and realized they were painful. But he hadn't decided to say no.

Grey noticed the growing hope in her expression. It occurred to him that his wife's love had been strong but cooler, her emotions matured by her years as a combat pilot. She had been a soldier long before they met, toughened by a brutal war. Shalli's love was uninhibited. Free of scars. Grey wasn't sure if he should be flattered or frightened by Shalli's lack of restraint, and the thought was communicated clearly in his eyes. Shalli burst into a smile and kissed him.

"You're going to tell me, aren't you?" she said, slipping her legs under the furs.

"Some of it. Only some," he decided, knowing too much knowledge of his background would be dangerous for her. "As I said, my world was at war with the Arikhan. I was a soldier in that war, trained to fight from childhood. Not just to fight the masters, but anyone who stood in our way. I'm good at my profession, but it's never who I wanted to be."

"You wanted to be a builder, didn't you?" Shalli said.

"A builder. An explorer. I had many dreams. I hate war, but I also thrive on the challenges. Now I'm here, and it's impossible to ever go home. This is my world. If I have to fight for it, I will."

Shalli rested her head against his chest with a sigh. She was not disappointed.

"I think I understand," Shalli said, dwelling on his words. "You're like them. The masters. That's what Frontra was trying to tell me."

"No, I'm not like them. But I'm not completely different, either."

"Being a warrior means being a killer, doesn't it?"

"That's usually what it means. Should I not have spoken?"

"No. Speaking the truth is never wrong."

"I know this isn't what you expected. I would understand if you'd rather spend your time with someone else."

"You fool," Shalli said, cuddling close. "I may be frightened by your past, but it won't stop me from loving you."

"I wish it would," he sighed.

"I know you wish that, but it's not going to be that easy for you. I'll never let it be that easy."

She suddenly moved to a straddling position, kissing him passionately and rubbing him with her body. Then she pulled off her tunic and shook out her long blonde hair, letting it drop down in his face. She felt warm and firm, the curves delicately round. Her flesh soft. Inviting. He could feel her excitement. And his own.

"This is going too far," he protested, trying to still the movements of her hips.

"You want me," she whispered.

"It wouldn't be right," he said.

"Don't try to deny it."

"I can't deny it, but it still wouldn't be right."

She continued moving back and forth. Grey squirmed involuntarily. Shalli put her hands on his chest to hold him down.

"Stop that," he said, trying to wiggle out from under her.

"Take me, my love. Take me now," she insisted, leaning close.

Grey lifted her up with both hands and rolled over, putting Shalli on her back in the fur as he struggled for breath.

"I'm not so ready as you think," he said, holding her wrists to prevent more mischief.

"Next time you won't say no," Shalli confidently predicted, kissing him with acceptance of defeat. "May I dare to say something?"

"Dare, my wild ignorant slave girl," he laughed.

"Your plan to trap Marne can be better."

"In what way?"

"Let me speak with Tak. If she agrees, your plan will be better."

"You haven't said how," he asked, worried by her elusiveness.

Shalli used one of Grey's own tricks, smiling without responding. Then she laid back to fall asleep in his arms.

* * * * * *

Clagg and Nole decided to let Grey visit Sparrow Camp, mostly because they felt unable to stop him. They also agreed to let Shalli and Tak go along to make the introductions, but only for the first trip.

"I'm still uncomfortable with this," Grey said as they walked along a northbound trail through the woods toward Sparrow Camp.

"We must do this. Isn't that right, Tak?" Shalli said.

"I want to see the wolves stopped more than anything, and even Ben said it's a good idea," Tak agreed.

"I said your plan is clever. I never said it's a good idea," Grey corrected. "And don't think destroying the wolves will solve every problem. It won't. Revenge can have a sour taste."

"This isn't about revenge," Tak said, embracing Grey's arm. "Ar said he wanted to get me alone next time. Marne and Carp have said the same thing about Shalli. If they come lurking around by themselves, you'll have a better chance against them."

"You're fighting the wolves for us. For what they've done, and for what they keep doing. Is it wrong for us to want to help?" Shalli asked.

"It's not wrong, but I wish we had told Nole and Clagg," Grey said.

131

"If we told them, they would have said no," Shalli disagreed.

He knew she was right, and understood their need to participate. He would have felt no different at their age.

"Stay alert and be ready to run. You're the bait, not combatants. I don't want you in my way if trouble starts," Grey ordered.

"We promise," Shalli said.

They emerged from the brushy tree-lined trail into a large meadow. Sparrow camp lay on the other side, twice the size of Deer Camp, with a dozen fair sized tents surrounding a rough log cabin. Unlike Ferret Camp, the lake and gardens could be seen from a nearby rise.

"Hello Sparrow Camp," Tak called out from forty yards away.

Enjoying the rest day, the people stirred from their midday naps, moving to the edge of camp. A few picked up stools for clubs should they be needed.

"Who calls upon Sparrow Camp?" a voice yelled.

"That's Old Ravo, their leader," Shalli told Grey.

"Tak of Deer Camp comes to visit. With me are Shalli and Ben of Ferret Camp," Tak shouted.

"No others?" Ravo asked.

"None," Tak said.

"Come forward and visit," Old Ravo agreed.

Tak, Shalli, and Grey crossed through the meadow. Though the yellow grass was dry from winter, Grey thought the soil good. With water brought down from the hillside, it could be irrigated.

"What brings two beautiful girls and a coward to Old Ravo's camp? Are you ready to be made women? All three of you?" Ravo asked.

Sparrow Camp's leader was a stocky man with a barrel chest. He wore a dark red shirt and short black pants that barely covered his knees. His bushy gray beard was the first Grey had seen in a long time. He guessed Ravo to be in his early fifties, possibly the oldest man in Karak. Grey thought he looked like a Viking.

"No thank you, Sparrow Camp leader," Tak said, attractive in her long blue skirt, fur jacket and rawhide boots. She also wore a white stone necklace to remind everyone that she was the daughter of a camp leader.

"We haven't visited in a long time," Tak continued. "We should visit more. You have never met Ben. He wishes to speak with Sparrow Camp."

"Already have we heard the coward's words. His pleas for mercy were loud all the way from the lake," Barris said as many laughed.

Just a few years younger than Grey, Barris bore a resemblance to Ravo but was much slimmer. His dark brown hair matched his piercing brown eyes. His black short-sleeve shirt showed the well-crafted strength of his arms. Barris also had an intelligent look to him, unlike Ravo, who appeared crafty.

"He wears black hands better than Thal," a man jeered.

"I'm glad to have provided Sparrow Camp with entertainment," Grey said, accepting the insults with good humor.

Many laughed again while sizing the stranger up. Neither tall nor short, slender nor stocky. A sharp, predatory look in the steel gray eyes. And a light, muscular bounce in his walk, almost like a big cat. Some decided not to laugh too loudly.

"Are we welcome to join you? We've brought our own provisions if needed," Tak said, holding up a knapsack.

"Join us," Ravo said with a sweep of his thick calloused hand.

They entered the camp and followed Ravo past the log cabin to an area where tree stumps were set in a circle around a fire pit. An old oak tree provided a shadowy canopy. Only a few Sparrow Camp members joined them, most choosing to watch from their own cooking fires.

"Ben of Ferret Camp, this is Bynar, Ravo's much beloved wife, and Barris, Ravo's son," Tak introduced.

Grey saw Bynar was older, too, her features much like Beknar, with long hair that was growing gray and bronze skin beginning to wrinkle. He wondered if they were cousins. Bynar's brown tunic showed a trim figure, the green eyes pleasant but worried. The woman smiled while saying nothing.

"The youngster is Rat, Ravo's nephew," Tak said, pointing to a scrawny twelve-year-old. "The big stupid looking oafs are Pixx and Jasper, team leaders of the dig. Sparrow Camp, this is Ben, a member of Ferret Camp and friend to Deer Camp. It was Ben who gave us the quarry."

Like the dig leaders of Ferret and Deer Camps, Pixx and Jasper were big men, simply dressed and loyal to their leader. Pixx wore his curly brown hair short with a trimmed beard. Jasper's straight black hair hung free down to his shoulders, his chin clean shaven. Both had tattoos of pick axes on their upper arms. Grey pitied the nephew, for he looked aptly named.

"A quarry your camp does not share," Ravo gruffly said as everyone sat down.

"You haven't been our friends," Shalli was quick to say.

"It's hard to be friends with those who have so many enemies," Barris replied.

"If we had more friends, we would not have so many enemies," Shalli responded.

"And you would have shared our quarry," Tak added.

"We do not consort with cowards," Barris said.

"You lick Marne's ass," Shalli accused, contemptuously flipping her hair over her shoulder.

"He's not so bad," Barris weakly defended.

"You've never been dragged to his torment pit," Tak said, staring angrily.

"Maybe you were asking for it?" Barris suggested.

Grey suddenly stood up, his eyes focused on Barris. A furious snarl curled his lip and a low, guttural objection rose from his throat. His fists were clenched, his position poised, the heart pumping with an adrenaline rush.

Barris, Pixx, and Jasper quickly jumped up, expecting the coward to retreat. They were surprised when Grey set himself, his eyes selecting which enemies to strike first. Tak took hold of his arm, tugging to make him sit down. Grey reluctantly stepped back but did not relax his stance.

"Allow me to apologize," Grey said, taking a breath to regain composure. "We've come to visit. It's rude for a guest to cause trouble. But if any of you, or all three of you, would like to go into the woods, I will not be a guest there."

He continued to stand, waiting for their response, more than ready to try his luck in the woods. Ravo watched the confrontation with interest. The coward wasn't what he expected.

"This Ben does not look afraid to me," Bynar finally said, breaking the tension. "Barris, apologize to Tak. Such words to a guest are shameful. Pixx, Jasper, sit down. This isn't your fight. Or does it take all three of you to fight one visitor? One you have called a coward."

"Hah!" Ravo shouted, clapping his hands together. "Does anyone speak so clearly as my Bynar? Barris, sit down before you make an fool of yourself. Pixx, Jasper, control your tempers or leave my fire."

All three men returned to their stools, Pixx and Jasper embarrassed. Barris was still startled by Grey's challenge. Grey remained standing, looking to Barris for the anticipated apology.

"I'm sorry, Tak. My words were rude," Barris said sincerely.

"Thank you, Barris," Tak graciously accepted.

Grey sat down, causing Shalli to let out a relieved sigh. Ravo noted the smitten look in Shalli's eyes, as Bynar had, and guessed something was brewing there.

"May we offer a midday meal?" Bynar offered.

"That would be nice," Shalli said, still shaken by the confrontation.

"Let us help," Tak said, the women leaving so the men could speak more frankly.

"My son apologized, but our grievances are real," Ravo said.

"I've not come so far on the rest day to hear old wounds," Grey said, unimpressed.

"Why have you come?" Pixx asked.

"To ask if Sparrow Camp wants a quarry like Ferret and Deer Camps," Grey explained. The men looked interested but suspicious.

"Is such a thing possible?" Jasper asked.

"I would need to survey your mine and test the ore," Grey said.

"We don't let anyone into our mine," Jasper immediately objected.

"Then I cannot help you," Grey said, rising from his stool.

"Exceptions have been made," Ravo quickly said, holding up his hand until Grey returned to his seat. "Do you believe it would be worthwhile?"

"My studies indicate the same veins running through Deer Camp's mountain run through yours," Grey said. "We would search for the most promising area and use small explosives to burrow in. If we find the ore we want, we'll blow a hole in the mountain and bring it down."

"And what do you demand in exchange for this magic? Our tents? Our women?" Pixx asked.

Grey took a moment to study the dig leaders. Pixx was about thirty years old, strong but getting used up in the mines. Somewhat younger, Jasper had a more pleasant expression. Neither seemed especially bright, but Grey had no intention of underestimating them.

"Ferret Camp has new tents and many women," Grey said.

"Maybe he wants protection from Marne?" Barris sneered.

"How could someone who licks Marne's ass protect me?" Grey asked. "Would you suckle him on my behalf?"

Barris flushed with anger. Ravo laughed. Pixx and Jasper smiled, already reevaluating the strange visitor.

"I have made no demands of Sparrow Camp," Grey said. "If we're unsuccessful, nothing is expected. If successful, then Sparrow Camp may speak with Clagg to decide what rewards are shared."

"That sounds fair," Jasper said.

"More than fair," Pixx said. "What should we do to get ready?"

"Shouldn't Sparrow Camp's leader have a voice in the decision?" Ravo interrupted. "Is there to be no debate?"

Jasper and Pixx felt chastised for their presumption. Barris appeared ready to object, but held back when Ravo cast him a discerning glance.

"Have your debate. We can talk again after the winter season," Grey said, starting to get up again.

"Wait! It doesn't hurt to discuss what plans are needed," Pixx urged, half out of his seat.

"Leaders of the dig must know what to expect," Jasper added just as strongly.

Grey paused, looking toward Ravo. The shrewd old goat responded with a sly grin. He knew Grey had no intention of walking away after having taken so much trouble to arrange the meeting.

"We can go over a few details," Grey said, retaking his seat.

"That's a beginning," Ravo said. "Where is Rat?"

"Here, uncle," Rat answered, the boy emerging from behind Pixx and Jasper where he had been hiding.

"Run to Bynar. Have her bring a pitcher of mauck. We're going to be here for a while," Ravo instructed.

A few hours later, Tak, Shalli, and Grey were on the trail going south, their business with Sparrow Camp concluded.

"Will you make them a quarry?" Shalli asked.

"It's possible. Ravo needs time to decide," Grey answered.

"Marne will be jealous. He might cause trouble," Tak suggested.

"Marne should be jealous. Sparrow Camp's mountain has rich potential. I don't think the good ore runs as far north as Wolf Camp," Grey speculated.

"Be careful, Ben. Ravo isn't trustworthy," Tak warned.

"Don't worry, I have no intention of trusting anybody," he replied.

They walked through the woods for nearly a kilometer enjoying the wintry forest. Occasional brooks and clearings crossed their path. Grey noticed that none of the trees were stout enough for the mines, the more robust timber having been depleted.

"Deer Camp is around the next bend, just past the creek," Tak said.

"I didn't see anyone trying to follow us," Shalli mentioned, looking back but trying to be subtle. The growth was thick in spots, sparse in others. A soft wind rustled the branches.

"Someone is nearby, moving parallel in the trees on the left," Grey whispered. "He's been stalking us since we left the ore tracks."

"Is it Marne?" Shalli asked.

"Not big enough. Maybe Logis or Carp," Grey guessed. "Let's stop in the next clearing. If you see movement in the trees, run for camp."

"Are you sure there's only one?" Shalli asked.

"Just be ready," Grey said.

The women tried not to appear concerned. Grey fell back a few paces and picked up a flat stone, clutching it close to his side. When they reached the creek, the sound of breaking branches close by put everyone on alert. He turned slowly, trying to look afraid so the attack wouldn't be discouraged. The plan was soon ruined.

"Shalli! Ben! There you are," Clagg shouted, coming up the trail from Deer Camp. With him were Nole, Sal, Hernet, and Turk.

"Tak, what's taken all day?" Nole asked, hugging his daughter.

Grey glanced back into the trees and thought he saw a movement, but it was going in the opposite direction. And fast. It may have been no one. Or the wolf that got away.

* * * * * *

As the winter season progressed, Myra and the mated women of Ferret Camp struggled to cultivate their garden, the seven of them not enough for the task. Missing Shalli, Pie, and fourteen-year-old Keep was causing them to fall behind. Myra was surprised one morning to see Bynar, Lupet, and Loto of Sparrow Camp approach for the first time in more than a year. Their brown tunics were better than those found in the southern camps, but not remarkably better.

"We would like to help irrigate your winter wheat," Bynar said, bundled in a red shawl against a cold breeze.

"Winter wheat is difficult this year with the water pump broken," Myra said.

"Ben has spent many days at Sparrow Camp when he could have been working Ferret Camp's mine. It's only fair," Lupet said.

Lupet smiled when she saw Myra. Close in age, they had grown up together at the desert camp and lost their fathers at the same time, making recent separations more difficult. Loto was young and attractive, her long golden brown hair tied back. Bait for the wolves if she hadn't been mated to Jasper. Nevertheless, it troubled Myra that Bynar would risk her in the gardens.

"We accept your help," Myra agreed.

The women dispersed to their duties, Bynar staying close to Myra as they prepared a new irrigation trench. Though Bynar was fifteen years older than Myra, both were the wives of camp leaders. They understood each other.

"Ravo thinks Sparrow Camp will make quota this season," Bynar said.

"I'm glad for your people. Winter season is always the hardest with weather so poor," Myra said. "Clagg expects us to make quota

138

again, thank Sherra. The Spring Festival will be joyful this year."

"Ben has made many small tunnels searching for the best ore. The signs are good. He says we'll soon have our own quarry," Bynar related.

"Ben is very smart. He knows the mountain," Myra answered.

"Bear Camp wants a quarry. They've come to visit Ravo on days when Ben is away. They ask Ravo to speak for them."

"I'd like Bear Camp to have a quarry. They've been better friends than some, but Ferret Camp needs Ben. We have quotas, too," Myra said, echoing Clagg's thoughts.

"Marne visited our camp yesterday," Bynar mentioned.

Myra stopped her work to listen. She had thought Bynar had arrived seeking favors. Now she realized that wasn't the case.

"Marne says strangers shouldn't be invading Sparrow Camp and making changes. He says we have a good mine and should be content," Bynar explained. "Marne says camps that make quota should share with Wolf Camp, which has not made quota."

"Maybe they would make quota if they worked harder," Myra responded.

"This is true, but Ravo dares not say it. Marne had five wolves with him. Ben was there, too, kept distant by Pixx and Jasper. Marne was not prepared to violate camp hospitality, so he shouted at Ben instead. He said if Ben didn't share his quarries with Wolf Camp, he would be lashed and bound for Gronar's pleasure."

"What disgusting animals they are," Myra whispered in outrage. "What did Ben say?"

"Ben did not speak, but he made a gesture with his hand. I don't know what the gesture meant, but I'm sure it was an insult. Marne thought so, too. Later, after all the visitors were gone, the men discussed if they should give Ben to Marne after the quarry is made."

"And some have called Ben a coward. I'm sorry, Bynar, but your men stink of fear."

"It's true of many these days, but not all. Barris hasn't been a friend to Ben, but now he resents Marne even more. Much has Ravo been forced to pull him in. I like Ben. He's kind to the children. I'll feel sad when Marne catches him."

"I fear that day, too. But what can be done? Ben won't stay within our camp as he should. He can't help Deer Camp or Sparrow Camp by hiding."

"I've said this to Ravo, but he wants the quarry. All of the men want the quarry," Bynar sadly reported. "There is other bad news. Ar and Carp were with Marne. They say Shalli and Tak have been too long from the gardens. That it shows disrespect. They say if they don't see them in the fields soon, they'll see them someplace else. Ar slapped his hands together in a foul way."

"This is bad, but I've expected it. Thank you for the warning, Bynar."

"I'm sorry we haven't been friends, Myra. Women shouldn't lose friendships because men play cruel games."

"Maybe someday it will be better," Myra hoped.

"There is a question I would ask about Ben," Bynar requested.

"No one knows much about him. Even in our own camp, Ben is a mystery."

"Is he a coward?"

"I don't think so."

"Some men still call him a coward, though few who work with him truly believe it. Ben never denies it. I know he's quiet, but why doesn't he deny it?"

"Ben is afraid of many things. He's afraid the children will go hungry. He's afraid the camp won't have adequate supplies. He's afraid Shalli's love for him will someday hurt her. He's afraid the masters will turn against us. Maybe that's why he thinks he's a coward?"

"All men who love their camps have these fears. Does Ben not understand this?" Bynar asked.

"Not all men feel they can control the future," Myra said. "They pray to Sherra and hope for the best. In this way, Ben is different. What Ben prays for, he expects to get."

* * * * * *

"Ben! We have introductions!" Ravo shouted.

Fifty yards away, from a small chemical-filled tent pitched in the

140

meadow, Grey slipped through the flap and crossed a warning line of torn rags toward Sparrow Camp.

"Ben, this is Jarten of Bear Camp and Seeak, his dig leader," Ravo said. "They've been asking about a quarry."

Grey found a square-shouldered man about his height and age, curly chestnut hair with sky blue eyes and a friendly smile, which he assumed was the Bear Camp leader. The muscular man next to him was short, dark and surly, unhappy to be begging favors. Full leather outfits, now beginning to fray, indicated a camp less prosperous than it once was.

"They haven't been asking me," Grey said, having received no greeting.

"Marne said they shouldn't speak to you," Ravo said.

"Then let Marne make a quarry for them," Grey replied, abruptly returning to the tent in the meadow through the yellow grass.

"Ben's in a bad mood today," Ravo apologized to his guests. "Barris, go ask Ben if he will speak with Bear Camp."

"If Ben wanted to speak with Bear Camp, he would not have walked away," Barris said.

"Tell him I would be grateful," Ravo urged.

"I will ask him," Barris agreed.

Following Grey to the canvas laboratory, Barris entered gently, as instructed many times. Numerous chemicals and mixing containers were laid out on the workbench, the bottles labeled in Arikhan. Grey sat on a tall stool wearing a leather apron with thin doe skin gloves protecting his hands.

"You shouldn't be here. It's dangerous," Grey said without looking up.

"The task doesn't go well?" Barris asked.

"It could take several more days. The chemical bases are dried out and the mixing solutions are unstable. I'm concerned that even a slight movement may set them off."

"Set them off?"

"If the chemicals combine in a bad way, they could explode, like the blasts we used to make the burrows," Grey said. Barris took a step toward the door.

"Would they not explode you, too?" Barris asked.

"That's what I'm trying to avoid," Grey said, squinting as he added more solution to a bowl of clear goop.

Barris scratched his head, wondering why the danger didn't concern Grey as it might concern others.

"If I must be exploded, it could happen in worse company," Barris said, moving close to the table.

"Let's try not to get exploded," Grey said with a smile.

"Ravo said he would be grateful if you would speak with Bear Camp."

"Grateful? I've not heard Ravo use such a word before."

"It's not common," Barris agreed.

"I will speak with Bear Camp," Grey said, storing the chemicals as best he could.

A few minutes later, the leaders of Sparrow Camp and Bear Camp were sitting around a council fire under the old oak tree. Grey was offered the head seat but declined.

"We've heard Sparrow Camp will make quota," Jarten said.

"We made quota yesterday, and with five days left in the season," Ravo bragged. "We didn't have time to make the quarry, but Ben created tunnels for us. With our quarry, the spring season will be better."

Ravo was happy, his camp filled with optimism.

"We aren't going to make quota," Jarten said. "Neither will Squirrel Camp. I don't believe any of the northern camps will make quota. There's much dissatisfaction."

"Is it Sparrow Camp's fault there is dissatisfaction?" Barris asked.

"No, but it's still there," Jarten said. "Bear Camp would like a quarry, but we don't want to anger Marne. To have a quarry made, we would be friends with Ben and Ferret Camp. But to befriend Ferret Camp is to make enemies in Wolf Camp. We come to you, Old Ravo, for your wisdom."

Ravo smiled, his yellow teeth shining through the gray beard.

"We'll have much reward for making spring quota," Ravo bragged. "That's why I bribed Marne to leave Ben alone until the end of season."

Grey looked at Ravo in surprise. For months he had waited for the anticipated ambush that never came, and at last he knew why. He was not pleased. Barris noted the expression and was curious, wondering why Grey appeared so angry.

"Perhaps Bear Camp can bribe Marne to leave Ben alone during spring season?" Ravo suggested. "In return, Ben might make a quarry for Bear Camp."

"Don't bother," Grey said, suddenly standing up. "I need to make a new quarry for Ferret Camp. I've promised one to Sparrow Camp. If all goes well, I'll try to help Bear Camp. But no one is to bribe Marne on my behalf. It's unacceptable. Old Ravo, though I respect you, you have disappointed me greatly."

Grey left the council fire despite an attempt to call him back. Many were mystified.

"We've heard he is much afraid of Marne. Why does he reject your protection?" Seeak asked, the voice a growling baritone.

"I don't know. I thought he would be thankful," Ravo said, baffled by Grey's reaction.

"How little you understand him, father," Barris said. "Ben isn't afraid of Marne. He doesn't fear Marne's wolves. He doesn't fear the mountain. You've presumed upon his honor."

"Honor will not protect him from the wolves," Ravo said without apology. "If I must bribe Marne to get my quarry, I'll bribe him. And if I must trade Ben to the wolves to protect Sparrow Camp, then I'll trade him. If you are to lead a camp someday, you must know to make these decisions."

"Isn't it more important for a leader to keep faith with his friends?" Barris asked.

"My son, a good leader has no friends," Ravo answered.

* * * * * *

On the last day of winter season, the people of Sparrow Camp huddled in the meadow. With them were five Arikhan sentries including Nabbatron and Frontra. All looked toward a gorge fifteen meters above the canyon floor where valuable ore strains had been discovered.

"With quota and a quarry, Sparrow Camp will have much to celebrate during spring festival," Frontra said, addressing Ravo, Pixx, and Jasper.

"Three days of meat and mauck are worth a celebration, mistress. We thank you for the bounty," Pixx said.

"You are fortunate to have the half-meat's help," Nabbatron said to Ravo. "It is said that Ferret Camp is displeased by his absence."

"I believe the southern camps will have other worries before long, master," Ravo answered.

Frontra overheard the remark and raised an eye-ring, but said nothing. It was not her place to interfere.

"The mountain explodes!" Jasper shouted as a loud boom echoed from the canyon.

A powerful vibration and the sound of bursting rock accompanied the blast. Hundreds of birds flew away as trees were thrown from the hillside and boulders crashed down into the gully that divided their zone from Deer Camp's. Within seconds, a plume of dust churned high into the morning sky, drifting east above the compound.

"We have a quarry!" Ravo announced somewhat prematurely.

Barris rushed forward into the gully first, followed by the men, then the women, the entire camp braving the dirt-choked air to inspect the fresh ore. The Arikhan guards lingered behind before starting back to their post at the main gate.

"What did Old Ravo mean?" Frontra asked.

"I do not ask such questions of food creatures, but the half-meat may have seen his last sunrise," Nabbatron speculated.

"Marne's reputation is much afflicted by your camps, Frontra," Bortro reported, his girth grown wider with better days. "It is said the wolf creatures intend a reckoning."

"Much has this day been feared," Frontra said. "It is sad. I am fond of Ben. The creature is like no other I have known."

"It was impertinent," Nabbatron said.

"That was part of the creature's charm," Frontra contended.

"I suppose you are right," Nabbatron agreed, clicking his tongue in sympathy.

For the next few hours, Sparrow Camp roamed through the new

quarry that filled the canyon floor, often stopping to stare up at the gaping hole where the rock had been blasted out. By early afternoon, they were satisfied that several seasons of excellent ore had been brought down within easy reach.

Brushing dust off his work shirt, Grey walked through the debris field, studying samples with a frown. Barris thought he was looking for something special but not finding it.

"You look disappointed," Barris said.

"I hoped for more variety. Still, this field should prove adequate," Grey explained.

"It's magic," Barris said.

"It's science. A science that was practiced here long ago."

"Could you teach me to do it?" Barris asked.

"It's not hard to learn, provided you're not prone to mistakes."

They walked toward the mouth of the canyon only to find the people had all vanished. Everyone except Ravo, Pixx, and Jasper.

"This isn't good," Barris whispered to Grey.

"Care to be more specific?" Grey asked.

"Marne was here last night. He argued with my father."

"Perhaps your father is not so grateful after all?" Grey suggested.

"When we reach the meadow, I'll distract them. Run for Deer Camp. Run as fast as you can. Only Jasper can run, and not very fast."

"We haven't been friends," Grey said.

"That doesn't make this right," Barris answered.

"Thanks for warning me, but I'm not running. Is it four against one?"

"No. I can't help you, but I'm not going to help them, either. Father knows how I feel. I'm sure that's why he didn't tell me."

"Stay back. I'll try not to hurt anyone," Grey offered.

"I don't understand," Barris questioned.

"You will," Grey said, quickening his pace.

Barris slowed to a walk, noticing that Grey approached the group nonchalantly despite knowing their intentions. He didn't know if it was courage or stupidity. *Does Ben think he'll talk them out of it?* Barris wondered. *Appeal for sympathy? If so, he doesn't know Ravo.*

"Are you pleased with your quarry, Old Ravo?" Grey asked.

"Very pleased," Ravo said, his feet solidly braced, arms crossed over his chest.

"And you, my friends of Sparrow Camp, are you satisfied?" Grey asked Pixx and Jasper.

"You have been true to your word. None can say different," Pixx replied.

"Much does Sparrow Camp owe you appreciation. I pray Sherra that you can forgive us, my small friend," Jasper said with a sad expression.

"In what manner should you be forgiven?" Grey asked.

"Marne has demanded a third of our quarry. Or you. We will not give up a third of our quarry," Ravo said.

Pixx and Jasper slowly shifted around Grey's flanks. Grey watched their shadows on the scrub-covered ground as he turned toward Ravo.

"Marne will not treat me kindly," Grey said, shifting a step to adjust his positioning.

"I did my best to urge mercy for you. Indicated the many ways you could help Wolf Camp. Marne's ears are closed," Ravo replied with regret.

"This is disappointing news indeed. Much have I enjoyed the company of Sparrow Camp. It's been a privilege to make a quarry for you," Grey said.

"We, too, have made a fondness, but this cannot be helped. The wolves must have tribute or our women will not be safe in the gardens. It's you they demand," Ravo said.

"Much is it easy to present a demand. Harder is it to collect," Grey responded.

Grey's left hand lashed out so quickly the motion was just a blur, the back of his fist smashing Jasper in the face. Blood spurted from the tall man's broken nose as he staggered backward. Grey wheeled around and kicked Pixx between the thighs, the motion executed with forceful precision. A thrust kick caught Pixx in the gut as he doubled over, then a flying roundhouse kick to the head put him down.

Spinning back on Jasper, Grey rabbit punched him in the kidney before delivering a powerful right hook to the chin, sending the hefty dig leader into the dirt. In hardly an instant, both Pixx and Jasper lay moaning on the ground. Grey whirled around to face Ravo, who hadn't moved.

"You are fast, and you know how to fight," Ravo realized.

"That's true," Grey agreed.

"You only pretended to be a coward."

"It seemed a wise choice at the time."

"I'm a strong fighter, better than Jasper or Pixx, and you won't take me by surprise," Ravo warned. "But I'm slow. Maybe you should run?"

"I don't think so," Grey said.

"You won't run?"

Grey glanced back at Barris, who stood ten meters away, watching but not interfering.

"I don't like running away. I'll stay and fight with my friend Ravo," Grey said.

"I'm twice your size," Ravo warned.

"Women find me more attractive," Grey replied.

"You will not run away?"

"Not today."

Ravo frowned and charged, his arms outstretched to grab Grey before he could defend himself. Grey sidestepped at the last moment, gripped Ravo's right arm, and used a judo throw to flip him upside down. Ravo crashed heavily to the hard ground, the impact leaving him breathless. Grey shifted to one side, feet braced and fists ready to continue the battle, but Ravo remained on his back staring at the sky, making no effort to get up. Grey approached cautiously and knelt beside him.

"You fight well. I was very frightened by the ferocity of your attack," Grey said.

"It's good to know that I'm feared," Ravo moaned, still wheezing.

"Would you like to fight some more?" Grey asked.

"No, I will rest here for awhile," Ravo responded.

Barris came forward, kneeling on the other side. Pixx and Jasper lay groaning, neither getting up.

"Are you all right, father?" Barris asked.

"I'm resting. It was a good fight," Ravo answered.

"I've learned a valuable lesson today about leadership," Barris said. "Sometimes it's better to keep faith with your friends. Especially if your friends make dangerous enemies."

"It's a wise lesson," Ravo said, slowly sitting up and rubbing his back.

Grey checked to make sure Ravo wasn't injured before going to Pixx, who lay curled in a ball.

"How fares my friend?" Grey asked.

"Impaired. Few will be the women entertained in my tent during the spring festival," Pixx groaned. He glanced up at Grey, looking at him without anger. "I'm grateful you didn't break my arms. I never wanted to be your enemy."

"I know," Grey said, patting him on the shoulder before going to Jasper.

"The bent nose looks good, my friend. The women will flock to you," Grey praised.

"Could you not have broken Pixx's nose instead?" Jasper sniffled, blood still running down his face.

"I kicked Pixx where it hurts most," Grey replied.

"A broken nose is not so bad. I didn't want to be your enemy, either. But Ravo is our leader. He has been leader for as long as anyone remembers."

"Ravo is a good leader, but even a good leader can make mistakes," Grey said.

Grey turned back. Ravo noticed his expression had transformed from genial adversary to one capable of great brutality. The gray eyes were cold. The brow bent. The half-smile on his lips changed to a thin, mirthless line.

"Hear me well, Old Ravo, for this will only be said once," Grey warned. "Do not make this mistake again. Next time, I will not be your friend."

Chapter Five
BLOOD AND PROMISES

Barris walked with Grey toward the gardens at the southern end of the lake, passing through a dry pasture and a bleak late winter forest. The pace was brisk. Barris saw Grey was worried.

"You could have hurt them, couldn't you? Hurt them bad enough for the pens," Barris asked.

"Pixx and Jasper were taken by surprise. Ravo knows nothing of martial arts. Anyone who takes an opponent lightly may get hurt."

"You beat them easily," Barris said.

"I was trained by a master of the ancient arts. There's no magic to it."

"I think you're better than you say. Maybe even better than Marne."

"I look forward to finding out," Grey confirmed.

Barris saw this was true.

"You should be angry with my father. More than angry. I don't understand why you don't hate every member of Sparrow Camp for betraying you," Barris pressed.

"Your people are afraid. They made a bad decision. I know what it's like to be afraid. I know what it's like to make bad decisions. Once the wolves are no longer a threat, life will be better for everyone."

"You should be angry with me," Barris felt compelled to say. "I suspected something last night, but I didn't say anything until it was too late."

"Your warning was unnecessary. I spent last night on the mountain deepening the blasting holes. When I saw Marne visit the camp, it took no imagination to guess what was going on."

Barris stopped in his tracks, his mouth open.

"And you still made the quarry for us?"

"Don't be fooled. My motives are not altruistic."

"Not what?" Barris asked.

149

"I didn't do it out of the goodness of my heart," Grey explained.

They walked on, leaving the woods around Sparrow Camp and crossing the ore tracks toward the gardens. It was a gray day, the sun hidden by threatening clouds.

"I understand," Barris said. "If Sparrow Camp is happier, we'll be better neighbors to Deer Camp, who is friend to Ferret Camp. The women will work together in the gardens again. By making quota, we'll have more goods to trade. Soon Bear Camp will feel prosperity, too. They'll also be better neighbors."

"You'll make a good leader someday," Grey said.

"Someday? We're almost the same age, but you're already a better leader than I'll ever be. Better than Ravo."

"I'm not a leader."

"I haven't been your friend, but I would like to be."

"Marne won't like that. You can't be friends with both of us."

"I was never friends with Marne. I pretended to be his friend out of fear," Barris admitted. "I would rather be your friend."

"I don't make a very good friend, Barris," Grey had to say.

"That will be for me to decide," Barris insisted.

Barris smiled and extended his arm. Grey looked deeply into the dark brown eyes and saw sincerity. Barris was not his father. Grey extended his arm, each gripping the other's forearm as the men of the camps did when affirming special bonds.

"Why do we travel to the gardens, my brother?" Barris asked.

"Marne's scheme to acquire me was bold. I'm concerned he may have larger plans in mind."

"It could be true. Spring festival is a good time for him to proclaim power over the weaker camps," Barris realized.

They reached the gardens to find only Myra, Beknar and an observer from Rabbit Camp present.

"Hello, Barris. Nice to see you again. Do you have a new mine?" Myra asked.

"Where is everyone?" Grey impatiently interrupted.

"They went back early to prepare for the festival. Not that many were here today with everyone watching you make the quarry," Myra said.

Grey and Barris looked at each other.

"Only Sparrow Camp came to the meadow. Ravo didn't invite the other camps," Barris said.

"That's strange," Myra remarked. "We didn't see Bear Camp here today, or Squirrel Camp. And only a few watchers from Rabbit Camp. What does it mean?"

"I'm going to find out," Grey said. "Barris, thank you for walking with me."

Barris looked at the empty fields with foreboding before turning back toward Sparrow Camp. After the observer from Rabbit Camp checked the baskets, Grey helped Myra and Beknar carry the food to Ferret Camp. Myra noticed Grey was unusually quiet.

"Shalli is hoping you'll have a surprise for her during the festival," Myra finally said to break the silence.

"What sort of surprise?" Grey asked, watching the trail for danger.

"Spring festival begins the new year. It's a time of singing. Dancing. And mating announcements," Myra elaborated.

"She expects a mating proposal?" Grey responded.

"A woman cannot expect such a thing. One may not presume upon a man in such a way, but she has high hopes. All think it's a good match," Myra said.

"Even you? You've kept your distance lately," Grey mentioned.

"Violence frightens me, but I don't think you enjoy hurting others. Not like the wolves. I'm sorry, I do have reservations, but it's still a good match."

"Do I decide this or the camp?" Grey inquired with some annoyance.

"Don't get into one of your moods. People talk. They wonder. They make opinions. It's only natural."

Grey nodded. He was edgy. Being angry with Myra wasn't going to help, and he appreciated her honesty.

They reached Ferret Camp to find everything normal. The older women were preparing for tomorrow's events, the younger women and girls were cooking or taking care of the children. Garn already had a fruit in his hand, his face dripping with juice. The men had not returned from the quarry yet, but soon would. Beknar and Myra went

151

to put their baskets away.

"Where's Shalli?" Grey asked.

"She went to visit Tak at Deer Camp," Pie said. "They're very excited about the festival. Someone hopes for a surprise."

Pie started to smile before noticing Grey's expression.

"What's wrong, Ben? You look so grim," she questioned.

"Bad karma."

"Is that a food they eat at Sparrow Camp?"

"Karma isn't a food, Pie, it's a feeling. Tell Myra I've gone to Deer Camp."

Of several trails north, Grey took the route through the woods past his private clearing rather than the one veering left to the quarry or right to the gardens. He decided not to pick up a club despite his apprehension. Carrying weapons was frowned upon by the people and forbidden by the Arikhan.

Grey studied the trail for signs of ambush. A sound from behind caused him to spin, ready to strike. It was Myra, running as fast as she could to catch up.

"Ben, what's wrong?" she asked, breathing hard from the sprint.

Grey didn't answer. He turned back toward Deer Camp with Myra struggling to match his pace. Well before they could see Deer Camp's tents, black smoke was rising into the hazy afternoon sky.

"That's not a cooking fire," Myra said.

"It's canvas. Their tents are burning," Grey said, picking up a broken branch from the trail.

They hurried to the shallow flat where Deer Camp had stood for the last eight years. The communal tent was in flames. Two smaller tents were also burning. In the middle of the camp, three women lay sprawled on the ground.

"Bless Sherra!" Myra yelled, rushing headlong into the clearing.

Grey entered more cautiously When he was sure the raiders were gone, he kicked over the smaller tents to put out the flames and pulled down the communal tent, robbing the fire of fuel.

"Court, what happened?" Myra asked, kneeling next to her friend.

"Wolves. They came. Right here, into our camp," Court whispered. "They can't do that. It's not allowed."

Court was bleeding from a head wound. Clubbed. Grey went to the other women who lay unmoving. One was Bab, Sal's mate. Her skull was bashed in. The other was Leet, the young mate of Medim. She had been run through the shoulder by a sharp object, possibly a short knife like the one Lace carried. Her breathing was labored but the bleeding wasn't critical. Grey used a moment to bandage the wound and make her comfortable.

"Where's the rest of your women?" Grey asked, going back to Court.

"They took the children. Ran for the quarry. The wolves have Tak. Myra, I'm so sorry. They took Shalli, too. We tried to stop them. We tried hard," Court managed to say.

"How is Bab?" Myra asked.

"Bab is dead," Grey reported.

"Oh, no. No, no, no. Is Leet dead, too?" Myra asked. She tore a piece off her dress to sop the blood on Court's forehead.

"No, but she has a bad injury. Where would the wolves take the girls? Back to their camp?" Grey inquired.

"No," Myra said, tears running down her face.

"Where?" Grey asked.

Myra was overwhelmed, unable to answer. He grabbed her arms trying to shake her out of it.

"Answer me. Where would they take them?" he demanded.

"Their torment pit," Court said when Myra couldn't reply.

Grey examined Court's wound, a hard blow to the left temple. The laceration was bloody but not deep. He guessed she may have a concussion, but hopefully nothing worse.

"Ben, get the men from the quarry. Maybe the other camps will finally help," Myra said through anguished tears.

"There's no time for a war council. Not if I'm to reach this torment pit before they hurt Tak and Shalli," Grey said, getting up to leave.

"Ben, don't. They'll kill you," Court warned, trying to grab his arm.

"They'll try," he answered.

From the smoking debris of the communal tent, he pulled out an oak tent pole. He hefted the shaft, gave it a swing, then a thrust. The balance was good, the thickness just right for a firm grip. Myra jumped up to block his path.

"Where are you going?" Myra asked.

"I'm going after them," he said.

"The wolves are too many."

"I won't know that until I find them," Grey said, trying to go around her. Myra blocked him again.

"There are too many. Wait for the men."

"The wolves aren't keeping the girls a moment longer than I can help it," Grey swore, his eyes blazing with a deadly determination. "I don't know what customs your people use to deal with situations like this. I don't care. I'm using my customs now, and the wolves are going to answer for kidnapping Shalli. They're going to answer for raping Tak. They're going to answer for killing Bab. Anyone who gets in my way is going to get hurt. Do you understand?"

Myra had never seen such an expression before. Not on Ben. Not on anyone. It was a cold, controlled rage. His resolve was firm. Fixed. Unchallengeable. The quiet Ben she had known was gone, replaced by a force of nature.

"I see you now. I see the warrior. And I'm not frightened anymore," Myra said. "It's not hatred or vengeance that makes you what you are. It's love."

Myra stood up on her toes to kiss him on the cheek.

"Bring the girls back safe, if you can," Myra whispered.

"By Sherra's Will," Grey said, gripping the staff as he left the camp.

Myra went to Leet and pulled her into the largest of the surviving tents, then returned to Court, putting a damp cloth on her head.

"My poor Tak. She won't come back to me this time," Court cried.

Myra held Court in her arms, thinking she might be right. And wondering if she'd ever see Shalli or Ben again.

Grey didn't know exactly where the so-called torment pit was, only that it lay somewhere on the west bank of the lake near the marsh. So far, only one path led in the right direction, but that would change once he left the woods. He hoped the trail wouldn't be too hard to follow.

Something moved up ahead. The leaves rustled. Grey slowed in time to see Tak emerge from a brushy ravine. She was naked, scratched by branches but otherwise uninjured.

"Ben!" she shouted, running on the dirt trail and throwing herself in his arms. "Ben, it worked, just like you taught me. Ar wanted to take me first. Alone. I didn't resist when he pulled me into the high grass. Let him push me down. Then, when he was full with excitement, I kicked him. I kicked him hard!"

Grey had expected Tak to be traumatized by the second kidnapping. Far from it. She was frightened, but she had kept her head, fought back, and hurt her attacker.

"You're very brave," he said, taking off his leather jacket and pulling it around her shoulders. "I'm proud of you, Tak. I don't know if I've ever been more proud of anyone."

Tak hugged him, tears just below the surface.

"I wouldn't be so brave if not for you," she said.

Tak looked behind him, expecting to see Nole and Clagg. Sal and Cot. Turk, Burne, Medim, and Hernet. The trail was empty.

"Where is everyone?" Tak asked.

"They'll be along soon. When I leave the woods, where do I find this pit they're taking Shalli to?"

"Follow the ore track toward Bear Camp. It's just past the old pier," Tak answered. She noticed the pole in Grey's hand and looked into his eyes. There was an intensity she had never seen before.

"Court and Leet are hurt. I think they'll be okay, but you'd better go help. Stay at Ferret Camp until this is over," Grey instructed, sliding around her and starting for the lake.

"You should wait. Shalli wouldn't want you to die for her."

"I'm not afraid."

"That's the problem. You're always afraid when you don't have to be, and not afraid when you should be. That's why no one understands you."

"Yeah, I kind of like that," he said.

"This is no time to make jokes," Tak protested.

"My guardian always said I use humor in desperate moments to deflect fear. I guess some things never change," he replied with a grim smile.

"Please, Ben. Please don't. Wait for the men," Tak pleaded.

"I won't wait. Too many have waited too long already," he insisted.

Grey kissed her on the forehead, looked deeply into the dark eyes one last time, and tucked the staff under his arm, running for the ore tracks. Tak watched him go, glanced at the trail south to Deer Camp, but turned to the northwest trail instead.

As Grey emerged from the woods near the lake, he began to formulate his thoughts. Anger was good; it would give him strength, but it couldn't rule his thinking. He didn't know how many wolves he'd need to challenge, and wasn't foolish enough to believe himself invincible. He dug down into the past he'd tried so hard to forget. The answers were there—if he had the courage to find them.

Though he had trained hard in martial arts at West Point, he was never at the top of his class. His best talents were small arms, but there were none to be had. Master Shao said he had a rare ability to reach inside, to bring mind and body together in a way few others could. To ignore fear. To put everything on the line. And he remembered the words of a childhood mentor: no one is better than you. You have the talent, the skill, the experience. Move fast! Strike hard! And if you've got no one to watch your back, send your enemies to hell.

Grey saw the ore track curve north, past the offshoots for Sparrow and Bear Camps. There was a well-worn path along the gardens on his right. Soon the carefully cultivated plots gave way to marshy grasses lining the lake's western edge. Up ahead, on the far side of a broad meadow, he saw a crowd of forty or fifty people. And at least a half dozen wolves.

Maybe most of the people are just watching, he thought, like curiosity seekers at an accident. He had to hope so. Reaching into his belt, he found a rag used to clean his hands in the chemical tent. His pants were still streaked with Leet's blood. He tore the pants leg open, dabbed the rag in blood, and tied it around his knee to make it look like a badly wrapped injury. Then he hobbled toward the loose-knit crowd using the tent pole as a walking crutch.

The first group of people to see him moved away. As he thought, they were only spectators. As he closed to fifty yards, several wolves saw him and passed the word. They formed a line, not for defense, but to enjoy the spectacle of the whimpering coward pathetically limping in their direction. There appeared to be eight wolves in all, seven men and a woman.

With the crowd thinning, Grey could see past the wolves. Adjoining the lake was a dry fishery, three feet deep and ten yards in diameter, with a tall stake planted in the middle. Shalli had been stripped naked and leashed to the stake by a halter fastened around her neck, her hands tied behind her back. She was staring in his direction, deeply frightened.

Marne stood close to the pit, and next to Marne was the biggest man Grey had seen since coming to Karak. The infamous Gronar, nearly seven feet tall with arms the size of most men's legs. Little wonder the wolves felt safe protected by such a goliath.

"Please, masters, let the girl go," Grey called out in his most pitiful voice as he continued to hobble forward.

The wolves laughed and three began walking in his direction. Marne and the others lingered behind, fully enjoying themselves.

"It's the cowardly quarry maker," one of the three said.

It was Ar, always the bold one, walking with a stiff gait from the kick delivered by Tak. The second was Logis. Easy to surprise, slow to respond. Grey hadn't seen the third one before, a husky teenager with unruly red hair. Possibly Marne's younger brother or a cousin. Grey backed up a step, then another, but slowly. The three quickened their pace.

"Please don't hurt me, masters," Grey said, coming to a halt on a flat piece of ground. The three wolves stopped before him, smiling with evil anticipation.

"We'll give him to Gronar, but not until we see how many lashes it takes to make him beg," Ar said, taking a short leather whip from his belt.

"He'll beg before the first stroke, not that it will do him any good," Logis said, reaching to grab Grey's wrist.

The red-headed teenager sought to take the staff, grinning with wolfish confidence, but not so bold as Ar. Grey guessed he had not been a thug long.

"Please, master. Please don't hurt me," Grey repeated. "Please don't—"

Grey whipped the staff around, catching Ar in his already sore groin, and then drove the pole backward, hitting Logis in the face. A spinning swing hit the teenager on the side of the head, the impact cracking bone.

Twirling the staff up and around, Grey struck the last victim a second time and heard the skull break. The youngster fell in the short grass, blood pouring from a torn scalp. The brown eyes glared up in confusion, the teenager looking for help, but there was none to be had.

Shifting back to Logis, who had somehow managed to keep his feet, Grey drove the pole into his stomach, spun it down on top of his head, and kicked him in the face as he fell.

"Stop. Stop," Logis moaned, scratching at the dirt.

For the moment, Grey did, turning back on Ar to stomp the man's left forearm and hearing the bones snap. Then he broke the right forearm with a slam of the pole. The arrogance disappeared from Ar's face, replaced by bewildered fear.

In a matter of seconds, all three opponents were down, injured but not yet neutralized. Grey looked toward the other wolves standing forty yards away. They were staring in shock, so stunned that not one of them had moved. Just as Grey hoped. Their complacency had proven costly.

He glanced down at Logis, took a quick breath, and used the staff as a pile driver to crush his skull. The red-headed teenager tried to drag himself away. Having no personal animosity toward him, Grey killed the boy with a single swift blow to the back of the head. Then he knelt before Ar, who lay curled in the yellow grass.

"Tak told me of your little adventure. Was it fun hurting her?" Grey asked.

Ar looked into his eyes. He saw no mercy there. No trace of the coward. He tried to crawl back toward the lake, his broken arms nearly useless. Grey swung the pole in a high arc and brought it down on Ar's lower spine with every bit of force he had. The vertebrae separated. Ar screamed. And screamed. Ar would be food for the pens.

The five remaining wolves finally reacted, drawing knives and waving clubs. Two of the wolves, young Winso and the female, Lace, advanced on Grey the quickest. He knew their strategy. They expected him to run. The youngsters would delay him until the other three caught up. It would have been a good plan if he felt like running.

Grey did take several steps backward, still pretending to limp, just to egg them on. When the distance between Winso and the remaining wolves was at its best advantage, Grey suddenly turned, whipping the pole around to catch the youngster in the ribs. Winso twisted to avoid a second blow, lunging with a steel knife. Grey spun around and brought the staff down on the boy's neck, knocking him off his feet.

When Lace jumped at him with a short bone-handled knife, Grey ducked aside and swung the staff to strike her behind the knees. Her legs flew up and she landed on her back with a grunt, rubbing her butt and looking at him with indignation. Grey whacked her on the forehead and she fell back in the grass semi-conscious.

Winso staggered to his feet, the knife held weakly in both hands. His eyes were glazed, the movements unsteady. The pitiful sight made Grey sad. The teenager was so badly overmatched, it felt like murder. It didn't stop him from killing Winso with a quick double-handed blow to the head.

Grey saw Marne, Carp, and Gronar running toward him. He turned away from Winso with barely enough time to set himself. Carp swung a heavy wooden club, the blow grazing the side of Grey's head. He sidestepped and delivered two swift blows with the staff, the last buckling Carp's knee, but the man was tough and wouldn't be down long.

Gronar closed in. At first the giant tried for a bear hug, but Grey ducked and faked a jab at Gronar's groin. Gronar bent to protect himself only to leave his head exposed. Grey twirled the staff and brought it down on top of the giant's skull so hard that the end of the pole cracked on impact. Gronar was hurt, but not enough to stop him.

Gronar quickly grabbed the staff and tried to wrestle it from Grey's grasp, surprised to find his smaller opponent so strong. After a desperate tug of war, the end of the pole broke off, leaving the giant holding a splintered stake. Grey jabbed with the length of staff he had left, catching Gronar in the belly, but the monster was close enough to thrust the stake at Grey's throat, cutting him just below the chin.

Ducking out of Gronar's reach, Grey turned to hit Carp in the face with the butt end of the staff, knocking him down again, and then paused to take a new defensive position, keeping all three enemies in front of him. He was breathing hard now, blood running down into his eyes that he needed to wipe away. He had been fortunate so far, but it would count for nothing if he grew careless.

Marne finally made his move, using his long reach to swing a sharp knife at Grey's arm. Grey used the staff to block the blow and countered with a jab at Marne's ribs, hoping to use the jagged end like a spear, but he couldn't get close enough to inflict an injury. Still on the ground, Carp made an effort to grab Grey's leg, forcing him to wiggle free. Marne moved in from the left. Gronar came straight ahead.

Grey backed away from Marne and Carp, bracing himself for Gronar's charge, but he wasn't sure how to stop him. The sheer mass of his enemy caused Grey to wonder if he could be stopped. Several ideas ran through his mind. Advice from Master Shao. Techniques taught by Peter Wingfoot at the academy. The Biblical tale of David and Goliath. Grey glanced around, wondering if there were any good stones to be found.

Suddenly there was a blinding pain in his back. A momentary numbness in his right arm. Grey twisted around to see that Lace, kneeling on the ground behind him, had stuck her knife in his right side just below the ribs. She was preparing to strike again.

Grey shifted the staff to his left hand, using it as a club to cave in her skull, then backpedaled away from Gronar and Marne.

"She got him!" Marne shouted.

"Save some for me," Gronar said, his deep voice hardly more than a brutish grunt.

"No, he's mine," Carp said, rushing to get at Grey first.

Grey wasn't sure how bad the knife wound was, though he could feel blood running down his leg. The blade had missed the spine, but if it found a vital organ, his life was measured in minutes.

"Maybe we can talk about this. I'd still like to be friends," Grey said, slowly backing away while trying to catch his breath.

"We'll show you friendship, wolf style," Carp muttered, taking a step forward.

It was the last thing Carp ever said. With a flick of his wrist, Grey brought the broken pole up and flung the splintered end deep into the tall man's throat. Carp fell back, hands grasping at the staff, twisting on the ground as he suffocated in his own blood.

Marne knelt at Carp's side but was unable to help, anguish in his expression. Grey guessed they had been close friends since childhood. Partners in crime. No doubt they had spent countless hours at the campfire boasting of their foul deeds. There would be no more campfires for Carp. No more boasting. No more deeds. Marne's grief gave Grey a great deal of satisfaction.

"Have you guys always been this stupid, or are you just having a bad day?" Grey asked, pretending the pain didn't matter.

But he gasped for air so hard that his enemies weren't fooled. Marne stood up from his friend's body. Several wolves lay dead. The ones that weren't dead were dying. Only he and Gronar remained. Marne had his steel knife. Grey had Lace's knife. Gronar pulled the long end of the broken staff out of Carp's throat and turned on Grey with an angry snarl, ready to run him through.

"You're going to die hard. I'll make an example of you that will keep the camps in fear forever," Marne promised.

"*Hoka hey,*" Grey answered, retreating two more steps before taking a stand.

"What's that supposed to mean?" Marne asked.

"An ancient saying of my people," Grey answered. "It means today is a good day to die. I've offered my blood to Sherra in exchange for yours. I'm content that it should be so."

Marne came to a sudden halt, believing that such an oath could only have dire consequences. He looked down at Carp, Winso, and Lace. Logis and the teenager lay off in the distance. Ar had stopped screaming, now lying still in the bloody grass. If other wolves were coming to help, they were taking their time.

161

"He wants Shalli. Let's see how clever he is with a blade pressed against the bitch's throat," Marne said, going back toward the lake.

Grey wanted to cut him off, but Gronar blocked the path and swung the staff at his head, landing a glancing blow.

"You go nowhere," Gronar said, the deep set brown eyes gazing with defiance.

When the giant grinned, the axe tattoos on his big red cheeks doubled in size. Two of his yellow teeth were missing. The man seemed to feel no pain.

"Stand aside," Grey ordered, looking for an opening.

Gronar swung the broken staff, forcing Grey backward. Grey waved the short knife and threatened to throw it, but he could not afford to give up his only weapon. Gronar ducked before realizing he'd been bluffed.

"I kill you quicker now," Gronar said, growing angry.

Anxious to catch Marne, Grey tried to sneak around Gronar, but the giant tripped him with the pole, causing him to fall hard. When Grey tried to get up, Gronar kicked him in the gut.

The fight was not going well. Grey rolled over only to find Gronar standing above him, the splintered staff poised to stake him through the heart. Grey twisted sideways as the jagged tip hurtled down, slicing through his shirt. Grey rolled over again, just barely avoiding a second thrust. With an impatient growl, Gronar put a foot on his victim's chest to hold him in place.

Grey struggled with all his strength, but Gronar's heavy boot had him thoroughly pinned. He slashed with Lace's knife, cutting Gronar's calf several times, but the angle was bad. The wounds didn't even faze him. Gronar hefted the stake and prepared to drive it through Grey's throat.

Suddenly there was a blur of movement. A flying shadow. Grey realized that somebody had jumped on Gronar's back. Thin legs wrapped partway around his huge waist. Slender arms gripped his neck. A wave of long black hair fanned out to fill the sky. It was Tak, a wild look in her blazing brown eyes as she bit down on Gronar's ear.

The giant roared and shook her off, putting a hand to the bloody lobe of chewed flesh. He turned with a vengeance only to find Barris standing behind him, Carp's heavy club in his hand. Barris swung with all his strength, hitting Gronar in the ribs. Gronar grabbed the club and ripped it from Barris' grip.

Tak jumped up and moved to one side, distracting Gronar. Barris jumped in the other direction. Gronar hesitated before reaching for Tak, snagging his thick grubby fingers in her hair. Tak tried to pull away but couldn't get free.

Barris didn't hesitate, rushing forward with a defiant yell and punching Gronar in the nose. Gronar dropped the staff and grabbed Barris by his rawhide jacket, holding him up in one hand and Tak in the other, waving them like rag dolls. For a moment, it looked like Gronar was going to smash the two troublemakers together, but he was suddenly kicked between the legs from behind.

With an annoyed snarl, Gronar dropped his victims and turned to see Grey standing behind him, bloody but ready for renewed combat. Gronar could hardly believe his eyes as Grey snatched up the heavy club and swung, but the blow was easily deflected.

Gronar responded with a lunge, nearly catching Grey flatfooted, but he managed to duck aside at the last second and club Gronar on the back of the head as he stumbled past. The big man fell to the ground, momentarily stunned.

"Marne! Marne, where are you? I'm hurt," Gronar shouted, staggering to his feet. He felt the back of his head, finding blood. His vision was blurred, the earth unsteady. The giant seemed astounded, never before having such an injury.

Grey did not wait for him to recover his composure, swinging for the knee. This time he heard bone crack and Gronar howled, limping several steps. Grey glanced down into the grass and saw the broken staff, the sharp end still red with Carp's blood. He grabbed the weapon with both hands and charged, aiming high for the giant's throat.

Gronar had turned to look for Marne, but the Wolf leader had already reached the dry fishery, hoping to use Shalli as a hostage. A hostage would not help Gronar. He turned back just as Grey drove the broken staff into his windpipe.

Gurgling with painful frustration, Gronar grabbed the staff with one hand even as he swatted Grey aside with the other, then he tried to pull the staff free. Grey found the club again and stood up, preparing to whack Gronar over the head, but a shooting pain in his side forced him to drop the heavy weapon. He fell to one knee, reaching back to where Lace had stabbed him, realizing the wound was tearing open.

Gronar pulled the staff out of his neck and clutched his throat, sucking in more blood than oxygen. Grey lunged forward armed only with Lace's knife, stabbing Gronar in the kidney. When Gronar grabbed his violent foe by the hair and yanked him up, Grey slashed the giant's eye. He almost slashed the other eye but was flung away, tumbling as he hit the ground.

Calling for Marne was impossible, for Gronar was choking. He groped around, looking for help that wasn't there. Grey got up on one knee, took a deep breath, and charged his huge enemy shoulder first, managing to knock him down. Then, gripping Lace's knife tightly in his left hand, he stabbed down with a vicious thrust, finding Gronar's jugular vein. And even then, the giant continued to battle as his life's blood drained away. When Gronar finally stopped moving, Grey rolled over into the bloody weeds barely able to breathe.

"You're hurt," Tak said, coming to help.

Grey removed the rag wrapped around his knee and stuck it over the wound in his back. Barris used his belt to hold the rag in place.

"Get me up," Grey whispered.

Barris reached under Grey's arms to put him on his feet. Grey double-clutched Lace's knife and turned toward the marshy pit.

The crowd of spectators had grown larger, perhaps fifty or sixty, but all were keeping a safe distance. Hardly a word was spoken by anyone. Marne stood in the pit behind Shalli, using her as a shield. She struggled against the leather restraints, the leash still wrapped around her neck. Grey reached the dry fishery first, followed by Tak and Barris. In the distance, from the direction of the ore tracks, two dozen men from Deer and Ferret Camps were approaching. From the north, members of Wolf and Raven Camps were coming, alerted that Marne's effort to cow the southern camps had failed. Hundreds of people were hurrying to see the fight.

"It won't take much to cut her throat," Marne warned, waving the large steel knife.

"Come out and fight. You and me. No weapons," Grey challenged, standing exhausted at the edge of the pit.

"You don't fight fair," Marne declined.

"I'm wounded. That should give you an advantage," Grey lied.

"Ben, don't," Shalli pleaded, more frightened for him than herself.

"What if I decide to cut her throat instead?" Marne asked.

Holding Lace's knife behind his back, Grey transferred it to his left hand. He wouldn't be able to throw right-handed with his side cut open, but he thought himself fairly good left-handed. What he needed was a clear shot.

"If you hurt her, expect to die slowly," Grey promised. "My people have paths to death that a coward like you can't even imagine. You would find the pens joyful by comparison. But that will come later. First I'll kill every man, woman, and child in your camp. They will curse your name before they die. All will know the coward Marne let his people suffer rather than accept a challenge from a wounded man. All the ghosts will fall down."

"The ghosts will do what?" Marne asked.

Shalli smiled. She had seen Grey fight the ghosts. She bumped Marne with her shoulder and dropped to the marsh-covered bottom of the pit. Marne looked down at her in surprise even as Lace's knife was flying through the air, sticking him in the chest.

"What the—" Marne grunted, staring at the knife as if it wasn't real.

Grey leaped from the pit's edge, found his balance, and charged, bowling Marne over before wresting the large steel blade from him.

On his knees, Marne pulled the bone-handled knife from his chest, probing the wound. It was painful but not fatal. But before he got up, Grey plunged Marne's own knife into his back between two ribs. Marne screamed and broke away, crawling to find help from the scores of people rushing from Wolf Camp. Grey staggered after him and stomped his leg. Marne rolled on his back to ward off the assault, swiping wildly with Lace's knife as Grey circled around him looking for an opportunity.

"Stay away! My people will seek revenge," Marne warned, terrified of the relentless stalking beast.

Grey felt no need to answer, kicking the flailing knife aside and pouncing. The wolf leader tried to throw him off, pounding with weakened fists. Grey pushed the blows aside, gripping Marne's metal slave collar with his right hand, holding the steel knife in his left.

"You don't fight fair," Marne whimpered.

"Tell that to Bab on your way to hell, you goddamn son of a bitch," Grey answered, plunging the knife deep into Marne's throat and giving it a rough twist. Blood spurted in every direction as the wolf leader struggled beneath him. Air bubbled through the ragged hole. After a moment, Marne stopped twitching. The eyes rolled back in a lifeless stare. Grey sighed with relief.

"Ben! Ben!" Shalli called out, still tethered to the pole.

Grey crawled over to cut the bindings loose, glad to see she wasn't hurt. Apparently the wolves hadn't had time to exploit their captive. Then he slumped slowly to the ground until Shalli caught him in her lap.

"They haven't killed you. I won't let you die," Shalli cried, holding him tightly.

"The wounds aren't so bad. A few stitches will make everything better," Grey said, sure he could stand up if the dizziness would go away.

"You bleed like a stuck quail," Shalli complained, showing him her hand where blood ran generously through her fingers.

"Don't worry, Marne wasn't able to kill me. It's not an easy thing to do," he said, sickened by the dank smell of the pit. Barris helped him to his feet, loaning an arm to keep him steady.

"Never has such a thing been seen," Barris observed.

From Marne's body in the pit to the bodies of Ar and Logis fifty yards away, eight wolves lay dead or dying. It was a field of unprecedented carnage. When Grey turned to scan the spectators silently watching the battle, they retreated from his gaze.

Members of Wolf Camp reached the pit, expressing shock and outrage, but at the same time men from the southern camps arrived, and not far away, the men of Sparrow Camp were running to help

166

Barris. People in the crowd from Bear Camp and Squirrel Camp began a subtle shift away from Wolf Camp. The people of Raven Camp left the scene entirely. Wolf Camp was isolated, their best fighters dead, and for the first time in memory, they were outnumbered. They turned and ran.

Grey went the other direction, limping to a grassy beach not far from the old pier where he sank painfully to the ground. He didn't think he had been wounded too badly. Then again, he could be wrong. Clagg and Nole came forward. Shalli started to wash off the blood using water from the lake.

"You've made much food for the masters," Nole said, thoughtfully considering the ramifications.

"I don't know if this is a good thing," Clagg worried.

"Now we must call a council. They won't say no this time," Nole insisted. "We should call it for sunrise so the festival won't be spoiled."

Grey looked at Nole in surprise, amazed the festival was on his mind at such a moment, but then he reconsidered. The people had so little to look forward to, and spring festival was that rare event everyone anticipated all year long. He couldn't blame them.

"Should I return to camp?" Grey asked, unsure if his membership was now a liability.

"You're not going to move," Shalli said. "Wart, go back to camp. Bring the bag of medicines. Get a tent and blankets. We'll stay here at the lake tonight."

"That's not necessary," Grey said, trying to get up.

"I'll decide what's necessary," Shalli demanded.

Grey was quickly stripped of the bloody clothing, laying on the grass as half a dozen women gasped at the cuts and bruises. Not that the injuries were bothering their patient. The wounds seemed like old business to him. Pie went to wash out the stains, hanging the torn garments on a tree branch. Others began tearing strips of cloth from their outfits to use as bandages.

"Don't make such a fuss," Grey moaned, not happy with the attention.

"You stay quiet," Shalli ordered.

167

After inspecting the battlefield, Clagg and Nole returned to find their injured friend surrounded. He was awake, though not alert. Perhaps dazed.

"Marne and his gang are dead," Nole confirmed. "We've not seen any of the masters yet."

"Clagg, have someone put the bodies in an ore cart," Shalli instructed. "Roll them to the gate before the masters come looking."

"Father, we must be sure Wolf Camp doesn't come back," Tak said, taking a shirt from Burne and wrapping it around Shalli's bare shoulders.

"They won't come back. Ravo and Jarten are following them. Their whole camps are following them. Most of Deer and some of Squirrel Camp, too."

Grey heard what Nole said but didn't think much about it. He was just glad the trouble was over. The wounds ached, and without a pain killer, all he had was cool water that Beknar brought from the lake.

The sun was setting as Burne and Hernet arrived with a tent and sleeping furs, Wart having arrived earlier with the medical kit. Shalli had them set up camp near the southwest corner of the lake. Grey was relieved when he was able to take a painkiller. He also had Tak sit before him while he scrubbed out her scratches, and he sent Myra instructions for treating Court's head injury back at Deer Camp, telling Nole to keep her still for a few days. Leet's shoulder would take more time, but Grey had no doubt the treatments he advised would prove effective. Akrona had been a primitive world before the Arikhan arrived, and though the Arikhan were not inventors, they were good at adapting technology from other planets.

The medical kit was a good example. The bag had everything a battlefield medic would want, and Grey had his fair share of training. What proved unfortunate was that he couldn't treat the injury to his back, the stab wound out of reach. And too deep to ignore. Shalli and Tak tried to help, taking turns with the suturing, but it seemed to get worse instead of better. After awhile, they were forced to give up, putting a bandage over the stitching and hoping the bleeding would stop. It wasn't until Grey woke from a light sleep an hour later that he noticed the fires.

"What's going on?" he asked, smelling smoke and seeing flames on the north side of the lake.

"The people are angry with Wolf Camp," Shalli said, sitting on the ground watching over him. Grey noticed all the men and many of the women were gone.

"Help me up," Grey said, reaching for Tak.

"You shouldn't move. The stitches could tear open," Tak warned.

"The canoe tied at the dock. Does it still float? Is there a paddle?" Grey asked.

"It belongs to Rabbit Camp," Beknar said with disapproval.

"I'm going. Help or don't help," Grey persisted, struggling to his feet.

Shalli and Tak helped him up until he had his balance. He picked up a spare tent pole, tucked Marne's knife in his belt, and limped toward the dock twenty yards away. Shalli and Tak followed.

"What are you going to do?" Shalli asked as she and Tak helped him into the canoe.

"I'm going to stop this," he said.

"You won't be able to. The people have been suffering for years. Wolf Camp has much offended," Tak said.

"Mob violence won't benefit our camp. It won't benefit the other camps. It will just create another group like Marne's," Grey responded.

"There's always someone like Marne," Shalli replied.

"Not when people have the courage to prevent it," he insisted.

The canoe glided over the passive water, Shalli and Tak using the paddles. The surface reflected the stars and one of the moons. Light came from the guard station far to Grey's right, beyond the darkened Rabbit Camp. Up ahead, several fires lit the area where Wolf Camp stood at the mouth of a deep canyon. Somewhat to the left, torches and campfires marked Raven Camp's location.

When the canoe reached the north shore, Tak jumped out first to assist Grey from the boat. He didn't feel the help necessary. The drugs had given him a boost, and the stitches were strong enough to hold provided he didn't do anything rash. Like walk fast or twist suddenly. He decided maybe a little help wouldn't be so bad.

As he stepped out, Grey leaned on the staff and turned to tell the women to take the canoe back. Each was holding a paddle, ready to fight. He didn't try to talk them out of it, knowing neither would listen.

Wolf Camp was thirty yards back from the lake at the mouth of a large canyon, a sprawling collection of tents and several well-built cabins. Grey guessed a hundred and fifty people lived there, though few were evident. There was no mob. Hardly any noise. Just two burning cabins and a makeshift bonfire.

They entered the camp finding discarded objects and overturned tables. If there was a fight it hadn't lasted long. Toward the rear of the camp, not far from the canyon, they found several dozen women and children huddled in the brush.

"Where are your men?" Shalli asked, shocked by the fear in their eyes.

"They left us. They ran to Raven Camp," one of the women said.

"Is anyone hurt?" Grey asked.

"We hid. They had clubs," an older woman said.

"They'll kill us all!" another cried.

"Our camps don't kill women and little ones. We're not like Marne," Tak said.

"Marne never harmed women and little ones," the first woman defended.

"Marne and his wolves hurt Tak and many others," Shalli replied. "They murdered Bab. They attacked Court and Leet. They robbed and terrorized. You lived well while Marne's victims went hungry. Do you think we're stupid?"

"Please don't hurt us," a young woman begged, clutching her baby.

"The mob has moved on," Grey said to Shalli and Tak. "How do I reach Raven Camp?"

"The lake trail is easiest at night," Shalli said, pointing toward the distant torches. There was enough light reflecting off the lake to make out a well-worn path near the water.

They soon reached Raven Camp, the women leading the way. Grey found an angry mob being held at bay by a crude log barrier. Though much of the mob was shrouded in darkness, he guessed their numbers at several hundred. Beyond the barrier, he saw the men of

Raven Camp and refugees from Wolf Camp. There was a great deal of shouting and insulting going on, the mob trying to gain courage for the assault, Raven camp and the refugees trying to scare them away.

Shalli noticed Grey frown as he marched toward the confrontation, the staff nimble in his hand, his eyebrows narrowing with determination. Her eyes widened while her heart beat faster. Shalli wasn't afraid. Not of him. Not for him. He was a champion. A warrior. He had held up the mountain, fought ghosts, talked with the gods, and destroyed Marne's wolves. And he belonged to her.

The two sides were standing ten yards apart, a few throwing stones, most waving clubs or shaking fists. Torches lit the mob, bonfires showed the readiness of Raven Camp to defend itself. Both sides fell silent when Grey suddenly appeared in the open ground between them carrying the staff in his left hand.

"What seems to be the problem?" he asked, studying both groups.

Yelling broke out but he raised his hand for silence, walking up and down the agitated battle lines. Once the crowds were focused completely on him, he stopped before the log barrier.

"My name is Ben. I would speak with the camp leaders," he said. It was not a request.

"I am Sharlot, leader of Raven Camp," a tall, broad-shouldered female said. She was about Clagg's age with long auburn hair, a wide flat face, and intelligent brown eyes. Raven Camp's leader stood bravely in the firelight, but she looked stressed.

The refugees milled about in confusion until an older male stepped forward, his thin hair prematurely streaked with gray.

"I am Vester of Wolf Camp," the shaken man said, representing the leaderless camp. He was clearly afraid. They all were. Even more so, now that the slayer of the wolves stood before them.

"Several camps are angry with you," Grey said. "Other camps seek opportunity in your downfall. Will you agree to have their grievances arbitrated?"

"Who will judge?" Sharlot questioned.

"The leaders and dig captains will meet to seek agreement. I believe we will find suitable compromises. Do you agree to participate, or must this violence continue?" Grey asked.

171

Sharlot looked at the ugly mob. She had many people to protect. Her goods and food supplies needed to be preserved. There seemed little choice.

"I agree to arbitration," the leader of Raven Camp said.

"Even if we agree, they will not," Vester said, pointing at the mob.

"They will agree," Grey assured them.

"How do you know?" Vester asked.

"Because I'll kill anyone who doesn't," Grey replied.

Sharlot had no doubt he spoke the truth. The way he gripped the staff, and the fierce glint in his eye, caused her to take heed. The Raven Camp leader was thankful she hadn't rejected his demand.

"Wolf Camp agrees," Vester said.

Grey turned to climb on a fallen log where he could address the mob, a twinge in his back telling him some stitches had torn. In the torchlight, no one would notice.

"This is over. Return to your camps," Grey said.

"We will have retribution!" someone shouted.

"Vengeance for Bab!" a Deer Camp member demanded.

"Justice for our daughters!" a third said.

"The leaders will meet on the morning sun. Come to my tent near the dock. We will talk," Grey announced.

"No, we finish this now," a voice yelled from the back.

Grey dropped into a fighting stance readying the staff, scanning the mob for its boldest members as he'd been taught so long ago. Against the backdrop of the bonfires, many thought he looked like a hawk searching out the most vulnerable rodent in the field.

"If violence is what you want, let your leaders come forward first," Grey said, giving the staff a dramatic twirl. "But expect no more mercy than I gave Marne, because you don't deserve it."

"We don't want to hurt you, friend," Bear Camp's leader said.

"Don't worry, Jarten. You won't," Grey answered, holding the staff steady before him.

The mob hesitated. Grey knew all they needed now was a push in the right direction.

"Clagg, Cot, Hernet, my companions in the mines, often have you called me brother. Where stand my brothers now?" Grey asked.

"Nole, people of Deer Camp, you have called me friend. Tonight you must prove it. Ravo, you have boasted of Sparrow Camp's gratitude for the quarry. Now you may show it. Jarten, you asked for my friendship to make a quarry for Bear Camp. Prove to me now what Bear Camp's friendship is worth."

The mob muttered, Ferret and Deer Camp being the first to disengage. Clubs and stones were dropped to the ground. Shalli and Tak came forward, then Barris, Turk and Burne, all of the youngsters ready to fight at Grey's side. Even little Wart held a tree branch.

"We will have a council," Nole said, leader of the most aggrieved camp. "Everyone, leave this place. Remember we have spring festival. The children and women must not be disappointed."

The crowd broke up, disappearing into the dark night. Clagg and Nole came forward as Tak helped Grey down from the log. Tak felt the blood and showed her hand to Shalli, but neither woman said anything. When Sharlot climbed over the barrier, Jarten and Ravo came forward.

"We will meet as Ben said, at the old dock when the sun rises," Sharlot promised. "Wolf Camp will want their property returned."

"Will Wolf Camp return Sal's mate to him?" Nole asked.

"Marne is dead. The debt is paid," Vester said, reflecting Wolf Camp's bitterness.

"No debt is paid so easily," Nole insisted.

"Enough for tonight," Grey said. "We'll discuss these problems tomorrow. They will be resolved to everyone's satisfaction."

"And if they can't?" Old Ravo asked.

"Then I'll resolve them to *my* satisfaction," Grey concluded.

* * * * * *

The first day of spring festival was subdued, but when the leaders returned to their camps for the midday meal, hopes soared that the next two days would be better.

"Never have I seen such a thing," Clagg said, sitting down with his camp to explain the decisions. "Ben permitted no shouting and only a little argument. He listened carefully, asked many questions, and then told each leader what they would agree to. He didn't ask if

173

they agreed—he told them." Clagg laughed heartily. It was a good joke.

"Will there be peace between the camps?" Myra asked.

"Yes, for now," Clagg answered, taking her into his arms and holding Garn on his knee. "Property will be returned or exchanged. Even Raven Camp has agreed to give up some of what they've taken. And Ben will help each camp find better ore in time to make spring quota. Everyone gives up something but gains more. I think Ben has done this before. He speaks like one accustomed to being heard."

"He's not so meek as many believe," Myra mentioned.

"With Marne now food for the masters, the fear is gone," Cot said. "The young women will return to the fields. The camps will have visitors. Many are going to the lake tomorrow to revive old friendships."

"We should all go. Take our food and the children. A few of the tents," Myra said.

"And the mauck," Hernet added.

"Let's not wait for tomorrow. Shalli is there with Ben. Let's go now," Pie said.

Everyone burst into activity, it having been many years since such an event was possible. They had just finished packing when several unexpected visitors arrived, led by Nole and Turk.

"Nole, what brings you here?" Myra asked.

"We've come to help carry your camp to the festival," Turk said with a smile. A smile that grew bigger when he saw Pie, who blushed.

"But we only just decided. How did you know?" Beknar questioned. The visitors from Deer Camp laughed.

"Everyone's doing it. Even Raven Camp. Bear Camp arrived just as we finished setting up. Many are gathering wood for bonfires," Nole reported.

"It's going to be the best festival ever!" Turk boasted.

The food, tents and children were quickly gathered up, the people excited to reach the lake as soon as possible. As they started on the trail north, Nole fell back to speak privately with Clagg and Myra.

"Ben does not thrive," Nole said. "Even with the medicines, the wound continues to leak blood. Tak and Shalli have tried to sew it, but I'm afraid they made it worse."

"It's my fault. I should have looked at it last night. I was so busy worrying about Court and Leet that I didn't think of going to the lake," Myra said.

"I should have, too, but we needed the remembrances for Bab," Nole explained. "Someone said Thal should be asked to help, but no one knows her demands."

"Or if she can be trusted," Clagg warned.

"I could speak with her. Ask what she wants," Myra said.

"Someone should, but someone also needs to speak with Shalli. She guards Ben's tent like a she-bear and won't have Thal anywhere near," Nole reported.

"I will speak with Shalli," Clagg suggested.

"She's in love, Clagg. Truly in love for the first time. Speaking to her won't be easy," Myra said.

"Then I will spank her," Clagg insisted.

They reached the campground, finding dozens of tents arranged in a big circle around a huge stack of wood. Several camps were merged together sharing campfires and babysitting duties. Clagg took his people to a gap between Squirrel and Bear, two camps they hadn't visited for some time, and quickly set up the tents. It wasn't long before crowds were circulating to renew old acquaintances, often with apologies for the missing years.

Set back from the circle, in the large canvas tent used for the council meeting, Grey lay on a grass mat pawing through the Arikhan medical kit. But it wasn't the medicines that were failing, it was the poor surgery.

Shalli, Tak, and Barris sat with him telling stories of festivals past. Grey found the tales interesting and laughed at many of them. He was not in pain because of the drugs, but the continued seepage was causing concern.

"Maybe we should call Thal?" Barris dared to suggest.

"No, never. Ben put black hands on Thal. She'll never forgive the humiliation," Shalli said. "She could poison Ben and seek protection at Raven Camp. They are the strongest now. If not for Ben, they would dominate like Wolf Camp did."

"They aren't so bad," Barris said.

"You said that about Wolf Camp," Shalli reminded him.

"I was afraid of the wolves. I'm not afraid of Raven Camp," Barris said. "And no one will ever permit another Marne. Ben has shown us that Marnes only exist when we allow them. We've all learned. Bad things like that will never happen to our loved ones again."

Barris looked at Tak, who dropped her eyes and blushed. Though they tried to be subtle, Grey noticed Barris take Tak's hand. They seemed happy. Shalli noticed, too. Grey hadn't known it before, but Tak did not run back to Deer Camp like he asked. She ran to Sparrow Camp instead, which was closer, and met Barris on the trail. They had jumped Gronar together. Grey suspected they would be doing more together in the very near future.

"Maybe we should ask Thal for help?" Tak said after changing another blood-soaked bandage. She showed the bandage to Shalli. Shalli still refused.

"The bleeding has slowed. It will stop eventually," Grey supposed.

"We would like it to stop now instead of later," Tak replied.

Outside the tent, bonfires were lit. Singing began. Food and ale were being served. Soon there would be dancing and the playing of log drums.

"Enjoy the festival. I'm going to sleep for awhile," Grey said, rolling on his side to find a more comfortable position.

"I like it here," Shalli said, making a pillow from a folded fur.

"You keep me awake," Grey complained.

"If you hadn't turned your back on Lace, we would be dancing tonight. Maybe we would be doing more than dancing," Shalli suggested.

"Everyone does foolish things," Grey responded, resting his head.

Barris led Tak from the tent, walking toward Raven Camp's lodgings near the woods.

"What are you going to do?" Tak asked, walking quickly to match his rapid pace.

"I don't know. Not yet. But I know what needs to be done. I'm going to think like Ben. He doesn't always know what to do, either. He watches, listens, and then does what's necessary."

"You're going to talk with Thal, aren't you? Shalli won't like it. Ben might not like it, either."

"Ben is my friend. My brother. I will fight for him whether he likes it or not."

An hour later, Tak ran through the camp waving her hands. Both moons were up, one red on the eastern horizon, the other hanging yellow in the dark sky, partially hiding behind a gray cloud. A large bonfire was burning rotting timbers leftover from Sparrow Camp's abandoned mine. Myra stopped Tak outside the council tent.

"Child, what's wrong?" Myra asked.

"Thal is coming," Tak said, eyes bright with excitement. "She says to make boiled water and clean wraps. And we need lanterns. Lots of lanterns."

"Shalli refuses her help," Myra warned. "I'm worried, too. Thal's pride may cause her to hurt Ben. What demands has she made?"

"You'll see. Shalli will see, too. Everyone will see!" Tak shouted.

Tak went inside the tent. Shalli looked up from a half-sleep, lying cradled in Grey's arm.

"We must move outside," Tak said.

"Why?" Shalli asked.

"Thal is coming. She's going to stop the bleeding," Tak answered.

"No, she will not come," Shalli refused.

Tak knelt down to take Shalli's hands. "Am I not your friend? Do I not love Ben? Is Barris not his friend?"

Grey woke up and twisted against the irritation. The drugs were wearing off. He had hoped the dosage would last longer.

"Thal comes," Tak said to him.

"Thal's a witch doctor. She upsets the women of Ferret Camp," he dismissed.

"She can help," Tak insisted.

"I doubt it," Grey said, trying to sit up. He couldn't. His whole body had grown stiff.

"Maybe you should talk less and listen to your friends more?" Tak protested. Her tone shocked Shalli and surprised Grey. He smiled.

"You've grown bold, my little warrior," Grey said, happy to see her with such confidence.

"I've had a good teacher," Tak smiled back.

"We will hear what Thal has to say, if she really comes," he agreed.

The camp outside suddenly went quiet. Grey emerged from the tent hearing only the bonfire, supported by Tak and Shalli. They slowly walked to the ring of tents where hundreds of people were staring at a strange parade.

Two teenagers tapping small drums entered the meadow, followed by Barris carrying Thal's medical kit. They walked slowly with shoulders squared, faces solemn. Scores of people murmured, wondering what it meant.

Ten members of Raven Camp came next, mostly children carrying baskets. The procession circled the campfire before stopping in the largest clearing. Then Thal came forward dressed in a simple white cotton tunic, the skirt short. She wore no sandals or jewelry. Her black hair lay loose around her slender shoulders. The children spread mats on the ground before the fire and emptied the baskets, revealing jewelry, trinkets, and valuables.

"Look, Myra, it's your mother's bracelet," Pie said, pointing to a shiny circle of silver.

"And my favorite scarf," a woman noticed.

"Falat, look, there's my lynx tooth necklace," another remarked.

Thal raised her hands for silence as the bonfire crackled behind her, filling the moment with drama.

"You see here what I've taken in payment for my skills," Thal loudly announced. "It is yours once more. Reclaim that which was taken from you."

Then, to everyone's astonishment, Thal took off the cotton tunic and flung it into the fire, standing naked before the dancing flames. On her body, visible to all, were black handprints on her breasts and buttocks.

"More than any other, a healer knows what it is to wield the power of life and death, and must be tempered by that knowledge," Thal loudly declared. "I had forgotten the teachings of my calling until last night, when a valiant spirit gave me cause to remember. I am grateful to him. And to make sure I never forget again, I am no longer Thal of

178

Raven Camp. I am Black Hands of the People."

The newly christened Black Hands walked from the fire through the circle of speechless spectators and knelt before Grey.

"It would be an honor for Black Hands to have you as her first patient," the physician said, her dark brown eyes searching Grey's expression for forgiveness.

"I don't know. I'm deeply impressed by Black Hands, but Shalli says she doesn't show enough humility," Grey replied.

Red-faced with embarrassment, Shalli took off her shawl to drape over Black Hands' shoulders and kissed her reverently on the cheek.

"My words were ignorant. Please, Ben, let Black Hands treat your wound," Shalli begged, kneeling next to her.

"Shalli's words were not ignorant, yet would I be of service," Black Hands said.

"I would be grateful for your help, healer of the people, if you will let me find you suitable clothing on a cool night," Grey answered.

Instantly several women came forward offering a shirt, skirt and boots.

The red moon was high in the midnight sky when Black Hands emerged from the tent, washing blood from her hands. Myra, Court, and Sharlot were with her, all relaxed.

"She did a fine job, Shalli," Myra said, hugging her sister-in-law. "Black Hands' skills may have come dearly, but never was there doubt of her ability."

"The stitching and poultice will heal him quickly now. He may even walk by the festival's third day, if he's careful," Black Hands advised.

Many breathed sighs of relief, looking at Black Hands with new respect.

"Would you have a cup of mauck?" Clagg asked, handing her a goblet.

"Thank you, Clagg. How's your leg?" Black Hands inquired.

"It walks well," Clagg said with a smile.

Black Hands pulled her borrowed jacket tighter and noticed a pile of goods lying on a mat next to her baskets. Blankets, bowls, and more clothing than one person would ever need. Shalli and Tak smiled.

"These are yours, Black Hands," Shalli said. "After everything was taken back, people came with gifts for you. There is enough to be comfortable."

"There certainly is," Black Hands said, holding back tears.

Grey wanted to be up and walking the next day, but no one would let him, so he waited for the festival's final morning to visit the camps. Myra and Clagg accompanied him, making introductions and having Grey hold Garn's hand so fewer would be afraid. The slayer of the wolves looked less fearsome with a smiling child at his side.

At noon, a great meal was held with the leaders giving speeches from a tree stump. Clagg spoke first, his booming voice echoing through the grassy fields. Grey was surprised to find Clagg could be eloquent when the occasion required, his words of brotherhood and mutual challenges finding a receptive audience.

Sharlot spoke next, assuring everyone that the former troubles between the northern and southern camps were now forgotten. All knew she was being optimistic, but they appreciated her effort.

The Raven Camp leader was followed by Barris, who made a few encouraging remarks on behalf of Old Ravo. Though bold in the quarry and in council, Ravo was known to be a poor public speaker, and none trusted his temper.

Nole declined his place on the podium, preferring to convey his thoughts to the camps privately. Jarten's words on behalf of Bear Camp were kept short and the leader of Squirrel Camp was equally brief. Without a formal leader, Wolf Camp declined to participate in the addresses, and Rabbit Camp was not invited to speak.

Several times during the proceedings, eyes turned toward Grey, who sat between Shalli and Tak near Ferret Camp's cooking fire. Apparently they expected him to say something. They were disappointed.

After the speeches and some afternoon sporting events, the cooks prepared to serve a final meal. Dishes were shared generously with every camp and the people were eager, but the celebration grew quiet when the Arikhan arrived.

"Welcome, masters," Sharlot said on her knees. As leader of the most powerful camp, the duty was gladly ceded to her.

"Someone has delivered much meat to the pens," Nabbatron said, scanning the assembled slaves. Behind Nabbatron stood Frontra and Bortro. All three were armed.

"There were disturbances, master, but they have been resolved," Sharlot said.

"Are all the camps here?" Frontra asked, recognizing a diversity of faces.

"Yes, mistress. For the first time in a great while, we dwell together," Sharlot confirmed.

"Where is the half-meat? It is the one I most expected to see," Nabbatron inquired.

"Here, master," Grey responded from the rear.

Barris and Turk helped Grey up and he slowly walked to the guards, kneeling again with some difficulty.

"I smell fresh blood. Is the wound disabling?" Bortro asked, his brown cheeks flushing with hungry interest.

"No, master. I will work again soon. Forgive me if it displeases you," Grey said.

"The creature is impertinent," Bortro complained, his fat tongue clicking with disgust.

"It matters not. I no longer yearn for its flesh," Nabbatron said. "But its aggression has lost us many strong workers. This must be accounted for."

The crowds murmured, much to Nabbatron's surprise. He was not accustomed to such a reaction

"Excuse me, master. May I speak?" Nole requested, rushing forward to kneel at Nabbatron's feet.

He was quickly joined by leaders from Ferret, Bear, and Squirrel camps. Impressive support, Grey thought, but not necessarily good.

"Speak," Nabbatron allowed.

"The wolves preyed upon our women and the weak. We could not work the fields or trade goods. Our camps will work harder now. Through cooperation, we will make quota more often," Nole explained.

"It is true, master," Sharlot said, still bowing low in supplication.

181

Grey was surprised to find the northern camp leader pleading his cause with so much to gain by his absence. Machiavelli would not have approved.

"Ferret Camp has prospered. Other camps will prosper," Clagg said.

Listening closely, Nabbatron did not detect rebellion in their speech. The alien eyed Grey again, suspicious but not unduly alarmed. Not yet. Grey knew just what Nabbatron was thinking, and Nabbatron could tell Grey was thinking it, too.

"The half-meat will come with us. The rest may continue the feast," Nabbatron decided.

Dozens of people began to rise, but not to continue their meals. There was a sense of dissension in the air that caused the sentries to put claws on their sidearms. Grey jumped up quicker than any of them, even though the sudden motion hurt. He put a hand on Clagg's shoulder to keep him down and held out a hand to Nole and Barris. The leaders retook their submissive positions, signaling for everyone to remain still. After a moment of hesitation, they held back. All except Shalli.

"That's wrong! All Ben did is protect us!" Shalli shouted, running up to Nabbatron and waving an angry finger in his face.

Before Nabbatron could react, Grey swept around with a gentle roundhouse kick, knocking Shalli's legs out from under her. She gasped with surprise as she fell, landing on her rear. Grey pressed her to the ground, almost sitting on her.

"Excuse the female, masters. She suffers from a fever of the brain," Grey said, preventing Shalli from speaking.

"This we have seen," Nabbatron responded without anger.

"Come, food creature," Bortro ordered, taking out a light chain and attaching it to Grey's slave collar. Grey gave Shalli a warning stare as he was led away to the main gate. Frontra lingered behind.

"You are a foolish creature, Shalli. It is good Ben has the wisdom you lack," Frontra scolded, using a claw to raise her up.

"I do not understand, mistress," Shalli said.

"Nabbatron will only question Ben about the fight so a report may be submitted to the Sarden Leader," Frontra said. "Ben is a clever animal. He will provide satisfactory answers. But if Ben becomes a focus of rebellion, he will be sent to the pens."

"Frontra speaks truly. Generous are the masters to overlook your words," Myra agreed.

"I am sorry, mistress. Please forgive my stupidness," Shalli said.

"You have a fever of the brain. It is called love. Do you think we of the superior race do not understand such things?" Frontra questioned.

"Even Nabbatron?" Shalli asked.

"Yes, foolish creature. Even Nabbatron," Frontra answered.

"Will you join us, mistress?" Myra asked.

"I will stay but a moment," Frontra agreed, aware her presence would chill the festivities. "But I would like a cup of mauck. Who was nearest the battle?"

"I, mistress," Tak said, standing up.

"And I," Barris said, quickly at her side.

"Was it Ben alone who slew the wolves?" Frontra wanted to know.

"Barris hit Gronar with a club," Tak mentioned, giving him a smile.

"Tak bit Gronar's ear," Barris boasted. "But Ben slew the wolves. He moved faster than a hawk. The blows of his staff struck with the force of falling rock."

"He was slower after Lace stabbed him, but not much slower," Tak said.

"Tell me everything. Leave out nothing," Frontra said, accepting a stool to sit on.

The people of the camps crowded around even though many had already heard the details. The story got better each time it was told. Frontra's eye-rings jumped with delight as Tak and Barris took turns acting out the moves, her tongue often clicking with excitement. She stayed for three cups of mauck.

The sun had set when Grey emerged from the guard post and staggered through the gate. Several people were there to meet him, all worried. Grey offered a weary smile.

"What's wrong? Did they beat you? Did they use the shock stick?" Shalli asked, rushing to support him.

"No, but Bortro enjoyed making threats," Grey said, his eyes red and legs weak.

"You don't look well. Let us carry you," Barris offered, motioning for Turk to help.

"I'd prefer to walk awhile," Grey declined.

Black Hands looked into his eyes, put her palm against his forehead, and smelled his breath.

"Ben is drunk," Black Hands announced.

"Drunk!" Tak shouted.

"You should see the masters. Most are passed out on the floor," Grey said with a chuckle.

"They didn't hurt you, did they?" Shalli asked.

"No. After the first round of questioning, they wanted me to tell about the fight again," Grey explained. "Dhartro thought to loosen my tongue with Lafarian wine, so we all started drinking and swapping tales. I must have told the story four times."

"It's a good story," Wart said.

"Are there going to be problems? Is the Sarden Leader displeased?" Barris asked.

"I'm not sure. Romtra gave us permission to expand mining operations provided we show results. As long as we make quota, everything should be fine."

Shalli gave him a hug, then placed herself under his arm to help him walk. Tak went to assist on the other side.

"Were there surprises at the festival this year?" Grey asked.

"A few. There will be more at the harvest festival," Barris responded, making sure Tak was paying attention.

"I'm sorry there weren't more surprises. I heard someone was hoping for one," Grey said, kissing Shalli on the forehead.

"You are too hurt for a surprise," Shalli complained. "Maybe you let Lace cut you on purpose so there would be no surprise."

"We're going to have a good spring season," Grey said. "With luck, every camp will make quota. The gardens will be full. When the harvest comes, it will be a joyful time."

Shalli jumped to kiss him, almost climbing up as she clutched his shoulders. Black Hands warned her to be careful.

"I'll be careful," Shalli said in her most sultry voice. "Until you feel better. Then you had better watch out."

Turk and Wart blushed. Barris and Tak smiled.

"Now, my friends, you see my life as it has always been, lurching from one danger to another," Grey said.

This time it was Shalli who blushed.

Chapter Six
SURPRISES

Grey had predicted the spring season correctly. There was excitement during the final weeks as each camp looked forward to making quota, some with double digit surpluses. With extra help in the fields, and Grey's new windmill driving the water pumps, the gardens produced a food surplus as well. But it didn't mean everyone was happy.

Where a temporary council tent once stood at the southwest edge of the lake, a timber frame cabin with a shingle roof was now used for meetings. A long pinewood table was set with nine chairs, one for each camp leader, one for Black Hands, and one for Grey. A chair Grey rarely used.

"Ben should be at these gatherings," Old Ravo demanded, scratching his shaggy gray beard with one hand and holding a cup of mauck in the other.

"We don't need him. His ways are strange," the new leader of Wolf Camp said, a tough miner with large hands and an angry glare. "And the explosive chemicals are dangerous. They shouldn't be allowed."

"Your resentment is clear, Birner. Ben broke the power of your camp, but he's also helped," Nole said.

"If he doesn't want the honor of this table, let him stay away," Birner insisted.

"Ben hasn't done anything for Rabbit Camp," Kaylo said, a thin older woman with stringy gray hair.

"What is there to do? All you do is move ore through the gate and prowl the gardens like field mice. None of you work," Ravo said.

"Our work is hard. No one appreciates Rabbit Camp," Kaylo lamented.

The other leaders laughed at her.

"Ben hasn't attended a meeting since the two moons. Does anyone know why?" Jarten asked, searching Clagg for an answer.

"Ben doesn't feel he belongs at this table. He's not a camp leader. He's not a healer of the people like Black Hands," Clagg explained.

"Maybe he just doesn't want responsibility," Eck grumbled. "We couldn't get a quarry at Squirrel Camp, so we tunnel instead. The tunnel Ben made could be better."

"Our tunnel should be better, too. We have lost property to make up for," Birner complained.

"He spends too much time in the gardens with the women," Eck protested. "Why irrigate so many new fields? There's nothing wrong with the old ones."

"Our quarry is good, but it won't last the year. He should spend more time searching for ore. Less time etching with those damn pencils," Ravo said.

"Should we vote?" Kaylo asked.

"Vote on what? What's the question?" Clagg asked.

"There is no question, only ungrateful camps who want unearned rewards," Nole said.

"You have a quarry. The best one," Eck replied.

"Your surpluses outweigh ours combined," Birner whined.

"The northern camps are not well served. What does Raven Camp think?" Jarten asked.

Sitting at the head of the table with Black Hands on her left, Sharlot looked at the men with disdain. Her reaction was noted.

"What's wrong?" Nole asked.

"You men sicken me. Send your women here next week so we can get something accomplished," Sharlot replied.

"What female insurrection provokes this?" Ravo asked with a condescending grin.

"Which camp does Ben belong to?" Sharlot asked, letting her long hair drop as she leaned forward. Her low cut tunic was a momentary distraction.

"All know it is Ferret Camp," Jarten said.

"How much time has Ben spent at Ferret Camp's quarry this season?" Black Hands asked, sharing Sharlot's contempt.

"Very little," Clagg said, the issue a well-known sore point.

"How can Ben spend time at Ferret Camp while working at all the other camps? And preparing explosives? And exploring the mountain for new ore?" Sharlot said. "What gratitude have you shown him? What compensation have you given Ferret Camp for his services?"

"Sharlot speaks what many women in the camps feel," Black Hands said, her dark eyes staring down the table. "Shalli cries because she thinks Ben is leaving her camp. He works all day, often without rest. While you men are at the campfires singing songs and sharing the day's troubles, he labors through the night with his strange drawings."

"And the masters watch him too closely. You have all seen it," Sharlot elaborated. "He's smarter than they are. A good fighter. They fear he may turn the workers against them. Ben would be wiser to stay at Ferret Camp, mate with Shalli, and sleep when the sun goes down as we do. Instead, he risks much to help our camps. Your ingratitude is outrageous. Am I a fool to expect more?"

"I've spoken of this to Ben. So has Myra. We want him to take a mate and settle down," Clagg said.

"Court and I have spoken as well. We've asked Tak and Barris to speak to him. If you wish to vote, let's vote that Ben must stay within his own quarry from now on," Nole suggested.

"You would like that, wouldn't you? Then only your camps would make quota," Birner said, eyeing Nole with jealousy, for many thought Deer Camp was growing strong at Wolf Camp's expense.

"You argue over nothing," Ravo suddenly shouted, his great fist pounding the table and making the cups fly. "Ben will do as he finds necessary. Always has it been so. But there's a truth here. I, myself, will find a way of showing appreciation."

"Like when you tried selling him to Marne?" Jarten asked.

Ravo's face grew red and he lunged across the table, arms outstretched, but Jarten jumped back out of reach. Clagg and Nole helped restrain Ravo until he calmed.

"We'll all make quota this season," Sharlot said. "The masters may give us a three-day holiday to celebrate. Let's make this a happy time for our camps. Let's not ask for more than Sherra gives."

"Blessings on Sherra," many at the table whispered.

After the meeting, Sharlot went to Clagg and Nole before they reached the south trail.

"Will there be any surprises at the harvest celebration?" Sharlot asked.

"I think Barris will have a surprise for Tak," Nole said. "Not long ago, I would have said no, but he's changed. It will be a good match."

"They're welcome to join Raven Camp if they want a new start," Sharlot offered.

"If there's a surprise, Barris has asked if he and Tak can join Ferret Camp. They have many friends among my people," Clagg mentioned.

"No surprises coming from Ferret Camp? Shalli must be well into her eighteenth year by now," Sharlot asked.

"I don't know. Shalli is nervous," Clagg said. "We haven't seen much of Ben lately. He's spends much time on the mountain searching for new mines."

"If there is a surprise, Raven Camp would like to make gifts," Sharlot said. "Our quarry is good and will last a long time. And we haven't forgotten what he did for us the night the wolves died."

"I'll let Ben know. It's good to have gifts when starting a new life," Clagg said. "Do you really think the masters may take Ben from us?"

"It would be best if he doesn't attract too much attention. Dhartro makes many inquiries, as does Romtra," Sharlot advised.

"Nabbatron, too," Nole mentioned. "What of Frontra?"

"Many times have I seen Ben and Frontra speaking. I don't think it's a bad thing," Clagg guessed.

"I hope you're right," Sharlot said.

* * * * * *

"There you are. No one has seen you in days," Shalli said, finding Grey in his old forest hiding place near Ferret Camp's quarry. The trees were tall enough and the brush thick enough to ensure privacy. The small rock damn holding back the pond steadily trickled water. Nearby, a fire was heating a pail of rocks for the sweat lodge.

"Many people have seen me," Grey disagreed. "I spent the morning at Raven Camp. Black Hands and I plan to build an infirmary in the maple grove. And I've started a new irrigation system in the meadow below Sparrow Camp. The soil there is rich. Eck also wanted me to take another look for a quarry, but the ore deposits above Squirrel Camp are poor. He's very unhappy."

"But Ferret Camp is your home. This is where you belong," Shalli insisted.

Finding the rocks hot enough, Grey used a pole to move the pail to the sweat lodge, setting it down just inside the door. Shalli waited for a response that he seemed reluctant to give.

Grey initially hesitated to undress, but when Shalli stripped down to nothing and crawled in ahead of him, he sighed and took off his clothes. Though casual nudity was not a custom in his home culture, the slaves of Karak could rarely afford such modesty.

"Don't you think I'm pretty anymore?" Shalli asked, raising her arms above her head as the first clouds of steam filled the tent. Her fresh young skin tingled in the flush of heat.

"There's no doubt you're pretty," Grey was forced to agree.

"Then what's wrong? You can't say I'm a child anymore."

"I have many more years than you. By Karak standards, I'm almost an old man."

"You're not so old. Why don't you tell me the truth?" Shalli pressed.

Grey poured a little more water on the rocks and leaned back on a grass bale to enjoy the steam. Shalli is right, he decided. She deserves the truth. Some of it.

"Shalli, I care for you. I care for you very much. But a mating wouldn't be fair. Someday the masters will find out who I am. When they do, they'll take me away. Even if they don't, marrying you would still be wrong. I already have a wife."

"A wife? pressed.? Where? Not someone in Raven Camp?"

"No, not in Raven Camp. On the world where I came from."

"But you haven't seen her in years, and you can never go back. Isn't that what you said? That you can never go back? How can she still be your wife if you'll never see her again?"

"We're still married. The distance doesn't matter."

"Your people think you're dead, don't they? You told me that once. You said everyone thinks you're dead, and even you sometimes think it's true."

"I'm sure they believe I was killed," Grey admitted.

"And the one who was your wife, she thinks you're dead, too?"

"Without doubt."

"Then she might have remarried already. Isn't it true that she might have a new mate? Doesn't your culture permit such a thing?"

"I hope she found someone. She's too young to live the rest of her life alone."

"So are you," Shalli said, leaning over to kiss him.

Grey gently pushed her back, though Shalli suspected he did so reluctantly.

"What was she like? Was she anything like me?" Shalli asked.

He laughed, thought the question over, and laughed again. Shalli frowned, her lip curled in a pout.

"You're being mean," Shalli complained.

"I don't wish to be, but it's funny."

"Tell me why it's funny," she demanded.

"Because you have almost nothing in common. She's a soldier. A butt-kicking, in-your-face fire-eater. She graduated from a famous naval college and won many awards for heroism. She's got black hair, blazing green eyes, and shoulders straight as Sharlot's. And she has a mouth on her that could shame a sailor. I've heard language that's left me blushing."

"And I'm just a stupid little slave girl," Shalli said. "I've never been to a school. Never held a weapon. Myra doesn't even like me to raise my voice. Is that why you don't want me? Because I'm not good enough?"

"You can't think that. Not ever," he said, pulling her into his arms. "It's not that I wouldn't want you if things were different. My wife could be very sweet, but you're lovable. She's an educated woman, but in many ways, you're just as smart. And you both care deeply about things that are important. Probably more than I do. You have nothing to be ashamed of. On my world, there would be legions of men fighting to be your mate. I might even be one of them."

Shalli rested her head against Grey's chest as he stroked her long soft hair. His touch was gentle. Sad. Shalli sensed that he still loved the wife he would never see again, but suspected something else was bothering him. Something that had nothing to do with a lost woman from his mysterious past.

"Why would the masters take you away?" Shalli suddenly asked.

Grey was surprised by her question, though on reflection, he realized it was a possibility he never should have revealed. Shalli could be very intuitive, and once again she had picked up on a careless comment.

"We were enemies in a war," he said, hoping she would drop the subject.

"The masters have lots of enemies. What makes you so special?" she asked, suddenly sensing his reluctance was more serious than he pretended.

Grey lingered on her question. He had been Ben ever since the night Clagg was injured, from the middle name of Benjamin given to him by the father he never knew. But his real name was too dangerous to reveal. It always would be. He wasn't prepared to put Shalli in harm's way.

"Maybe I'll seek a new mate someday, when I'm ready. But that might be a long time from now. You shouldn't wait," Grey urged.

"That's for me to decide," Shalli replied.

She leaned up to kiss him, and this time he returned her kiss, though not with the enthusiasm she hoped for.

Grey had not been on Ferret Camp's mountain for more than a month. The star chart he had carved on the limestone cliff was weathered but still readable, the calculations revealing the convoluted descriptions of three-dozen star systems. One of the star systems was the place of his birth, where a minor moon orbited a minor planet orbiting a minor sun. He remembered being close to tears the day the chart was finally completed, but those days were gone now, replaced with new responsibilities.

There was a noise in the brush, too loud to be a small animal. The experiences of Grey's youth caused him to reach for a sidearm that wasn't there. But this wasn't the land of his youth; it was a weed-covered hillside on a warm spring day twelve hundred light-years from home.

"Be not alarmed, half-meat," Frontra said, emerging from the overgrown trail. Grey relaxed, not that he would have fought any of the guards.

"Welcome, Frontra. What brings you to my camp?" Grey inquired.

Frontra clicked her tongue in amusement.

"When did a cave of dead leaves become a camp?" Frontra asked.

"When did the masters begin to inspect caves of dead leaves?"

"I inspect nothing. I seek the impertinent food creature who causes endless controversy."

"He's not here right now, but I'll gladly take a message," Grey said.

Frontra clicked her tongue even more rapidly, demonstrating how much she appreciated the jest.

"Mauck?" Grey asked, producing a clay jug.

Frontra took a seat on a flat rock next to Grey where they could look at the star chart. Though not an astronomer, she had no trouble deciphering the basic patterns.

"Which system holds your world?" Frontra asked.

Grey poured a generous amount of mauck into his cup, gave the cup to Frontra, and kept the jug for himself.

"It is better we not talk of it," he said.

Frontra glanced at him with her large black eyes, her long pale tongue lashing briefly from her thin mouth. Her posture didn't change, but Grey knew she was curious.

"It must be far away," Frontra guessed.

"All the stars are far away," Grey answered.

"For a slave, they are far away. Even for a camp guard, the journeys are long. How far away are they for you?"

Grey was intrigued. He and Frontra had spoken of many things. The slave culture. The wolves. Religious philosophy. Arikhan civilization. He could not remember her ever asking such specific questions about his past.

"Are we friends?" Grey asked.

"To the extent our positions allow."

"Then tell me why you make such delicate inquiries?"

"I ask because I think you are far away from home. Perhaps too far to ever return. Do I think falsely?"

"You do not."

"Then why must you hesitate?"

"Hesitate?"

Frontra took a deep breath of the warm air before raising her slender chin. Her eye-rings rose with obvious pique. Her brown cheeks gathered the slightest trace of gray. She was not angry, but she was annoyed. Grey refilled her cup.

"You give the food creatures courage, Ben," Frontra explained. "You have wisdom cherished by Sherra. Knowledge that brings wealth. Strength in times of crisis. Yet you stand aside from your people. How can they embrace your unique faith if you refuse to be one of them?"

"Pardon me, mistress, but your words are dangerous. What are you suggesting?" Grey asked with alarm.

"Not insurrection, if that is what troubles you. But I know, to the depth of Sherra's Soul, that exploiting sentient life as we do is an abomination. Our empire must change. It must be inspired to change. For change to occur, the food creatures must prove they are not food creatures. As you have."

"I am sorry, Frontra, but you *do* speak of insurrection. Well do I know the Arikhan temperament. To even hint of the changes you suggest would send me to the pens and take much of Ferret Camp with me. Let us finish the mauck and say no more about it."

"You do not deny my philosophy. I also glimpse that elusive glimmer in your eyes. The shine that summons old memories. Have you no truth to share?"

Grey took a deep swig from the clay jar. He had always liked Frontra. He had risked his life for her.

"It has been a long time since I shared radical thoughts with one such as yourself," Grey recalled. "You remind me of days long ago where another world struggled with similar challenges. They, too, oppressed slaves in ignorance of Sherra's teachings."

"In what manner were this planet's issues resolved?"

194

"In blood, my friend Frontra. And the issues were not resolved."

Frontra took a moment to study Grey, attempting to find clues to his thoughts. She had wondered if the planet of his origin had been a violent world, and now she knew.

"Drink deeper of the jug, half-meat. I surpass you," Frontra said.

"This is a pleasant day to share good talk, but you still have me in mystery. Why did you seek me out?" Grey asked.

Frontra seemed particularly delighted by his question. And she refused to answer.

That evening, just as the sun was setting, Clagg saw Grey coming down from his old burrow on the mountain. Grey looked tired and troubled.

"Ben, I've been waiting for you," Clagg said.

After washing off in the shallow creek below the old mine, Grey sat for a moment on the sandy embankment. The stars were coming out in force. Clagg thought there was a particular grouping that seemed to have Grey's attention.

"You've had much on your mind lately," Clagg said.

"It seems to always be that way," Grey replied.

"Have you been thinking about a surprise?"

"I've given it consideration."

"Why must you think so much? Shalli loves you. Everyone thinks it's a good match."

"I don't want to hurt Shalli, but I already have a wife," he explained.

"Out there? In the stars?" Clagg asked.

"Yes, out there in the stars. It hurts to know I'll never see her again. I wouldn't want Shalli to feel like that if I suddenly disappear someday. She should find someone else."

"Are you worried about the masters, too?"

"Frontra warns that the Sarden Leader requests frequent reports on my activities."

"I've not heard you suggest rebellion. They have no reason for fear."

"You really don't know me very well, do you?" Grey said, almost smiling.

"No one does, but that isn't our fault."

Grey nodded, the smile disappearing.

"My friend, we live in a slave camp on a conquered world," Clagg lectured. "Life can be short. If you bring Shalli happiness, even for a brief time, wouldn't it be worthwhile? If Shalli can bring you happiness, then it's much earned. Would Shalli make you happy?"

"Of course. She's bright and sassy. And smarter than many think," Grey confessed.

"There's only a week left in the season. Many would like to make gifts. What should I tell those who ask?"

Grey glanced up at the darkening sky, looking toward a star not quite bright enough to be seen in the twilight. Clagg put his on hand on Grey's shoulder.

"The one who was your wife. The one who may still be your wife. Would she want you to be happy?" Clagg asked.

"Yes, she would."

"Then maybe it's time. The life we have here isn't the one you knew, but it still has much to offer," Clagg stressed.

Grey reflected on Clagg's words. And remembered what he had said to his friends those many years ago, when he knew attacking *Bellerophon* might be his final mission. He urged them to be happy. To move forward. And suddenly he realized why Frontra had come to him on the mountain. Apparently even the Arikhan sentry could see that which he did not.

* * * * * *

A few days before the end of the season, Ferret Camp stopped work early in the afternoon. They were already above quota and didn't want to make the other camps more jealous than necessary. Moved from its old site to be nearer the quarry, the moth-eaten tents were gone now, replaced by sturdy huts. Adjoining the new fire pit was a stone oven for baking bread. Several lanterns hung from tree branches. They soon had visitors.

"How was the surprise?" Myra asked with a grin.

"I was shocked. Who would guess that Barris would choose me?" Tak said, still breathless from the proposal.

Barris smiled, holding Tak's hand. Shalli's eyes were wide with happiness for her friend. She looked down the trail, but it was empty.

"Isn't Ben with you?" Shalli asked.

"Ben is still visiting Deer Camp. There were many unmated women left after I picked Tak," Barris said. "I think some are disappointed. We haven't gone back to Sparrow Camp yet, so our promise isn't confirmed. Because Nole and Ravo aren't on good terms, Ben is going with us. He'll speak on Tak's behalf to my father. There are many unmated women at Sparrow Camp, too. I hear they seek a surprise."

"Ben isn't interested in anyone from Sparrow Camp. Or Deer Camp, either," Shalli said, her chin tucked in.

"Many women want Ben. Gifts have been offered," Myra said.

"No, he doesn't care about gifts," Shalli denied, crossing her arms.

"Raven Camp thinks he should live there," Clagg said offhandedly.

"Ben would never leave Ferret Camp. Would he?" Shalli asked.

"Raven Camp is strong now. And much grateful," Myra said. "Sharlot thinks Ben would make a good match for Black Hands. They build the infirmary together and speak far into the night on ways to help the people. Together they would wield great power."

"Black Hands is old. Old and wrinkled," Shalli protested.

"Black Hands and Ben are the same age, Shalli dear, and she's quite lovely," Myra responded. "Wouldn't such a match benefit Ferret Camp, Clagg?"

"It's something to think about. But first we need to talk. Barris came to me with a question that only the camp can answer."

"We welcome you Barris, friend from Sparrow Camp. Ferret Camp would like to hear your question," Myra said in formal greeting.

Barris stood before the cooking fire where all could see him, holding Tak's hand. He was dressed in his best brown leathers, she wore an attractive blue dress with a long skirt. The late afternoon was warm but not unpleasant. Many of the people sat back in the shade of the trees, though a few children gathered close.

"Tak and I are promised to be mated, but there's a problem," Barris said. "I'm the son of Old Ravo, leader of Sparrow Camp. Tak is daughter to Nole, leader of Deer Camp. Our camps have not always been friendly. Someday Tak and I would like to start our own camp, but until then, we wish to join Ferret Camp where we have many friends."

"It's a good question," Clagg said. "Barris came to me several days ago. Myra would welcome them. Would anyone else welcome them?"

"I would welcome them," Beknar said, standing next to Myra.

"And I," Seenar said, tugging up her long cotton skirt as she rose.

"I also say welcome," Hernet agreed, rising from his stool to show approval.

"I would welcome you," Cot agreed. "But would you still want to live here if Ben goes to Raven Camp?"

"Ben will not go to Raven Camp!" Shalli shouted, causing many to exchange glances.

"Yes, we would still want to live here," Barris said.

"Are you willing to accept the risk?" Clagg asked.

"What risk?" Barris replied.

"Even though you are promised, Tak is still unmated. If we accept you, she'll remain available until the mating ceremony. Someone else may want to surprise her," Myra explained.

"Like Ben, for instance," Cot said, walking around the couple to appraise Tak's attractions, of which there were many. He tugged at her shoulder strap, touched the softness of her hair, and motioned to the men how worthy she would be as a mate.

"Everyone knows Ben loves her greatly," Cot added. "She is beautiful and healthy, with good hips for child bearing. Her father is leader of Deer Camp and well thought of."

"It would be a good match," Seenar agreed.

"Maybe Ben would not want Black Hands if he could mate with Tak and stay here? We could offer gifts," Hernet suggested.

Many nodded. Shalli was not pleased.

"I will accept the risk," Barris said, though he sounded nervous.

"Are there any other questions?" Clagg asked. There were none. "Then it's agreed. If Barris and Tak mate, they will become members of Ferret Camp at the end of season. All will make them welcome."

The congratulations were still being made when Grey appeared on the trail from Deer Camp. He was dressed in a fine deerskin outfit and rawhide boots, a broad brim straw hat, and a new green scarf around his neck. There was a bounce in his stride and a pleased look in his eyes. Many were startled to see him smiling.

"Greetings brothers and sisters of Ferret Camp," Grey said. "Welcome, my friends, Barris and Tak. Deer Camp comes to share a meal with us. They will be here soon."

"Ben, we have told Ferret Camp of the surprise and asked to become members. We have been welcomed," Barris announced.

Grey stepped forward and gripped Barris' arm. Many suspected Barris had become his closest friend, which influenced their decision to accept him.

"Clagg, with my friend Barris soon to be mated, perhaps it's time I choose a mate. What do you think?" Grey asked.

"You're not getting any younger, little brother. Maybe it's time," Clagg agreed. "Ferret Camp has several unmated women. One may be selected if you are worthy."

Grey took off his shirt and rolled up his pants, showing strong lines of hard muscle. For those who remembered the day Frontra had first brought the skin and bones stranger to their camp many seasons before, the transformation seemed remarkable.

"As you see, I am healthy and a good worker," Grey said. "I have helped make quota. There are people who will speak for me."

"All this is known. You are a worthy match," Clagg confirmed.

"Which unmated women are available?" Grey asked, putting his shirt back on.

"There are several," Clagg said, waving his hand.

Shalli, Pie, and Keep quickly lined up near the fire, even though Keep was still a year too young. The younger girls were all smiles. Shalli looked anxious when Grey held back, standing between Cot and Hernet, consulting with them in soft whispers.

"Are there no others?" Grey asked.

"Barris agreed Tak could be selected," Clagg said.

"It's true," Barris acknowledged, releasing Tak's hand and sending her to the group.

Now Shalli grew worried, for all knew Grey and Tak were close friends. Closer than friends. Shalli looked to Tak for a reaction, but Tak appeared pleased to join the group, shaking out her long black hair and opening her top to reveal more cleavage. She fluttered her long eyelashes and dipped her head submissively.

"It's still a small selection," Grey said. "There are four times this number at Raven Camp. Many were the generous offers when I visited there this morning. Sharlot said many want to make gifts."

"If you would like to wait for Deer Camp, Nole has more young women who might be acceptable," Clagg suggested.

Grey sighed with impatience.

"Let me look at these first," Grey opted, going to Pie and then Keep.

The young women flashed shy smiles and looked down, their cheeks flushing. Then Grey went to Shalli, looked at her briefly but with little interest, and went to Tak at the end of the line. When Grey took her hands, Tak smiled with delight, ignoring Shalli's stunned disappointment. Tak whispered in his ear. Grey laughed, his gray eyes sparkling with delight. They hugged, Grey pressing her head into his shoulder with genuine warmth.

"Perhaps the choice isn't so hard after all," Grey conceded, standing back and looking Tak in the eyes. She moistened her lips.

"Have you made a selection?" Clagg asked even as many were looking toward Barris for his reaction. The smile had disappeared from the young man's face, replaced by an apprehensive frown. Shalli saw the frown and felt her heart pounding with trepidation.

"Yes, I've made my selection," Grey said.

"Who will be your mate?" Clagg asked.

"I select Shalli," Grey answered.

"Me? You've picked me? Ben, I love you! I love you so much!" Shalli shouted, leaping into his arms and smothering his face with kisses.

The camp applauded while exchanging suggestive remarks. Tak ran back to Barris, laughing as she gave him a kiss. Clagg and Myra also grinned, looking at others who were enjoying the joke.

"I think she was surprised," Myra said.

* * * * * *

A three-day holiday was granted due to the outstanding success of the spring season, every camp having made quota. Many rewards were expected to make the fall season comfortable.

The camps used the first day of the holiday to relax, enjoy their achievements privately, and prepare for the festivities. By dawn of the second day, tents were appearing at the lake. A great circle was gradually being formalized, white stones marking a ring around the beginnings of a bonfire. The new slate roof on the council cabin was so strong that some used it as an observation platform.

By late morning the camps had arrived and cooking fires were lit. The mating of Tak and Barris created extra excitement, for the children of camp leaders always received more attention than common workers. The mating of Shalli and Ben, though not the children of leaders, was also an event of heightened significance.

By habit rather than design, the men gathered near the council cabin at the edge of the lake while the women prepared for the ceremony at the far end of the circle closer to the woods. Flowers were cut for the two brides as many helped them dress. Myra had never seen Shalli so happy, and Court was proud of her courageous daughter.

"Is it time yet?" Shalli asked.

"Soon, dear," Myra consoled. "Try to calm down. Enjoy the day. Think about First Night."

"Shalli's not waiting for First Night. She's going to drag Ben into the bushes the moment Black Hands mates them," Pie laughed.

"Pie! Don't speak such nasty things," Myra scolded.

"It's true. Isn't it true, Shalli?" Pie said.

"Waiting for dark will be hard," Shalli admitted, showing off the wide cotton skirt Beknar and Seenar had made for her.

Tak was also splendidly dressed and the brides exchanged tokens for the bond they would share.

"You've always been my best friend," Shalli said, giving Tak a red scarf embroidered with strands of silver thread.

"Sharing the mating day makes it more special for me, too," Tak said, giving Shalli a necklace of finely polished stones.

"It's beautiful. Thank you, Tak," Shalli responded.

"A fitting gift," Court pronounced, helping Shalli put the necklace on. "Our camp did not struggle as yours did. You lost many good men in the cave-in, and the wolves were ungenerous. Now all will see that Ferret Camp deserves a place of honor."

On the men's side of the circle, mauck was shared and lewd remarks made about First Night. Some agreed with Pie that Shalli might not wait for dark. Grey took the teasing well, as did Barris. Both were handsomely dressed in tanned leather outfits, wide belts, high boots and broad brim hats.

"Nervous?" Barris asked.

"Just a little," Grey said. "You?"

"Very nervous," Barris admitted. "What was it like the first time you mated?"

Grey looked up at the clear blue sky and felt the brilliant sun. The grass beneath his boots was green. The nearby lake rippled in a gentle breeze. Only a few hundred people filled the meadow, not the thousands who had witnessed his first wedding.

"This is different, but the feelings are similar," Grey said.

"It's time," Clagg announced, slapping a heavy hand on Grey's shoulder. "Often do men of the camps call each other brother, but today, as you mate my sister, you are truly my brother. Myra, too, gains a brother. Garn gains an uncle. We're happy to have you in our family."

Grey remained quiet, unable to find proper words.

They went to the head of the circle where a timber platform had been erected. Black Hands was pacing behind the stage muttering chants under her breath as Nole and Sharlot stood nearby.

"Black Hands has never conducted the ceremony before such a large crowd before. She may be more nervous than the brides," Nole reported.

"It's not so hard," Grey recalled.

"Have you performed mating ceremonies before?" Sharlot asked.

"One of my former duties was magistrate of a mining colony. I conducted marriage ceremonies on several occasions," he explained.

"The camp you led was bigger than ours, wasn't it?" Barris guessed.

"This is my world now. What happened before doesn't matter," Grey answered.

"There are some who think our camps could produce more, and get more reward, if we worked together," Nole said. "Some think you're the person to help us. A leader all the camps would respect."

"Not all the camps," Grey said. "Before long I would spend most of my time negotiating grievances and being criticized. Nothing would get done. No, Nole. I appreciate your confidence, but I like the work I do now. I'm looking forward to spending my nights with Shalli. Becoming a father. I don't want to be a leader."

"You might not have a choice," Nole warned. "But that is for another day. This is a time of great festivities, and you have a hard night ahead."

The men laughed and took positions near the platform. Soon drums and wooden flutes were played as the procession began. The mates of the leaders entered first carrying the symbols of their camps mounted on long poles. Some of the standards featured animal heads carved from wood, others were decorated with large bows made of ribbons and traces of lace. The children followed, throwing blossoms. Then the brides made their appearance.

Shalli and Tak walked side-by-side, Tak on the right as was due her rank. Their outfits were simple but alluring, with deep necklines and flowing blue skirts, their hair adorned with colorful flowers. Their nervous smiles filled with excitement. Barris poked Grey with his elbow.

"It would be dangerous to say which is the most beautiful, but I think Tak has the claim," Barris bragged.

"Dangerous indeed. Especially as you are wrong," Grey disagreed.

The standards were planted in a semi-circle and the couples joined together on the platform. Black Hands stood before them wearing a long buffalo robe bleached white for important occasions. The drum beating subsided as a single flute played a wedding tune, the melody familiar to all but Grey.

Then the flute suddenly stopped. Many looked around to see why, the song not yet complete. Four Arikhan sentries had taken positions behind the gathering, all holding weapons and wearing body armor. Two more guards appeared on the left not far from the dock, and three on the right from the direction of the main gate. One of the three was Romtra, coordinating their movements. Another was Nabbatron, watching for trouble. Frontra was maintaining a forward position.

The camps pulled together in a circle, the men on the outside, the women and children at the center, all wondering what had brought the guards out in such force. There was murmuring, then silence. Many trembled. All kneeled with heads down, awaiting an explanation.

Only Frontra approached the circle, the other guards maintaining watch from a secure distance. She walked through the outer ring, stepped over the cowering women, and went to the platform where the wedding party knelt.

"Ben, you must come with us," Frontra ordered, a claw on her weapon should drawing it be necessary.

"Why? Why, Frontra?" Shalli asked, clinging to Grey's arm.

"It is not permitted for slaves to ask questions without permission," Frontra responded, looking toward Clagg.

Clagg took the hint, climbing up on the stage to hold Shalli's shoulders. Nole did the same for Tak. There was no one to hold Barris back, but Grey put out his arm.

"You're needed here. Don't do anything foolish," Grey whispered.

"What's this about?" Barris asked loud enough that those in the immediate area could hear. Including Frontra.

"I've expected this for a long time. I'm only sorry it didn't happen sooner," Grey answered, seeing the distress in Shalli's eyes.

He stood up, but Shalli lunged, grabbing his leg.

"Don't go," she implored. "Fight them. You can fight them all!"

"Shalli, you must be brave," Grey said, kneeling down and prying off her hands. "Be brave for me. For your family. And for Sherra's sake, don't threaten the masters. Such words put everyone in danger."

"Don't go," Shalli said more quietly, tears running down her face.

"The call is made," Grey sighed with resignation.

He waited for Clagg to get a good grip on her before jumping down off the platform.

"You might not return, Ben. If you wish to say anything, I have a moment of patience," Frontra offered.

Grey could tell Frontra wasn't enthusiastic about her assignment. No doubt her popularity with the camps was the reason she'd been selected to make the arrest. He looked at the many confused expressions, but there wasn't much to say.

"Clagg, Myra, Ferret Camp, I've been happy living with you. You'll always have my respect. To my other friends, it's been a privilege."

Grey wiped tears from Shalli's face and kissed her slowly on the lips.

"I was prepared to love you. Don't ever forget that you deserve to be loved," he whispered.

"Come back to me," Shalli said.

"If I can," he promised.

Grey went with Frontra, walking near the lakeshore to avoid the thicker crowds. As they reached the outer ring, Grey saw Wart kneeling in the short grass, his eyes watery. Grey stopped and stripped off the fine clothing and boots, keeping only the breechcloth. It was more than he had worn while entering the gate two years before.

"I won't need these," he said, handing Wart the folded bundle. "Work hard and you'll grow into them."

"I won't grow to be a digger. I'll grow up to be a warrior and kill the enemies of my people," Wart said, glaring at Frontra.

Grey pushed Wart's head down to keep him from saying anything more and left the circle, walking to Nabbatron and Romtra.

"Follow us, half-meat. Make no sudden moves," Nabbatron instructed.

"I will do nothing to endanger the people, master," Grey said, wondering if he should try something after leaving the compound. But he quickly dismissed the idea. He would have to hurt several guards, including Frontra, and he didn't see anything good coming from that.

The point became moot. As they crossed the line of painted yellow rocks before the main gate, Bortro tied Grey's hands behind his back and attached a chain to his slave collar. The Arikhan sentries weren't taking any chances with their potentially dangerous prisoner.

"What is this about, mistress?" Grey asked Frontra as they passed under the brick gatehouse arch, walking across the railroad tracks and over a narrow wooden bridge to the camp headquarters on the opposite side of the narrow valley. It occurred to Grey that it was the first time he had been outside the compound since the day he arrived.

"No one but the Sarden Leader knows," Frontra replied. "He has been reading reports. Trying to find something that is hard to find. He is much frustrated. He may be angry."

"What does it have to do with me?" Grey asked, trying to sound clueless.

"He has been gathering your records," Frontra said.

Grey stopped asking questions. He had long thought it was only a matter of time before the Arikhan figured out that the slave Ben was also the destroyer of *Bellerophon*. Earth's hero was last seen wearing a Quexelian meteor suit. Ben was found in a Quexelian meteor suit. And Ben had foolishly spoken English when captured, a language the crew of the *Link* had never heard, but one their Council of Warriors would have in their database. As for how he could be found floating outside the Laros stargate more than a year after the battle, that remained a good question. He had no answer, but that didn't mean the Arikhan scientists hadn't discovered one.

Grey was led up rough flagstone steps to the headquarters on the hill overlooking Karak. The wood frame building was painted dull green. The tarpaper roof was covered with gravel tiles. Large glass windows gave the building light.

From the tree-lined path, Grey could see all the way down the valley where the railroad tracks crossed a rickety suspension bridge. The wide river was deep blue. The tracks gradually disappeared north into the prairie. Somewhere beyond the prairie were refining centers, factories for making components, and assembly plants. Akrona had once made warships for the Arikhan fleet. Now the planet was a forsaken backwater making an occasional cargo transport.

Except for Romtra, the guards returned to their duties at the gatehouse. Frontra took a final sad look at Grey before he was pushed through the wooden door.

The headquarters had improved since his previous visit. A red woven carpet covered the center floor area, the stools were finely carved tree trunks, and the walls were decorated with sculptures of various Arikhan deities made of twisted swamp wood.

Grey was put on his knees in the middle of the carpet and ordered to stay. Then, to his surprise, Romtra unclasped the chain and left the building, locking the door on her way out. Presumably to prevent escape. Odd, he thought, because the room had eight wide open windows and no bars.

He sat on the carpet by himself for a quarter of an hour, providing plenty of time to study the room. A communications globe was active, the images showing Arikhan officials providing reports, but the sound was off. Grey considered trying to read their lips, or beaks as the case may be, but decided it wasn't worth the effort.

There was a desk for administrative work in the far corner, and a long table for meals off to his right. Small tables near the north window held some of the games of chance the Arikhan liked to play. He remembered Mordari showing him several of the Arikhan pastimes. Some games used sticks with symbols on the edges, others had objects shaped like teeth the size of dice. Grey discovered his poker skills came in handy when playing Bones & Skulls.

Finally, a door down the rear corridor opened and Sarden Leader Gamtro entered the room. Grey didn't remember their initial meeting, only the one near the ore cart after the first quarry was made. Gamtro was still physically impressive, but his eyes were more sunken. Tired. His long bluish face was lined heavily below the high cheek bones, and the chin looked more pointed. Grey didn't know if it was age or stress that caused the weary appearance, but he had no doubt the alien was still a robust leader. He wore a plain olive green tunic, gray trousers, and high brown boots.

"We have not spoken in several seasons," Gamtro said in roughly worded Akronos, squatting just a few feet away.

"No, master," Grey replied in well-pronounced Arikhan, putting his forehead to the floor.

"Sit up. I wish to see your eyes when we speak," Gamtro ordered, reverting to his native language.

Grey rocked back on his heels, hands still bound behind his back, folding his feet underneath him. Gamtro moved forward, kneeling close enough that Grey could feel the alien's breath on his face.

"They say you are not a slave. They say you are a dangerous creature. A warrior," Gamtro said.

Grey sat passively, listening but doing his best not to react. Gamtro grew impatient, his narrow bird-like eyes darting about for clues.

"Answer, food creature, before I have you hung by the heels and drained for carving," Gamtro threatened.

"I have not been asked a question, master," Grey replied.

"Very well. Respond to the accusation," Gamtro ordered.

"The accusation is less than true, but not entirely false," Grey said, trying to return Gamtro's intense stare without being bold.

"In what manner is the accusation false?" Gamtro asked.

"It should be obvious, master. I sit on your floor, bound with a collar around my neck, completely at your mercy. I have worked your mines, struggled to fill your quotas, and obeyed your guards. Clearly I am a slave."

"You speak impertinently."

"I have not claimed to be a perfect slave."

"You are a warrior," Gamtro asserted.

"In another life, that was true. But now I am a slave of the Arikhan. One cannot be both a warrior and a slave."

"I am not sure of that. Are you as dangerous as my guards say?"

"I have not harmed any of your guards."

"Could you kill me if you wanted to?" Gamtro asked. "I am bigger than you. Stronger. So is Nabbatron. Frontra thinks you could kill Nabbatron in an equal fight."

"It would not be equal," Grey said.

"Then you call Frontra a liar?"

"No, I only say the fight would not be equal."

Gamtro stood up and walked around Grey, poking his shoulders, studying the musculature, noting the posture. Nearly naked with its paws tied behind its back, the Sarden Leader did not see how the creature could be dangerous. But he had no intention of being complacent.

Grey half-expected to be kicked or punched at any moment but made an effort not to appear apprehensive. He was only partly successful. Arikhan were good at reading the body language of their prey. Gamtro returned to the squatting position before him and drew a polished steel hunting knife.

"If you wait for me to beg, save yourself the time," Grey said in an angry voice. He raised his chin and closed his eyes. Gamtro put a claw in Grey's hair, holding his head still, and put the knife against his throat. Grey felt the coolness of the blade.

"Are you ready for death, food creature?" Gamtro asked.

Grey struggled to remain brave. He had long expected such a moment. Had long ago determined to keep his nerve to the end. Nevertheless, his breathing grew quicker. His shoulders trembled. He clenched his jaw to maintain composure.

Gamtro remained calm, still holding the knife against Grey's throat. After a moment, he slowly pulled back.

"Put your head on the floor," Gamtro demanded.

Grey bent over, his forehead in contact with the rough carpet. He felt Gamtro pull at his arms and suddenly the bindings came free.

"Sit back," Gamtro said.

Grey rocked back on his heels again, rubbing his wrists, wondering what Gamtro wanted from him. The alien appeared pleased to have aroused the captive's curiosity.

"You do not prepare for death like a slave. You abide in a warrior's courage."

"I was afraid," Grey disagreed.

"We are all afraid with a blade pressed to our throats," Gamtro answered, slowly waving the knife. "My guards insist you are dangerous. Not being warriors of the first rank, they may exaggerate your skill."

Grey grabbed Gamtro's wrist in a motion so quick the Sarden Leader hardly realized what had happened, then bent the claw back and twisted the knife free. In a heartbeat, Grey was pushing forward, driving with his legs, forcing Gamtro backward on the carpet. The alien tried to fend Grey off, seeking to block the assault with his powerful arms, but Grey was too fast, pouncing on Gamtro's chest to pin him down. The blade was soon pressed tightly against Gamtro's windpipe.

Now Gamtro was breathing hard, his eyes wider than normal, the cheekbones shimmering in a darker shade of blue. He struggled but Grey's hold was firm, the knife carefully poised. Grey was breathing heavier, too, from a brief adrenaline rush, but he wasn't excited. The attack was swift and professionally executed, just as he'd been taught by Captain Wingfoot many years before.

Once Gamtro ceased resistance, Grey drew the knife back.

"Have you found out what you wanted to know, master?" Grey asked.

"Much of it," Gamtro said.

Grey stuck the knife in the floor, crawled back to the center of the carpet, and resumed his original sitting position, crossing his hands behind his back. Gamtro pulled the knife out and put it close to Grey's throat.

"You could have killed me," Gamtro said.

"It would prove nothing."

"Now I have another chance to slay you."

"You could have done that yesterday, or a few minutes ago. You can do it now, or you can do it tomorrow. You are the Sarden Leader. I live at your discretion."

Gamtro put the knife back in its sheath.

"For several seasons I have gathered reports of your activities," Gamtro revealed. "Your engineering skills are beyond question, but when I suggested compelling you to do more, Frontra said neither fear nor intimidation would prove successful. I see now that Frontra has spoken truly."

"What is it you want, master?" Grey asked.

"When we are alone, you will call me Gamtro," the Sarden Leader said.

The alien stood up, went to a cabinet, and took out a bundle of clothing.

"This outfit was made by Denesians," Gamtro explained.

"Captured from a smuggler who foolishly sought to evade our stargate's defenses. I don't know what the material is made of, but it is tougher than leather and keeps a good temperature in heat or cold. It is yours."

Grey accepted the gift, a full-length black uniform cut to his size. He put the suit on and admired the fit. He was not able to identify the material, but he found it particularly comfortable. Gamtro added a pair of fine leather boots to complete the outfit.

"The bribe is impressive, but you still have not revealed what you want," Grey said.

"More production," Gamtro answered.

"In exchange for what?" Grey inquired.

Gamtro looked surprised. "You yourself have admitted being my slave. I need not exchange anything."

"I am your slave," Grey said. "You may beat me, torture me, or kill me. All is within your power. But if you want my engineering skills, you must pay me. And my services do not come cheap."

Gamtro pounded the nearby table with a clenched claw, but he wasn't angry.

"Nabbatron is right. You are impertinent beyond words," Gamtro said, his tongue clicking with amazement. "What payment would you demand?"

"That depends on how much production you need, and whether or not the workers are willing to cooperate."

"We have never had trouble getting them to work," Gamtro said.

"They are good workers," Grey agreed. "But to increase production, their labor needs to be reorganized. New skills learned. I would also need power tools, spare parts, better nutrition, and rewards adequate enough to make them want to change. As your guards would need to change."

"This is more than I expected," Gamtro said, a worried clip at the end of the sentence.

"If all you want is marginal improvement, then much can remain as it is. But not if you want an appreciable increase."

"How much of an increase is possible?" Gamtro asked.

"One hundred percent in the first year. More after that, if we get the right equipment. I do not think a one thousand percent increase within the first three years is an unreasonable expectation."

Gamtro sat on a stool, stunned by the prediction. His claws quivered.

"Are you sure of this?" Gamtro asked.

"I was born on a mining colony. Engineering is my profession, but that does not mean it will be easy. And the people must be rewarded."

"I could make life very comfortable for you. And a few of your fellow food creatures," Gamtro offered.

"No, Gamtro. I am not Marne."

Gamtro shifted on the stool, embarrassed he had made the suggestion. His cheeks subsided to a soft aristocratic blue. The black eyes grew thoughtful.

"Nabbatron said my offer would not impress you. He believes your integrity is such that your flesh should be dedicated to Sherra when the time comes."

"Which begs an important issue. If we embark upon this endeavor, I want a promise that no one from this camp will be sent to the pens unless we both agree."

"That is presumptuous," Gamtro said, cutting his words sharply.

"Would you let your people be sent to the pens?" Grey asked.

"No, but these are not your people. You are not of Akrona."

Grey let the statement hang in the air, wondering if Gamtro would elaborate. Gamtro noticed the reaction.

"You have a greater secret," Gamtro suddenly realized, pointing at Grey with his claw. "When you came in here, you thought I knew the secret. You expected to die."

Grey did not respond. There was no point. Regardless of what he said, Gamtro would be curious enough to do his own research.

"Maybe this gives me more bargaining power?" Gamtro speculated.

"If you think so, you're a fool," Grey said.

Gamtro was shocked. Angry. Then he thought for a moment before slowly clicking his tongue.

"I tested your resolve. Now you test mine," Gamtro observed.

"I do not test your resolve, Sarden Leader. All know life at Karak is short for some, longer for others. For myself, I have few illusions. War has been my life, an early death the inevitable destiny. If you want my skills, you must offer more than threats."

Gamtro paced the room as he studied the prisoner, perceiving the determination in the creature's eyes. The defiant posture. Clearly it was not afraid of death. Gamtro doubted it could be intimidated, nor was it greedy. It had not seized power after slaying the wolves, nor gathered spoils from needy camps.

Nabbatron is correct, Gamtro thought. *This creature holds itself to a high standard. It's almost Arikhan.*

"Would you share bruno with me? I have a superior vintage," Gamtro invited.

Grey was taken off guard, which pleased Gamtro. For the first time since he entered the room, Gamtro felt he had broken a piece of the creature's reserve.

"Thank you, Gamtro," Grey said, unable to hide his curiosity.

* * * * * *

Several hours later, after more than one bottle of imported wine, Grey and Gamtro were speaking freely. Grey was surprised to find he liked the Sarden Leader, whose flexibility of mind was atypical of the Arikhan.

Gamtro was even more surprised. For a reason he didn't understand, he found it impossible to think of Grey as a food creature.

"Frontra is fond of you," Gamtro said, sitting opposite Grey at the small gaming table.

"Frontra is fond of many. She has a good heart."

"It was no accident she was sent to take you at the ceremony."

"It was a good strategy. Why did you wait for the mating ceremony to bring me here?"

"I thought to maximize the pressure. If you could be broken, it would be today, in a moment of great distress," Gamtro explained.

"I am not so easily disconcerted, though I fear Shalli is heartbroken," Grey said.

"Perhaps I may make amends. I will declare an extra day of

holiday. That should provide sufficient opportunity to complete the ceremonies."

"That is generous, Gamtro," Grey appreciated.

"I find this event most strange," Gamtro remarked, pouring Grey another cup. "If anyone had told me I would enjoy sharing bruno with one of your kind, I would have thought them mad. Maybe there is something to be said for the Voice of Sherra."

"Voice of Sherra?" Grey asked.

"A new movement among my people. I have given it no heed. Most do not. But there are some who listen, such as Frontra. I do not believe, but maybe I will listen more carefully."

"Among my people, new ideas have great power. What is this new thought?"

"A warrior of much experience is declared by some to be a high priestess. Her followers call her the Voice of Sherra. She claims it wrong for the Arikhan to exploit sentient creatures as we do. She proclaims the decline of our empire is a sign of Sherra's displeasure. She says the Arikhan will prosper only when we respect the rights of alien cultures."

"This would be a great change for your people. As a food creature, I am inclined to sympathize with this philosophy," Grey said.

"You are no food creature."

"I am a member of a food creature species, Gamtro. Either we are all food creatures or we are not. I do not see how it can be otherwise."

"This is a difficult thought," Gamtro agreed, scratching the fine webbing on the side of his head. "Perhaps it will become clear if Mordari ever returns."

"Mordari!" Grey shouted, rising from the stool.

"Yes, Mordari. She is scout of the 44th Camp, held prisoner by food creatures in a far off star system," Gamtro explained. "Do you know of Mordari?"

Grey was feeling enough of the wine that he almost answered. Almost admitted a much more personal knowledge of Mordari than Gamtro could ever imagine, for he and the alien scout had spent countless hours together on missions. As allies, and as enemies.

Once again, Gamtro realized there was more not being said. His thin eye-rings lowered, the aristocratic gaze probing. But he did not pursue the thought. For now.

"The sun has set," Grey mentioned.

"Are you ready to return to camp?"

"Yes."

"I will have the planning materials you requested delivered, and Nabbatron will announce the extended holiday," Gamtro said.

"Do the people think I dwell in the pens?" Grey asked.

"No word is given. Even my guards do not know of our agreements. For now, it is best they abide in ignorance."

"Your wishes will be respected. I do have a request. A spoonful of flash powder. There is a stunt from an old entertainment I would like to try."

"A colorful one, no doubt," Gamtro agreed.

* * * * * *

The sun had already set on the festival campground but the mood was less than festive. Though some simply shrugged at Grey's misfortune, particularly those from Wolf Camp, many others were sad to lose such a valuable asset. For Ferret Camp, the holiday was over. They would share the evening meal and return along the south trail to mourn their loss. Shalli was trying to be brave.

"Maybe he's not sent to the pens?" Shalli said.

"Maybe," Clagg said. "Black Hands is offering prayers for him. Many are gathering at the lake to hear her words."

"We should go, too," Tak said, holding Shalli's hand.

"You should have completed the mating," Shalli said. "You were so beautiful. You and Barris should be having First Night, not watching over me."

"You're our friend. So is Ben. He would want us here with you," Barris said. "Let's go and hear Black Hands' prayer."

The group told Myra where they were going and started off, walking slowly through the camps to the edge of the lake. Darkness had crept all around, the central bonfire and the cooking fires being the primary sources of light. They found Black Hands sitting on the wedding platform studying the stars for a sign. They could see she

215

had been crying.

"Is there hope?" Tak asked.

"There's always hope," Black Hands said, trying to wipe the tears. "The masters have not returned with ill news. The yellow moon is full. Several stars and planets are in harmony. And Ben is friend to the mountain. I think the signs are good."

Three dozen people gathered around as Black Hands finished her observations and raised her hands to the dark sky.

"Sherra, goddess of prosperity, hear our humble pleas," Black Hands said, her sincerity undoubted by all who listened. "Our brother is taken from us, we know not why. He is much needed, and much loved. Look upon us with kindness that our brother might be returned."

Suddenly, a bright red flash appeared at the rear of the platform accompanied by a short boom that echoed off the lake. The brief burst of flame was followed by a plume of white smoke. As the startled group looked up, Grey stepped from the smoke dressed in the black uniform Gamtro had given him.

"It's Ben! Ben has returned!" Tak yelled.

"Ben!" Shalli cried, climbing on the platform to hug him.

"It's a miracle. A miracle right here for all to see," Pie said.

"Black Hands, how did you do it?" Barris asked. "How did you bring Ben back?"

"I don't know," Black Hands said, surprised as anyone.

Hundreds of people began running toward the lake, many bearing torches to light the way. As crowds formed, Grey took Shalli into his arms and gave her a long kiss. Then he drew Black Hands up on the platform.

"Thank you for bringing me back, Black Hands," Grey said above the noise. He wrapped an arm around her shoulders so all might see him and the former healer of Raven Camp standing together in the torchlight.

"I could not have brought you back. It's one of your tricks," Black Hands whispered.

Grey smiled to let her know it was true, but didn't say so. The myth would enhance her stature, as they both knew. He helped Tak climb the timber steps to share a hug. Barris jumped up with her, gripping Grey's forearm.

"Welcome back, my brother. It's good to see you've not been claimed by the pens," Barris said, in awe of his miraculous reappearance.

"It would seem Sherra has other plans for me. Shall we reschedule the mating ceremony for tomorrow?" Grey asked.

"No! We'll do the mating ceremony right now," Shalli insisted. "I won't wait for something else to go wrong."

"Shalli is desperate for First Night," Barris laughed.

"So am I," Tak said, giving Barris a passionate kiss.

"What do you think?" Grey asked Barris.

"Are you able?" Barris questioned.

"Were you beaten? Tortured?" Tak asked.

"No, I spent the afternoon drinking bruno with the Sarden Leader," Grey said.

"Drinking? I've been scared to sickness," Shalli said.

"Better to share refreshments with the masters than be the refreshment," Grey said.

All paused to dwell on his words. Though spoken lightly, as he often did, many knew him well enough to recognize the dark humor that lay beneath.

An hour later, with the meadow lit by a hundred torches and blazing bonfires, the healer known as Black Hands joined two couples. The first was Barris and Tak, son of Sparrow Camp and daughter of Deer Camp. The second couple was Shalli and Ben of Ferret Camp. The brides were beautiful, the men handsome. Black Hands spoke the words of the ancient ritual, and with all her heart, wished the couples long and happy lives together.

It was not meant to be.

Chapter Seven
THE LADY GAMTRA

The former Sarden Leader of Karak, now Baron Gamtro of Akrona, paced in the light gravity of the orbital space station. By coincidence, he was looking through the viewport when he saw a bright flash from the stargate fifty million kilometers away.

"Is it the Lark?" Gamtro asked, rushing to the inquiry desk.

"Yes, Baron," the clerk responded, checking her communications globe. "A day late, but undamaged and under full power."

The outer ring of the large station rotated to maintain gravity, the floating wheel based on technology stolen from another culture centuries before. Once a contact point for dozens of visiting cargo ships, all but two of the space station's service bays were now mothballed. Akrona was no longer the thriving center of commerce it had been eighty years before, though recent history had shown improvement.

The interior of the station was comfortable without frills. Long curving corridors made of gray polymers accessed storage and crew compartments. The lighting was bright, the temperature generally warm. Occasional portholes allowed views of the sun, planets, and stars.

Gamtro noticed the desk clerk was bored with her duties, pausing often to smooth the curling webbed membrane on her head or adjust her dark purple tunic. Her skin was a commoner's brown, as were most of the space station workers. As dreary as life could be administering production on a remote planet, certainly duty on a cargo dock was worse. Gamtro counted himself fortunate.

The stargate was not a physical structure, but a ring of harmonic energy that surrounded the star maintained by resonance fields and solar winds. Twenty small satellites relayed communications. Another fifty satellites were armed to discourage intruders. Gamtro studied a strategic scanner to see if the *Lark* traveled alone or with an

218

armed escort, recalling that, in better days, no escort would be necessary.

"Is that the Bos'pher?" Gamtro asked, seeing a second ship. It was a destroyer class warship, lightly armed but maneuverable.

"Bos'pher is now assigned to this sector," the clerk confirmed.

"I once commanded a destroyer, in my young egg days," Gamtro fondly remembered. "It was an old ship, but worthy. The Na'vat. Probably scrapped for spare parts by now."

The clerk said nothing, uncomfortable making small talk with such a high official. A moment later, Gamtro saw the second image disappear back through the stargate. Only the *Lark* continued forward.

The small cylindrical passenger craft, twenty-five meters long and six meters in diameter, had traveled twenty-one light years to reach the Laros star system. And eighteen light years from the star before that, bursting through the subspace openings with all six thrusters burning. A large spacecraft, such as a first line battle cruiser, might jump sixty light years at a time if the stargates were in alignment. Minor craft had to cope with shorter ranges.

Eight hours after entering Laros space, the transport finally reached the space station, allowing the tired passengers to disembark through the docking port. Among them was a tall, intelligent female dressed in a shimmering gold tunic, the fine membrane covering her head longer than most Arikhan. Her thin blue face was free of wrinkles, and there was a dance of curiosity in her rust-brown eyes. Any who saw her instantly recognized an aristocrat.

"Dogra," Gamtro greeted, rushing to brush claws.

"Gamtro," Dogra said. "Many years has it been since I've felt the touch of my beloved. Or must I now call you Baron Gamtro?"

"As I may now call you Lady Gamtra," Gamtro said with a happy rise of eye-rings.

"Lady Gamtra. A beautiful sound, do you not agree? I am so proud of you, my mate. Nine years ago Festro exiled you to the most worthless camp on the most worthless planet in the empire, and now in but a short space of time, we are restored in wealth and high with rank. A baron no less. Director of all mineral production on Akrona."

"The years have been prosperous, but you are much missed," Gamtro said.

"Attaché to the Ministry of Central Planning is not glamorous work, yet for generations my family has served the high committees. Our work is necessary."

"How fares our legacy?"

"The eggs we devoted to the academy survive. I fear only two will reach maturity, but there may be a warrior among them."

"We will provide a heritage worth boasting of," Gamtro promised.

After collecting the Lady Gamtra's traveling trunks, they went to the departure gate for the flight down to the planet. The waiting area was not crowded, scanners checking each individual's identity and travel status while a lone guard insured order. An airlock allowed admittance to a flexible tunnel accessing the shuttle's boarding hatch.

"Akrona sees much change," Gamtro said as they strapped down in the bucket seats of a small passenger compartment.

Vintage but well-maintained, the shuttlecraft held twelve seats, six on each side with an aisle down the middle. Only a few other passengers shared the vehicle, a short-winged sho'ker with two primary thrusters. Mounted above the hatch to the pilot's compartment was Governor Zenatro's formal crest, crossed platinum swamp leaves, marking it as an official government transport.

Generous windows allowed the passengers to see the planet to starboard. From space, Akrona appeared to be an unremarkable ocean world with most of the land mass confined to a single continent. A few large islands and hundreds of small ones spread like a chain around the world's equator.

"Our colonies are west of the mountain range," Gamtro said, pointing to an area above the equator near several great lakes.

Dogra saw most of the continent was divided by a snowy mountain range. Prairies to the west, thick forests to the east, and large river valleys in the south. The northern coastline was cut with glacial badlands.

"Is Karak not beyond the Varish Expanse? Next to the Rellina River above the Ognak Fork?" Dogra asked.

"You have been making studies," Gamtro said, his tongue clicking with satisfaction.

"Have we no colonies east of the mountains? I see no roads or cities."

"There is little of value east of the mountains," Gamtro said, declining to elaborate.

"Much is your work discussed at the ministry's conference tables, and in the social gatherings after. There is a proposal to build warships here again. The contracts will make the production managers powerful with wealth. You are much credited for reviving this forgotten world."

"A share of credit may be accepted. The new mines are rich. Several refining facilities have been retooled to process more efficiently. Young engineers arrive to improve our assembly plants. We even have plans for two new cargo vessels."

The sho'kar separated from the space dock, dropping into a long glide path toward Va'ragashant, Akrona's colonial capital. The noise of the wing jets allowed Dogra to whisper.

"They say you risk much, treating the food creatures with such deference," Dogra said.

The rumor seemed to worry her. Gamtro understood.

"There is much to say, and this is not the place," he said, looking at the other passengers. "But the cooperation we have achieved costs little, yet gains much. Prosperity is not a crime."

"Since being released by the Sol creatures last year, Mordari has visited six worlds. Her sermons move some hearts but anger more. Jealous voices say you hear her words," Dogra suggested, unsure what his answer would be.

"I am not in league with heresy," Gamtro grunted. "This planet follows a new path to strength. No apologies are needed."

"None call Mordari a heretic. Not yet. But you travel a path she would praise," Dogra said. "You are brave to do so. More brave than in your youth. Much does your bravery make me look forward to a coupling."

"How long may you stay?" Gamtro asked, affirming her desire with a brush of claws.

"Only a season. The marauders grow bolder. With fleet on

assignment, it grows difficult to protect our stargates. Even craft such as the Lark must await escort."

"Waging war against the rocks leaves much vulnerability. If we can maintain production here and produce new ships, maybe this marauding can be suppressed."

"Prophecy says the Sword of Sherra will be forged in the mines of Akrona," Dogra recalled. "*Bellerophon* was not Sherra's Sword as we all believed. It may yet wait to be forged."

The shuttle glided to the planet's only operational landing strip, setting down at the Lo'cosan Spaceport with a gentle bounce. The passengers disembarked on the tarmac and took an open tram to the terminal building. The temperature was warm, the clear sky a lovely blue-green. She noticed rich forests on the surrounding hillsides.

The simple terminal was not large or particularly busy. Built in a series of cubes with light plaster walls painted in a modest green, Dogra thought the structure drab except for its colorful marble flooring.

"Is there so little activity?" Dogra asked, noticing that only two of the spaceport's hangars were in service.

Though the large airfield was surrounded by high walls made of white stone, even the guard towers had been abandoned.

"Until recently, there was little need for more staff. We are trying to recruit new ground crews from Kavas'tak by offering bonuses," Gamtro explained.

"Are crews so difficult to find?" Dogra inquired.

"Skilled crews are. They expect more comforts than Akrona offers, but we are improving. There is a new tavern on Scrabbage Hill, and we reopened the theater."

"Only one theater?" Dogra laughed, clicking her tongue softly.

Gamtro wasn't sure, but he suspected Dogra was mocking the colonial world's attempt to develop culture.

Given precedence, Gamtro and Dogra boarded a private ground transport, her baggage taking up most of the eight-wheeler's cargo space. The seats were comfortable, the driver wise enough to remain quiet among his superiors. The vehicle moved smoothly except where the old stone road grew rough. Large windows provided a good view of the green landscape.

After thirty kilometers of forested highway, they reached a low hill overlooking a vast grassy plain. Out in the middle of the plain, bordering two glistening blue lakes, was a small city.

"Va'ragashant was important once. Two hundred thousand colonists lived here," Gamtro said. "Now we barely have sixty thousand."

Dogra saw a handful of tall buildings dominating the city center, but few were over eight stories high. Most of the commercial structures were low roofed and joined together by covered walkways. Private dwellings were most obvious by their broad sundecks.

"I had thought the capital more worldly," Dogra said, finding nothing inspiring in the old-fashioned hive architecture.

They exited the vehicle in the city center. Before them was an ancient stone fort, the walls too low for a realistic defense, and a wide plaza surrounded by produce stalls. Merchants and a few soldiers loitered in the plaza where a small sandstone temple allowed travelers to leave offerings for Sherra. Dogra noticed two of the lesser deities where also honored; Ro'gak, the god of strength, and Darri, the god of fortitude.

Beyond the fortress gate stood an impressive administration building with tall arched entrances. Wide balconies on each of its eight levels allowed government workers plenty of fresh air and daylight.

"The new residences on Zilif Heights are quite elegant, but I rarely stay there," Gamtro said, pointing to a row of dwellings on a ridge across the river. "Zenatro and I are not on good terms. In the morning, I would like to return to Karak for a few days."

"I had not expected to take my sabbatical in a slave camp," Dogra objected.

"If you find the camp beyond toleration, the remainder of your stay can be here," Gamtro offered.

"That is fair. Is it true that even greater increases in production are expected?"

Gamtro's answer was interrupted.

"Any fool can increase production if he is a thief," a gravelly voice burst.

They turned to see Governor Zenatro waddling in their direction from the administration building. Barely Dogra's height but twice her weight, the big alien moved in jarring steps rather than the graceful glide typical of their species. His emerald tunic was of the finest quality, his leather boots smartly oiled. Deep shades of blue in his cheeks and neck indicated an aristocratic heritage, though not of Dogra's lineage.

"Your mate has stolen a thousand slaves from other camps, closed the pens, and pirated the best supplies. He is a monster, Lady Gamtra. A monster. Sherra's dark shadow," Zenatro complained, clicking his tongue rapidly.

"It is good to see you again, Zenny," Dogra replied, amused by the governor's exasperated tirade. But despite the jesting manner, she sensed genuine tension between the two. Zenatro's career had stalled on Akrona while her mate's was soaring.

"Have the new analyzers arrived yet?" Gamtro said, unimpressed with Zenatro's teasing.

"Not yet," Zenatro replied.

"We need that equipment to expand operations at Gotsha'ka. Why double mineral production if we cannot process the best ore?"

"You made no such demands when you were Sarden Leader of Karak. Now you have twenty camps, and each week you have twenty more demands," Zenatro complained.

"Do you want enough Akronium to build warships, or should we go back to making copper kettles?" Gamtro taunted.

"I will locate the analyzers for you, provided there are sufficient rewards," Zenatro hinted with a discreet click of his thick tongue.

"There is profit enough for all," Gamtro said, reluctantly agreeing to the bribe. Dogra saw her mate was unhappy with Zenatro's attitude.

"Commander Cordaris sends me a new assistant. Amartro. You met him at the desert conference," Zenatro mentioned. "I will instruct him to supervise the delivery."

"I require no help from the Contingent. They hamper production," Gamtro protested.

"Is that your opinion, or the opinion of your pet?" Zenatro

grumbled, shoulders straightening.

"New contracts are worthless without product," Gamtro answered.

"Amartro will be urged to restraint," Zenatro agreed.

"The Contingent knows no restraint. They are brooding flanta with the grace of vvleen," Gamtro cursed, clicking his tongue boldly.

"Do not trouble yourself over the ambitions of commoners," Zenatro impatiently replied. "Think on tonight's Grand Formal."

"A formal?" Dogra asked.

"The reception is in your honor, great lady," Zenatro proudly boasted, waving his claw toward a large tent near the administration building. Servants were busy rushing in and out.

"I am not on ministry business," Dogra said, surprised.

"That may be true, but still do we humble provincials wish to offer tribute. Not often does a high official visit such a Sherra forsaken world as this," Zenatro explained.

"I look forward to your company, Zenny," Dogra said. "There are fine wines in my baggage, the grapes grown in the bosom of Arikhan. You can tell me of all the terrible crimes committed by your Sarden Leader. Oh, excuse me. I mean Baron Gamtro."

Zenatro raised eye-rings in mock insult, looking forward to an evening with one as beautiful and cultured as the Lady Gamtra.

* * * * * *

"The politics of these backwater planets never fail to astound," Dogra said on the train two days later. "At committee, we argue over the disposition of fleet resources protecting twenty-five planets. How to structure governing boards without promoting corruption. Even treaties, such as the one with these foul Sol creatures. Here the bickering is worse, and all over a handful of worthless food creatures."

"Nothing has been revealed of the negotiations. Will we truly honor a truce with Sol?" Gamtro asked.

"We must for now. Our fleets are spread thin and the Western Belt reeks with pirates."

"I did not realize Sol had established a permanent stargate."

"They did not have a stable resonance field until last year. The technology was stolen when they captured Bhast. The gate is not powerful enough to window a battlecruiser, and the Sol creatures breed small warships like solets in heat. As they pose no threat to our worlds, the Council of Warriors have chosen to postpone the problem for another time. Praise Sherra the hostages are finally released."

"Is it true all our warships were lost? All of the warriors killed?" Gamtro asked, sharing the astonishment most Arikhan felt at their invasion's defeat nine years before.

"A thousand colonists from Bhast were captured, and a regiment of warriors who landed on the planet were forced to surrender, but it is true that all three warships perished," Dogra lamented. "Only now are we getting full reports on the battle. We know the Sol creatures were alert to our approach, and they were not the primitive culture our studies anticipated. They fought tenaciously and accepted deep losses. Most vitally, they had determined leadership. Sol possesses a species of food creature our empire has rarely encountered. We will study them carefully before invading again."

"Did the Sol creatures brainwash Mordari during her captivity?"

"No, that is a fiction put out by the Ministry. Mordari truly believes Sherra frowns upon our treatment of these lesser species. Now that she is called the Voice of Sherra, her claims grow ever bolder. If she does not curtail her activities, she will most certainly be arrested. And all who sympathize with her."

"Are you providing warning?" Gamtro asked.

"No. Merely advising."

The train, consisting of four dozen cargo tenders and one passenger car, was pulled by a sturdy hydrogen powered engine. As they left the green pastures around the capital, the train passed a series of dreary industrial plants before entering a vast prairie. Near a rundown processing center they saw a group of slaves digging salt. The plight of the slaves, though only visible from a distance, was obvious to the passengers. They looked thin, weary, and dreadfully dressed in white linen rags.

"As I thought," Dogra said, refusing to see more. "I pity those who staff these wretched outposts. It was cruel of Festro to send you here. And these poor animals. The pens would be more merciful. At least the stockyards don't torture the poor things."

"It does not need to be like this," Gamtro said, eye-rings dipping.

"I suppose your camps are better?"

"In the beginning, my camps were such as the one you see, but much improvement has been made."

"A slave is a slave. A camp a camp. All is misery leading to the pens," Dogra said.

"I know one who says these things are relative," Gamtro mentioned.

"He would not say so if he were a slave. As for slaves, what is this pet of yours everyone speaks of? I could not tell if Zenatro admires the creature or hates it, so sharp were his words."

"Ben provokes much controversy," Gamtro agreed.

"It even has a name? Ben?"

"They all have names, my mate. They have personalities. They have loves. Hates. Resentments. We may destroy them if we choose, but these traits cannot be denied."

"I have never spoken to a food creature," Dogra said with some apprehension. "I have seen pictures of them before they enter the pens, but the meat looks different after it reaches the distribution centers."

"Few of our people have contact with food creatures," Gamtro said. "The populations that once inhabited the inner systems are extinct. The survivors on the outer worlds are few in number. Even here on Akrona, there are but a few thousand left. You will meet some of them today. Perhaps they will surprise you."

"I am afraid, my mate. Are your guards heavily armed?"

"Never would my beloved be exposed to danger," he answered, brushing her claw. Dogra sighed with relief and looked out the window at a tall mountain range in the distance.

After many hours and several short stops, the train slowed as it approached a great river. On the other side of a long suspension bridge, Dogra saw a stretch of cultivated land.

"Those are farms!" Dogra exclaimed, jumping from her seat to look at acres of green vegetation running from the hills down to the river's edge.

The train crossed a creaking hundred-year-old bridge, the farms to their right, a forested hillside on the left. A narrow valley loomed ahead, the tracks and a creek running down the middle. Not far from the tracks, beyond an electrically powered fence, were the famous Karak mines at the base of a frightening rock mountain. And there were strange structures littering the landscape.

As the train moved up the valley, Dogra saw a group of slaves, but they were not the pathetic specimens of the salt camp. These slaves were dressed in colorful clothing and appeared well fed. A dark-haired female carried a child in her arms and looked happy. Dogra turned to Gamtro and saw him watching the group. There was pride in his gaze.

"That is Jarten, leader of the Bear Camp, and his mate, Seak. Their baby is named Fronny. She's a year old now," he said.

"They do not look like slaves," Dogra said, her eyes wide.

"As I said, our camps are managed differently. It is an important part of our success."

The train halted near the loading platforms where ore carts were lined up. Crews rushed forward, eager to fill the waiting cargo holds. Gamtro and Dogra went out the other side, walking up the flagstone path to the camp headquarters located on the hillside.

"I must apologize," Gamtro said. "No doubt you would have found better comforts in town. Our facilities are more primitive than some, but these last few years have been busy. We have not made time for luxuries."

"It will only be a few days. The facilities cannot be worse than those tiny staterooms on the Lark," Dogra acknowledged.

As they approached the wooden building at the top of the path, Gamtro was startled to see it had a fresh coat of jungle green paint. White and yellow stripes gave it texture. The door was decorated with swirling strings of pinecones. Frontra and Nabbatron stood outside, dressed in their best leather uniforms, jaunty yellow feathers tucked in their wide brim hats.

"Welcome back, Baron Gamtro. You were gone longer than expected," Nabbatron said, his tongue clicking in respect.

"Greetings, Lady Gamtra. We are honored by your visit," Frontra said, her eyes reflecting great admiration.

"Beloved, this is Nabbatron, head of my guard, and Frontra, supervisor of the workers," Gamtro introduced.

"It is my honor to meet those who have served my mate so loyally these many years. If ever you visit Arikhan, you are welcome to our estate at Kal' Tree," Dogra said.

"Thank you, Lady Gamtra," the sentries said with deep appreciation.

"Has all progressed well in my absence?" Gamtro asked.

"All is as it should be," Frontra said, standing aside to let them enter the headquarters.

Again Gamtro was amazed. New rugs had been laid throughout the building, the walls decorated with rustic artworks. The tables and kitchen were scrubbed clean. Baskets of fresh food gave the quarters a friendly smell. Gamtro looked toward the corridor where his small sleeping chamber was. The room was gone as if it never existed.

"My mate's baggage is on the train," Gamtro said to Nabbatron. "Are my quarters still here somewhere?"

"Up the stairs to the left," Nabbatron said, trying to keep eye-rings low.

"Stairs? What stairs?" Gamtro asked.

"Your mate makes light of his efforts, Lady Gamtra. You must need rest from your long journey," Frontra said.

With Gamtro following, Frontra led Dogra into the corridor and up a flight of newly cut plank steps to a spacious room perched on the edge of the hill. Through large glass windows they could see all the way down the valley to the river. The floor was sanded oak, the walls a light-colored pine. A large sleeping platform was made with woven bedding of the finest quality and shaped into a giant nest. A sitting room off to the left held stools and a work table. To the right, Dogra found clothing cupboards and a private water closet. Through a sliding glass door was a wide balcony to enjoy the evenings.

"Gamtro, much have you fooled me," Dogra said. "These are beautiful rooms. What amenities in town could be better than these?"

Gamtro glanced at Frontra, who was very pleased with herself.

"Is this Ben's doing?" Gamtro whispered as Dogra went out on the balcony.

"And many others, though it was his idea," Frontra confirmed.

"Five years now have we worked together, yet still does he surprise me," Gamtro confided.

"Many are his skills, though Romtra, Shalli and I provided advice," Frontra said.

"Where is he?" Gamtro asked.

"He seeks extension of the Squirrel Camp mine. He suspects a new vein of Akronium broader than the last one," Frontra answered.

"I have ordered him not to enter those tunnels. He ventures into unstable areas."

"He seeks treasure from the mountain," Frontra said.

"Will the mountain replace him if he is lost?" Gamtro asked.

"I will have him recalled," Frontra agreed.

"Immediately. And fail not to mention my displeasure," Gamtro said with a sharp click of his tongue.

"I am sure he will be much afraid," Frontra said, rolling her eye-rings.

Gamtro blinked acknowledgment. Both knew there was little chance their errant engineer would be impressed by Gamtro's displeasure.

"Invite Ben and Shalli to dine tonight with the Lady Gamtra and myself. And schedule a meeting for the senior staff. Have all wear their best," Gamtro instructed.

"Yes, Baron," Frontra said, going to issue the orders.

Gamtro joined Dogra on the balcony, enjoying the view as much as she did.

"This is a breathtaking place," Dogra said. "The river is beautiful, and the forest is so green. The mountains stand like purple giants. I can hear birds sing. Those structures, across the tracks, what are they? The ones made of rock with thatched roofs."

"Those quarters belong to the workers," Gamtro said.

"I thought slaves lived in tents and caves, if they lived in anything at all."

"A few years ago, that was true. Much changes. We built a timber mill to cut wood and acquired power tools for digging, which has freed labor to improve camp conditions. The ovens make bricks and pottery. While off-duty, guards hunt game, and we have extended the gardens all the way to the river, providing a surplus that we barter at the city markets. We work better, smarter, and faster, and this brings many rewards."

"Better, smarter, and faster? That sounds like a proverb," Dogra said.

"The proverb of my chief engineer. I question if you will like him. Some are offended by his bad manners."

"Beloved, I once served the diplomatic corps. I interact well with all types."

"We will see if that is true," Gamtro said.

* * * * * *

After their long separation, Dogra and Gamtro did not wait long for a coupling, thrashing about in the big nest among lashing tongues, gripping claws, and tossing bedding everywhere. Little of the afternoon remained when they decided to wash up.

"The refreshment closet has a shower. Heated water," Gamtro said, testing the new plumbing.

"Is that a surprise?" Dogra asked, wondering where her traveling clothes had gone and knowing her baggage had been left downstairs.

"Yes, my beloved, a surprise which I will explain later. It should make an interesting story. Enjoy the shower. I will bathe in the guardroom and find Nabbatron. There are reports to study before meal time."

As Gamtro went downstairs, Dogra took a shower in a newly tiled stall built of intricately combined slate and shale. The hot water did not last quite so long as she wanted, but still satisfied. Then she stood before a mirror, admiring her smooth leathery skin, still free of unsightly spots, and the long membrane behind her ear holes which gave her such a distinctive appearance. The four-digit claws were perfectly formed, the hard nails clipped to her taste. Her skin held a delicate blue tint with only the slightest traces of tan. Sure evidence of a noble heritage.

Not bad looking for a middle-aged countess, Dogra thought, finding a towel as she returned to the nest room. Then she stopped

231

cold, her heart beating fast as her breathing grew short. There was a food creature. Right there in her room.

Surprised by Dogra's sudden appearance, Shalli dropped the bedding she carried and instantly fell to her knees in the posture of submission.

"Forgive me, mistress," Shalli said, her head bowed low.

Dogra regained her composure. The female slave was a little more than twenty years old, with long blonde hair and creamy skin. It was a small creature that did not appear menacing.

"Look up," Dogra said.

Shalli obeyed, her big blue eyes searching for something in Dogra's stare. Dogra sensed curiosity. The creature is intelligent, she realized.

"Have you a name?" Dogra asked.

"Yes, Lady Gamtra. My name is Shalli," Shalli answered in a clear Arikhan, her accent better than some provincials. "I am sorry to have disturbed you, mistress. I wanted to bring up your bags and straighten the bed."

"That is very thoughtful of you, food crea ... Shalli," Dogra said, charmed by the obedient creature. "Please stand and remove your false hide."

Hesitant at first, Shalli stood up and undressed, dropping her elk skin dress on the floor, then removing her moccasins and deerskin underwear, standing naked before Dogra's inquiring stare.

"You are lovely," Dogra said in surprise, admiring the well-formed breasts, graceful limbs, and nicely proportioned body structure. She noticed Shalli's face turning red but it took her a moment to guess why.

"Are you embarrassed?" Dogra asked.

"Yes, mistress," Shalli said, looking down at the floor.

Embarrassed? Dogra thought, scarcely able to believe it. Gamtro is right, these creatures have sensibilities. At least, this one seems to. And it is very sweet, not some roaming brute like food creatures are portrayed in the theatres. Perhaps this one is an exception?

"I am sorry, Shalli. Please dress," Dogra allowed, watching how she did it. Another surprise. The creature dressed just like anyone else.

"You are helping with my luggage?" Dogra asked.

"If it pleases you, mistress," Shalli replied.

"An instruction from Baron Gamtro?"

"Excuse me, mistress?"

"You are ordered to serve?"

"No, mistress!" Shalli said, her eyes bright with disagreement. "We have known for months you would be visiting. Everyone has worked hard to make your stay pleasant. I had to draw lots with Pie and Keep for the honor. Tak wanted to draw, but the twins keep her busy."

"You have sought this duty? In truth?" Dogra asked.

"Yes, mistress. Often has Baron Gamtro told of the illustrious Lady Gamtra. Of your great education and high culture. All are excited to meet you."

Dogra was truly perplexed. It had never occurred to her that she would be a celebrity among food creatures, or that one could be so pleasurable as this Shalli.

"Have you no hatchlings to keep you busy, like your friend?" Dogra asked.

Shalli's smile disappeared as her head dropped.

"My little Jaime died last year," Shalli replied, choking back the words. "He was very smart and beautiful. I miss him terribly."

"I mourn your loss," Dogra said, realizing she meant it. "Soon you will have more."

"Yes, mistress. I pray to Sherra daily for the blessing," Shalli responded.

Dogra gasped. The creature worshipped Sherra! Of course, its simple mind could not be expected to comprehend the all-encompassing greatness of the Arikhan deity, but that Shalli would even imagine an appeal to Sherra was a staggering concept.

"Have you seen the clothing worn by females of my world?" Dogra asked, going to one of the trunks. "Not guard uniforms or provincial wear, but the lovely silks and satins of civilization."

"Only bits and pieces, mistress," Shalli admitted, looking with eagerness as the trunk was opened.

"Then come, Shalli, and help me unpack from a long voyage," Dogra said. "I stay here at Karak for the season. I will enjoy having another to share these with."

Just before sunset, Dogra went downstairs dressed in a comfortable dark blue leisure suit, stopping in the corridor to look for Gamtro. Shalli had returned to camp a few minutes before, bouncing happily with a gold silk scarf wrapped around her neck. Dogra found half a dozen guards gathered at the conference table in the main room, Gamtro sitting at the head. Introductions were made before the guards left.

"You were with Shalli for nearly two hours, beloved," Gamtro said, moving to a stool at the gaming tables where a bottle of fine bruno sat. Gamtro poured her a cup. "If the food creature frightens you, I can station an armed guard at your door."

"You are right to tease me. How could anyone be afraid of Shalli? She is a dear thing, and very bright," Dogra answered, surprised the find the wine of an acceptable vintage.

"Did you expect an ugly monster?" Gamtro asked.

"There is a new theatre on Arikhan. *The Keepers*. It portrays food creatures as bloody vvleen capable of hideous murder. Everyone who attends is frightened."

"I only guess, but in the early days of the empire our first conquests were of primitive worlds," Gamtro said. "Those creatures probably *were* barbaric vvleen. But not all worlds are like that. Two centuries ago, Akrona was just emerging from barbarity when we enslaved the population. There were millions of them then."

"Perhaps exposure to our culture has helped civilize them? I heard Shalli offer a prayer to Sherra."

"We may hope that is true. Sherra shapes the universe according to Her will. This may be Sherra's plan," Gamtro said. "But our will is not negligible. I have arranged for us to have privacy tonight. My staff is staying at their lodges where they find more comfort."

"Comforts? Here?" Dogra said.

"Each senior member of my staff is wealthy now. When they rotate out at the end of their enlistment, they will have fine homes for retirement," Gamtro said. "Zenatro is too dense to realize that

234

revenues from the lumber mill and farms produce as much as our mining bonuses. The glass factory we started at Ka'lan last year utilizes deposits of river sand. No one else on Akrona makes good quality glass."

"Such enterprise," Dogra said, brushing his beak with hers. "Never have I dreamed you could be such a merchant, my mate."

"It is a learned skill," Gamtro said, careful in his response. "Dogra, my beloved mate, much do I long to reside in your esteem, but there are things not yet disclosed. All will be known soon. Keep open your thoughts, and know that it takes many to accomplish things worthwhile."

"This I already know, my mate," a puzzled Dogra said. "My career is spent in committees. Teamwork is always the source of success."

"It gladdens me that you understand. The evening meal will wait until sundown. I would visit the pens while there is still light."

"The pens! Zenatro said you closed the pens," Dogra said, instantly thinking of Shalli.

"Workers are not sent to the slaughterhouses, but there are herd creatures on the prairie to exploit. We call them buffalo. As an experiment, we captured a group and fenced them in a box canyon."

"This is not a new practice, my mate. On several worlds, herd animals are bred on ranches. It lowers the cost and increases supply. Few Arikhan will engage in such work, but those who do make much profit."

"We wish to prove it can be done here," Gamtro said, surprised to learn his mate had studied so far from her field.

"Many talents do you acquire on this world. If our circle back home knew, you would gain much admiration."

"We may hope that is true. Would you like to see the buffalo? They are more fearsome than Shalli."

"Will you tease me of this for long?" Dogra asked, raising graceful eye-rings highlighted with ruby streaks.

Dogra followed Gamtro south along the deep creek, wider now than in the past due to a levee supplying water to an orchard. The camp was to their right, the forest on the left. Many of the trees to the west of the creek had been harvested where the ground gave way to a long sloping hill.

At the end of the tracks, she saw a large maintenance building made of wooden planks held together with steel bolts. Dogra guessed the structure big enough to service train engines should they require repair.

As the valley grew wider, a canyon appeared on the east side. There, behind a sturdy stockade fence, Dogra saw a herd of large hairy beasts milling around an artificial pond. She thought the hides would make wonderful coats if properly cured.

"Greetings, Lord Gamtro," a stocky middle-aged researcher said.

Dogra recognized the markings on his sea-green tunic as those of the Guild of Agriculturalists. She had not known the guild had a chapter on Akrona, let alone an investigator at Karak.

"Thank you, Tameron. How fare the beef-creatures?" Gamtro asked.

"They thrive. My report will remark favorably on your project," Tameron said, the accent sophisticated. Dogra wondered if Tameron was descended from a distinguished family.

"This is the Lady Gamtra. She has come to see the buffalo," Gamtro introduced.

"All know of Lady Gamtra and her work for the high committees. I am honored," Tameron said, his cheeks flushing light blue. Dogra dipped her head, acknowledging his homage.

"We are considering expanding the herd," Gamtro said.

"Diverse genes are necessary for good breeding, but you will need a larger water supply and more grass than you have in this canyon," Tameron explained. "And who will tend them? It is not fit work for your guards."

"Perhaps you can provide recommendations?" Gamtro requested.

"It would be an honor, Baron," Tameron eagerly agreed, clicking his tongue with pleasure.

Dogra took a sideways glance at her mate, approving of his skill in gaining the guild member's cooperation. And surprised to find him so diplomatic.

Just after sunset, Dogra walked alone up the poorly lit path to the headquarters. The tall dark trees loomed over her with foreboding shadows. The late spring brush seemed to hide lurking dangers. The forest did not feel so friendly at night. She was glad Gamtro would be along soon, having stopped at the rail station to authorize cargo manifests.

When she saw a light coming from an open door at the top of the path, Dogra hurried her pace, entering the headquarters with relief. She quickly noticed the conference table had been cleared of the day's work and set with large candle holders. There was no one in the main room, but noise came from the kitchen.

"Frontra? Romtra?" Dogra called out, approaching slowly.

Then she stopped with a gasp of terror. A horrible blood-soaked monster was standing in the doorway. A half-mad food creature! It wore a white apron splotched with red stains and held a long bloody knife in one paw. Sweat streaked its fierce brow and piercing gray eyes glared out from a narrow, sun-bronzed face. Its tousled brown hair grew wild in every direction.

Dogra prided herself on a brave heritage. It was not deemed fitting to cry out in fear, but it took all her nerve not to scream. The creature studied her, seemed to notice her reaction, and raised the knife. Dogra almost took a step back toward the door but could not bring herself to flee. Then, to Dogra's great relief, the creature made a half turn, threw the knife back into the kitchen basin, and dropped to its knees, the forehead making complete contact with the floor.

"Forgive me, Lady Gamtra," the creature said, the voice not unpleasant. And the Arikhan pronunciation was nearly perfect, though clipped with a strange accent.

"What is your purpose here, food creature?" Dogra said, regaining her composure.

"Preparing your meal, mistress," Grey said.

Dogra looked past the creature into the kitchen. A slab of freshly cut venison lay cooking on the grill. Spices were laid out on the counter. Colorful ceramic plates were stacked on serving trays near freshly cleaned utensils.

"Oh, for Sherra's sake," Dogra said, realizing now why the creature was covered in blood. And feeling especially foolish.

Gamtro entered.

"What's wrong?" Gamtro asked.

"Nothing, my mate. I did not realize ... nothing is wrong."

"What are you doing on the floor?" Gamtro asked his kneeling servant, his tongue clicking with displeasure.

"I fear the Lady Gamtra was startled, master," Grey said, maintaining the position.

"Our ways are strange to her," Gamtro said. "Do you fare well, my beloved?"

"Yes, but I do not understand. It is male. A food creature. Why does it prepare our meal when there are females available?" Dogra asked.

"A fair question. What is the answer?" Gamtro asked. "And get up. Stop groveling on the floor like a slave."

Grey stood and took several steps backward before removing the apron. His expression was still contrite. Dogra now saw it wasn't a blood-soaked monster, but a male of medium height, average weight, and a proportional build. The sweat came from working in the warm kitchen. The eyes shone with a searching intelligence. And there was sadness. This creature carried a world of experience on its shoulders.

"Shalli wanted extra time to dress. This is a special evening for her. I volunteered to cook the meal," Grey explained.

"It knows Shalli?" Dogra asked.

"I apologize for my negligence," Gamtro said. "Lady Gamtra, this is Ben, Shalli's husband. They are joining us for the evening meal. Ben, this is my most beloved, informally called Dogra, now the Lady Gamtra."

"You are Ben? Gamtro's famous pet?" Dogra asked.

"The master has been kind to me, mistress," Grey said, bowing deeply.

"That's enough," Gamtro objected, eye-rings hard and tongue clicking with dissatisfaction. "Beloved, in private Ben does not address me as master, or Baron. He simply calls me Gamtro. He has been my chief engineer for the last five years. He is responsible for cutting the new mines, for building the timber mill, the glass factory, the buffalo pens, and for many other projects that central planning is still unaware of. And he helped me reorganize the new camps assigned to my department. We would not have our exalted rank if not for him."

"My master speaks too generously," Grey disagreed. "Production is controlled by his authority. If failure is his to accept, so is the success. He is the one who raised the financing, found the extra labor, and risked ridicule to try new methods. If not for his boldness, I would have been sent to the pens years ago."

"We both know that is not true," Gamtro protested.

"We both know that it is," Grey responded.

"The creature is impertinent, is it not?" Dogra asked, adding a click of disapproval to the end of her question.

"Always has it been so. Ben is also my friend," Gamtro replied.

Dogra studied her mate's expression and realized it was no exaggeration. He truly felt affection for the creature. She would claim no expertise in reading a human being's expression, but she sensed that Ben felt the same way about Gamtro.

It suddenly struck her just what they were saying. The mines, the timber, the new wealth, all a result of their partnership. Even her new rank. Dogra's knees suddenly went weak.

"Let me find you a stool. Ben, find wine for us," Gamtro said.

As Grey scurried back into the kitchen, Gamtro helped Dogra sit down and loosened her collar for better breathing.

"I am sorry. I should have explained sooner, but this is not something to discuss in a public communication," he apologized.

"Certainly not. Never have I heard of such a thing," Dogra said.

"I hope you are not angry," Gamtro said.

"No, beloved, not angry. Just concerned," Dogra answered. Then she lowered her voice to a whisper. "Is it really responsible for as much as you say?"

"By Sherra's Oath."

"Remarkable."

Grey returned with two cups of imported wine, passing the first to Dogra, then the other to Gamtro before stepping back. Dogra noticed Gamtro's eye-rings curl sharply.

"Are you going to do this all evening?" Gamtro said to Grey.

"Do what, master?" Grey questioned.

"Pretend to be my servant. Lady Gamtra is my mate. A sacred bond in our culture. Do not play the fool with her," Gamtro insisted.

Dogra saw Grey frown. Clearly he was not comfortable with the situation. He didn't want to question Gamtro, especially about so sensitive an issue, but he wasn't ready to offer his trust, either. The dilemma was obvious in the creature's eyes.

"Ben, get yourself a cup and sit," Dogra ordered, leaving her stool. "Gamtro, take your seat. I will finish making the meal."

"Excuse me, Lady Gamtra, but the meal will be ready soon and you need to change clothes. Let me finish the preparations," Grey requested.

"I will let you finish the cooking if you will call me Dogra when we are alone," Dogra bargained.

Grey sighed as if it was a bit much to ask, then nodded and went into the kitchen.

"I am not sure it will obey," Dogra said in amazement.

"These creatures have many reasons not to trust the superior race, but Ben makes his own decisions, and they are always based on us as individuals. I think he trusts Frontra more than many of his own kind. In time, he will trust you, also."

"Shalli and I will spend some afternoons together. There is much I wish to learn about these people," Dogra said, getting ready to go upstairs.

"People?" Gamtro said.

"No doubt the majority of this planet's population is barbarian, but Shalli and Ben do not seem like food creatures. I have no doubt Shalli is an exception, of course. And Ben is obviously from a civilized race."

Shalli arrived wearing a lovely deerskin dress embroidered on the hem, soft beaded moccasins, and her hair bundled on top of her head tied with her new silk scarf. Grey changed into a deerskin shirt, bleached goat hide pants and buffalo hide boots. When Dogra looked downstairs and saw the trouble Shalli had gone to, she selected a sleek brown dinner suit with an ermine collar that matched the rustic occasion. Gamtro merely dressed as he always did, in a simple camp uniform.

"That was an excellent meal, Ben," Dogra said. "For someone who does not eat meat, you certainly know how to prepare it."

"Ben is good at everything," Shalli said, hanging on his arm.

Dogra could see that Shalli adored her mate. And he seemed fond of her, though he was much older. They made a good match.

In the course of the dinner conversation, Dogra lost all doubt that Ben was an engineer of exceptional talent. He could explain complex projects in ways that were easy to understand. Weave together diverse theories, means and goals that even a full committee would find confusing. And even then, he wasn't discussing everything he was thinking, only that which needed to be known. It made Dogra very curious about his origins. Certainly he was not native to a primitive world like Akrona.

"Thank you for a lovely evening, Dogra," Shalli said as they prepared to leave.

"You are welcome, child. I shall anticipate a visit with your friends," Dogra said, even fonder of Shalli than before.

"We can still postpone the hunting trip," Grey suggested.

Gamtro considered the offer but Dogra gave him encouragement with a wiggle of her thin eye-rings.

"We should go. We know little of the best game trails this late in the spring," Gamtro said. "Maybe the females can go with us?"

"No thank you!" Dogra and Shalli said at the same time. Shalli laughed and Dogra clicked her tongue.

After Shalli and Grey left for the compound, Dogra sat down next to Gamtro.

"Their table manners are not bad," she said. "Not cosmopolitan, but not bad."

"Better manners than Zenatro," Gamtro remarked.

"Does Ben never eat meat? Shalli does. She seemed to enjoy the grilled deer."

"She certainly did. She ate so much I thought we might have to go out for another," Gamtro said, clicking his tongue rapidly. As Dogra did. "I have only known Ben to eat meat on rare occasions, but he does hunt. And one of his first projects after we formed our partnership was to restock the lake with fish. He said it would provide

241

a more balanced diet for the workers and attract game birds from the river. As always, he was correct."

"Partnership is a dangerous word. Are you truly partners?" Dogra asked.

"No, I suppose not," Gamtro said.

"What troubles you? If Ben merely serves, none may criticize."

"They will criticize, my mate. Make no mistake."

Gamtro walked upstairs, removed his uniform, and went to sit on the balcony. Campfires lit the west side of the valley. Stars and one of the moons shone above. Dogra removed her dinner outfit and followed in a thin silk shift.

"What is wrong?" she asked, sitting next to him on a log bench.

"I find it disturbing. If Ben and I were true partners, we could pursue our projects as equals instead of master and slave. There is so much more we could achieve."

"What more can you do for Ben? He is a food creature, subject to the laws of the Empire," Dogra said.

"That is not what troubles my thoughts. While we grow in honor, everything Ben does is for his people. What little he keeps is for Shalli's sake. There are times I grow embarrassed by the arrangement."

"Has he asked for more?"

"No, Ben knows the law as we do. Perhaps better. He does his best. He knows I do my best. He also knows nothing lasts forever. In two more years, my term of office will expire. What will happen to the camps then?"

"Surely, my mate, someone else will wish to profit as you have, and gain recognition," Dogra said even as she began asking herself the same question.

"But will they accept advice from a food creature? Tolerate Ben's insolent ways? I have thought, my mate, that I should try to take the governorship from Zenatro."

"Sarden Leader to governor in a mere nine years? Beloved, even if the ministry would entertain such an idea, you would make powerful enemies. You would be undermined at every turn. If you must seek protection for these creatures, find another path."

"You speak wisely," Gamtro said, brushing her claw.

"Have you spoken to Ben of this?" Dogra wondered.

"Ben will say little, only that it lies with Sherra to decide. But I sense he agrees with you. No encouragement is offered."

"That is strange," she said.

"Strange?"

"I would think he has much to gain if you succeed, and little to lose if you fail," Dogra suggested.

"You do not yet understand, my beloved."

* * * * * *

On the third day of her visit, Dogra walked down the path from the headquarters and crossed over the footbridge to the main gate. It was a nice morning, not too cold, and she dressed casually in a light blue tunic and low boots.

From the outside, Karak was notably unimpressive. A few old tool sheds and the train station were common to any industrial facility. The shimmering blue energy barrier that reached to the river on her right and curved deep into the mountains on her left was barely visible in the bright sun. Though appearing harmless, attempts to penetrate the energy field could be extremely painful, forming an effective prison. Several portals showed where the ore carts were rolled up to the loading docks. The landscape was generally dry despite the many trees growing on the hillsides.

The two-story brick guardhouse was still there, though the ground floor meeting room offered a few more comforts. A tall spiked gate prevented unauthorized departures from the compound, reminding Dogra that she was visiting a slave camp.

Dogra saw Shalli waiting for her just inside the fence wearing a simple brown dress and sandals. The sentry on duty opened the iron gate and then locked it after Dogra passed through. Frontra joined her.

"Sherra's blessing on the morning," Frontra said, in full uniform with several weapons attached to her belt.

"And to you, Frontra. Are you my escort?"

"It must be so. Not all of the animals are tame," Frontra replied, though by her manner, Dogra suspected the senior guard of harboring a secret resentment.

"Greetings, Lady Gamtra," Shalli called out, waving as Dogra crossed the line of yellow stones into the compound.

"Hello, Shalli. No friends, this morning?" Dogra asked.

"They have quotas, mistress. We can meet them at the midday meal," Shalli explained.

Quotas, Dogra thought. *And here I thought to meet a crowd of admiring food creatures vying for my attention.*

They walked toward the first of the camps, Dogra and Shalli side by side with Frontra trailing behind. They passed Rabbit Camp, now constructed of timber huts with thatched roofs, and entered the gardens at the southern end of the lake, now larger due to the extended irrigation.

"These are the old gardens," Shalli said. "Mostly used by Ferret and Deer Camps. Rabbit Camp spends its time down at the river with the newcomers."

"Newcomers?" Dogra asked, watching as Shalli turned the irrigated soil over to show the richness.

Shalli pointed to the north end of the lake where the foothills around Wolf Camp gave way to the valley. Just beyond the gap, near the first of the farms leading down to the river, was a large village.

"They are all new, gathered from other camps. Some from the desert camps. Some from the old processing center. They were so frightened when they came here. So naked and hungry. They thought they were going to the pens. Now they have homes. Warm clothes for the winter. Their little ones thrive. My Ben gave them this. My Ben and your Baron Gamtro," Shalli said, her voice quivering with emotion.

Shalli looked up at Dogra, making sure the great Arikhan lady understood the gratefulness in her heart. Gradually, Dogra did come to understand, and it helped explain why the food creatures were so eager to please her. It was not fear, or subservience, as she initially assumed. At least on Shalli's part, it was genuine appreciation.

There were many women working the gardens, tilling the soil and clearing ditches to bring water down from the windmill driven pumps near the lake. Some young boys and girls were fishing. The work was hard but the laborers looked content. None stopped to greet the visitors, but several did nod in their direction.

Shalli took Dogra to a two-story stone building on the west side of the lake where a council tent had once stood years before. The simple structure had windows facing east to the lake and west toward the mines. A single wooden door opened on a broad porch from the south side. A dozen chairs and nearly fifty stools were in the immediate area. Dogra saw an outside staircase that accessed the second floor.

"Our home is on the ground," Shalli explained. "My husband has his office in the sky. Would you care to sit until meal time?"

"Thank you, Shalli," Dogra said, following her inside. Frontra took a seat on the porch as one accustomed to being there.

The interior of the stone house was a shock. Dogra had seen several huts at Rabbit Camp with their primitive wicker furniture and straw-covered floors. This building resembled an Arikhan dwelling, with sanded wood floorboards, a colorful throw rug, and a well-designed dining table with eight chairs. A brick fireplace was usable for warmth or cooking, though a cast iron stove in a nearby alcove served a small kitchen. There was even running water from a corner sink.

In the rear, sectioned off by red curtains, was a sleeping chamber with a large bed. The comfortable living room had canvas paintings on the walls.

Dogra stopped to take a closer look at the paintings. They were not the usual landscapes. One showed a lonely lunar outpost on a desolate meteor-pocked plain. Another featured a dangerous asteroid belt perilously close to an unsuspecting planet. The largest had a stunning starfield being drawn into an unforgiving black hole. Even the smaller paintings had poignant, almost wistful yearnings emerging from comparatively simple images. Dogra stared at the paintings for a long time, moved by the deep feelings they invoked.

"Such strength. Such emotion. No one here could have painted these. Where did they come from?" Dogra asked.

"My husband paints them. He was working so many hours, the

245

leaders conspired with Baron Gamtro to make him take recreations. Do you find them interesting, mistress?"

Dogra could tell Shalli was not impressed, either with the forms or the subjects. A culture accustomed to fertility totems could hardly understand the great contrasts between Sherra's all-encompassing universe and the fragility of individual mortality.

"Shalli, these are superb works of art. Not the work of a master, of course, but highly evocative," Dogra said.

"I am sure Ben would want you to have one. If it were my choice, you could have them all. They frighten me. I think there are dark spirits in the worlds he sees."

"That is the beauty of them, child. And I would very much like to have one. Let us wait until the males return from their hunting trip. We will speak of it again."

Before long, women arrived to start cooking fires, many setting up near the lake. With them were babies and young children. Many women had more than one child to care for, sharing their duties.

As introductions were made, Dogra noticed the majority of women were far more reserved than Shalli. Respectful, but not trusting. They were not overwhelmed by the Lady Gamtra's exalted status in a society they knew nothing of, but most did express gratitude for her mate's generosity.

Their reserve did not extend to Frontra, who babysat several infants while their mothers prepared food. Dogra saw it was a duty Frontra eagerly accepted.

"I am sorry the people were not more friendly, mistress," Shalli said as they walked back to the main gate late in the afternoon.

"They were friendlier than I expected, child. This has been a very informative day. Your mines. Your farms. The dwellings. All are interesting. I wish more of my people could see Karak. It would open many eyes."

"What do you mean, mistress?"

"It is hard to explain. Perhaps another time," Dogra said, not wanting to confuse her with false hopes.

"Here is the gate, Lady Gamtra. I have duties on the north side," Frontra said, taking her leave.

"Thank you, Frontra. I shall commend your service to Baron Gamtro."

Frontra lowered her eye-rings and left, walking casually toward Rabbit Camp. Dogra noticed the ease with which she strolled through the camps, her authority based on respect rather than fear. There was a lesson there.

Dogra and Shalli went to the iron gate guarding the entrance, stopping just short of the sentry booth. Two guards, both new to the compound, came to attention. Shalli stopped short at the line of yellow rocks. Dogra looked at her with a question.

"This is as far as I am allowed, mistress," Shalli explained.

"Thank you, Shalli, you are a dear. You have brought joy to my day," Dogra said.

"You are welcome, mistress," Shalli answered, bowing her head.

Dogra acknowledged the guards as she passed through the gate, again feeling a cold shadow creep through her as she walked beneath the imposing brick arch. She turned to look at Shalli standing in the fading afternoon light with the slave camp behind her. The small creature looked so alone. So vulnerable. It would take nothing more than an angry guard, or a hungry one, to extinguish the light in those beautiful blue eyes, and not a law in the Empire would protect her. Suddenly Dogra felt a sense of foreboding, and an empathy that never would have occurred to her only a few days before. She turned back.

"Shalli, I feel lonely with the males gone. Would you keep me company until they return?" Dogra asked.

"It would be an honor, mistress, but I should gather something more appropriate to wear," Shalli answered, holding out the plain skirt of her work dress with embarrassment.

"Do not fret, child. I have plenty of material and a sewing kit. We will entertain ourselves by making a civilized outfit for you."

Shalli's face brightened with a smile as she rushed to the gate, jumping through to Dogra's side as the guards made way for her. Dogra experienced a unique satisfaction from Shalli's excitement and wondered if her fondness for Shalli was anything like the fondness Gamtro felt for Ben. She suspected it was. And she suspected it could make life very complicated for all of them.

* * * * * *

"Are you sure this is a good idea?" Grey asked as he and Gamtro disembarked from the hovering sho'kara.

"It has been done often. Not so much on this world, but on my home world," Gamtro said, removing his backpack from the hovercraft's cargo compartment and taking a second backpack for Grey.

The small cargo transport was bouncing lightly on four support jets, a powerful gyroscope aiding an anti-gravity effect. The side hatch allowed movement in and out of the craft without actually landing. Grey took his backpack and stepped back as Gamtro waved the vehicle off.

"Do not worry. It will be back in two days. We may enjoy this primitive planet without fear of civilization," Gamtro said.

"We are a hundred sectors southeast of the camp. Are you sure you will not get lost?"

"I am sure," Gamtro said.

"You did not take a communicator."

"I do not need a communicator."

"None of your people stray this far from your colonies. What if there is an emergency?"

"We have a compass, a medical kit, and weapons. What could happen that is beyond your abilities to combat?" Gamtro asked.

"You show much faith, my friend, but what if I am the one who gets injured?" Grey laughed.

"Then I will wander the forest and die, but I will wander the forest and die in good company," Gamtro said with clicks of amusement.

They watched the sho'kara as it disappeared to the west over a low range of mountains. An unseasonable frost had left the mountaintops white with snow. Grey unleashed the long bow from his shoulder to nock the string, then helped Gamtro with his bow. Both were dressed in hunting leathers with tall brown boots and broad felt hats.

"Try not to shoot me in the back this time," Grey said.

"I did not shoot you in the back. I missed by several claws," Gamtro protested.

248

"You missed by several teeth."

"Maybe we should look for a campsite instead of debating trivial accidents," Gamtro suggested.

They walked down from the rock hilltop where the hovercraft had paused, finding a wooded glen near a shallow creek. They dropped their backpacks and Grey started setting up camp.

"I will erect the tent," Gamtro said.

"Let me do it," Grey replied.

"I can do it," Gamtro insisted.

"It will fall down if you do it."

"You are not here to be my servant."

"If the tent falls on you, it falls on me too," Grey pointed out.

"That is true about many things, is it not?"

"What falls on who lies in Sherra's providence. At least I can set up the tent," Grey answered, opening the carrying bag and laying out the polymer poles.

Gamtro gathered materials for a fire, piled rocks for containment, and used his great strength to drag logs nearby to sit on. By the time Grey had erected the tent, Gamtro was making vegetable stew over a small fire.

"What do you think of Dogra?" Gamtro asked.

"She is very intelligent. For an Arikhan."

"You do not trust her."

"Your mate is an attaché for the ministry. The Empire is troubled, looking for scapegoats. I do not know enough about your politics to understand all, but we tread dangerous ground. It is hard to trust anyone with so much unknown."

"You must understand that in our culture, Dogra and I are one. We may disagree, but betrayal is impossible. What I tell her stays between us," Gamtro said.

"I have no doubt she is a fine mate. I find her very open-minded for one of your species. But time is not our friend. We have enjoyed several good years. We should have two more. After that, anything may happen."

"I could gain the governorship," Gamtro said.

"Did Dogra agree?"

"No, she thought the effort would fail," Gamtro admitted.

"Dogra is right. It would be foolish to endanger your career for a lost cause. You have learned much. Learned the need for change. One day you will win a governorship, maybe even rise to the High Ministry itself. On that day, you will be able to help more than a few thousand slaves on a forgotten world."

"You have also learned much. Working together has brought both of us new wisdom," Gamtro said.

Grey grew quiet, listening to the forest around them. Looking up at the tall green pine trees and hearing the babbling creek. Feeling an ancient freedom.

"If Sherra chooses to replace you with a generous heart, what we have built may thrive," Grey said. "But if there is a reaction to your practices, as I suspect there will be, then you alone will carry the lesson."

"I do not understand your words," Gamtro said.

"You will," Grey replied, stirring the cooking fire with a stick.

"Dogra would understand, would she not?" Gamtro asked.

"I suspect she will," Grey said, eating his stew without tasting it. "Gamtro, the laws of your Empire are very strict. Exceptions are difficult, but if there is a way, I would have you take Shalli away at the end of your term. Make her a servant on your estate, or a pet, or whatever is required. Do not leave her at Karak."

"If it comes to that, I will take both of you," Gamtro said.

"That will never happen. Everyone knows about Gamtro's pet food creature. Some even suspect I influence production. If they research my records, it might be more complicated than that. Shalli is merely a female. No one cares what happens to her."

"My people are not renowned for their record keeping."

"So far I have been lucky, but one day someone will grow curious. It surprises me you never asked more questions."

Gamtro's interest was aroused by this admission.

"All these years we have labored together, you have never mentioned your past. Never hinted it should be investigated. Why do you challenge me now?"

"Dogra appears fond of Shalli. She has power. If something is going to happen to me, maybe it should happen while Shalli can still find protection. We have accomplished much together. Given time, we can do more. But if my time runs out today, it will not be a tragedy."

"It would be to me," Gamtro said, clicking his tongue softly with indignation. "And to a thousand others who love you. And to millions who have not learned of our work, and need to learn of it, for the sake of your people and for mine. You wrong my species to underestimate yourself in this way."

"I mean no disrespect. If you knew all, you might feel differently," Grey said, sorry he had made the baron angry.

Gamtro glanced about the forest also. Seeing the same trees, the same creek, though with less yearning for the freedoms they offered, having sufficient freedom already. But the habit of looking for eavesdroppers was a necessary habit.

"What's wrong?" Grey asked.

"None will find your records. Those fools on the Link never classified them properly, and the Link was destroyed by marauders a year later. Every record you have ever generated is classified under my ancestral seal."

"I do not understand."

"Yes, you do. You do not trust me enough to say it."

"I confess you are right," Grey said with some embarrassment.

"Then let me say it. Years ago, before Ben became a slave of the Arikhan, you were known by another name. You were commander of the fleet that opposed our invasion of Sol. You were personally responsible for the destruction of Bellerophon and her crew."

Grey leaned back, astonished. The bowl dipped so low in his hand that Gamtro had to catch it before the contents spilled.

"How long have you known?" Grey asked.

"After the day I held the knife to your throat, and you held a knife to mine, I started a search. It took six seasons to find the answers. It does not speak well for our intelligence service that they failed to put such obvious data together. It took another season to gather all your records. After that, there was nothing to investigate. And there never will be."

251

"You have not said anything."

"Neither have you."

"What should I say? That I have slain hundreds of your warriors?"

"That is where you do not understand, my friend. It is true there are forces that would seek vengeance. Others, like myself, know you fought to protect your people. Just as we fight to protect our people. Since coming to Akrona, you have not waged war against us. You have sought to protect your adopted people. Cooperated to build mutual advantages. And you have served me well under thankless circumstances. Do you think me unaware of the criticism you receive from your own kind? Am I unaware of the riches you produce while demanding nothing for yourself?"

"You shame me," Grey said, confessing he had not thought Gamtro so insightful.

"You are not shamed. You have strong reasons to keep your past secret. I suspect even Shalli knows nothing. The precaution is wise. I have never told anyone. But know I am not your friend out of ignorance."

"I would have gone to the pens years ago if not for you. Never think that is not understood," Grey said.

"If you had gone to the pens, I would still be an arrogant Sarden Leader without wealth or prospects. Never think that is not understood."

"Are we going sit around all day or go hunting?"

"You do not eat the game."

"I cook it for my friend. That is good enough."

"Before we go, there is a question that has always puzzled me," Gamtro said. "You were seen to be killed when the molecule weapon destroyed Bellerophon. Your sacrifice was captured on visual recordings and replayed many times. Why were you not killed? How did you reach the Laros stargate?"

"You ask a good question. Many years have I pondered this problem and still only have an unproved theory," Grey said.

"I enjoy unproved theories. They provide distraction during the quiet hours."

"Do you understand the energy fields used to protect your

battleships?"

"I know that weapons cannot penetrate them," Gamtro said.

"Bellerophon was protected by a negative energy envelope generated by a step-two variable reactor," Grey explained. "A negative envelope diverts potentially destructive levels of energy into subspace dimensions. I floated through this screen carrying a deactivated nuclear warhead, allowing the shock to disrupt my central nervous system. After the biological nature of my wiring allowed me to recover, I cranked a generator to charge the warhead's battery and set the detonator."

"Is it true you activated the warhead manually?"

"I had no choice. Garthon discovered my presence on the hull and sent Varbatro to stop me. There wasn't enough time to set the timer and jump free as I hoped."

"But you must have been close to the explosion?"

"Within meters. Seconds before the warhead exploded, the ship suddenly increased rotation, throwing me off. I must have been inside the negative energy field at the moment of detonation. The explosion tore a hole in the subspace fabric where all atomic particles have a resonance signature. If my theory is correct, I was carried along with debris as it sought its original resonance source. I emerged through a stargate where the signatures were strongest."

"Laros. Bellerophon was built of minerals from this star system," Gamtro realized.

"That is my theory," Grey confirmed.

"It is a good theory. Astrophysics is not my highest skill, but I once commanded a destroyer escort. Stargate management is a mandatory study. There is one problem with your theory."

"More than one. Which have you selected?" Grey asked.

"Twelve hundred light years is far beyond the range of any known stargate," Gamtro said. "Assuming such a length could be traveled, you would spend months, perhaps years in a sub-dimensional state. In what manner could you be resurrected after so long a journey?"

"I have no answer, my friend. I lack the research to answer your question."

"Then we have much to contemplate," Gamtro said, gathering his bow and a quiver of arrows. "But let me suggest a solution that might elude you."

"A suggestion would be welcome," Grey granted.

"You do much for your people. Much that might one day return prosperity to my people. Perhaps Sherra has a plan for you."

Grey thought Gamtro was correct about one thing. It was an answer that would have eluded him.

After a day stalking through lush green meadows, the two hunters returned to their camp with a pair of rabbits. Gamtro skinned and cleaned the kills while Grey started a fire in the rock pit.

"You should have let me shoot the big meat creature," Gamtro said, finding the rabbits skinny.

"We are hunting elk and deer, not horses," Grey said.

"They have more meat than elk."

"Tougher meat, too. Your old teeth could not chew it."

"By Arikhan standards, I am not so much older than you, and my teeth chew well. You did not want to kill them."

"On my world horses are used for work and recreation. Sometimes they are eaten, but not often. My first wife loved horses. She rode them often. I even went riding with her on a few occasions."

"Rode? On the creature's back?"

"I do not recommend it. They are fierce animals," Grey said.

"How would a horse work?" Gamtro asked.

"Normally they are put in a leather harness to pull things. Wagons, plows. Even trolleys," Grey remembered.

"We have trouble bringing timber down from the slopes. Could horses be used for this purpose?"

"Gamtro, that is quite a leap in imagination for you," Grey complemented.

"Imagination does not come easy, but I learn. Each season the practice grows easier."

"To answer your question, horses would be much better than man-hauling, but they need to be cared for. They require food, training, and pastures. We don't have enough space in the camp for a ranch."

"Again I hear ranch. Dogra spoke of ranch also. What is a ranch?" Gamtro asked.

"Your people must have ranches?" Grey questioned.

"So I am told, but I am unaware of their operations."

"Well, excuse the poor analogy, but a ranch is like a slave camp but without the gross mismanagement. Animals are kept within designated areas. The best animals are kept for breeding. Some are used for producing products. Wool, milk, eggs, meat. If you eat all of your animals, as the Arikhan have done on too many worlds, you lose your reproductive stock. That is why good management is so important."

"Like what we are attempting with the buffalo, only on a larger scale. I understand now. I also understand that preying upon sentient beings is unnecessary. There are other ways for the Empire's needs to be met."

Gamtro watched for Grey's reaction. He expected Grey to boldly support the supposition. Criticize the Arikhan for their bloodlust. Grey merely shrugged in a manner that confirmed Gamtro's opinion.

"Are you not angered that so many die unnecessarily? Do you not hate us for it?" Gamtro asked, eye-rings bent in question.

"I might, if food was the only issue," Grey said.

"Explain," Gamtro demanded.

"Your people destroy the populations of conquered worlds for food, but also to make room for colonization. My people have much experience with this. A long history of genocidal practices. It is said a conqueror named Genghis Khan once massacred millions of harmless peasants to make grazing land for his war horses. We often kill those who oppose us. We clear the land of inconvenient inhabitants and rationalize the immorality of it. We even eat sentient creatures that are less evolved than ourselves. Do not feel badly, Gamtro. You may belong to a bloodthirsty culture, but at least you are not hypocrites."

"You do not approve of genocide. You despise it."

"Wasting so much potential is never good," Grey agreed.

"Do you want your people to be better than they are?"

"Yes, I would rather mankind was a more noble species."

"Then we have much in common. Like you, I have come to think the killing of sentient creatures is wrong. Creatures who could be our friends, as you are my friend, should not be food. I would also belong to a nobler species."

Grey heard the sincerity in Gamtro's voice. The pain of realizing the suffering his civilization was inflicting, and knowing he was part of it.

"It is what I have long suspected. At heart, you are a better soul than I am," Grey decided. Gamtro leaned back in surprise. He did not believe Grey's opinion correct.

After their meal, Gamtro and Grey settled down with a bottle of bruno and watched the stars, speculating on which ones had the most importance. It was near sack time when they heard a noise in the dark forest around them, the cracking of a fallen tree branch. Grey stood first, studying the woods with one hand on his hunting knife, an iron skillet in the other. Gamtro was just getting up when a soft shuffling of leaves increased the alarm.

"Get down, back from the fire," Grey said, listening carefully for movement.

Gamtro didn't obey the instruction, moving forward with a claw on his holstered pistol. Then, as he motioned to draw the weapon, a flat shape spun out of the darkness, flying with deadly force right at Gamtro's throat. Grey dove over a fallen log and raised the skillet, deflecting the object at the last second. When Gamtro knelt to pick the object up, Grey pushed him down and sat on him.

Another weapon whirled by, the aim high and wide. A warning? Grey wondered. There was more rustling in the bushes, then silence.

"Stay," Grey whispered, disappearing into the forest.

Gamtro stayed down for a moment, then drew the pistol and straightened up. The air-charged pellet gun was capable of firing with deadly force, but with Grey lost in the darkness, how could he tell friend from foe?

Gamtro retreated to the tent, kneeling just off to the side in the shadows. He wasn't afraid, but didn't want to be a target either. A cloud layer moved in, cutting off the stars and leaving the forest black. Better known for their sense of smell than their night vision, the Arikhan was forced to sit quietly while scanning the area.

After half an hour, Gamtro grew angry at Grey for leaving without

256

permission, wondering if he was following the intruders or lying dead someplace. Not until the second hour did Grey struggle back to camp. His jacket was torn by his dash through the woods. His hat was lost but he didn't appear hurt.

"I am displeased," Gamtro said.

"There were four of them," Grey reported, weary from a strenuous hike. "Bipeds, but I do not think they were apes. Fast, too. I lost them at the lake."

"You should not be chasing phantoms," Gamtro said.

"That boomerang was no phantom," Grey said, looking around the camp. The weapon was not there, only ashes in the fire where Gamtro had thrown it.

"They were phantoms. Do not speak of them again."

"Are you not curious?"

"There is nothing to be curious about. Pockets of primitives litter this world's remote areas. Special teams spent many years tracking them down. They even used slaves to lure them into traps. After a time, the primitives began killing the slaves. We burned the forests. You will ignore them. That is an order."

Grey sensed this was a sensitive issue. Precisely why could only be guessed. And it wasn't worth angering Gamtro over.

"It never happened," Grey said. "Let us get a few hours sleep and try our luck with the bows. I found a deer trail that looks fresh."

Gamtro accepted the change of subject without comment. The only alternative would be to obey his standing orders. Kill primitives whenever possible. And kill any slave who sees them.

Chapter Eight
FATEFUL DECISIONS

"Here they come!" Shalli shouted as the sho'kara appeared above the low treeless ridge to the southeast.

As Karak had no formal landing pad, the craft maneuvered on stubby wing jets to an area south of the compound where the railroad tracks terminated, touching down near the maintenance shed. Nabbatron drove up on a tractor towing a flatbed trailer. Dogra and Shalli rode with him.

"Greetings, my mate," Gamtro said, disembarking from the side cargo hatch.

"How fared the hunt?" Dogra asked.

"A bull elk," Gamtro said, very pleased.

"A bull elk?" Dogra asked.

"Like a killian, but larger," Gamtro explained, extending his arms to indicate the wide antlers.

"And four rabbits," Grey said, holding up the kills as he jumped off the transport.

Shalli ran to hug him, kissing so passionately that Dogra wondered if they were about to couple. They didn't, but Shalli made it clear they soon would.

The guards helped unload the elk, putting the carcass on the trailer so all could see as they were towed past the camp. There would be fresh meat for the guards, skins and antlers for the slaves. Shalli would get the rabbits.

Grey surrendered his hunting equipment to Nabbatron, who showed no fear they might be misused, and went with Shalli to the main gate. More than a dozen people waited at the yellow rocks to meet him, all from Ferret Camp. There would be a celebration at sunset.

Gamtro took a trophy hoof from the bull elk and walked back to his headquarters with Dogra while Romtra gave him a preliminary report.

"The ore train departed on schedule, Baron Gamtro," Romtra said. "The workers are quiet, production on schedule. Work on the Bear Camp mine goes slowly. They request more blasting, but Ben recommended no blasting while he was away. Wolf Camp produced most quickly. Black Hands reports worker health good. A new pup was born to Deer Camp."

"I was there," Dogra said. "Shalli's friend Trebeca gave birth to a male. A live birth. So much screaming and blood. I thought setting down eggs was hard, but this was much worse. It was exciting, too. I was allowed to hold it."

"That is rare. Unless coerced, the food creatures never render up their young to such as us," Gamtro said.

"Except Frontra," Romtra corrected.

"Frontra is much accepted," Gamtro agreed.

As Romtra veered off to the guardhouse, Gamtro and Dogra went up the path to the headquarters. Back in their private room, Gamtro noticed scraps of material and sewing supplies on the table.

"How have you spent our separation?" Gamtro asked as he washed in the refreshment closet.

"I walked to the river with Frontra where we could view the farms through the fence," Dogra said. "Frontra said the newcomers are too unruly to visit inside the screen. Shalli said so, too. She was very upset when I suggested we go north of the lake without escort."

"Her advice was wise. Guards only walk the north section in pairs. And always armed," Gamtro said.

"It is interesting. In the north, near the river, we are hated. You can see the lust for violence in the eyes of the slaves. But Ben is worshipped there. In the southern camps near the lake, we are tolerated, and you are much respected, but Ben is treated coolly. Some even seem to resent him. Are the politics of these creatures so sophisticated?"

"Their ways are not so difficult to understand. Ben only arrived a few years ago, but soon cast a large shadow. The older camps vie with him for leadership. The newcomers arrived from brutal camps where life was lived at the edge of the pens. Ben's efforts to bring them here saved a thousand lives. He gave them food and decent

259

quarters. For them, his leadership is unquestioned. This adds tension among the camps. But make no mistake, my beloved. They may complain and criticize, but even in the older camps, Ben is much honored."

"The dynamics would make an interesting study. Perhaps we could bring in a research committee? Examine the groups to better understand their culture."

"I would resist such an investigation," Gamtro said.

"But why, my mate? Such a study would be discussed at every academy."

"This is not the time to draw attention. It could be dangerous," Gamtro said.

"Dangerous for whom?" Dogra asked.

Gamtro stepped into the shower, scrubbed down with military efficiency, and emerged to brush claws with Dogra. He avoided her question.

"Have you been mending?" Gamtro asked, looking again at the sewing kits.

"Shalli and I created outfits. She stayed with me while you were gone. I apologize if rules were broken."

"Shalli is assigned to serve you. You alone decide how that is best accomplished," Gamtro answered.

Dogra sighed with relief. "I was worried we had taken liberties. Shalli even stayed here at night instead of returning to camp."

"You shared the same nest with a food creature? What would your friends say?" Gamtro teased.

"I could never think of Shalli as a food creature. She is sweet and caring. Harming her would be a crime."

"Harming her is not a crime. Someday our laws may send her to the pens," Gamtro warned.

Dogra's eyes went flat, a gray film appearing over the yellow irises. Her breath paused.

"I did not mean to sadden you," Gamtro said, taking hold of her claws. "Shalli is safe in our camp. They all are. Sherra will see to their future."

"My beloved, are you a follower of Mordari?" Dogra asked.

"No, my mate. There is wisdom in Mordari's words, but I do not believe her divinely inspired. Our empire struggles. There is much we can do better. But Sherra's blessing do not rise or fall on the fate of food creatures. If it did, we would have faltered centuries ago."

Dogra went outside to sit on the balcony, watching the camp beyond the tracks. As sunset came, fires were started and people gathered for their evening meals. Singing could be heard.

"Some of the creatures are violent, much as they are portrayed in our theatres," Dogra said when Gamtro joined her. "They should all hate us, but they do not. Not Shalli or her camp. Why is that?"

"Some have known Frontra for many years. She is respected," Gamtro speculated. "Ben knows that all Arikhan are not the same. He sees us as individuals, and much do his views influence others. Brutal guards are still hated, and slaves who see us only as masters may always hate us, but a few respect us for who we are."

"If the slaves who are treated brutally were treated well, would they still hate us? Where does the responsibility lie?"

"You begin to echo Mordari, my beloved," Gamtro said.

"I fear what Mordari's message may mean for us. To be called a traitor would break my heart, but I cannot close my eyes. I will not forget what I have learned here."

* * * * * *

"Your departure schedule leaves little time for error, but you will have an extra day to enjoy the festival," Gamtro said.

"This has been a wonderful visit. Difficult to believe we have but a breath of season remaining," Dogra sighed, snuggling next to him in their disheveled nest.

"Never has time traveled so fast," Gamtro agreed. "If you do not object, I would have Ben and Shalli share our meal on the rest day. Near end of season, they are busy with their duties. We may not have another chance to dine privately."

"Can you not excuse them from their duties, all-powerful Baron Gamtro?" Dogra asked.

"Ben is studying improvements for the next season. Shalli will be planning the festival. The responsibilities are to their people, not to me," Gamtro explained.

"They work hard. Everyone here works hard, including you, my beloved. It would be pleasant to share a final meal with Shalli and Ben."

"Your love for Shalli is well known. Have you warmed to Ben?" Gamtro asked.

"I respect him, but he does not invoke the feelings I have for Shalli. And his background disturbs me. Clearly he is not of this star system. I have considered making inquiries."

"Inquiries are unnecessary. I have his records," Gamtro said.

"I have not found them in the register," she mentioned

"They are confidential files."

"By whose order?"

"My own. And I will not release them. Should the ministry ever request more information, there is a false file identifying Ben as a survivor from Kappapek, a destroyed timber camp on Laggerate's eastern slope."

"This mystery worries me. What secret involving Ben can warrant such a breach of procedure?"

"Have you no suspicions?"

"I had a suspicion once, but it could not be true. I reviewed the chronology and found my suspicion wrong."

"Let us leave it at that," Gamtro urged.

"One day I will ask again. I shall expect an answer," Dogra said, angered by her mate's reluctance.

A few days later, as Baron Gamtro spent the morning reviewing end of season reports, Dogra joined Frontra on her morning rounds in the compound. Though Frontra carried her sidearm, as she always did when escorting the illustrious Lady Gamtra, Dogra did not find the precaution necessary. The women of the southern camps had come to accept her daily visits.

"You stay busy in the evenings. Romtra says you burn your recorder," Frontra said as they approached the gate.

"I am writing a chronicle of my camp experiences," Dogra said. "Though in deference to Baron Gamtro, it downplays Ben's contributions to Karak's success. Much of my story centers on Shalli, though I have not told her of this. I would not have her feel inhibited."

"It is sad no one will read such a work," Frontra remarked with a soft click.

"They will read mine."

"I have little faith our people will give up their cherished perceptions."

"To have impact, my readers will need to know these abused creatures are not the mindless brutes of popular culture," Dogra explained.

Dogra strolled a little faster as they passed Rabbit Camp and approached the gardens where Shalli and her friends were working.

When Shalli saw Dogra coming, her face brightened with a smile. The trowel she held dropped into the soil and Shalli ran through the plots, ignoring the late season plants.

"Dogra!" Shalli yelled, forgetting to use Dogra's formal title in public as she was supposed to. Dogra knew she should be displeased, but Shalli was so filled with joy she could not be angry.

"It has happened," Shalli said, jumping high to kiss Dogra on her bony cheek and hugging her big frame with all her might. Dogra was impressed by the small creature's strength.

"What has happened?" Dogra said, brushing the spot where Shalli's lips had kissed her. She could not remember ever seeing such a demonstration of affection from a slave. She looked at Frontra, who was equally surprised.

"The blessing, mistress. I have received Sherra's blessing," Shalli said.

Dogra knew what it meant to Shalli, having seen the envy in her eyes as she watched other mothers tend their young.

"That is wonderful, child," Dogra said, clumsily returning the hug. And finding satisfaction in the gesture. "I am sure it will be a beautiful, healthy male."

"I do not want a boy. I want a girl, to honor you. To bless the good fortune you have brought," Shalli said.

Frontra gasped. Dogra also caught her breath. To acknowledge such a bond would have profound implications.

"That is thoughtful of you, Shalli," Dogra said, slowly

disengaging. "But such an honor belongs with one of your own kind. Myra or Court. You must speak to them."

"But it is you and Baron Gamtro who have made our lives so special," Shalli said.

"Your mate brought you much, including this gift. Your mate and Sherra's generosity. Your offer pleases me, but it is not suitable," Dogra tried to explain.

Shalli's smile faded. Dogra brushed back the long blonde hair and looked deeply into the big blue eyes.

"I wish you were my egg, but Sherra has cast us in different roles. Please understand," Dogra consoled.

Shalli nodded, trying unsuccessfully not to let Dogra see her disappointment. Myra waved. Shalli returned to her garden.

"The food creature truly loves you, Lady Gamtra. Never have I witnessed such a thing," Frontra said, eye-rings round in awe.

"Shalli is not a food creature, Frontra. You know as much. It distresses me to see her trapped in this horrid place. Come, I need a quiet place to reflect."

Dogra and Frontra skirted the gardens, walked along the edge of the lake, and approached the porch of Shalli's house.

"Frontra, sit with me," Dogra said, offering the commoner a rare privilege.

"Thank you, Lady Gamtra," Frontra accepted, taking her usual stool near the railing overlooking the lake.

"How do you cope?" Dogra asked, her tongue clicking sharply in frustration. "I know you have affection for these creatures. As they have for you. How can you bear seeing them like this day after day?"

"If I do not watch over them, someone else will have the duty. Someone who does not care for them. Someone who does not realize that Sherra's spirit resides within them."

"You believe that?" Dogra asked.

"It is not a matter of belief. It is Sherra's Truth."

"You speak like Mordari."

"None speak so eloquently as the Voice of Sherra," Frontra said, clicking her tongue with reverence.

"A follower of Mordari, a guard in a slave camp? What strange lives we lead. How is it you see these slaves as more than food?" Dogra asked.

Frontra turned sad, looking out toward the lake.

"One of my early assignments on Akrona was with the Contingent, hunting primitives on the eastern slopes," Frontra recalled. "We slaughtered a small village, nearly all women and children. Under a slain mother, I found a pup struggling to feed on the dead breast. It was so helpless. It reached for me. I took the pup back to our barracks and fed it. Cared for it. It grew, and smiled, and laughed. I thought it a wondrous pet. Then one day it spoke. It called me mother. I called her Gammy."

Frontra was forced to pause, her throat choked with emotion. Her claws trembled. Her eyes stared distantly. Dogra had never imagined the stoic guard so sentimental.

"A day came when I was on assignment," Frontra eventually continued. "As a joke, a barracks mate sent the child to the pens. I was too late to save it."

Dogra reacted in horror, her cheeks flushing the brightest of blues. She knew she shouldn't be shocked. Slaves were routinely sent to the pens. But somehow this was personal. It had hurt Frontra.

What if it was Shalli who had been sent to the pens? Dogra wondered. What if I had come to the camp today, and instead of being warmed by her joy, learned she had been sent to the butcher shop?

"I know frontier life is difficult," Dogra said, struggling to control her emotions. "Our soldiers eat meat wherever they find it. Our distribution centers are filled with food from captive worlds. Must it be this way? I do not believe our people would tolerate such practices if they knew creatures like Gammy and Shalli."

"I may not say, mistress. I have not seen Arikhan since my fourteenth year," Frontra replied. "There were twenty-five years spent in fleet. Three years with the Contingent. I have been a guard at Karak for the last ten. I do my best, knowing these creatures have little future. What else may I do?"

Dogra realized there was nothing else an aging veteran like Frontra could do, and it was far more than most would even attempt.

"You serve nobly, Frontra. When I return to Arikhan, I will write of Akrona. I will ask my friend Gretnar to do a theatre," Dogra promised.

Frontra said nothing. Her posture displayed no enthusiasm.

"What is wrong? Should action not be taken?" Dogra asked.

"Sherra turns her face from us. Few believe what all should be able to see," Frontra answered. "Change does not come easily. I once spoke to Ben of this, hoping he could shed light on the brutality. Hoping he could see an end, much as you do. He spoke of a time on his own world when slavery tore at the better hearts. A rebel leader arose who fought the slavery without compromise. He was captured and executed. In his final words, he said the sins of a guilty land may only be washed away in blood. Much have I come to think on these words. I fear they are true."

"Our people may be wiser than his. What do you know of Ben?"

"We are friends, as much as he is friends with anybody. He holds back his feelings. Disguises his thoughts. He cares deeply but will not let himself show it. He is freer than any member of this camp, because he fears nothing. And more slave, because he fears everything."

"Have you seen Ben's paintings? Gretnar says paintings are windows into the soul."

"I purchased the colored oils for him while on leave at Va'ragashant," Frontra said with pride.

Dogra stood up and went inside the dwelling intending to give the paintings closer study. They were gone. The walls were bare except for one recently made picture of a sunrise. The painting wasn't very good.

"Where are they?" Dogra asked.

"Upstairs, in the office," Frontra said.

Dogra backtracked to the outside staircase and ran up the steps, bursting into Grey's office. On the walls she saw maps and production charts, not just of Karak, but of a dozen different mining camps, but no paintings. Frontra pointed to the corner where the canvases were rolled together in a stack.

"Why? Why?" Dogra asked.

"Ben fears they distress Shalli. With a new baby coming, he chose to take them down in place of happier images. He plans to offer them to Baron Gamtro. Or burn them. He has not decided."

"Burn them? No. Never. Pick them up. All of them. Pick them up now," Dogra ordered. "I will apologize later, but these must be saved. Saved and taken back to civilization where they can be appreciated. Our people will realize this slavery is wrong when they see Ben's paintings."

"It would prove nothing," Frontra denied.

"What do you mean?"

"The paintings would prove nothing. Ben is not a slave."

"Not a slave? Explain."

"It is not my place, Lady Gamtra," Frontra said, sorry to have spoken so freely.

"I order you to explain," Dogra insisted.

"Ben is a prisoner of war," Frontra answered.

* * * ** *

Later in the afternoon, Baron Gamtro and Nabbatron toured the compound, letting the workers know that each camp was on schedule to make quota. The harvest festival, now only a few days away, would be memorable.

The last visit on their tour was Ferret Camp, now a robust community of eighty people living in well-built timber cabins. Dogra and Frontra were there helping the women prepare a late afternoon meal.

"Baron Gamtro, I would speak with you," Dogra said.

"Beware, Baron. The Lady Gamtra has spikes for eyes," Nabbatron warned.

Myra and Shalli looked up from their baskets even as young Garn, now eight years old, ran to tug on Gamtro's tunic.

"Welcome to Ferret Camp, my Lord," eight-year-old Garn said in perfect Arikhan, adding a click of his tongue at the end.

"You grow well, Garn. Soon you will work beside your father in the quarries," Gamtro praised, patting the child on the head before sending him back to Myra.

Gamtro allowed Nabbatron to make the formal announcement.

No one was surprised. All knew quota had been reached the week before but it was nice to hear the festival would last four days.

Dogra would wait no longer, dragging Gamtro off to a hillside not far from the abandoned mine entrance.

"It is time you tell me of Ben," Dogra demanded. "Soon I return home to take a new position in the ministry. A high position due our rank. I also write an essay in which Ben may not be ignored."

"You know Ben is not of Akrona. Does it matter where he comes from?"

"Why does Frontra call him a prisoner of war?"

"Frontra should not do so."

"She has. It must be explained."

"Follow," Gamtro instructed.

He turned toward the mountain and climbed a steep trail, pausing on a hill that overlooked Karak. Dogra followed, her breath short when she reached the top.

"Interesting," Dogra observed, looking down on Ferret Camp, then toward the lake.

"In his first season at this camp, Ben dwelled up here. Alone. Feeding off the wild growths. He would take his place in the mines, but would not reside among the people," Gamtro said.

"Sherra's Spirit, why?" Dogra questioned.

"Ben did not speak the language of the natives, and was deeply disturbed by the loss of his previous life. Ferret Camp thought him a spy. Frontra says they insulted him. Took his food. Some even threatened him. Ben came to this camp with nothing.

"Back then, the people were poor. Their tribe had been devastated by a cave-in and could not make quota. They lived in rotting tents with barely enough food to survive. I did not help them. It did not seem necessary. I thought a failing camp might supply fresh meat for the pens."

Dogra looked down at the happy camp now filled with young children. She could hardly believe it was the same place.

"Ben did this, my beloved," Gamtro said, a wave of his arm indicating the entire Karak compound. "After a time, I helped. It was to my advantage. And later, it was my privilege. But in the beginning, his shoulders alone carried these people back from the edge of oblivion. And never once, in all these years, has he asked for thanks. Or gracefully accepted gratitude."

"But who is he? Where did he come from?" Dogra asked.

Gamtro went farther up the mountain through weeds and scrub trees until reaching a shallow canyon. One of the cliff walls was covered in worn etchings.

"These scratches were made years ago, during Ben's first season at Karak," Gamtro said. "The years have obscured many of the marks, yet small portions may still be seen."

"A star chart," Dogra quickly said, rushing to examine it.

Her rapid deduction surprised Gamtro. It had taken him half an hour to reach the same conclusion.

"Here is Laros," Dogra said, immediately recognizing the central diagram.

She stood before the fascinating sandstone wall tracing with her forward digit, looking at the many tracks that ended without resolution. Though half the etchings were unreadable, she could reconstruct most of them through logical conjecture.

"There are several possible solutions," Gamtro warned.

Dogra paid him no mind, concentrating on the puzzle until one variation stood out.

"Sol," she whispered in dread. "Nearly twelve hundred light years away. But the Sol creatures did not open a stargate until last year, and Ben has been here more than seven."

"He may have drifted in space even longer," Gamtro guessed. "This must not be revealed. I have told no one, not even Frontra. Ben was found outside our stargate, floating in a debris field. The patrol ship that discovered him was later destroyed by marauders. After interrogation by the Contingent, he was sent here as a slave."

"The battle of Sol was eight years ago. Have you seen the visuals brought back by the survivors?"

"We witnessed the images released during the homecoming. Only one warrior defending Sol wore an armored suit like the one Ben was found in. The same warrior who destroyed *Bellerophon*."

"Technical aspects of the battle are classified, but every report says the curl was killed in the explosion," Dogra related.

"Ben is not a demon, and he was not killed. Somehow, he was thrown through the Laros stargate to be found by the *Link*," Gamtro said.

"This human was not just an ordinary soldier. He was their leader. The invasion would have succeeded if not for his efforts. He is an enemy of the empire!" Dogra declared.

"The same empire that would send Shalli to the pens," Gamtro countered.

"That is not fair," Dogra complained.

"Nothing of this is fair. I only know Ben has been a friend to the people here. He has been my friend. He has taught me new ways of thinking, and new ways for our empire to prosper. The title I should have had years ago if not for Festro's jealousy is finally mine. Tell me, beloved, if I betray Ben, what glory would Sherra grant us? What glory would we deserve?"

"Despite your obligation, I believe we must tell the Council of Warriors," Dogra said. "I fear you do not know this creature so well as you assume. I have not seen all the records, but intelligence reported him as cunning. A deceiver. Most dangerous when apparently defeated. I see now why he dominates this camp. He is a wolf among cattle."

"I am not cattle," Gamtro said, eye-rings bent hard with anger. "I thought you learned much on your visit here. It was my hope that you would. Now I fear you have learned nothing."

Gamtro walked away, going farther up the hill until reaching a small meadow. Dogra followed.

"Forgive me, Gamtro. You have had years to overcome your doubts, I but a season. It is much to think on. Rest well knowing nothing will be said until we both agree the time is right," she promised.

"Write your chronicle. Your friend Gretnar can do a theatre. Be sure you understand your subject. Listen to Frontra's wisdom. Hear the skepticism of Nabbatron. Do not portray these creatures as lovable pets, for they are not. They are good and evil, kind and hateful. They are much like us. And if you see the worst in Ben, be able to recognize the best."

"I will strive to see as you do," Dogra said, unhappy to have spoiled their day together.

They started back down the hill veering toward the trail above Ferret Camp before coming upon an old prospector's shack. Nearby was a covered opening in the ground.

"Someone has been up here recently," Gamtro said, finding footprints in the dirt. He took a solar lamp from the repaired shack and went to inspect the shaft, pushing the wooden cover to one side.

"This must be the ventilation tunnel Frontra told me about," Gamtro said. "It was dug long ago, before Karak was even built. Ben is said to study the mountain's geology from here."

"It is dangerous. Leave the hole to those who crawl in such places," Dogra urged.

"I just want a short look," Gamtro replied, turning to back down into the shaft. He reached with his foot, found a ladder, and put his weight on it. The rung held, so he tried another.

"Come back. The hole looks unsafe," Dogra said, tongue clicking nervously.

"There is a ladder bolted to the wall. It feels sound," Gamtro said, going down another rung.

Soon only his head appeared above the surface. He used the lamp to peer down. Small falling stones were causing an echo.

"The shaft is deep. I see a branch tunnel," he said.

Gamtro felt his foot slip. He regained his hold. The rung slipped more.

"Perhaps this is not so safe," Gamtro realized. "I will—"

The rungs below his feet broke loose. Gamtro grabbed for rungs higher up but his great weight was more than the old supports would hold. He looked at Dogra with sudden surprise. Then he disappeared down the shaft.

"Gamtro? Gamtro!" Dogra yelled, rushing to the edge.

She heard crashing. Breaking beams. The sounds seemed to come from faraway.

"Gamtro?" she called one last time.

He didn't answer. There was no noise.

Desperately seeking the correct direction, Dogra ran down the hill through the overgrown brush, reaching the ledge above Ferret Camp. The small village was still a hundred yards away, but she could see people moving around.

"Frontra! Frontra!" Dogra summoned.

Frontra came running from the camp, breathing hard because of the sprint. Nabbatron was close behind. Several women and children were with them.

"Baron Gamtro has fallen down a hole. A deep hole. We need help," Dogra shouted.

Nabbatron was first to climb the hill. Frontra took out her communicator, sending an alert to the main gate. Myra turned to Garn, and with a whispered word, sent him running. Then she, too, began to climb the steep trail.

As Nabbatron and Frontra reached the crest, Dogra looked down to see even more help coming. Shalli was among them, running faster than she thought the creature could go, carrying a black medical bag clutched in her arms. In the distance, she saw men coming from the quarry. A dozen of them, many carrying tools.

Dogra led the rescue party back to the ventilation shaft, relieved to find the shack without much effort. Other than Karak's guards, she wasn't sure if any of the others had ever been there.

"Here. He fell here," Dogra said.

Nabbatron knelt at the hole seeing nothing but blackness. Myra lay flat on the ground, her ear bent for the slightest noise.

"There is a rustling. Maybe dirt falling. I don't know," Myra said.

Nabbatron tried to test the ladder but few of the upper rungs survived. He studied the shaft again.

"We need rope," Nabbatron decided.

"In the shed," Frontra indicated.

Someone, Dogra wasn't sure who, found a coil of rope and returned.

"It is not enough," Nabbatron said, finding a bare ten meters.

Shalli arrived with the medical bag. She looked distressed to find only the hole and no sign of Gamtro.

"Where is he?" Shalli asked.

"He has fallen down the shaft, dear," Myra said, still listening for clues.

"We need more rope. Rope and lamps. This shaft may be hundreds of claws deep," Nabbatron said.

"Hundreds? Gamtro, what has happened to you?" Dogra whispered into the darkness. Shalli went to her side.

"The master will return. You will see. Gamtro is good. Sherra will not abandon him," Shalli said.

"I pray you are right, Shalli. Please, Sherra, please bless us at this moment," Dogra responded, feeling an inescapable despair.

Nabbatron and the handful of people standing nearby bowed in reverence, for none could ignore such a plea.

Suddenly, all heads turned with sighs of relief. Even the guards. Dogra saw Grey hurrying up the trail, his brow furrowed with concern, his expression gritted in determination. Against her will, she felt her heart soar with hope.

"Stand back," Grey ordered, making everyone move away from the shaft. No one dared disobey, not even Nabbatron.

"Barris, have the men build a platform over the hole," Grey commanded. "Turk, get two pulleys from the shed and all the rope you can find. Wart, get lamps from the camp. Everybody, hurry!"

Grey listened from the top of the shaft as Myra had done, but he was able to hear more, sensing the mountain as one long acquainted with its ways. Shalli knelt at his side.

"Can you hear him?" Shalli asked.

"I hear something," Grey said.

He pulled Shalli close, gave her a deep kiss, and rolled sideways into the hole, disappearing almost instantly.

"Has he fallen?" Dogra asked, unsure what had happened.

"I do not see him," Nabbatron said, equally mystified. The shaft was quiet, and dark. It seemed as if Karak's engineer had simply vanished. Dogra was unnerved, and even Nabbatron seemed puzzled.

"Do not be afraid, mistress. Ben will not let the mountain claim your mate," Shalli said, standing at her side.

Dogra looked at the people nodding their heads. Even Frontra agreed.

273

Grey grabbed the good rungs, skipping the ones he knew to be weak, and dropped to the first ledge. Everything below was black. Above him, the light was growing small. He knew of a larger ledge farther down and hoped Gamtro had managed to land on it, so he climbed rapidly to the next offshoot tunnel and reached into a niche where a lamp was stored.

The niche was empty, the rungs nearby torn from the wall. When Grey reached the large ledge, he found it was gone, too. Gamtro had landed on it with such force the entire landing had broken free.

He continued down past several more tunnels, most of which he had explored. There was no further evidence of Gamtro until he approached the bottom of the shaft. Just where he expected to find the fallen victim, there was nothing. Not even a floor. Grey probed with his foot while hanging tightly to the lowest rung, but all he found was empty air. He paused, listening carefully for breathing. He did not hear any, but he did hear moving water.

"Gamtro? Gamtro?" Grey called.

No voice, but a splash.

"I need a lamp," Grey yelled up the shaft, the echo distorting his voice.

He couldn't see anything specific at the top, only shifts of light. Then a stronger light bounced back and forth as it dropped closer. It felt like ages until the solar charged lamp finally reached him.

"Ben?" a voice said.

It was Dogra's voice coming from Frontra's communicator, the small black transmitter clipped to the rope.

"Yes, Lady Gamtra," Grey said, pulling in the equipment.

"Have you found him? Does he live?" Dogra asked.

"Remain hopeful," Grey replied.

Grey used the lamp to inspect the bottom of the shaft. The floor was gone, smashed through. The walls around the missing floor had caved in, revealing a dark cavern five meters below him. A cavern he never knew existed. Had the floor been a false bottom all along?

Water reflected below him. It moved briskly from the west toward the creek south of Ferret Camp. Not rapid, but churning enough to cut the dirt walls.

Grey tugged on the rope. It wasn't the best quality.

"Barris, will the rope hold my weight?" he asked into the communicator.

The communicator buzzed.

"Barris says the rope will hold your weight, but not more. They are making a stronger one," Dogra answered.

More line was loosened, giving some play. Grey tied the end under his arms, made a simple knot, and swung out into empty space. The pull caused him to drop rapidly until he splashed into a pool of cold, knee-deep water.

Grey looked up the shaft with the lamp. Gamtro's impact on the false flooring had created a crater in the ceiling. An occasional bright reflection hinted at the cavern's secret. Diamond deposits. After all the years of searching, he had finally found them, but there was no time for treasure hunting.

The cavern was wide near the bottom of the shaft but quickly narrowed as it went downstream. Grey suspected the water level was rising, debris from the cave-in having clogged the channel. After probing the water immediately below the shaft, he began following the flow. Hardly more than five meters away, he spotted a pile of mud and broken timbers piled against the wall. And Gamtro, pinned beneath. A glance at the roof indicated an unstable situation.

"Baron, are you hurt?" Grey asked, wading to his side.

"If anyone would venture into this dismal hell, it would be you," Gamtro answered weakly.

"This is not a good place. I think we should leave," Grey said, trying to lift a timber. It was heavy. Water-soaked and wedged tight. He looked around for a lever.

"The roof comes down. The walls grow weak. In just a few minutes the water has risen above my waist," Gamtro said.

Grey found a broken timber and levered a beam off Gamtro's chest, then reached underwater and dragged a smaller beam off his thighs. A final beam had Gamtro's left ankle pinned in the mud. Holding his breath, Grey ducked under the surface and tried to dig Gamtro's leg free, but he found solid rock underneath.

"Ben? Ben?" Dogra was saying when Grey resurfaced for air.

"He's here, Lady Gamtra," Grey said, attaching the communicator to Gamtro's shoulder strap.

"Beloved?" Gamtro said, his voice a whisper.

"Your speech is not strong, my Lord," Dogra said.

"We fare poorly. There is much water at the bottom of the cave. Our space grows smaller."

And suddenly it did, a section of the wall giving way in a big splash of mud and rock. One boulder hit Grey on the forehead so hard he went under, resurfacing with difficulty. The collapse caused the water level to rise higher.

"Lady Gamtra? Barris?" Grey called.

There was no answer. The communicator was either too wet or damaged.

"I think the cave grows larger. It's only our portion that grows smaller," Grey suggested.

"You jest at bad moments," Gamtro reprimanded.

"I had hoped the bad moments were behind us. Let me try to move the beam again. Be ready to pull your leg free."

Grey found the best lever he could, set a fulcrum in the tight space, and tried to lift the beam. It wouldn't budge, and the dark water made it impossible to see why. Grey ducked into the stream again, probing and digging along the length of the obstacle. There was mud everywhere that seemed to fill in as quickly as it was dug away.

"Not much success," Grey said, coming up for air.

More rocks fell from the roof. Larger boulders were barely held in place.

"Perhaps you should leave," Gamtro said.

"Perhaps not," Grey disagreed, searching for alternatives.

"I order you to leave."

"With all respect, master, I refuse."

"You may not refuse a direct order," Gamtro said.

"I have never been good at obeying orders. Even as a child, I was much punished."

Again Grey dove, seeking an angle that might work. As he shoved the lever against the timber's highest end and pushed the fulcrum in a secure spot, the beam suddenly shifted with his forearm caught underneath. He struggled to pull free, kicking with his legs, but as his air ran out he began to panic. Bubbles burst on the surface when water started replacing air in his lungs. At the last moment, a great claw secured a hold on his metal slave collar and yanked him up.

"You do not breathe well underwater," Gamtro observed.

Grey coughed. His arm hurt. While Gamtro's grip steadied him against the current, Grey felt the bone and cursed himself for a fool. His right ulna bone was fractured just above the wrist.

"We need better cloth in this camp," Gamtro said, holding scraps of Grey's shirt. Grey discovered his tunic was torn to shreds, apparently by Gamtro's effort to save him.

"This is not a good situation," Grey concluded.

"Always have I admired your keen powers of observation," Gamtro replied.

A boulder splashed down, narrowly missing them.

"The collapse of the false floor might have raised an underground spring. If so, it may run itself out," Grey said.

"It would already have done so. Soon this entire cavern will be mud. Much wealth have I taken from the mountain. Now the mountain demands payment."

Grey tried one last time to shift the beam or dig under it, but Gamtro was right. It was held down by more shifting mud than he could move.

"The mountain is in a bad mood today," Grey agreed.

"You should leave now," Gamtro said.

"I think it better to stay here with my friend. Maybe something will happen."

"Did you break your arm?"

"I fear so."

"You should be more careful."

"It is not me who has a foot pinned beneath a log in a cave filling with mud."

"No, but you are stupid enough to sit next to one who has," Gamtro responded.

"You are smarter than me today. This does not happen often."

"You are impertinent."

"Always has it been so," Grey replied with a laugh.

Gamtro clicked his tongue in amusement.

"Did you bring a saw?" Gamtro asked.

"The beam is too thick to cut underwater," Grey reported.

"My leg is not. Maybe the mountain will take my leg and let the rest of me go."

"Are you sure? Such is not the way of your people," Grey mentioned.

"Will you leave without me?" Gamtro asked.

"I have not decided. Maybe I will abandon you if I grow afraid."

"Get a saw. We are running out of time."

Grey stood up, the water almost to his waist, and shoved a timber against the wall above Gamtro's head to retard slippage. Then he waded back until he could look up the shaft. The top was only a tiny circle of light. He tested the rope, wondering if it could be tied around the timber pinning Gamtro and then hauled from above, but he quickly saw it wasn't a good plan. The rope would slice into the roof, collapsing the chamber even faster.

"I will return in a few minutes," Grey said, tugging the rope. A moment later he felt himself being lifted.

Grey studied the shaft on the way up, pushing back projections and loose rungs. The light grew bigger, then bright. Barris and Nabbatron grabbed his arms, pulling him into the sunlight.

"I need a bone saw, the sharpest we've got. And a First Aid kit," Grey said, squinting against the blinding sun.

Gradually, as he was able to see again, he noticed Black Hands had arrived and was sorting through her supplies. Barris and Nabbatron were rigging a stronger sling. Shalli and Myra prepared a stretcher as a dozen others gathered materials. Dogra knelt at his side.

"How fares my mate?" she asked.

"All is not the best, but he will come back," Grey assured her.

"Have you the strength to bring him back? Even with a broken arm?"

"My arm is fine," Grey protested.

Dogra grabbed his wrist and squeezed. Grey yelped and pulled away.

"The arm is broken," Dogra said.

"If you want Baron Gamtro back, I suggest you put off sending me to the pens," Grey replied, glaring at her.

Dogra was surprised he would say that. And insulted. Black Hands came with splints, medical tape, and a pain killer.

"How did you know?" Grey asked.

"The transmitter still works. You could not hear us, but we could hear you," Black Hands explained. Grey looked at Dogra.

"Then you know what is planned?" he asked.

"My mate is brave. Not many would accept such a compromise, but his work is unfinished. Do you have enough time?"

"I will try my best. But if I do not come back, promise to take Shalli away from here."

"And if I do not? Will the destroyer of Bellerophon refuse to rescue my mate?"

Grey sighed. Though it wasn't her intent, Dogra's remark struck him like a cold wind. His eyebrows flattened. The shoulders dipped.

"I wish you would help Shalli, but I have no time to argue with an official of the Arikhan food creature eating ministry," he snapped.

As Black Hands finished wrapping his arm, she looked at Grey with many questions. She had heard the entire conversation and knew him well enough to guess the pessimism in his thoughts.

"The splints will not hold if you're rash," Black Hands warned.

When Black Hands went to help with the stretcher, Grey called for Nabbatron. Lady Gamtra stayed close, watching everything.

"May I give advice, master?" Grey asked.

"Say what must be done, half-meat. There is no time for insincere formalities," Nabbatron ordered.

"I am going to loop the rope under Gamtro's arms. After the severance, I will drag him directly beneath the opening. Pull him upright, let me wrap the wound, then have Clagg, Barris, and Turk haul on the rope. Pull steady, do not yank. Summon a sho'kara from Va'ragashant."

"Such a craft is already on the way," Nabbatron said.

"I think Baron Gamtro may have internal injuries. If you have a civilized yarbel ky on this planet, make mention that his condition is serious," Grey advised.

"It will be as you say," Nabbatron confirmed, clicking his tongue in confirmation.

Grey let Barris secure the rope around his chest, then crawled back toward the shaft. Frontra arrived with a bone saw which Grey tucked in his belt. Then there was a somber moment of silence. All seemed to sense that their lives were about to change, and maybe not for the better. Grey, in particular, was looking at the people of the camp as if he may not see them again. Shalli gave him a kiss.

"Don't be afraid. You are stronger than the mountain," Shalli urged.

Grey looked at Dogra, unable to read her expression. He studied Nabbatron and Frontra. Whatever Dogra knew, it seemed they didn't. Not that it would ultimately matter.

"Be brave. Never forget I love you," Grey said, giving Shalli another kiss. Then he dropped back into the shaft, feeling the tight grip of the rope under his arms.

Within minutes, Grey was back on the bottom of the shaft, wading through the cold water toward Gamtro. The water was up to Gamtro's neck. Soon it would no longer be possible for him to breathe.

"Did you bring the saw?" Gamtro asked.

"Yes. Do you still want me to use it?"

"What choice is there?" Gamtro questioned.

A rush of water pushed Grey downstream. He grabbed Gamtro's shoulder to pull himself back.

"This is delicate. Your mate hears all we say," Grey warned, spitting water.

"Speak," Gamtro ordered.

"Lady Gamtra knows the name I once had. We both knew this day would come. I have asked Lady Gamtra to take Shalli away if I am unable to return. I think that might be for the best."

"You have a dark view of life. Have you always given up so easily?"

"If I have little time left, I would give the balance to Shalli and our baby."

"It is no less than I would expect from you, but I fail to share your gloom. I will not give up. You must not give up. Saw the leg so we can leave this cursed place."

Grey ducked underwater and cut Gamtro's pants leg open with a knife. He used an injector from Black Hands' medical bag to apply a pain killer, then went up for a final breath before starting on flesh and bone with the saw, cutting just above the ankle. It was a good saw, taking only a few more breaths to finish.

Gamtro floated free of the timber just as the water reached a critical level. Grey towed him back to the opening, tied Gamtro securely in the harness, and gave the signal. He was hoisted high enough to clear the water line, giving Grey a chance to wrap the stump.

"How does it look?" Gamtro asked, the drug making him sleepy.

"A clean cut. Are you ready to be pulled up?"

There was no answer. Gamtro had lost consciousness. Grey finished wrapping the wound and ordered the pullers to continue, watching as Gamtro became a shadow against the small light at the top of the shaft.

The cavern was turning into quicksand, but Grey wasn't afraid of being trapped there. The question of survival didn't belong to the mountain. He considered Gamtro's words while waiting for the rope to drop back down, and was almost disappointed when it did. But the decision was made. He tied the rope around his chest and signaled.

By the time Grey was pulled from the muddy cavern, Gamtro had been carried down the hill to Ferret Camp. The hovercraft arrived, the whine of the landing jets rumbling off the cliffs. Black Hands kept Grey back to treat the broken arm. Shalli was close by to make sure the injuries weren't more serious. By the time they made their way down the mountain, the sho'kara was gone.

"You did well, half-meat," Nabbatron said, eye-rings curled in approval.

"Thank you, master," Grey said, accepting permission to sit down in the cooking area between the two largest cabins. Many in the camp looked relieved, but not Grey. He was tired, and hurt, and could not shake off a persistent sense of doom.

Chapter Nine
THE VOICE OF SHERRA

Six months after Baron Gamtro's fall into the mountain, a heavily-armed transport emerged from the Laros stargate with ten VIP passengers enroute to Va'ragashant. Protecting them was an Arikhan destroyer escort, the warship's crew alert for trouble. When the space lanes near the stargate proved safe, the travelers proceeded toward the planet alone.

"You will see," Dogra said to the brown-robed visitor sitting next to her. "Baron Gamtro performed wonders on this world. Not only do the mines produce more than ever before, but the workers grow their own food. They are happy to be so well-treated."

Dogra's guest clicked her tongue softly and looked out the porthole without comment. Dogra's private secretary was bolder.

"Production is down, my Lady Gamtra. Down so greatly the reports are suppressed," Vistra said, young and elegant in her purple tunic. Strong shades of blue blossomed in her cheeks, the reddish brown eyes gleaming with a fine education.

"Have no fear, Vistra, our committee will discover why. These lapses in communication are no doubt due to the recent outrages of the marauders," Dogra said.

"We may trust it is so," Vistra replied, her pronunciation precise.

The studious secretary continued to review graphs on the electronic globe resting in her lap, adjusting inputs with finely manicured claw tips. Occasionally she would click her tongue softly with dissatisfaction.

Accompanying Dogra and her secretary were seven members of her ministry staff, all nervous about adventuring to such a remote and dangerous outpost. The tenth member of the group showed no such anxiety, having ventured to farther and more dangerous worlds as a scout of the 44th Camp. But Mordari was a scout no longer.

"The world you praise sounds blessed by Sherra," Mordari finally

282

conceded. "Your chronicle makes a strong case for this new way, well supported with statistical evidence. But you report nothing of what has occurred since Baron Gamtro's injury forced him into retirement."

"Baron Gamtro is not retired. He convalesces at Kal' Tree."

"Is it true they grow him a new foot?" Mordari asked.

"The process is hard, but the procedure is working. Already he is offered new assignments. Maybe even another military command. Such honor has always been his dream."

The transport passed the numerous defense satellites guarding the stargate. One of the satellites was a huge nuclear powered dish capable of sending messages through the stargate's sub-space void.

"The communications array appears in order, Lady Gamtra. There is no evidence of pirate activity in this sector," Korbatro said.

A young aristocrat eagerly enjoying the adventure, Korbatro was short for an Arikhan, less than two meters, and somewhat slender. His emerald green tunic, trimmed at the shoulders with silver thread, indicated a wealthy ancestry.

Looking out the porthole, Dogra had the same impression. But she was not an expert on such things. She glanced over to Mordari, who was. Mordari appeared to agree with Korbatro's assessment.

"After the pirates we encountered at Gorthan, I felt certain they were responsible for the poor communications coming from Akrona," Dogra said.

"It is generous of the *Bos'pher* to provide escort. I have already spent enough time imprisoned by our empire's enemies," Mordari said.

"Were you ill-treated by the Sol creatures?" Vistra asked, the others leaning close to hear Mordari's answer.

"No. We were fortunate they hold to a higher standard of civilization than most species," Mordari said, looking out at the stars.

"What do you mean, mistress?" another assistant inquired, her young eyes keen for a response. Dogra looked around, pleased to find her staff so interested. As the younglings of important families, they represented the empire's future.

Mordari softly clicked her tongue. It was not the first time youthful admirers had sought her memories of the war.

"After our warships were destroyed, *Bhast* was overrun by squads of enemy warriors. All who survived were captured. Twelve hundred and fifty of us," Mordari remembered. "Before its destruction, *Bellerophon* had bombarded their planet. Many cities were destroyed. Hundreds of thousands killed. We expected to be massacred in revenge, for our forces had shown no mercy. Yet some of the Earth creatures spoke against such barbarity. Loudest was the voice of a female. A warrior of great courage. She was deep in grief for a husband lost in battle, but still was she firm in her resolve.

"At first, we were interned on their moon, our ultimate fate unknown. Then a new leadership emerged among the Sol creatures. I think perhaps there was a power struggle. Afterwards, we were sent to a place called Houston, there to live in a park filled with trees and lakes. All were well-fed and given access to entertainments."

"Entertainments?" Korbatro asked.

"They are a creative species," Mordari recalled with some fondness. "After a period of isolation, our people were allowed to interact with the natives. A few can be unpleasant, but most are easily appreciated."

"Some say your broadcasts were provoked by dire threats. Others say the Sol creatures twisted your spirit," the oldest assistant said, a tall brooding male named Sarantro who was close in age to Dogra. Some thought him rude, but Mordari showed no offense.

"Those who deny the truth will find reasons to justify their ignorance," Mordari responded. "There were no threats. Long had I suspected our people need a new path. While living on Earth, I met thousands of humans. Farmers and scholars. Merchants and priests.

"Then one day, I visited a shrine dedicated to a heroic Sol creature. A creature who had been my most hated enemy, yet it was he, in his final instructions, who decreed that no vengeance be sought against the Arikhan prisoners. Sherra spoke loudly in that holy place. She said her blessings belong to all sentient life. Now, through me, Sherra continues to speak."

Those who listened shuddered at Mordari's declaration, espoused without the slightest doubt. The older staff members were especially unnerved, fearing what consequences her ministry might bring. The young staff members held no such fear, curious to learn of this new faith.

They reached Va'ragashant half a day after entering Laros space, but Dogra did not want to be bogged down with bureaucratic delays. After sending her staff to find rooms in the Citadel, she slipped away with Mordari, seeking transport to the train station.

"This world is still somewhat primitive," Dogra apologized, the tram uncomfortable in the chill wind. The town had not changed since her visit two seasons before, though there seemed to be a stronger military presence in the plaza.

"Scouts of the 44th Camp are accustomed to hard duty," Mordari said, dismissing the complaint. "We live in our sho'kars. Burrow on small planetoids. Ryndari and I spent many years spying on Sol before the fleet arrived, often living in our bubble pod. For such as us, even fresh air is a luxury."

When they reached the train station, the two dignitaries attracted attention despite efforts to remain inconspicuous. Lady Gamtra, already known to the local population, was tall and well-dressed in fine satins. Mordari wore her brown woolen robe highlighted with streaks of gold thread throughout the folds. None had ever seen her in person, but the controversial priestess was easily recognized. Not necessarily with favor, given her outspoken criticism of Arikhan society.

"Not all stares are hostile," Dogra encouraged.

"By this time next month, I will be on Arikhan answering charges of heresy," Mordari mentioned. "You are brave to be my companion."

"I have not claimed to support your vision, though many see similarities between my chronicle and your philosophy," Dogra said.

"Our views are not the same," Mordari agreed. "You are new to Sherra's word. Still probing. You do not feel Her truth in your heart. For you, it is merely an intellectual exercise."

"It is more than that," Dogra protested.

"No, not yet. But someday, maybe you will understand. You knew the creatures in your chronicle for a season. They were subservient, often viewed through a fence. Their lives, their families, all they care for were at your mercy. The Sol creatures I lived among were not slaves. They are intelligent, determined, and rich in culture. Such qualities do not shine without a divine spark. I speak plainly, Lady Gamtra. Our people will pay a heavy price if we do not learn this lesson. Sherra frowns upon those who will not hear Her words."

"Our race is not stupid. We learn. Wait until you see Karak. The workers are prosperous. None go to the pens, not even the sick or injured. They are but a small step from living freely. They will be an example for other camps throughout the empire."

"I have seen our camps. They are miserable places run by closed hearts. Someday you will know this. Be prepared for a bitter lesson," Mordari warned.

"And your solution?" Dogra asked with impatience.

"Our people will be forced to accept change. I will continue to speak, but a new empire will not emerge until the Sword of Sherra appears to spread fear through evil hearts. Only then will the darkness be lifted."

"What is this sword? What does it look like?" Dogra asked.

"That is unclear to me. When my eyes behold, I will know."

Dogra felt a shiver at Mordari's words, and realized why so many had gathered to her vision. The priestess spoke with unquestioned confidence. Could she really dwell so close to Sherra? Dogra was not inclined to believe so. Her world was more orderly than that of mystics. But she could not help wonder.

The old train station was quieter than in the past, the long wooden benches empty. Only a few travelers loitered near the loading platform. The plaster walls needed paint, the coating beginning to peel. The train also appeared tired even though the engine was only pulling a dozen ore tenders. A passenger car was attached at the end, the cushioned seats losing some of the feathered stuffing.

Hours passed as they left the northern settlements and entered the Varish Expanse, the vast wasteland of rolling prairie and low, scrub covered hills offering little interest. Several stops were made along the way, the small number of passengers steadily shrinking until only a handful were left. Along the way, they saw the salt camps near the dry lake beds, several processing centers, and an occasional ghost town.

As the train approached the Rellina River, they noticed a brown haze hanging over the hills surrounding Karak.

"We are almost there," Dogra said, straining for a view.

Mordari rested comfortably in her seat, giving no hint to her thoughts.

When the train finally crossed the final bridge, Dogra and Mordari looked out the windows to the right. Even though it was still winter, Dogra expected to see robust crops running from the old fence down to the river. Possibly winter wheat, or the new orchards that had been planted before she left. There were none. Even the stone village of the newcomers was gone, replaced by piles of rock and canvas tarps strung over broken timbers. The camp looked like it had been hit by an earthquake.

Up from the river, along the creek where the railroad tracks ran, they entered the valley of the mining camps. The cabins around Wolf Camp were gone. Trees had been knocked down for barricades. Instead of seeing dozens of people going about their daily chores, only a few poorly clothed slaves were visible.

The train pulled into the ore depot slowly. Dogra saw a troop carrier parked to the left just down the hill from the camp headquarters. The armored vehicle's rotating energy cannon dominated the valley floor. On the right, a new two-story brick barracks had been erected fifty yards from the main gate. A handful of ore carts were rolled out. In the past, there would have been fifty.

"Disembark to the left. Mind the security zone," a grim soldier said as several guards boarded the train.

Dogra recognized Amartro, Cordaris's surly appointee, now wearing an officer's bronze leaf. The impudent commoner paid her no homage, though the other guards were respectful.

Given precedence, Dogra and Mordari disembarked the passenger compartment first. There were troops everywhere, most wearing black armor. Some were positioned below the headquarters around the troop carrier, others at the ore tracks, more at the main gate. The number of guard towers had tripled, each holding an alert sentry.

"What is this? I demand to see Romtra," Dogra asked the first brown tunic she found, a leathery trooper whose insignia indicated former service with the Contingent.

"Group Leader Romtra was transferred, Lady Gamtra. Lord Kanatron now commands this camp," the trooper said, a burly male with a lofty expression.

"*Lord* Kanatron? How did Zenatro's sniveling lackey gain such an exalted title?" Dogra asked, eye-rings rising in indignation.

"The title is honorary until the commission is confirmed," the trooper said, clicking his tongue in defiance. Dogra looked for someone she recognized. All the faces were unfamiliar.

"Where is Nabbatron? Or Bortro?" Dogra asked.

"All disloyal guards have transferred. All but Frontra, and she will not remain much longer," the trooper said, leaving without permission.

Dogra looked at Mordari with embarrassment, not accustomed to such treatment from one so far beneath her station. Mordari reacted calmly as if it was nothing unexpected.

Leaving her travel bag on the train platform, Dogra marched to the enclosure, not even checking in at headquarters as protocol required. Mordari followed without being asked.

"You may not enter, Lady Gamtra. Access is restricted," the sentry on duty said from the main gate. The brutish guard was well-armed, the accent lacking refinement.

"Do not attempt to stop me," Dogra said. "I represent the Committee of Commerce. Threatening a ministry representative is a criminal act."

"The camp is dangerous, lady. Wait until Lord Kanatron returns, or let me summon Group Leader Amartro."

"Stand aside," Dogra demanded.

The sentry hesitated, the black eyes angry. The sentry grew angrier when Frontra arrived to intervene. Dogra immediately thought Frontra looked older, the eye-rings drooping, the once straight shoulders bent. Her drab brown leather uniform lacked the jaunty decorations she had worn just two seasons before. There was no yellow feather in her hat.

"I accept responsibility," Frontra said.

"It is not Lord Kanatron's wish," the sentry objected.

"I am senior guard until my replacement arrives," Frontra insisted.

The sentry backed away, returning to a watch position above the gate.

"Paratro speaks true, Lady Gamtra. Karak is dangerous. Go back to the train. Leave this place," Frontra urged.

"Understand my words, Frontra. I have come three star systems to show this camp to Mordari. We will not turn back now," Dogra demanded.

"Mordari?" Frontra questioned, suddenly recognizing Dogra's companion. "Forgive me, priestess. This is a high honor. Name the request and it is granted."

"Not all would agree the honor so great, Frontra," Mordari said, finding the veteran guard interesting. "Lady Gamtra has taken much trouble on my behalf. I would see this paradise her mate carved from the mines of Akrona."

"It was never a paradise, but for a short time, it was a place of soaring spirit. All is gone now. I beg you to leave. Remember Karak as it was," Frontra said.

"I will enter," Dogra pressed.

"Please be our escort," Mordari softly urged.

Frontra signaled for the iron gate to open, passing a squad of worried guards. The first thing Dogra noticed was the timber mill burned to the ground. Now only the two large circular saw blades stood in the burnt rubble, both twisted by the heat.

The cottages of Rabbit Camp were still standing, though the thatched roofs showed holes and the flower pots had disappeared. There were several women present, all maintaining a distance. Dogra did not see any children.

Dogra hurried past the camp toward the southern end of the lake where Ferret Camp kept their gardens, walking fast enough to keep Frontra several steps behind. There were only a few women working the soil. And again, no children. With relief, Dogra recognized Shalli, Myra, and Pie. But the moment the women saw the Arikhan coming, they grabbed their baskets to flee.

"Stop! Stop!" Dogra shouted, running to catch them.

Most of the women kept going even after Frontra fired her weapon in the air, but Shalli stumbled. Nearly eight months pregnant and undernourished, she wasn't able to escape. Myra and Pie returned to be with her, all kneeling in submission as Dogra approached. Their outfits were little better than rags.

"Shalli, it is me. Lady Gamtra," Dogra said.

Shalli said nothing, keeping her forehead down in the cold winter soil. Dogra put a claw on Shalli's shoulder. Shalli trembled.

"Child, look up. Speak," Dogra said, eye-rings bent.

Shalli looked up, tears in her eyes. Tears of fear, anger and hatred. Dogra staggered back. Never in her life had she experienced such an expression.

"What is wrong, Shalli? Where are the other women? The children? Where are Tak and her twins?" Dogra asked.

"Tak is dead. Beaten by your guards until she could bleed no more. Tak's babies are taken for food by Kanatron," Shalli said. "But you will not eat my baby. When my time comes, I will go into the woods where you cannot find us. Then I will cut her throat and bury her under a tree."

"You cannot mean to slay your own child. The one you wanted so badly. Where is Ben?" Dogra asked.

"My husband lies dead on Vulture Rock," Shalli said, pointing to the far side of the valley.

Dogra looked above the fence and across the tracks, seeing a chained figure laying spread eagle on a barren hilltop not far from the camp headquarters. It was too distant to observe details, but the body showed no movement.

"My husband did not surrender his blood quietly," Shalli said. "He killed your guards. Avenged Tak. He has shown us how to fight, and one day we will kill you all!"

Shalli jumped up and ran away as fast as her girth would allow, the other women following without ever uttering a word. Mordari came forward.

"If that is the friendly food creature in your chronicle, I do not relish meeting the hostile ones," Mordari dryly remarked.

Dogra rubbed her claws, her eyes filming over.

"Frontra, what has happened?" Dogra asked.

"What did you expect, my Lady?" Frontra said, her tongue clicking in resentment. "After you abandoned these people, Kanatron sought to increase production with starvation and the whip. Like all camp commanders do. And the more he failed, the crueler were his methods."

"Do you hate me, too?" Dogra asked in hurt.

"You do not belong here. Go back to your chronicles and society meetings. Have a theatre. Let these creatures die with courage. At least Ben has taught them that."

Frontra started for the main gate, forcing Dogra and Mordari to follow. Dogra grabbed Frontra's arm.

"I demand an explanation," Dogra said.

"You have no power to make demands here. Only violence rules Karak," Frontra said, breaking Dogra's grip.

"Then in Sherra's name, allow me to beg an explanation," Dogra said, bowing her head in the posture of submission.

Frontra was startled that Dogra would use such a gesture to a mere commoner. Even Mordari was surprised. But the great Lady Gamtra's humility achieved the desired result, as Mordari suspected it would.

"It began a few weeks after Baron Gamtro's accident," Frontra reluctantly recalled. "Lord Kanatron arrived with new guards. Romtra was pushed aside for Amartro, an evil beast fresh from duty with the Contingent. They ate the buffalo, and once the meat creatures were gone, Kanatron reopened the pens, seizing a worker who had broken his leg."

"Could they be so stupid? Could they not see the disruption it would cause?" Dogra asked.

"They were beyond stupid, mistress. Production slowed. Tension increased. Harsh penalties were instituted. Crops were burned as punishment. Huts demolished. The senior guards warned Kanatron that quota would not be met with such tactics, but he would not hear. There came a day Kanatron himself was in the yard punishing prisoners who moved too slowly. One was young Garn, forced under too heavy a burden."

Frontra paused, her eye-rings quivering, the claws clenched tight.

"The shock stick was applied to Garn's flesh. And applied again when he cried out. The youngling fell. Myra sought to protect him and was clubbed. When Kanatron raised the shock stick a third time, Nabbatron had endured too much. He wrenched the stick from Kanatron's grasp with noble defiance. 'You have dishonored us enough, my Lord,' Nabbatron said. Then he broke the stick in half and threw the parts to the ground. Nabbatron was transferred the next day along with the other senior guards. Now only I remain of those who once served Baron Gamtro."

Frontra turned to look at the burned timber mill. Farther up the valley, she saw the empty pens where the buffalo had been kept. To the west, clouds of smoke hung over the compound.

"Six days ago, Amartro stole Tak's babies from the gardens. When she fought back, the guards beat her to death. Ben attempted to save Tak, but he was too late. He slew four of Tak's killers before shock sticks brought him down. The workers would have no more. They burned the factories. A hundred slaves died in the fighting. Now the workers attack any who venture beyond the lake. Production has stopped. All that Karak was is ash."

Dogra saw that Frontra's words were truly spoken. Mordari saw the pain in Dogra's expression, but was not ready to sympathize with her. She turned to Frontra.

"Sister, I feel Sherra's spirit in your heart. Is there nothing that can be done?" Mordari asked, leading Frontra away from the gate for more privacy.

"These people had but one hope, and he lies dying on Vulture Rock," Frontra said.

"This creature still lives?" Mordari asked.

"Yet does he linger, but without shelter from the night he will not last much longer."

"Lady Gamtra's description of Ben in the chronicle is vague, but he reminds me of another I once met," Mordari said. "A warrior who sacrificed his life to save his people. Is Ben such a spirit?"

"Ben was my friend. When I leave this duty, I will never again serve our empire. The Voice of Sherra speaks truly on the blindness we suffer."

"I would see this Ben. Take me to him," Mordari said.

The trio crossed the narrow valley, skirted the train depot, and went up the weeded hillside north of the headquarters building. The exposed rock wasn't more than ten meters from the canyon floor, an easy climb for Dogra and Mordari through the winter scrub brush. Frontra waited at the bottom of the hill.

Dogra realized the nest she and Gamtro had shared, the room Ben and Shalli had built for them, looked down on the spot where the prisoner lay. He didn't move as they approached, nor were any guards in the area. His arms and legs were chained to the rock, the bruised body streaked with dry blood. As they got closer, Dogra found herself praying Ben was still alive.

"I feel like a fool," Dogra confessed to Mordari.

"Embarrassed your chronicle will be exposed as a fraud?" Mordari asked.

Dogra grabbed Mordari by the elbow, rage in her reddish brown eyes. Her cheeks flushed bluer than any Mordari had ever seen. For a moment, the priestess thought Dogra might strike her.

"Do you believe I care about that?" Dogra angrily growled. "I love Shalli. She loved me. When I see the misery of this camp, and Frontra's resentment, and Shalli's hatred, do you think I care about my chronicle?"

"What does anyone care about?" Mordari asked. "You and Baron Gamtro earned much wealth and position before abandoning these people to Kanatron's malice. Kanatron sought rank and profit, yet reaps failure. It appears this Ben you speak of sought accommodation with his slave masters, but brought death to his people. This is why we seek Sherra's Truth, and when we find it, we fight for it. If necessary, we die for it. There can be no compromise. No middle path."

Mordari freed herself of Dogra's grip and walked the last few yards up the hill. The unconscious human lay on the crest of the rock, the flesh browned by the sun. The general build was similar to the Sol creatures Mordari had known during her years of captivity, but there was something eerily familiar about this one. Dogra came up beside Mordari as she stared down at the prisoner.

"I did not learn to appreciate him," Dogra said. "Many times did

293

Baron Gamtro explain Ben's qualities, but knowing what I did, I could only suspect an enemy."

"Is a slave not a slave?" Mordari asked.

"Not always."

Mordari knelt to study the limp creature, turning its head so she could see the face. The long brown hair was tangled in knots, the thin beard turning gray.

"This is not possible!" Mordari exclaimed, reeling back in shock. "This creature is dead. He died many years ago."

Mordari jumped up, retreating to the edge of the rock, her claws shaking.

"You recognize him?" Dogra asked.

"Recognize him? It is the first Sol creature I ever met. But he died. Millions witnessed his death. How can he be here?"

"My mate has known of his past but chose to keep the secret. Which I have respected with some reluctance. I did not realize he would have such a profound effect on you."

"You are a stupid child, Dogra," Mordari said, kneeling down and pulling a vial from under her cloak.

Dogra noticed the bottle contained a green fluid, one believed to treat illnesses with astonishing swiftness. Dogra wondered where Mordari had obtained it, knowing the medicine was expensive and only available to commoners through black markets.

"Governor? Governor, can you hear my words?" Mordari asked.

Mordari put the bottle to Grey's lips and made him take a sip. Then another. Grey stirred, blinded by the sun hanging high in the hazy cloud streaked sky. Mordari took off her wide brim hat to shield his eyes.

"Can you hear me?" Mordari said, clicking her tongue intensely.

"Yes, mistress," Grey whispered.

"Indeed must you fare poorly to address your old foe in such a manner," Mordari said, supporting his head with her claw.

Dogra rushed to the other side, sitting down to rest his head in her lap. Grey squinted, trying hard to focus.

"Mordari? It cannot be. Earth has no stargate," Grey said, adding a click of astonishment to his words.

"Earth took the stargate technology when *Bhast* was captured," Mordari explained. "For a star's turn have I been free. I and many more. Your instructions to spare our lives were obeyed. A superior question is how you came to be here without a stargate."

"It does not matter. Am I forgiven for slaying Ryndari?"

"You gave him a warrior's death. No Arikhan could wish for more," Mordari replied.

"How is my family?" Grey asked.

"They thrive, and your mate is given much honor. But you would have earned more, had you lived. Have you been here all these years, a slave to these closed hearts?"

"All hearts are not closed. The Voice of Sherra knows this. Every race has good hearts and bad. Do I see Lady Gamtra?"

"Yes, Ben. I return in shame," Dogra said.

"I regret you were not more thoughtful," he agreed. "But still do you owe a debt. If you know honor, take Shalli away. Do not let our child be food for the pens."

Grey closed his eyes. His limbs were weak. Mordari gave him more liquid from her bottle.

"He fades," Dogra said.

To her astonishment, Dogra saw Mordari lean over and touch Grey on the forehead with the tip of her tongue. A gesture of devotion.

"Come," Mordari ordered, a desperate conviction in her voice.

Mordari hurried back down the hill and pulled Frontra aside where none could overhear. Dogra was curious and went to join them. Mordari warned her off.

"This is not for your hearing, Lady Gamtra," Mordari said.

"Something has happened. What is it?" Dogra asked.

Mordari took Frontra by the arm and walked down the valley toward the river, whispering intently. Frontra squared her shoulders. Dogra would not be put off, rushing to pull Mordari into the trees. Then the proud Lady Gamtra dropped to her knees before Mordari.

"I beg you, mistress, whatever it is. Accept me into your service," Dogra pleaded.

"You cannot know what you ask," Mordari said.

Frontra came up, having heard the request. She also kneeled in submission to Mordari.

"Mistress, do not dismiss the Lady Gamtra. We need her. She alone has the authority to challenge Lord Kanatron," Frontra advised.

"You ask much," Mordari said.

"You question if Lady Gamtra can be trusted. I believe she can," Frontra said.

"Do you believe she will commit treason?" Mordari asked.

"Treason?" Dogra supported.

"A language we have learned to speak. Do you still wish to help?" Mordari asked.

"If it means helping Shalli and her people, I will not fail you," Dogra swore.

"By Sherra's Oath?" Mordari asked with a black stare.

"By Sherra's Oath," Dogra agreed without hesitation, a claw tapping her breast.

"Very well, let us consider what must be done. Know that our lives mean nothing. Freeing Ben is everything," Mordari said.

"Why, mistress? What brings this urgency?" Dogra asked.

Mordari looked to Frontra, who also had many questions, but Frontra needed no convincing. The veteran guard appeared ready to act regardless of the consequences.

"All is made clear to me," Mordari said, her eye-rings gravely curled. "Sherra has spoken so loudly even the deaf can hear. This warrior was killed at the Battle of Sol, yet here he lives again among our people, sent by Sherra to show us the true path. A teaching you advocated quite profoundly in your chronicle. A truth demonstrated by Baron Gamtro's prosperity. But this sacred wisdom has been repudiated by closed hearts. A shadow of blood cast upon Her blessing. A shadow that only blood may wash away."

"You perceive great significance in these happenings, priestess?" Frontra asked.

"It is no coincidence that I am called to this place at this time, nor chance that the Lady Gamtra brings me," Mordari explained. "The obligation has fallen upon us to free Ben from these chains. Free him to fulfill the destiny carved for him from the beginning."

"Destiny? I do not understand," Dogra said, feeling a chill.

"Then understand this. The creature you call Ben is the one spoken of in our prophecies. He who is sent to free us from darkness. That which was foretold will now be brought to pass. Strive boldly, my sisters, for the honor and glory of Sherra."

* * * * * *

By the time Lord Kanatron returned to Karak, six of Lady Gamtra's staff had flown in from Va'ragashant and taken over the headquarters. To the resentment of the guards, the ministry officials were searching records and compiling reports.

"What is this?" Kanatron asked, climbing the flagstone steps carrying his travel bag. The breezy wind was turning cold. Growing lean, Kanatron looked tired from the journey. Group Leader Amartro sat outside the front door, the hulking brute looking particularly displeased.

"Lady Gamtra and her young eggs," Amartro reported, eye-rings flat with anger. "Tread lightly, my Lord. They seek mischief."

"An investigation? Here?" Kanatron asked.

"Blue blood bleeds everywhere," Amartro replied, citing an old commoner's proverb.

Kanatron opened the door slowly, taking in the situation. Dogra was waiting for him.

"You have much to answer for, my Lord," Dogra said, disapproval in the bent of her eye-rings.

Kanatron stood in the doorway finding his files rifled and recorder access codes overridden. Dogra spoke sternly but her color was calm.

"Do not sell your chronicle of nonsense here, Lady Gamtra. I have acted within my rights," Kanatron said.

"No one denies your authority over the food creatures. Where are your quarterly reports? Why are no production statistics on file? Why has Baron Gamtro's share of the dividends not been paid?" Dogra asked.

"We have tried," Kanatron said, finding himself in an argument he was unprepared for. "The quotas are high. The workers rioted. They tore up the ore tracks."

"The Ministry of Commerce is not interested in excuses, and

Baron Gamtro requires payment of his fiefs," Dogra said. "Vistra, is this not so? Are there not serious irregularities?"

"You face charges of malfeasance, my Lord," Vistra said, the young secretary's eyes glaring with the sharp intelligence of her aristocratic breeding. "At the very least, you need to bring Baron Gamtro's accounts up to date from your personal funds."

"Funds? I have no funds. All went to bribe—that is, all went to compensate Governor Zenatro for this post," Kanatron protested.

Several staff members came and went showing Dogra reports on their portable globes. Dogra frowned at each new revelation, making Kanatron ever more nervous. He went to the long table where the reports were being complied, trying to discover what the aggressive investigators were searching for.

"How can revenue be down sixty-eight percent?" Dogra asked. "Have resources been diverted into forbidden markets?"

"We have no forbidden markets. The food creatures caused this," Kanatron said. "Now that their leader is punished, the rest will work harder. When I kill that sow of his and eat the flesh of his spawn, all resistance will cease."

"The creatures you refer to are Ben and his mate, Shalli?" Vistra asked. "We have a file request on them."

"They are the property of Karak. Soon they will be the property of the pens," Kanatron said, clicking his tongue with eagerness.

"That is the law," Vistra agreed.

"Bynatron, has Mordari reported her findings?" Dogra asked.

"Mordari comes now," Bynatron said, a tall blue-cheeked noble training with Dogra's committee.

The young assistant declined to acknowledge Kanatron's presence, as did the other junior staff members. Kanatron remained subdued, fearing to make enemies among those who would someday hold high office.

Mordari entered the room wearing her brown, gold-trimmed robe, her haughty posture setting her apart from the others. She glanced at Kanatron with disdain, nor did she give much attention to Dogra's busy staff.

"You entered a protest on our report. Are you ready to explain?"

Dogra asked.

"It is as I suspected," Mordari said. "The food creature Ben is not of Akrona. The creature is likely a smuggler from Gorthan, or perhaps Rog. It may even be involved in espionage."

"Espionage?" Kanatron said.

"You pretend not to know?" Dogra questioned, turning on Kanatron. "Could it be you have ordered this creature's death to conceal your complicity? Is this where the missing funds have gone, diverted into black markets?"

"There may be an even more serious offense, Lady Gamtra," Mordari suggested.

"What offense? I am Sarden Leader in Governor Zenatro's service," Kanatron said.

"Then you accuse Zenatro of complicity in the conspiracy?" Vistra asked, holding the recording device up for his response.

"You cannot trick me. There is no crime. No conspiracy," Kanatron said, backing toward the door.

Bynatron blocked the exit, not that Kanatron was actually going to flee. But the inference appeared damning.

"If Ben is proven a spy, then he is a prisoner with valuable strategic information," Mordari said.

"That would classify the creature as an enemy of the empire," Vistra said, adding the thought to her notes.

"By whose authority do you execute him? Only the Council of Warriors may order the execution of a state prisoner," Dogra asked.

"To presume such authority is treason," Vistra said, punching an entry on her recording globe with a deadly finality.

"Treason?" Kanatron whispered, sitting on a stool near the window.

"The spy must be placed under arrest, its health restored so it may be questioned by the Council investigators," Dogra demanded. "If it dies, all will assume you killed it to destroy evidence of collusion."

"It will be placed in a protected area. The healer of the food creatures will be summoned to revive it," Kanatron agreed, withering under the suspicious stares of Dogra's staff.

"It may be clever to let the mate visit," Mordari suggested. "Their

299

discussions might reveal secrets."

"Opportunities to gain intelligence should not be overlooked," Vistra agreed.

"What is your opinion, Lord Kanatron?" Dogra asked.

"I have only been here two seasons. None of this is my fault," Kanatron said.

"Then you have no objection?" Dogra asked.

"No, the visits will be authorized," Kanatron agreed.

"What about these production reports?" Vistra asked. "The figures are incomplete. Failure to meet quota will undermine work on the new cargo vessels requisitioned by the fleet. Should charges of malfeasance be filed?"

"As Lord Kanatron says, he has only held the duty two seasons. Perhaps the contrast between Baron Gamtro's methods and these new practices have created confusion. Is that possible?" Dogra asked.

"It is possible," Kanatron gratefully agreed.

"If given additional time, may the discrepancies be corrected?" Dogra asked. "If so, we may delay our report until the findings reflect better on your administration."

Kanatron looked out the window at the camp. At the bottom of the hill, he saw dozens of empty ore carts.

"There has been violence in the camps. Some workers choose death rather than work. Even with guard strength up to four squads, it is difficult to make progress," Kanatron complained.

"We will proceed with the indictments," Vistra said, opening a new file.

"Wait. Let me speak with Lord Kanatron," Mordari requested. Eye-rings of the younger staff members rose in curiosity, but none objected.

Mordari led Kanatron out the front door, glanced at Amartro firmly enough to make him retreat, and strolled down the brush-lined path where they could converse privately among a grove of evergreens.

"My philosophy is well known," Mordari said. "Even now, I go to answer charges of treason. Charges you may face as well, for it seems you have many enemies. Commoners such as we who challenge the Great Houses rarely prosper."

"My birth is not so low," Kanatron responded, his cheeks showing the faintest traces of blue.

"Do you know of Vistra's family? Or Korbatro's? Would you have Gretnar write a theater about you?"

"I only sought the prosperity that Baron Gamtro achieved."

"Sherra's blessings must be earned," Mordari said, eye-rings bent in resolve. "If I can convince the slaves to work, what promises would be kept?"

"What would you want?" Kanatron asked.

"I have read Lady Gamtra's chronicle. It is a silly piece of foolishness, but it appears that modest rewards and a closing of the pens provide effective motivation."

"I have run this camp as all camps are run. As they have always been run," Kanatron protested.

"If that is your decision, then I will greet you again on Arikhan," Mordari said, turning to go back inside. "Bring a fur coat. The prisons are not heated."

"Hold, sister. Perhaps Baron Gamtro's methods may be used again, for a time, until production improves. Then the food creatures may be taught the lessons they deserve."

"What happens in the future is beyond my concern. Give Lady Gamtra a promise of four seasons. I will ask the food creatures to cooperate."

"I accept these terms, but the mate of the rebel chief must be exempted," Kanatron demanded. "I have sworn to eat the beating heart of her pup. Nothing will break my oath."

"This is a hard exemption. Let us keep it secret. After the pup is whelped, perhaps an accident will happen. So small an amount of meat should not be allowed to disturb production," Mordari advised.

"I like you, priestess. I thought you less practical regarding these lesser beings," Kanatron said, eye-rings relaxing.

"I was scout of the 44th Camp. First on the frontier, spear point of the 8th Regimental Segment. Now my calling is to strengthen the empire by reducing conflict within our borders. My philosophy advances this goal. But even I occasionally enjoy a taste of blood in my mort. Though these days, it must be non-sentient blood. I have an image to protect."

Mordari added a clicking sigh at the end of her sentence. Kanatron lashed his tongue in sympathy.

* * * * * *

As the afternoon grew late, the slaves in the compound saw half a dozen guards unchain their prisoner from the hillside and carry him down toward the maintenance shed at the southern end of the railroad tracks. They assumed he had died. When Black Hands was summoned by Amartro, none wanted her to go.

"I should accept," Black Hands said.

"You should not," Clagg objected.

"Let's consider this carefully," Nole cautioned.

The leaders stood near the old dock on the west side of the lake. Broken timber had been thrown up as a stockade. Many held staves, slings, and pickaxes.

"The safe conduct is brought by Frontra. She has never betrayed us," Black Hands said.

"Frontra may be overruled," Jarten warned.

"The risk must be taken," Black Hands insisted. "If the masters would have secrets from Ben's spirit, we should know what they seek."

"Ben was always strange," Old Ravo remarked. "What secrets might remain now that he is dead?"

"He was a warrior. Warriors always have secrets, even in death," Black Hands said.

The leaders reluctantly agreed. Black Hands gave her medical bag to Myra so it could not be confiscated and walked toward the gate. Just as she reached Rabbit Camp, she was suddenly flanked by Frontra and Sub-leader Bractro. Both were heavily armed. The day was cold, the late sun partially hidden by winter clouds. Beyond the gate, eight nervous guards watched for trouble.

"Is there something I should know?" Black Hands dared to ask in well-spoken Arikhan.

"Remain silent," Bractro grunted, swinging his long arms as he walked. Frontra said nothing, careful not to reveal her thoughts.

They passed beneath the brick arch and went south. Bractro departed for the headquarters, waving for his squad to stand down. Frontra placed a claw under Black Hands' elbow, hurrying her along.

"What is this?" Black Hands asked once they were alone.

"Have I been a friend?" Frontra said.

"Yes, mistress."

"Then have patience."

At the end of the tracks, Black Hands saw a mysterious brown-robed figure standing near the maintenance building.

"I will return later," Frontra said, suddenly turning back toward the camp headquarters.

"Frontra? Frontra? Where are you going?" Black Hands called, but Frontra did not respond. Black Hands paused, frightened but unwilling to show it.

"You are the healer," the stranger said, emerging from the shadows.

"I am Black Hands of the People," she answered, chin held high. The dark eyes glistened with defiance.

"Among my people, healers may have great power. Are you such?"

"The greatest power I have known died on Vulture Rock. I am but his shadow."

"You will serve my needs," Mordari concluded.

There was a footlocker set next to the door. When the top was opened, the healer realized the container was well-stocked with drugs and medical instruments.

"This is a rich bounty, mistress. What must I do to earn it?" Black Hands tentatively asked.

"You must not address me as mistress without knowing my name. I am Mordari."

"The Voice of Sherra?" Black Hands said, struggling to maintain her composure.

"Has my infamy reached so primitive a shore as Karak?"

"Great truths are hard to hide."

"Harder to hide from some than others," Mordari sighed. "The medicines will be delivered to your camp without obligation, but I would beg a favor."

"If you wish me to cut some secret from my brother's body, the answer is no. I will not desecrate his spirit."

"Come into the depot," Mordari urged.

The large door was pushed open, the iron hinges creaking. The old shed was poorly lit by streaks of daylight creeping through cracks in the woodwork. Oily tools hung on the walls, repair equipment littered the floor. There was a dank, musty smell.

Near the back wall, Black Hands saw Grey lying on straw, his collar chained to a pole. Two guards stood inside the doorway, looking bored with their assignment. Mordari motioned with a wave of her claw and the guards slowly filed out. They did not appear worried about an escape.

"You have a patient," Mordari instructed.

"Ben lives?" Black Hands said in surprise.

"I have done what I can. I am not a healer. Use the chest of medicines. He must be strong for the times ahead."

"Will there be times ahead, mistress? Is all not come to dust?"

Mordari placed her claws on the sides of the healer's head, staring deeply into her eyes. Black Hands felt great power in the gaze.

"Frontra says you were reborn once. Before long, you will be reborn again. Do not despair," Mordari counseled.

As Mordari departed back toward the compound, Black Hands pulled the medical chest inside and closed the door.

"Ben?"

"Who speaks?" Grey softly answered.

"Black Hands."

She knelt at his side, finding him stronger than expected. Creams were used to heal the cuts. Ointments soothed the squinting red eyes. She noticed his lips were stained with a moist green coloring.

"Shalli?"

"She is safe, for now. The masters know there will be no production if they kill everyone."

"They've killed enough."

"If Tak's murder had not led to revolt, another event would have.

304

This is not your fault."

Grey suspected it might be true, but it didn't make him feel better.

"What does Nole intend?" he asked.

"No one knows what to do. Not Nole. Not Clagg. Even Old Ravo is afraid to offer his thoughts. What should we do?"

"Maybe Lady Gamtra has a plan."

"Why is Mordari here? Why would the Voice of Sherra take an interest in you?"

Grey looked to the door, wondering if their conversation was being overheard, but realized they were alone.

"There is something you should know," he whispered.

"About your past?" she guessed.

"Mordari and I have a history that goes back many years. To a war that was fought on another planet. Save the secret deep in your heart. Perhaps one day the knowledge may help your people."

"*Our* people," Black Hands insisted.

"I don't know if that's true anymore. I'm not sure if it was ever true."

"Do you have a plan?"

"Not yet. But if I get the chance, the masters will regret the day they unchained me from that rock."

* * * * * *

An hour after Black Hands left the camp, the gates opened again and an Arikhan appeared garbed in the brown robes of a priestess. All were surprised when the unwelcome visitor entered the compound alone.

Sixteen hundred slaves were formed in groups but ready to scatter if the guards came forward with their energy weapons. Most were stationed in a crescent west of the lake near the cabin where Grey and Shalli once lived. A cabin that was now a burned-out shell. Timber had been erected for barricades at the edge of the woods, trails providing a retreat to the old mines if necessary.

Clagg, Nole and the other camp leaders stood on a platform where they could see the gatehouse, ready to issue instructions. Barris paced near the lake with a steel knife in his hand, ready to kill the first

Arikhan to come within reach. Nole had convinced him not to throw his life away after Tak's murder, but now that his best friend was dead, Barris was determined to die with Arikhan blood on his blade.

The lone Arikhan walked toward the gardens where Dogra had found Shalli earlier in the day. As darkness fell, torches were lit. Hundreds of curious people watched the stranger approach, looking toward the gate to see if armed guards were coming. The gates were closed.

"You were here before, with Lady Gamtra," Myra said, being the first to speak. She approached cautiously ahead of the men, anxious to avoid unnecessary violence. Mordari thought her quite brave.

"Your name?" Mordari asked.

"I am Myra of Ferret Camp, wife of Clagg."

"You may be my escort," Mordari said, taking her arm.

Mordari continued forward with Myra at her side until they stood among a large crowd, most armed with clubs and shovels, ready to kill if provoked.

The visitor paused, searching out the ground, and spied a fallen log that would allow her to address the throng. She looked to Myra for assistance, holding out her arm. Myra gave Mordari a boost without even thinking about it.

"You should not be here," someone in the crowd shouted.

"Leave while you still can," another threatened.

"I urge you to listen for just a moment, for I have traveled a great distance to meet your people," Mordari said, her voice loud but not shouting. "I have an important message for all of you."

"Who is the message from?" Nole asked.

"The message is from Sherra," Mordari answered.

Many drew back in fear. Even Barris momentarily withheld his knife.

Myra motioned for the crowd to make room, helping Mordari down and leading her to Shalli's burned-out house. The camp leaders stood together, Old Ravo holding Barris back from rash action.

Mordari stepped up on what was left of the stone porch, pausing as the crowd gathered.

"Who are you? What do you want?" Nole asked.

"My name is Mordari. I come to speak from this place, for it is holy ground," Mordari replied.

"Who?" someone from the back shouted.

"Mordari," Myra said, the name repeated throughout the crowd.

"The Voice of Sherra?" Lupet asked.

"Such cannot be," Sal whispered.

"I think it is," Hernet said.

The crowd murmured restlessly, pushing for a closer look with a mixture of anger and curiosity.

"Many have doubts, mistress," Myra nervously said, standing in front of Mordari trying to shield her from harm.

Mordari clicked her tongue with appreciation and gently moved Myra aside, positioning herself where all could see.

"Myra says many have doubts. That is as it should be," Mordari announced, raising her arms. "Look into your hearts, my children. Sherra's Truth is not hard to find."

"You have come far to speak with food creatures," Nole said, unsure what to think.

"I am Sherra's Voice. No distance is too great to share Her words," Mordari answered. "Where is Shalli?"

Kept safe by a crew of hardened miners, Shalli emerged from the crowd and stood before Mordari, her expression filled with fear.

Mordari folded back the hood of her robe, waited for the crowd to grow quiet, and touched Shalli's forehead with the tip of her claw.

"Your husband lives," Mordari said, her black eyes shining in the torchlight. "Black Hands gives him food and medicine. You will be allowed to visit him. It is not his destiny to die in this place."

In an instant, Shalli dropped to her knees, followed by Myra and many others. The people murmured, sharing the words with those farther back that now encompassed most of the camps.

Shalli reached to take Mordari's claw. Mordari accepted the gesture. There was a sense of suspense as Mordari stood tall among the kneeling people and lit torches. All seemed to acknowledge some degree of homage except Barris.

"Listen to me now, for it is Sherra's voice that speaks," Mordari said loudly enough for all to hear. "Much have you suffered due to blindness and closed hearts. The suffering is not over. Not all will know blessed days, but do not give up hope. The liberator of your legends is coming. Await the arrival of Akeem."

Barris lowered the knife. Many shivered from the enormity of the moment.

"How may we serve you, mistress?" Myra asked.

"I would speak with your leaders," Mordari said.

A few minutes later, in the rubble of Shalli's home, Mordari sat in council with ten camp leaders. Mordari sought to explain the terms of Kanatron's offer, and the importance of accepting them.

"You must put Kanatron at ease. Give us time," Mordari urged.

"Can you tell us of Akeem?" Nole asked.

"I may say no more," Mordari apologized.

"You ask much, priestess," Old Ravo said.

"Trust is not easy. There is no reason it should be. Have faith. Though the Arikhan know Akeem by a different name, our prophecies also speak of one sent to free us from darkness. For this reason I am raised to Sherra's calling, and in Her vision will the martyrs of Karak live in eternal glory. It is not for us to question Her divine plan, I may only plead that those who are your friends be allowed to act."

"We will take all into consideration," Nole promised.

Mordari stood up and left the building, pausing outside the door where the crowds were watching. Well-practiced at her calling, she waited for silence before speaking.

"Be patient, my children. The day of liberation is not today or tomorrow, but it comes as surely as the morning sun and evening moons. Abide not in fear, for Sherra holds you in her heart," Mordari declared.

Mordari walked toward the main gate accompanied by Myra and Pie, the crowds parting for her in waves. The leaders retreated to a canvas tent hidden in the woods, speaking far into the night. The imminent danger posed by Kanatron, and the hope inspired by Mordari, were hard to reconcile.

Black Hands returned the next morning escorted by Bractro and a squad of armed guards. Nole and Clagg met them at the gate, the remaining leaders staying back with the people in case of treachery.

Beyond the shimmering force-field fence, Group Leader Amartro was seen standing on the troop carrier, keeping clear of the proceedings, for his presence would only incite trouble.

Just a few yards from the gatehouse, the slaves stood on one side of the yellow line, the Arikhan on the other. Nole noticed a strange young Arikhan female standing next to Bractro, her cheekbones bluer than any he'd seen except for Lady Gamtra. She was finely dressed in a jungle green uniform and tall black boots.

"Have you made a decision?" Bractro inquired with a grunt, eye-rings bent in displeasure. The guard looked fatigued from a lack of sleep. His blue-dyed leather jacket was stained.

"How do we know Kanatron will keep his word?" Clagg asked.

"*Lord* Kanatron," Bractro said.

"Not our lord," Clagg replied.

"Lady Gamtra and her committee stand witness," Vistra said, stepping forward. She waved a delicate claw, her fine webbing lifting slightly. Her reddish brown eyes danced with curiosity.

"You are Lady Gamtra's secretary?" Nole perceptively asked.

"I am Vistra, Countess of Alan' Tay. A servant of Lady Gamtra's committee. My father and Lord Gamtro share an ancestral spirit."

"Lord Gamtro was our friend," Clagg said.

"Lord Gamtro is a treasured member of my family," Vistra replied.

Clagg and Nole glanced at each other.

"Production will resume," Nole agreed.

Several of the guards noticeably relaxed. Nole sensed the failure to meet quotas had them under great stress.

"Lord Kanatron expects no less, for much of the season has been wasted," Bractro said, anxious to assert his authority. "And now Shalli must come with us."

"No. Kanatron's malice is well known," Clagg refused.

"She will return in safety, as promised," Bractro said, insulted by the questioning of his honor. Shalli shied back until she saw Frontra waiting outside the gate. Vistra raised her eye-rings with reassurance.

"I will go," Shalli said.

Frontra took custody at the gatehouse and walked Shalli up the tracks toward the maintenance shed. Three guards were on duty, two near empty ore tenders and a third at the door. Frontra's posture was stiff as she took Shalli inside, never saying a word. Mordari was waiting for them.

"He is weak but undamaged," Mordari said. "Special foods are ordered from Va'ragashant."

Grey sat cross-legged on the floor, weary but alert, his hands shackled and a chain around his neck. Someone had dressed him in a rough woolen tunic and long trousers. He struggled to his knees as Shalli rushed to hug him.

"Everyone thought you were dead," Shalli cried.

"That happens to me a lot," Grey replied, relieved to see her well. "Thank you, Mordari. We owe you a great debt."

"I have little to risk. Many think me guilty of heresy. After the trial, it will be confirmed. It is Lady Gamtra who deserves your praise. She gambles all on your behalf."

"I have cursed your people. Can you forgive me, mistress?" Shalli asked.

"If my people are cursed, it is Sherra's Will. Forgiveness will come when it is truly earned," Mordari answered, eye-rings reverently dipped.

"What happens next?" Grey asked.

"Lady Gamtra's plans are unknown to me, but she is much determined," Mordari said. "Now that you are a prisoner of the empire, Kanatron's authority over you is weakened. Gamtra's staff believes you will be transferred to Arikhan, there to face a military tribunal. I fear Shalli faces more immediate peril."

"Our world is destroyed, priestess. Each new day is a gift," Shalli said, standing on her toes to give Mordari a kiss on the cheek. Mordari was not flustered as Dogra had been. Grey assumed she had been kissed by humans before.

"Enjoy this time together, for the future is full of danger," Mordari advised, leaving them alone.

"All the camps are proud of you, my husband," Shalli said, snuggling close.

"They have little cause to be. For too long I sought cooperation with the masters. All it brought was death. To Tak. To her babies. To a hundred others. All I've struggled for has failed."

"There is no longer dissension between the camps. Tak is avenged. And a truce is negotiated until the day you bring our people freedom," Shalli said.

"Freedom?" Grey asked.

"Mordari has brought word of a vision. She would not explain, but I needed no explanation. You are Akeem, my husband, the liberator of our people."

Grey looked out a narrow window toward the compound several hundred yards away.

"You don't seem surprised," Shalli said.

"I've never been lucky," he answered.

* * * * * *

At midday, Frontra took Shalli from the maintenance shed, still declining to speak with her. The guards exchanged bent eye-rings as Shalli passed, but she ignored them. They walked along the tracks until reaching the train station, then up the steps to the old headquarters perched on the hill. The main room still held Dogra's staff, though the work was less frenzied.

All in the room stopped to look at Shalli, their expressions searching. Shalli wondered if they had ever seen a living food creature before, remembering Dogra's stories about their homeworld. One came up to greet her.

"I am Livy, second secretary to the Lady Gamtra," an elegantly attired alien said. "We are pleased to meet you. We wish you well."

"Thank you," Shalli said, sensing the greeting was sincerely spoken. Though why this group of important administrators would give her a second thought was a complete mystery. A moment later, Dogra came down the stairs from the upper room.

"My companions, this is Shalli, whom you have read about," Dogra introduced. "Shalli, these are my associates on the Committee of Commerce. They are helping me repair the damage caused by that fool Kanatron. Though they are not followers of Mordari, all believe relations between our peoples can be better. You deserve much credit for teaching this lesson."

"Me? I am no one special," Shalli said, her Arikhan adequately pronounced.

Dogra's staff approved of her modesty. Shalli felt admired by them.

"Come, child, we must speak," Dogra said, taking Shalli upstairs.

The room was no longer the lovely vacation suite it had been six months before. Kanatron had used it for a barracks, replacing the large nest with pads of straw. Dogra made Shalli sit down on a mat before bringing her hot broth and a plate of roasted duck.

"You should not be so thin this late with child," Dogra said.

"Winter is a hard time, mistress. Especially with our crops burned," Shalli answered. She immediately regretted the rebuke, setting the bowl aside and putting her forehead to the floor in submission. Dogra noticed Shalli trembling.

"An apology is called for," Dogra said.

"Please forgive me, mistress," Shalli said, her voice choking on a sob.

"You do not understand, dear heart. I am the one who apologizes," Dogra said, drawing Shalli into her lap. "Eat more of the broth. It has special ingredients to give you strength."

"Thank you, mistress," Shalli appreciated, her hands still shaking.

"Dogra," Dogra insisted, peeling a piece of wing and feeding it to her.

"Thank you, Dogra," Shalli corrected, fear still in her eyes.

Dogra stroked Shalli's long dirty hair and sniffed her shoulder. The human was not bathing regularly. The meat was not robust.

"When we left here, Baron Gamtro was seriously injured. We returned to our estate on Arikhan where it took several moons for his health to stabilize. We were visited by dignitaries, given honors, and I wrote a chronicle that received high praise. Then I was offered a new post and gained leadership of a committee," Dogra explained.

"The Baron and I made attempts to contact Akrona, but we only received a few official replies from Governor Zenatro. We should have tried harder, Shalli. We should have made sure all was well. I will never forgive myself for what has happened. When Baron

Gamtro learns how your people have been mistreated, he will be outraged. Those responsible will be held to account, but that will not return those you have lost. Or the trust. Please forgive us."

Shalli didn't know what to say. An explanation was unexpected.

"Have you ever seen one of these?" Dogra asked, showing her a reading globe.

"It's a recorder. Ben used one for keeping records until Amartro wanted to confiscate it. Ben gave it back, but not until a big rock accidentally broke it," Shalli said, trying not to smile.

"We use recorders for viewing images and words," Dogra said. "I wrote a chronicle after returning home. A story about you. Millions of my people have read it. Millions more will read it. That is why my staff is so interested."

"I do not understand, mistress. Why would you make words about me? Why would anyone read them?" Shalli asked.

"Come here, my lovely innocent," Dogra said, pulling Shalli against her breast. "Let me pretend you are my egg, like we did once before. Know that I love you."

Shalli snuggled warmly in Dogra's arms, tears running down her face.

"I am sorry I spoke so meanly to you," Shalli said.

"I know. Now rest quietly. My committee can only be here a few days. We will take testimony. Compile records. I will write another chronicle, and this time it will not be an egg's tale. The truths will be hard, but they will be heard. I want you to get strong. And I will do whatever is necessary to get you out of this terrible place."

"It does not matter what happens to me," Shalli said. "If not for Baron Gamtro, all of Ferret Camp would have gone to the pens years ago. If you can do anything, help my husband. Only he can save my people. And if you can, make my baby live in freedom."

Dogra held Shalli in her arms, praying for way to make her wish come true.

* * * * * *

Four days later, the train station was active with Dogra's staff loading their equipment. None would miss life at Karak, the major disagreement being who was worse, the angry slaves or the brutal guards. All agreed that Shalli was everything Lady Gamtra's chronicle had claimed.

Early in the morning, after a final visit with Dogra, Mordari walked with Shalli back to the compound. Two armed guards lagged behind, watchful but less worried than they had been a few days earlier. Women had returned to the gardens, and the sound of mining activity echoed off the mountain.

"Your husband will not be transferred to Arikhan until the military sends a warship. None yet suspect his true identity," Mordari softly told her.

"I do not understand, priestess. My husband was a warrior on another world. Is that so uncommon?" Shalli asked.

"No, but your husband is. He will be a subject of much interest by the Council of Warriors."

"What will they do?"

"Patience, Shalli dear. Most only know your husband as Ben, a slave of Akrona. That is for the best," Mordari said as they reached the gate.

The guards allowed them through without question. Mordari and Shalli had made many trips from the camp in the previous few days, and no mere guard cared to question the Voice of Sherra, regardless of their personal opinions.

"Lady Gamtra is quite upset she could not free you from this camp," Mordari said. "She tried all, even bribery. Kanatron is indeed a vengeful spirit."

"I will not let them have my baby. Tak fought to the end to protect her twins. I will, too," Shalli said, her hands around her belly.

"It takes courage to strive in times of great risk," Mordari advised. She looked around, made sure they were well within the compound away from prying eyes, and handed Shalli a wicker basket.

"More food? Lady Gamtra would make me fat," Shalli said.

"This is not food, dear. It is hope," Mordari answered, opening the basket cover. Inside was a fully charged energy pistol and extra power packs. Shalli tried not to stare as Mordari closed the lid.

"The train leaves this afternoon," Mordari informed. "Lady

Gamtra and I fly to Va'ragashant in the morning with Kanatron. When Frontra comes for you at dusk, bring the warmest clothes you have. And winter clothes for Ben. We will have food and equipment ready. When Frontra leaves to file her report, kill the guards and free your husband. Flee into the mountains."

Shalli was dumbfounded. Never had she imagined that one Arikhan would instruct her to kill another. Nor was Shalli sure she could do it.

They came to the southern gardens where several women were planting seedlings. Court was among them, a rage in her eyes from which Mordari was not immune. Shalli saw Barris approach and grew afraid, standing in front of Mordari to protect her. Barris stopped just a few yards short, a hand poised on the knife in his belt. Nole and Clagg ran up to prevent trouble, but Barris pushed Nole away.

"You should not roam freely in our camp. You might get hurt," Barris warned.

"Not while I have you to stand beside me, Barris," Mordari said, stepping past Shalli to take Barris by the arm. "I had a dream of you last night. A most powerful dream."

"You do not know me. I do not talk to Kanatron's spies," Barris said.

"You are the friend of Ben. His closest friend," Mordari answered.

"I am his brother, now and forever. He killed the monsters who murdered my wife and children. He taught us to fight."

Mordari put her claws against the sides of his head, staring deeply into the fierce brown eyes with a mesmerizing gaze. Barris felt the energy of her touch. There was no fear in Mordari's eyes. None. Not of him. Not of anything. Barris was forced to wonder if the alien really was one with the gods.

"Ben will need such brothers in the difficult times ahead," Mordari said. "Be true to him always. You believe yourself rash. You think Ben keeps your balance. This is false. You are the balance."

A dozen people gathered around. Shalli, Myra, and Clagg. Garn and Pie. Turk, Byrne, and Keep. Even Court. But none were more interested than Barris. Mordari looked for a place to sit and was provided with a tree stump.

"There is something I could say, but much discretion is required," Mordari hinted, lowering her voice to a whisper. "Shalli, are there any here who would betray your husband?"

"All are family, priestess," Shalli said.

"Would you hear my words, Barris? And Court, you who have been so dreadfully wronged. Will you open your heart?" Mordari asked.

"I will hear your words," Barris agreed.

Court sat down, frowning but willing to listen. Nole put an arm around her shoulders. Clagg went to hold Myra.

"I first met Ben nearly twenty years ago on the moon of another planet," Mordari explained. "I was scout of the 44th Camp, the most honored advance guard in our service. Ben was soon to be leader of the planet's resistance, though he kept that secret. We were enemies, and in a strange way, companions on a journey.

"Along with my partner, Ryndari, Ben and I traveled together. We shared meals. Became drunk on mauck. Exchanged thoughts. And sometimes we fought, for above all else, we were opponents in a great struggle between two civilizations. The Arikhan, old and set in our ways, unbelieving of defeat. And Ben's people, young and strong, unwilling to contemplate surrender. I saved Ben's life several times. On several occasions, he saved mine.

"Then the day came that Ryndari discovered Ben had played us falsely. They fought, and when Ben slew Ryndari, I hated him for it. But as the years passed, I came to see Ryndari had been given a warrior's death, and that no great cause can be waged without sacrifice.

"In the final battle of our war, Ben surrendered his life to save his world. Deeply have his people mourned his loss, for he had a wife and many friends. In time, I also mourned. Long have I sought Sherra's wisdom to understand the order of Her universe. The search for Her truth has led me here."

Mordari paused, her brown cheeks turning gray as her shoulders sagged. The black eyes stared as if in a trance. It appeared the speech was taking a toll on her, as if Sherra herself was using Mordari as a vessel to express her thoughts. Even Barris and Court were awed by

316

the experience.

"Listen now, for you have become his people. In this you have gained a sacred responsibility. Know that Ben is more audacious than any of you may imagine. He will do anything to defend those he loves. Anything to achieve a goal he holds necessary. But there are times he does not see the true path. Times he is consumed by failures of perfection, for the mentors of his youth were exacting in their demands. I charge you not just to serve him, but to be his center. He will need your strength.

"Though she has not shared her thoughts with me, I sense that Shalli has guessed why Ben stands so greatly in my thoughts. Shalli, you are not wrong. Share this secret with those you trust most deeply, but no one else. In your heart, you hold the fate of worlds."

Mordari paused again, her voice growing weaker. Shalli went to keep her steady, quickly joined by Myra. All were breathless with anticipation.

"I have a message for Barris," Mordari finally said, holding out a claw to touch his arm. "My people have believed that only we travel to the Great Nestings after death, there to celebrate eternal blessings. I have always thought this true, even after living on another world and communing with their powerful gods. I was mistaken. I now understand that eternal blessings belong to all, and I truly believe, beyond all possible error, that Tak is called as messenger to sit at Sherra's feet. Do not hurry to meet her, Barris. You have much to do, and Tak is proud of you.

"Court, mother of this sacred spirit, do not despair. Hold patience close to your heart, for it is Sherra's will to grant you the greatest of all gifts."

Suddenly Mordari stood up, glanced around at her surroundings, and slowly walked away, her stride graceful.

"I have never known a creature like her," Barris said, watching Mordari disappear into the darkness.

"Look," Shalli whispered, opening the basket.

Barris saw the weapon and glanced to Shalli for the meaning.

"Mordari has arranged for me to escape tonight. With Ben," Shalli explained. "We'll go into the mountains where my baby will be born in freedom."

"Mordari does this?" Barris quietly said.

"She is very brave," Shalli answered, taking Barris by the arm. "Tomorrow she travels home, there to stand trial. They may even execute her. But Mordari will not be silenced. She says Sherra has decided to act. I don't know what it means, but I'm frightened."

"I wanted to kill all the masters, but how can I hate Mordari, who offers her life for our people?" Barris said. "Ben is right. Ben is always right. We may not judge all masters because some are evil. Marne was evil, too. Do you think Mordari's words are true? Does Tak sit with Sherra?"

"Mordari is Sherra's voice. That's why so many fear her," Shalli said. "If she says Tak sits at Sherra's feet, then you know it's true. There's also the secret she spoke of. A very dangerous secret."

Chapter Ten
A FINAL MESSAGE

Just before sunset, Shalli gathered up her warmest clothing. Clagg worked on putting together things Grey would need, including the black thermal suit Gamtro had given him years before. Myra held two-year-old Bern in her lap while having young Garn gather sleeping furs. Everyone was sad to see Shalli going, believing they would never see her again.

"There is something more," Myra said as she helped Shalli pack.

"Yes, Myra?" Shalli asked.

"Clagg and I have talked. We want Garn to go with you," Myra said.

"Garn? With us to the mountains?" Shalli questioned.

Garn came forward, a backpack slung over his slender shoulders, his dark brown eyes filled with apprehension. Though already close to Shalli's height, he seemed small by the light of the campfire. He shared the wide, soft-brown face of his mother, and the curly auburn hair of his father. His arms and legs were long, the body thin with youth.

"We don't know what will happen here," Clagg said. "We don't know what will happen to Ferret Camp when the truce ends. Garn is nine now. Strong for his age. This is his best chance to be free. If Bern wasn't so young, and if you weren't so heavy with child, we'd send him, too."

"I want my nephew to be free, but this will be dangerous. I'm afraid of what might happen," Shalli said.

"We're all afraid," Myra replied, giving Shalli a hug.

They looked toward the eastern trail and saw Frontra coming, the only guard who dared walk alone among the slaves. All knew it was for the last time. Frontra would be leaving in the morning, her replacement having finally arrived.

"Garn will go with Shalli," Myra said the moment Frontra entered

319

the camp. Frontra looked at the faces around her. She could smell the fear.

"Garn, would you like to take a walk?" Frontra asked, extending her claw.

"Thank you, mistress," Garn said, taking a final moment to hug his parents.

"Remember us," Myra said, unsuccessfully holding back tears.

"Do what Shalli and Ben tell you," Clagg said.

"I won't forget," Garn he assured his father.

"Frontra, we thank you. We thank you for many years of being our friend. None here are blind to that which lies in your heart," Clagg said, tall enough to stand eye to eye with the big Arikhan.

"Perhaps one day we will meet again," Frontra said. "I have heard of a former guard who feels as I do. He bought a ranch on the western peninsula and purchases slaves to work it. His ranch has no chains or pens, and the prosperity is shared by all."

Shalli gave her camp tearful hugs and let Frontra carry her pack as they started for the gate. Frontra slowed her pace so Shalli would not need to struggle, taking a look at the gardens in the moonlight.

"What does Garn know?" Frontra asked.

"Only that we go on a journey," Shalli said.

"Let no more be said. Be brave. Do what must be done. Is that Mordari's basket?"

Shalli nodded, not sure if Frontra knew the contents.

"Allow me to carry it," Frontra said, straightening her shoulders.

The guards did a light search of the slaves as they exited the compound, holding too much contempt for food creatures to believe a pregnant woman and a child dangerous. Frontra almost wished she had let Garn carry the basket just to teach the arrogant fools a lesson. They went slowly up the tracks where several ore tenders were waiting for repair. The maintenance shed was off to the right, two guards near the front door and another inside.

"Greetings, Nartro. The food creatures bring travel wear for the prisoner in accordance with Lord Kanatron's orders," Frontra said, exaggerating the instructions.

"I thought you did not consider them food creatures," Nartro said, a stocky veteran bored with his duties.

"They are what they are. The laws of nature do not change," Frontra replied.

Nartro raised an eye-ring in agreement, looking at the succulent food creatures with longing. Particularly the young calf meat in Shalli's extended girth.

As Frontra backed away, Shalli and Garn entered the old shed, finding Grey still chained to a post in the far corner. A guard stood a few meters away, tall with long arms and a narrow face, a Contingent badge on his shoulder. It was Farlatro, one of Amartro's most hated minions.

"Stay behind me," Shalli whispered to Garn.

There was only one dim fluorescent light hanging from the high ceiling, leaving Grey sitting in shadow. The guard was easier to see. As Shalli approached, the guard gave her a hungry stare, knowing Kanatron's plans for her. And sure Garn could be added to the menu.

"You must be searched. Strip off your false hide. Remove everything," Farlatro ordered, eye-rings bent in expectation.

Shalli made a motion to remove her heavy bearskin coat, but pulled out the energy pistol instead, a trim metallic weapon with a trigger button on the handle. Farlatro was initially startled, but quickly regained composure.

"Release my husband," Shalli ordered, aiming the weapon's stem without precision.

The guard could have drawn his pistol, but decided to pull his hunting knife instead. Grey stood up and strained against the chain.

"I will have a taste before surrendering you to Lord Kanatron," Farlatro said, stepping directly under the dim light.

Shalli pressed the button on the blaster's grip with her thumb, firing the weapon. A bolt of red hot energy passed a meter to the right of the Arikhan's head. She fired again, shooting high and to the left. Her hands were shaking. Instead of firing a third time, she started to back up. Farlatro was excited by the panic in the food creature's eyes. Sharp yellow fangs emerged beneath the thin upper lip.

"No longer do I need permission to taste the rebel sow's blood, though raw meat is not always the best. The filth in your belly I save for Lord Kanatron," he said, slowly advancing.

A second later, Farlatro's eager expression disappeared, replaced by a stunned look. Shalli cried out as an explosive pellet shot over her shoulder from behind, the steel ball passing so close to her head that she felt the pressure against her ear. The pellet struck the guard dead center in the chest. He clutched at the wound, uncomprehending, then weakly reached for his pistol.

Shalli dropped to the floor as a second shot tore into the guard's throat. He fell to his knees clutching at his neck, blood spurting from his windpipe, and finally toppled over, dying with a final twitch of quivering eye-rings. Shalli turned to see Frontra standing near Garn, a pistol in her claw. If Frontra had strong emotions about killing one of her own kind, she didn't display them.

"Thank you, mistress," Shalli whispered.

"Hurry," Frontra urged, disappearing out the door.

Grey was already digging in the guard's belt for the key. The moment he was free of the chain, he picked up the hunting knife and motioned for Garn to stay quiet. Garn nodded. He had been afraid at first, but not anymore. Grey gave Shalli a quick but passionate kiss.

"Have our supplies ready to go," Grey said in a hushed tone, slipping out the door.

Shalli hurried to gather the extra backpack Mordari had mentioned, finding condensed food rations and heat lamps. She let Garn carry the energy pistol.

Hardly a minute later, Grey returned dragging a dead guard, the hunting knife streaked with Arikhan blood. Shalli and Garn saw the guard's throat had been slashed all the way to the spine. Grey took their weapons and hid both bodies behind a stack of rails.

"Where's Nartro?" Shalli asked.

"I don't know. Maybe he left with Frontra," Grey guessed.

"Clagg and Myra want Garn to come with us," Shalli said.

"I'm glad they did," Grey responded, giving his nephew a hug.

They went out the side door wrapped in their bear coats and turned south. Within minutes, they had climbed over a low ridge and passed through a timber yard where logging operations would make tracking difficult. Having worked in the area for years, Grey knew the trails even in the darkness.

* * * * * *

Frontra walked with Nartro back to the camp headquarters, leaving him at the bottom of the steps. She went up the stairs slowly, looking south for signs of trouble. The area appeared quiet, dark but for a few dim lamps. The cold night would keep the sentries indoors.

With Dogra's committee having returned to the capital by train, the main room was once again being used by Kanatron's senior staff. Some watched the communications globe while others prepared food in the kitchen. Many were resting and staying warm. Frontra went into the rear office where Kanatron and Dogra were in conference, a bottle of fine bruno on the desk. Group Leader Amartro sat on a stool in the corner.

"Travel wear is being delivered to the prisoner as ordered," Frontra reported.

"Are you packed for departure?" Dogra asked.

"Yes, my Lady. We keep few possessions here at camp. The company agent will forward my assets when I find resettlement," Frontra explained.

"Lord Kanatron suggests we take the prisoner with us in the morning. Have you an opinion?" Dogra requested.

"The prisoner is dangerous, well-schooled in combat by a blood thirsty culture. A squad would be preferable, but four guards will suffice if you keep him chained," Frontra answered.

"You rate this creature too highly," Amartro complained, leaning back on his stool. "If we lash the thing often enough, it will give us no trouble."

Dogra looked to Kanatron, who appeared unsure. Amartro squared his shoulders, confidently clicking his tongue. Frontra noticed he had not been invited to share Kanatron's bruno, holding a goblet of mauck instead.

"Amartro knows these animals better than I. His advice will be respected," Kanatron said.

"If you say beatings make the creature manageable, that will be sufficient," Dogra gracefully conceded. "By law, the prisoner remains your responsibility until the formal transfer takes place in Va'ragashant. I have reported as much to the Ministry, crediting you with its capture."

"Thank you, Lady Gamtra," Kanatron appreciated.

Amartro stood up, gazed out the south window for a moment, and set his goblet aside.

"I have duties," Amartro announced, suddenly leaving without permission. Frontra offered a final salute and quickly followed.

"Your Group Leader shows little respect," Dogra observed once they were alone.

"I do not trust him," Kanatron confided, his tongue curling.

"Has he plotted against you?"

"What do you mean?" Kanatron asked, eye-rings going up.

"The slaves were productive until Amartro killed Tak and stole her babies. Did he deliberately provoke the workers to undermine your administration?"

Kanatron rose from the stool, glanced into the empty hall, and drew Dogra to an outside balcony. It was a dark night, the clouds hanging heavy in the western sky.

"You are much in secrecy, my Lord," Dogra said.

"Before entering my service, Amartro served the Contingent. He may be conspiring with my enemies. If the camp continues to fail quota, Zenatro may revoke my commission while keeping the fees I used to secure this post."

"Did Amartro abolish the accords that Lord Gamtro used to motivate the camps?"

"No, that was my decision."

"Your decision was ill-advised," Dogra sighed, eye-rings bent in rebuke.

"I was within my rights to do so," Kanatron insisted.

"My Lord, the Ministry of Commerce is preparing contracts for a new generation of cargo ships," she said, offering confidential information. "Contracts that require Akronium. Eighty percent of all Akronium is mined at Karak. What will Governor Zenatro say when the contracts cannot be filled? What of his lieutenants, who will not receive bonuses? What will every factory manager on Akrona think when their plants remain idle? Do you think they will be impressed that you incited insurrection merely to exercise your rights?"

"What should I do, great lady?" he begged, head bent in submission.

"Maintain what relations you can with the slaves. Ensure the Akronium supply. By next year, you may receive a promotion. Then these problems will be left for another to resolve."

"You are indeed wise, countess. It will be as you say. What of Amartro?"

"The one called Ben has sworn to rip Amartro's heart from his chest," Dogra said. "Maybe you will get lucky."

* * * * * *

"I can't see the trail," Shalli worried, the moon obscured by drifting clouds.

"We know the way," Grey answered, putting a hand on Garn's shoulder.

"The buffalo pens were down this canyon," Garn said, leading the way. "We can follow the brook to the low pastures."

"There's a river flowing south toward the lakes. We should reach the first tributary before dawn," Grey said.

They walked briskly on the well-beaten path, being careful not to stumble. Large tree branches loomed overhead, creating deep shadows. The air was frosty but not uncomfortable. The hoot of a night owl was heard in the distance.

"There is someone up ahead," Garn warned, coming to a halt.

Grey put Shalli behind him as they approached slowly. The stocky intruder was alone, blocking the path with arms crossed. It was an Arikhan.

"Greetings, food creatures," Amartro said, emerging from the darkness into soft moonlight. He was wearing light armor, a sidearm holstered on his hip.

"You are far from camp, Group Leader," Grey said, drawing one of the stolen pistols he'd taken from Farlatro's body.

"Not so far that a shot will not echo off the hills," Amartro replied, drawing his own weapon.

"I may shoot anyway," Grey warned.

"You are too sly," Amartro responded.

"Why don't you fire?" Grey asked.

"You will make a better prize taken alive, now that I have discovered your secret. Much will be my rewards. Perhaps I will even gain command of Karak, with that corrupt fool removed."

"You are much in power," Grey agreed, putting the pistol back in the holster. Then he drew the hunting knife taken from the dead guard.

"You make the game interesting," Amartro said, holstering his own weapon and drawing a sharp blade.

"Ben, don't. Amartro is too strong," Shalli said, grabbing his arm.

"Amartro is strong, and braver than I thought," Grey said. "Braver than when he stole babies from a defenseless woman. What secret inspires such courage?"

"I remember you now. From many years ago. You are the spy brought from the Link, found in the alien suit. While you were held in Contingent custody, Commander Cordaris questioned you. When he could gain no information, he sent you to these mines."

"Such is commonly known," Grey lied.

"Commonly known among traitors. I have watched the conspiracy between Lady Gamtra and the heretic. Frontra betrays us, too. All will face retribution once their treason is exposed."

"Shalli and Garn know nothing of this. I will send them away while we bargain."

"I seek no bargains."

"We have business to discuss," Grey calmly insisted. "Garn, show Shalli the way to the pasture. I will meet you at the great tree that was struck by lightning."

"We will not leave you, husband," Shalli said.

"You will do as I say," Grey ordered. "Leave now. Do not look back."

"Come, Shalli. We must obey Akeem," Garn said, dragging her off.

Shalli resisted for a moment, and then reluctantly complied. Grey and Amartro stood in silence until they were gone.

"Akeem? You are much exalted," Amartro sneered.

"What does the superior race know of Akeem?"

Amartro pondered the question, studying Grey with a dubious eye. At first he thought the food creature was feigning ignorance, but after a moment of reflection, he clicked his tongue softly.

"You truly are a barbarian," he said.

"You are not a font of enlightenment."

"This is the heretic's doing. She gives inspiration to the slaves, telling them their liberator has arrived. Perhaps this plot is larger than I suspected."

"Are three escaped slaves such a threat to the empire?"

"I am not so dull as you believe. The heretic spreads a dangerous philosophy, abetted by Gamtra and her chronicle of weakness. I suspect now that even Lord Gamtro seeks advantage by destroying our sacred traditions. Do not think to benefit from their schemes."

"The night grows late. My absence will soon be noticed."

"Why do you think I let you escape? Much will be the humiliation of Kanatron. Even Zenatro will not be able to justify such incompetence. When he turns to the Contingent for support, Cordaris will grant me many rewards."

"It is a clever plan. Is this why you brought death to these camps? To bring down Kanatron?"

"There was no plan. It is the natural order for slaves to serve their masters, and when that service is complete, to provide food for the pens. Your resistance merely provided an opportunity."

"You practice a cruel philosophy."

"I will not kill you. When you are taken to Va'ragashant in chains, I will bask in honor."

"I would make a worthy prize," Grey agreed.

* * * * * *

On their final night in Karak, knowing they may soon be separated forever, Dogra rested with Mordari in the conductor's lounge near the train station. A furnace kept the room warm despite Mordari's insistence on leaving the door partially open.

"What troubles you?" Mordari asked.

Dogra stared out the window toward the slave camp. A few fires burned in the distance. The sense of danger was fading.

"Priestess, during his years in this camp, Ben struggled not to fight his masters. Do you believe he will fight now? Even though he has Shalli and the youngling to care for? Would Ben not be wiser to seek a quiet refuge deep in the forest?"

"Wise? Without doubt it would be wiser, for the greater wisdom lies in peace. But I believe it is his nature to fight," Mordari replied. "Solets do not abandon their young, nor does a vvleen return to the nest hungry. The one you call Ben may choose to be quiet for a time, but someday he will return to the stars. Akrona is not the only conquered world that requires hope. That is why I kept one secret from him."

"A secret I should know?" Dogra asked.

Mordari dwelled on her question, knowing it was more of a demand than a request.

"Perhaps someone should know, but not now. There is much to accomplish."

"Can it be so grave?"

"Who can say what might change our destinies?"

"I have given all, priestess. Please do not deny me."

Mordari glanced again out the window before speaking.

"Ben has a daughter he does not know of. On Sol. She is a lovely, intelligent child, but without a father. The world of the Sol creatures is a dangerous place, filled with rivalries and betrayal. If Ben knew of his lost daughter, he would not rest until he believed her safe."

"He is stubborn beyond forbearance," Dogra agreed, clicking her tongue with impatience. "But he is also a creature of high obligation. I do not believe this knowledge would deter him from his destiny, if he truly has such a calling."

There was a presence at the door. A guard was standing in the shadows, holding a box.

"Enter," Dogra said.

The husky commoner, wearing a thick covering to protect from the cold, hesitantly stepped forward to place a metal storage container on the table.

"There was a disturbance, mistress," the guard said. "On the south perimeter. This cube was found with your mark on it."

The guard rushed from the room. Dogra thought he seemed unnerved, perhaps by the presence of the strange priestess.

Mordari walked to the box, released the straps, and peered inside.

"Sherra bless me," she whispered, quickly closing the lid.

"What is it?" Dogra asked.

"We must go for a walk," Mordari suddenly announced.

They strolled down to the creek, then slowly up the stone-covered hill where the prisoner had been chained just a few days before. Only pegs remained in the rock.

"There are many stars tonight. Notice how the clouds are moving away," Mordari observed.

To the north, Dogra saw the flowing river and imagined the Arikhan colonies far beyond the Varish Expanse. To the south, she saw the mountains, high and formidable, with their tall trees and steep cliffs. Dawn started to break through the morning mist.

With a soft click of her tongue, Mordari sat on the crest of the hill, taking the green bottle from her pocket and sipping gingerly. Dogra wondered if her health was not good.

"It was here that everything changed," Mordari finally whispered. "Never would I have imaged Sherra casting so great a light in so dark a place."

"Has so much truly changed? All appears as before," Dogra said.

"When I was prisoner among Ben's people, the captivity was much resented. Often did I yearn for retribution. But then Sherra allowed me to grasp Her Truth. With vision came enlightenment. With enlightenment, came resolve."

"Yet you seem sad," Dogra remarked.

"It is not sadness, my child. I do not know why Sherra chose me as her messenger, but now I will face my enemies with a sturdy heart. A warrior's final battle."

"The indictments may not be so severe. You have many followers, and the Supreme Council does not want a martyr."

Mordari sighed, scratching at the dirt with her claw.

"I do not fear the Supreme Council. Nor do I fear their judgment."

"Then what troubles you?" Dogra asked, seeing the faraway look in her black eyes.

"I was scout of the 44th Camp. First upon the frontier. I would not leave my mission incomplete."

"You have much life remaining."

"There is a legend among the Sol creatures. A prophet led his people through the wilderness for forty years, only to be denied his place in the Promised Land. Now I feel a wind blowing from the east and fear I may not live long enough to savor its blessings."

"But mistress, there is no wind. It is perfectly calm," Dogra disagreed.

"You may not see the wind, nor yet feel the wind, but by the Will of Sherra, the wind comes."

"How can you be so sure?"

"The box."

"The one brought by the guard?" Dogra asked. "What was inside?"

"A sign of things to come, dear," Mordari replied. "It was Amartro's head."

Novels by Gregory Urbach

Dashiell Hammett and the Hearst Castle Mystery
When a body is discovered on the Hearst estate, America's
foremost mystery writer is given 48 hours to solve the crime

Dashiell Hammett and the World's Fair Mystery
When Albert Einstein's letter containing vital secrets is stolen,
America's foremost mystery writer must save it from Nazi spies

Custer at the Alamo
Sent 40 years in the past by Chief Sitting Bull, General Custer
and the 7th Cavalry join Davy Crockett to defend the Alamo

Custer and Crockett: After the Alamo
Stranded in time, General George Custer and
Davy Crockett set out to win independence for Texas

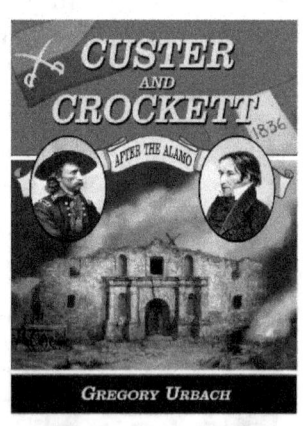

Dinosaur Blitz
Science fiction and romance with dinosaurs,
a moon base, alien visitors, the end of the world,
and movie stars

Slave of Akrona
A mysterious castaway finds new love while
challenging his overseers on a conquered alien planet

Rebels of Akrona
A soldier from another world struggles to
defeat an oppressive alien empire

Magistrate of the Dark Land
A cowardly lawyer seeks two kidnapped
girls in a war-torn medieval land

Rachel From the Edge
A shy yet brilliant woman is hounded by a merciless
press following the death of her billionaire boyfriend

Rachel Running on Empty
Forced to make a life-changing decision, a gifted
scientist is caught up in a web of corruption and murder

Rachel the Warrior
When cyber-terrorists take control of a nuclear-armed
space station, a shy mathematics prodigy is sent to take it back

Diminished Capacity
Accused of shooting the president, a troubled war veteran
seeks redemption for his crime. But is he guilty?

Diminished Capacity 2: Second Chances
An accused assassin and the slain president's daughter
seek a new life in the glare of a relentless media

Twilight on the Road Home
Rescued from vicious kidnappers, a young woman
struggles to survive criminals, courts, and lawyers

This futuristic science fiction series, taking elements of *Tarzan of the Apes* and *Clan of the Cave Bear*, follows the journey of a lunar orphan from his childhood on the moon to his last stand against fierce extraterrestrial enemies

Tranquility's Child
Tranquility's End
Tranquility's Heirs
Tranquility Besieged
Tranquility in Darkness
Tranquility Down
Tranquility Divided
Tranquility Under the Eagles
Tranquility's Last Stand

About the Author

An avid student of history, Gregory Urbach has been writing adventure stories for 30 years. From his days working for a campus newspaper, he has also pursued an interest in politics and popular culture. His degree in Urban Studies proved useful when writing the nine-book Tranquility science fiction series. The author's books reflect worlds where the concepts of good and evil are challenged by complicated realities.

Dashiell Hammett's grave at Arlington National Cemetery
A veteran of World War I and World War II